LINDA HOWARD

MACKENZIES' HONOR

MIRA®

ISBN 0-7783-2267-X

MACKENZIES' HONOR

Copyright © 2005 by MIRA Books.

The publisher acknowledges the copyright holder
of the individual works as follows:

MACKENZIE'S PLEASURE
Copyright © 1996 by Linda Howington.

A GAME OF CHANCE
Copyright © 2000 by Linda Howington.

MIRA and the Star Colophon are trademarks used under license and registered
in Australia, New Zealand, Philippines, United States Patent and Trademark
Office and in other countries.

www.MIRABooks.com

Printed in U.S.A.

CONTENTS

MACKENZIE'S PLEASURE

Mackenzie's Pleasure is dedicated to all the wonderful fans who fell as much in love with the Mackenzies as I did.

Prologue

Wolf Mackenzie slipped out of bed and restlessly paced over to the window, where he stood looking out at the stark, moonlit expanse of his land. A quick glance over his bare shoulder reassured him that Mary slept on undisturbed, though he knew it wouldn't be long before she sensed his absence and stirred, reaching out for him. When her hand didn't encounter his warmth, she would wake, sitting up in bed and drowsily pushing her silky hair out of her face. When she saw him by the window she would slide out of bed and come to him, nestling against his naked body, sleepily resting her head on his chest.

A slight smile touched his hard mouth. Like as not, if he stayed out of bed long enough for her to awaken, when they returned to the bed it wouldn't be to sleep but to make love. As he remembered, Maris had been conceived on just such an occasion, when he had been restless because Joe's fighter wing had just been deployed overseas during some flare-up. It had been Joe's first action, and Wolf had been as tense as he'd been during his own days in Vietnam.

Luckily, he and Mary were past the days when spontaneous passion could result in a new baby. Nowadays they had grandkids, not kids of their own. Ten at the last count, as a matter of fact.

But he was restless tonight, and he knew why.

The wolf always slept better when all of his cubs were accounted for.

Never mind that the cubs were adults, some of them with children of their own. Never mind that they were, one and all, supremely capable of taking care of themselves. They were *his*, and he was there if they needed him. He also liked to know, within reason, where they were bedding down for the night. It wasn't necessary for him to be able to pinpoint their location—some things a parent was better off not knowing—but if he knew what *state* they were in, that was usually enough. Hell, sometimes he would have been glad just to know which *country* they were roaming.

His concern wasn't for Joe, this time. He knew where Joe was—the Pentagon. Joe wore four stars now, and sat on the Joint Chiefs of Staff.

Joe would still rather strap on a metal bird and fly at twice the speed of sound, but those days were behind him. If he had to fly a desk, then he would damn sure fly it the best it could be flown. Besides, as he'd once said, being married to Caroline was more challenging than being in a dogfight and outnumbered four to one.

Wolf grinned when he thought of his daughter-in-law. Genius IQ, doctorates in both physics and computer sciences, a bit arrogant, a bit quirky. She'd gotten her pilot's license just after the birth of their first son, on the basis that the wife of a fighter pilot should know something about flying. She had received her certification on small jet aircraft around the time the third son had made his appearance. After the birth of her fifth son, she had grumpily told Joe that she was calling it quits with that one, because she'd given him five chances and obviously he wasn't up to the job of fathering a daughter.

It had once been gently suggested to Joe that Caroline should quit her job. The company that employed her was heavily engaged in government contract work, and the appearance of any favoritism could hurt his career. Joe had turned his cool, blue laser gaze on his superiors and said, "Gentlemen, if I have to choose between my wife and my career, I'll give you my resignation immediately." That was *not* the answer that had been expected, and nothing else was said about Caroline's work in research and development.

Wolf wasn't worried about Michael, either. Mike was the most settled of all his children, though just as focused. He had decided at an early age that he wanted to be a rancher, and that's exactly what he was. He owned a sizable spread down toward Laramie, and he and his wife were happily raising cattle and two sons.

The only uproar Mike had ever caused was when he decided to marry Shea Colvin. Wolf and Mary had given him their blessing, but the problem was that Shea's mother was Pam Hearst Colvin, one of Joe's old girlfriends—and Pam's father, Ralph Hearst, was as adamantly opposed to his beloved granddaughter marrying Michael Mackenzie as he had been to his daughter dating Joe Mackenzie.

Michael, with his typical tunnel vision, had ignored the whole tempest. His only concern was marrying Shea, and to hell with the storm erupting in the Hearst family. Quiet, gentle Shea had been torn, but she wanted Michael and refused to call off the wedding as her grandfather demanded. Pam herself had finally put an end to it, standing nose to nose with her father in the middle of his store.

"Shea *will* marry Michael," she'd stormed, when Ralph had threatened to take Shea out of his will if she married one of those damn breeds. "You didn't want me to date Joe, when he was one of the most decent men I've ever met. Now Shea wants Michael, and she's going to have him. Change your will, if you like. Hug your hate real close, because you won't be hugging your granddaughter—or your great-grandchildren. Think about that!"

So Michael had married Shea, and despite his growling and grumping, old Hearst was nuts about his two great-grandsons. Shea's second pregnancy had been difficult, and both she and the baby had nearly died. The doctor had advised them not to have any more children, but they had already decided to have only two, anyway. The two boys were growing up immersed in cattle ranching and horses. Wolf was amused that Ralph Hearst's great-grandchildren bore the Mackenzie name. Who in hell ever would have thought?

Josh, his third son, lived in Seattle with his wife, Loren, and their three sons. Josh was as jet-mad as Joe, but he had opted for the Navy rather than the Air Force, perhaps because he wanted to succeed on his own, not because his older brother was a general.

Josh was cheerful and openhearted, the most outgoing of the bunch, but he, too, had that streak of iron determination. He'd barely survived the crash that left him with a stiffened right knee and ended his naval career, but in typical Josh fashion, he had put that behind him and concentrated on what was before him. At the time, that had been his doctor—Dr. Loren Page. Never one to dither around, Josh had taken one look at tall, lovely Loren and begun his courtship from his hospital bed. He'd still been on crutches when they married. Now, three sons later, he worked for an aeronautics firm, developing new fighter aircraft, and Loren practiced her orthopedic specialty at a Seattle hospital.

Wolf knew where Maris was, too. His only daughter was currently in Montana, working as a trainer for a horse rancher. She was considering taking a job in Kentucky, working with Thoroughbreds. From the time she'd been old enough to sit unaided on a horse, her ambitions had all centered around the big, elegant animals. She had his touch with horses, able to gentle even the most contrary or vicious beast. Privately Wolf thought that she probably surpassed his skill. What she could do with a horse was pure magic.

Wolf's hard mouth softened as he thought of Maris. She had wrapped his heart around her tiny finger the moment she had been placed in his arms, when she was mere minutes old, and had looked up at him with sleepy dark eyes. Of all his children, she was the only one who had his dark eyes. His sons all looked like him, except for their blue eyes, but Maris, who resembled Mary in every other way, had her father's eyes. His daughter had light, silvery brown hair, skin so fine it was almost translucent, and her mother's determination. She was all of five foot three and weighed about a hundred pounds, but Maris never paid any attention to her slightness; when she made up her mind to do something, she persisted with bulldog stubbornness until she succeeded. She could more than hold her own with her older, much larger and domineering brothers.

Her chosen career hadn't been easy for her. People tended to think two things. One was that she was merely trading on the Mackenzie name, and the other was that she was too delicate for the job. They soon found out how wrong they were on both counts, but it was a battle Maris had fought over and over. She kept at it, though, slowly winning respect for her individual talents.

The mental rundown of his kids next brought him to Chance. Hell, he even knew where Chance was, and that was saying something. Chance roamed the world, though he always came back to Wyoming, to the mountain that was his only home. He had happened to call earlier that day, from Belize. He'd told Mary that he was going to rest for a few days before moving on. When Wolf had taken his turn on the phone, he had moved out of Mary's hearing and quietly asked Chance how bad he was hurt.

"Not too bad," Chance had laconically replied. "A few stitches and a couple of cracked ribs. This last job went a little sour on me."

Wolf didn't ask what the last job had entailed. His soldier-of-fortune son occasionally did some delicate work for the government, so Chance seldom volunteered details. The two men had an unspoken agreement to keep Mary in the dark about the danger Chance faced on a regular basis. Not only did they not want her to worry, but if she knew he was wounded, she was likely to hop on a plane and fetch him home.

When Wolf hung up the phone and turned, it was to find Mary's slate blue gaze pinned on him. "How bad is he hurt?" she demanded fiercely, hands planted on her hips.

Wolf knew better than to try lying to her. Instead he crossed the room to her and pulled her into his arms, stroking her silky hair and cradling her slight body against the solid muscularity of his. Sometimes the force of his love for this woman almost drove him to his knees. He couldn't protect her from worry, though, so he gave her the respect of honesty. "Not too bad, to use his own words."

Her response was instant. "I want him here."

"I know, sweetheart. But he's okay. He doesn't lie to us. Besides, you know Chance."

She nodded, sighing, and turned her lips against his chest. Chance was like a sleek panther, wild and intolerant of fetters. They had brought him into their home and made him one of the family, binding him to them with love when no other restraint would have held him. And like a wild creature that had been only half-tamed, he accepted the boundaries of civilization, but lightly. He roamed far and wide, and yet he always came back to them.

From the first, though, he had been helpless against Mary. She had instantly surrounded him with so much love and care that he hadn't been able to resist her, even though his light hazel eyes had reflected his consternation, even embarrassment, at her attention. If Mary went down to fetch Chance, he would come home without protest, but he would walk into the house wearing a helpless, slightly panicked "Oh, God, get me out of this" expression. And then he would meekly let her tend his wounds, pamper him and generally smother him with motherly concern.

Watching Mary fuss over Chance was one of Wolf's greatest amusements. She fussed over all of her kids, but the others had grown up with it and took it as a matter of course. Chance, though…he had been fourteen and half wild when Mary had found him. If he'd ever had a home, he didn't remember it. If he had a name, he didn't know it. He'd evaded well-meaning social authorities by staying on the move, stealing whatever he needed, food, clothes, money. He was highly intelligent and had taught himself to read from newspapers and magazines that had been thrown away. Libraries had become a favorite place for him to hang out, maybe even spend the night if he could manage it, but never two nights in a row. From what he read and what little television he saw, he understood the concept of a family, but that was all it was to him—a concept. He trusted no one but himself.

He might have grown to adulthood that way if he hadn't contracted a monster case of influenza. While driving home from work, Mary had found him lying on the side of a road, incoherent and burning up with fever. Though he was half a foot taller than she and some fifty pounds heavier, somehow she had wrestled and bullied the boy into her truck and taken him to the local clinic, where Doc Nowacki discovered that the flu had progressed into pneumonia and quickly transferred Chance to the nearest hospital, eighty miles away.

Mary had driven home and insisted that Wolf take her to the hospital—immediately.

Chance was in intensive care when they arrived. At first the nursing staff hadn't wanted to let them see him, since they weren't family and in fact didn't know anything about him. Child services had been notified, and someone was on the way to take care of the paperwork. They had been reasonable, even kind, but they hadn't reckoned with Mary. She was relentless. She wanted to see the boy, and a bulldozer couldn't have budged her until she saw him. Eventually the nurses, overworked and outclassed by a will far stronger than their own, gave in and let Wolf and Mary into the small cubicle.

As soon as he saw the boy, Wolf knew why Mary was so taken with him. It wasn't just that he was deathly ill; he was obviously part American Indian. He would have reminded Mary so forcibly of her own children that she could no more have forgotten about him than she could one of them.

Wolf's expert eye swept over the boy as he lay there so still and silent, his eyes closed, his breathing labored. The hectic color of fever stained his high cheekbones. Four different bags dripped an IV solution into his muscular right arm, which was taped to the bed. Another bag hung at the side of the bed, measuring the output of his kidneys.

Not a half-breed, Wolf had thought. A quarter, maybe.

No more than that. But still, there was no doubting his heritage. His fingernails were light against the tanned skin of his fingers, where an Anglo's nails would have been pinker. His thick, dark brown hair, so long it brushed his shoulders, was straight. There were those high cheekbones, the clearcut lips, the high-bridged nose. He was the most handsome boy Wolf had ever seen.

Mary went up to the bed, all her attention focused on the boy who lay so ill and helpless on the snowy sheets. She laid her cool hand lightly against his forehead, then stroked it over his hair. "You'll be all right," she murmured. "I'll make sure you are."

He had lifted his heavy lids, struggling with the effort. For the first time Wolf saw the light hazel eyes, almost golden, and circled with a brown rim so dark it was almost black. Confused, the boy had focused first on Mary; then his gaze had wandered to Wolf, and belated alarm flared in his eyes. He tried to heave himself up, but he was too weak even to tug his taped arm free.

Wolf moved to the boy's other side. "Don't be afraid," he said quietly. "You have pneumonia, and you're in a hospital." Then, guessing what lay at the bottom of the boy's panic, he added, "We won't let them take you."

Those light eyes had rested on his face, and perhaps Wolf's appearance had calmed him. Like a wild animal on guard, he slowly relaxed and drifted back to sleep.

Over the next week, the boy's condition improved, and Mary swung into action. She was determined that the boy, who still had not given them a name, not be taken into state custody for even one day. She pulled strings, harangued people, even called on Joe to use his influence, and her tenacity worked. When the boy was released from the hospital, he went home with Wolf and Mary.

He had gradually become accustomed to them, though by no stretch of the imagination had he been friendly, or even trustful. He would answer their questions, in one word if possible, but he never actually *talked* with them. Mary hadn't been discouraged. From the first, she simply treated the boy as if he was hers—and soon he was.

The boy who had always been alone was suddenly plunged into the middle of a large, volatile family. For the first time he had a roof over his head every night, a room all to himself, ample food in his belly. He had clothing hanging in the closet and new boots on his feet. He was still too weak to share in the chores everyone did, but Mary immediately began tutoring him to bring him up to Zane's level academically, since the two boys were the same age, as near as they could tell. Chance took to the books like a starving pup to its mother's teat, but in every other way he determinedly remained at arm's length. Those shrewd, guarded eyes took note of every nuance of their family relationships, weighing what he saw now against what he had known before.

Finally he unbent enough to tell them that he was called Sooner. He didn't have a real name.

Maris had looked at him blankly. "Sooner?"

His mouth had twisted, and he'd looked far too old for his fourteen years. "Yeah, like a mongrel dog."

"No," Wolf had said, because the name was a clue. "You know you're part Indian. More than likely you were called Sooner because you were originally from Oklahoma—and that means you're probably Cherokee."

The boy merely looked at him, his expression guarded, but still something about him had lightened at the possibility that he hadn't been likened to a dog of unknown heritage.

His relationships with everyone in the family were complicated. With Mary, he wanted to hold himself away, but he simply couldn't. She mothered him the way she did the rest of her brood, and it terrified him even though he delighted in it, soaking up her loving concern. He was wary of Wolf, as if he expected the big man to turn on him with fists and boots. Wise in the ways of wild things, Wolf gradually gentled the boy the same way he did horses, letting him get accustomed, letting him realize he had nothing to fear, then offering respect and friendship and, finally, love.

Michael had already been away at college, but when he did come home he simply made room in his family circle for the newcomer. Sooner was relaxed with Mike from the start, sensing that quiet acceptance.

He got along with Josh, too, but Josh was so cheerful it was impossible not to get along with him. Josh took it on himself to be the one who taught Sooner how to handle the multitude of chores on a horse ranch. Josh was the one who taught him how to ride, though Josh was unarguably the worst horseman in the family. That wasn't to say he wasn't good, but the others were better, especially Maris. Josh didn't care, because his heart was wrapped up in planes just the way Joe's had been, so perhaps he had been more patient with Sooner's mistakes than anyone else would have been.

Maris was like Mary. She had taken one look at the boy and immediately taken him under her fiercely protective wing, never mind that Sooner was easily twice her size. At twelve, Maris had been not quite five feet tall and weighed all of seventy-four pounds. It didn't matter to her; Sooner became hers the same way her older brothers were hers. She chattered to him, teased him, played jokes on him—in short, drove him crazy, the way little sisters were supposed to do. Sooner hadn't had any idea how to handle the way she treated him, any more than he had with Mary. Sometimes he had watched Maris as if she was a ticking time bomb, but it was Maris who won his first smile with her teasing. It was Maris who actually got him to enter the family conversations: slowly, at first, as he learned how families worked, how the give-and-take of talking melded them together, then with more ease. Maris could still tease him into a rage, or coax a laugh out of him, faster than anyone else. For a while Wolf had wondered if the two might become romantically interested in each other as they grew older, but it hadn't happened. It was a testament to how fully Sooner had become a part of their family; to both of them, they were simply brother and sister.

Things with Zane had been complicated, though.

Zane was, in his own way, as guarded as Sooner. Wolf knew warriors, having been one himself, and what he saw in his youngest son was almost frightening. Zane was quiet, intense, watchful. He moved like a cat, gracefully, soundlessly. Wolf had trained all his children, including Maris, in self-defense, but with Zane it was something more. The boy took to it with the ease of someone putting on a well-worn shoe; it was as if it had been made for him. When it came to marksmanship, he had the eye of a sniper, and the deadly patience.

Zane had the instinct of a warrior: to protect. He was immediately on guard against this intruder into the sanctity of his family's home turf.

He hadn't been nasty to Sooner. He hadn't made fun of him or been overtly unfriendly, which wasn't in his nature. Rather, he had held himself away from the newcomer, not rejecting, but certainly not welcoming, either. But because they were the same age, Zane's acceptance was the most crucial, and Sooner had reacted to Zane's coolness by adopting the same tactics. They had ignored each other.

While the kids were working out their relationships, Wolf and Mary had been pushing hard to legally adopt Sooner. They had asked him if that was what he wanted and, typically, he had responded with a shrug and an expressionless, "Sure." Taking that for the impassioned plea it was, Mary redoubled her efforts to get the adoption pushed through.

As things worked out, they got the word that the adoption could go forward on the same day Zane and Sooner settled things between them.

The dust was what had caught Wolf's attention.

At first he hadn't thought anything of it, because when he glanced over he saw Maris sitting on the top rail of the fence, calmly watching the commotion. Figuring one of the horses was rolling in the dirt, Wolf went back to work. Two seconds later, however, his sharp ears caught the sound of grunts and what sounded suspiciously like blows.

He walked across the yard to the other corral. Zane and Sooner had gotten into the corner, where they couldn't be seen from the house, and were ferociously battering each other. Wolf saw at once that both boys, despite the force of their blows, were restraining themselves to the more conventional fisticuffs rather than the faster, nastier ways he'd also taught them. He leaned his arms on the top rail beside Maris. "What's this about?"

"They're fighting it out," she said matter-of-factly, without taking her eyes from the action.

Josh soon joined them at the fence, and they watched the battle. Zane and Sooner were both tall, muscular boys, very strong for their ages. They stood toe to toe, taking turns driving their fists into each other's faces. When one of them got knocked down, he got to his feet and waded back into the fray. They were almost eerily silent, except for the involuntary grunts and the sounds of hard fists hitting flesh.

Mary saw them standing at the fence and came out to investigate. She stood beside Wolf and slipped her small hand into his. He felt her flinch every time a blow landed, but when he looked at her, he saw that she was wearing her prim schoolteacher's expression, and he knew that Mary Elizabeth Mackenzie was about to call the class to order.

She gave it five minutes. Evidently deciding this could go on for hours, and that both boys were too stubborn to give in, she settled the matter herself. In her crisp, clear teaching voice she called out, "All right, boys, let's get this wrapped up. Supper will be on the table in ten minutes." Then she calmly walked back to the house, fully confident that she had brought detente to the corral.

She had, too. She had reduced the fight to the level of a chore or a project, given them a time limit and a reason for ending it.

Both boys' eyes had flickered to that slight retreating figure with the ramrod spine. Then Zane had turned to Sooner, the coolness of his blue gaze somewhat marred by the swelling of his eyes. "One more," he said grimly, and slammed his fist into Sooner's face.

Sooner picked himself up off the dirt, squared up again and returned the favor.

Zane got up, slapped the dirt from his clothes and held out his hand. Sooner gripped it, though they had both winced at the pain in their knuckles. They shook hands, eyed each other as equals, then returned to the house to clean up. After all, supper was almost on the table.

At supper, Mary told Sooner that the adoption had been given the green light. His pale hazel eyes had glittered in his battered face, but he hadn't said anything.

"You're a Mackenzie now," Maris had pronounced with

great satisfaction. "You'll have to have a real name, so choose one."

It hadn't occurred to her that choosing a name might require some thought, but as it happened, Sooner had looked around the table at the family that pure blind luck had sent him, and a wry little smile twisted up one side of his bruised, swollen mouth. "Chance," he said, and the unknown, unnamed boy became Chance Mackenzie.

Zane and Chance hadn't become immediate best friends after the fight. What they had found, instead, was mutual respect, but friendship grew out of it. Over the years, they became so close that they could well have been born twins. There were other fights between them, but it was well known around Ruth, Wyoming, that if anyone decided to take on either of the boys, he would find himself facing both of them. They could batter each other into the ground, but by God, no one else was going to.

They had entered the Navy together, Zane becoming a SEAL, while Chance had gone into Naval Intelligence. Chance had since left the Navy, though, and gone out on his own, while Zane was a SEAL team leader.

And that brought Wolf to the reason for his restlessness. Zane.

There had been a lot of times in Zane's career when he had been out of touch, when they hadn't known where he was or what he was doing. Wolf hadn't slept well then, either. He knew too much about the SEALs, having seen them in action in Vietnam during his tours of duty. They were the most highly trained and skilled of the special forces, their stamina and teamwork proven by grueling tests that broke lesser men. Zane was particularly well-suited for the work, but in the final analysis, the SEALs were still human. They could be killed. And because of the nature of their work, they were often in dangerous situations.

The SEAL training had merely accentuated the already existing facets of Zane's nature. He had been honed to a perfect fighting machine, a warrior who was in top condition, but who used his brain more than his brawn. He was even more lethal and intense now, but he had learned to temper that deadliness with an easier manner, so that most people were unaware they were dealing with a man who could kill them in a dozen different ways with his bare hands. With that kind of knowledge and skill at his disposal, Zane had learned a calm control that kept him in command of himself. Of all Wolf's offspring, Zane was the most capable of taking care of himself, but he was also the one in the most danger.

Where in hell *was* he?

There was a whisper of movement from the bed, and Wolf looked around as Mary slipped from between the sheets and joined him at the window, looping her arms around his hard, trim waist and nestling her head on his bare chest.

"Zane?" she asked quietly, in the darkness.

"Yeah." No more explanation was needed.

"He's all right," she said with a mother's confidence. "I'd know if he wasn't."

Wolf tipped her head up and kissed her, lightly at first, then with growing intensity. He turned her slight body more fully into his embrace and felt her quiver as she pressed to him, pushing her hips against his, cradling the rise of his male flesh against her softness. There had been passion between them from their first meeting, all those years ago, and time hadn't taken it from them.

He lifted her in his arms and carried her back to bed, losing himself in the welcome and warmth of her soft body. Afterward, though, lying in the drowsy aftermath, he turned his face toward the window. Before sleep claimed him, the thought came again. Where was Zane?

Chapter 1

Zane Mackenzie wasn't happy.

No one aboard the aircraft carrier USS *Montgomery* was happy; well, maybe the cooks were, but even that was iffy, because the men they were serving were sullen and defensive. The seamen weren't happy, the radar men weren't happy, the gunners weren't happy, the Marines weren't happy, the wing commander wasn't happy, the pilots weren't happy, the air boss wasn't happy, the executive officer wasn't happy, and Captain Udaka sure as hell wasn't happy.

The combined unhappiness of the five thousand sailors on board the carrier didn't begin to approach Lieutenant-Commander Mackenzie's level of unhappiness.

The captain outranked him. The executive officer outranked him. Lieutenant-Commander Mackenzie addressed them with all the respect due their rank, but both men were uncomfortably aware that their asses were in a sling and their careers on the line. Actually, their careers were probably in the toilet. There wouldn't be any court-martials, but neither would be there any more promotions, and they would be given the unpopular commands from now until they either retired or resigned, their choice depending on how clearly they could read the writing on the wall.

Captain Udaka's broad, pleasant face was one that wore responsibility easily, but now his expression was set in lines of unhappy acceptance as he met the icy gaze of the lieutenant-commander. SEALs in general made the captain nervous; he didn't quite trust them or the way they operated outside normal regulations. This one in particular made him seriously want to be somewhere—anywhere—else.

He had met Mackenzie before, when both he and Boyd, the XO, had been briefed on the security exercise. The SEAL team under Mackenzie's command would try to breach the carrier's security, probing for weaknesses that could be exploited by any of the myriad terrorist groups so common these days. It was a version of the exercises once conducted by the SEAL Team Six Red Cell, which had been so notorious and so far outside the regulations that it had been disbanded after seven years of operation. The concept, however, had lived on, in a more controlled manner. SEAL Team Six was a covert, counterterrorism unit, and one of the best ways to counter terrorism was to prevent it from happening in the first place, rather than reacting to it after people were dead. To this end, the security of naval installations and carrier battle groups was tested by the SEALs, who then recommended changes to correct the weaknesses they had discovered. There were always weaknesses, soft spots—the SEALs had never yet been completely thwarted, even though the base commanders and ships' captains were always notified in advance.

At the briefing, Mackenzie had been remote but pleasant. Controlled. Most SEALs had a wild, hard edge to them, but Mackenzie had seemed more regular Navy, recruiting-poster perfect in his crisp whites and with his coolly courteous manner. Captain Udaka had felt comfortable with him, certain that Lieutenant-Commander Mackenzie was the administrational type rather than a true part of those wild-ass SEALs.

He'd been wrong.

The courtesy remained, and the control. The white uniform looked as perfect as it had before. But there was nothing at all pleasant in the deep voice, or in the cold fury that lit the pale blue gray eyes so they glittered like moonlight on a knife blade. The aura of danger surrounding him was so strong it was almost palpable, and Captain Udaka knew that he had been drastically wrong in his assessment of Mackenzie. This was no desk jockey; this was a man around whom others should walk very lightly indeed. The captain felt as if his skin was being flayed from his body, strip by strip, by that icy gaze. He had also never felt closer to death than he had the moment Mackenzie had entered his quarters after learning what had happened.

"Captain, you were briefed on the exercise," Zane said coldly. "Everyone on this ship was advised, as well as notified that my men wouldn't be carrying weapons of any sort. Explain, then, *why in hell two of my men were shot!*"

The XO, Mr. Boyd, looked at his hands. Captain Udaka's collar felt too tight, except that it was already unbuttoned, and the only thing choking him was the look in Mackenzie's eyes.

"There's no excuse," he said rawly. "Maybe the guards were startled and fired without thinking. Maybe it was a stupid, macho turf thing, wanting to show the big bad SEALs that they couldn't penetrate our security, after all. It doesn't matter. There's no excuse." Everything that happened on board his ship was, ultimately, his responsibility. The trigger-happy guards would pay for their mistake—and so would he.

"My men had *already* penetrated your security," Zane said

softly, his tone making the hairs stand up on the back of the captain's neck.

"I'm aware of that." The breach of his ship's security was salt in the captain's wounds, but nothing at all compared to the enormous mistake that had been made when men under his command had opened fire on the unarmed SEALs. His men, his responsibility. Nor did it help his feelings that, when two of their team had gone down, the remainder of the SEAL team, *unarmed*, had swiftly taken control and secured the area. Translated, that meant the guards who had done the shooting had been roughly handled and were now in sick bay with the two men they had shot. In reality, the phrase "roughly handled" was a euphemism for the fact that the SEALS had beaten the hell out of his men.

The most seriously wounded SEAL was Lieutenant Higgins, who had taken a bullet in the chest and would be evacuated by air to Germany as soon as he was stabilized. The other SEAL, Warrant Officer Odessa, had been shot in the thigh; the bullet had broken his femur. He, too, would be taken to Germany, but his condition was stable, even if his temper was not. The ship's doctor had been forced to sedate him to keep him from wreaking vengeance on the battered guards, two of whom were still unconscious.

The five remaining members of the SEAL team were in Mission Planning, prowling around like angry tigers looking for someone to maul just to make themselves feel better. They were restricted to the area by Mackenzie's order, and the ship's crew was giving them a wide berth. Captain Udaka wished he could do the same with Mackenzie. He had the impression of cold savagery lurking just beneath the surface of the man's control. There would be hell to pay for this night's fiasco.

The phone on his desk emitted a harsh *brr*. Though he was relieved by the interruption, Captain Udaka snatched up the receiver and barked, "I gave orders I wasn't to be—" He stopped, listening, and his expression changed. His gaze shifted to Mackenzie. "We'll be right there," he said, and hung up.

"There's a scrambled transmission coming in for you," he said to Mackenzie, rising to his feet. "Urgent." Whatever message the transmission contained, Captain Udaka looked on it as a much-welcomed reprieve.

Zane listened intently to the secure satellite transmission, his mind racing as he began planning the logistics of the mission. "My team is two men short, sir," he said. "Higgins and Odessa were injured in the security exercise." He didn't say *how* they'd been injured; that would be handled through other channels.

"Damn it," Admiral Lindley muttered. He was in an office in the U.S. Embassy in Athens. He looked up at the others in the office: Ambassador Lovejoy, tall and spare, with the smoothness bequeathed by a lifetime of privilege and wealth, though now there was a stark, panicked expression in his hazel eyes; the CIA station chief, Art Sandefer, a nondescript man with short gray hair and tired, intelligent eyes; and, finally, Mack Prewett, second only to Sandefer in the local CIA hierarchy. Mack was known in some circles as Mack the Knife; Admiral Lindley knew Mack was generally considered a man who got things done, a man whom it was dangerous to cross. For all his decisiveness, though, he wasn't a cowboy who was likely to endanger people by going off half-cocked. He was as thorough as he was decisive, and it was through his contacts that they had obtained such good, prompt information in this case.

The admiral had put Zane on the speakerphone, so the other three in the room had heard the bad news about the SEAL team on which they had all been pinning their hopes. Ambassador Lovejoy looked even more haggard.

"We'll have to use another team," Art Sandefer said.

"That'll take too much time!" the ambassador said with stifled violence. "My God, already she could be—" He stopped, anguish twisting his face. He wasn't able to complete the sentence.

"I'll take the team in," Zane said. His amplified voice was clear in the soundproofed room. "We're the closest, and we can be ready to go in an hour."

"You?" the admiral asked, startled. "Zane, you haven't seen live action since—"

"My last promotion," Zane finished dryly. He hadn't liked trading action for administration, and he was seriously considering resigning his commission. He was thirty-one, and it was beginning to look as if his success in his chosen field was going to prevent him from practicing it; the higher-ranking the officer, the less likely that officer was to be in the thick of the action. He'd been thinking about something in law enforcement, or maybe even throwing in with Chance. There was nonstop action there, for sure.

For now, though, a mission had been dumped in his lap, and he was going to take it.

"I train with my men, Admiral," he said. "I'm not rusty, or out of shape."

"I didn't think you were," Admiral Lindley replied, and sighed. He met the ambassador's anguished gaze, read the silent plea for help. "Can six men handle the mission?" he asked Zane.

"Sir, I wouldn't risk my men if I didn't think we could do the job."

This time the admiral looked at both Art Sandefer and Mack Prewett. Art's expression was noncommittal, the Company man refusing to stick his neck out, but Mack gave the admiral a tiny nod. Admiral Lindley swiftly weighed all the factors. Granted, the SEAL team would be two members short, and the leader would be an officer who hadn't been on an active mission in over a year, but that officer happened to be Zane Mackenzie. All things considered, the admiral couldn't think of any other man he would rather have on this mission. He'd known Zane for several years now, and there was no better warrior, no one he trusted more. If Zane said he was ready, then he was ready. "All right. Go in and get her out."

As the admiral hung up, Ambassador Lindley blurted, "Shouldn't you send in someone else? My daughter's life is at stake! This man hasn't been in the field, he's out of shape, out of practice—"

"Waiting until we could get another team into position would drastically lower our chances of finding her," the admiral pointed out as kindly as possible. Ambassador Lindley wasn't one of his favorite people. For the most part, he was a horse's ass and a snob, but there was no doubt he doted on his daughter. "And as far as Zane Mackenzie is concerned, there's no better man for the job."

"The admiral's right," Mack Prewett said quietly, with the authority that came so naturally to him. "Mackenzie is so good at what he does it's almost eerie. I would feel comfortable sending him in alone. If you want your daughter back, don't throw obstacles in his way."

Ambassador Lindley shoved his hand through his hair, an uncharacteristic gesture for so fastidious a man; it was a measure of his agitation. "If anything goes wrong…"

It wasn't clear whether he was about to voice a threat or

was simply worrying aloud, but he couldn't complete the sentence. Mack Prewett gave a thin smile. "Something always goes wrong. If anyone can handle it, Mackenzie can."

After Zane terminated the secure transmission he made his way through the network of corridors to Mission Planning. Already he could feel the rush of adrenaline pumping through his muscles as he began preparing, mentally and physically, for the job before him. When he entered the room with its maps and charts and communication systems, and the comfortable chairs grouped around a large table, five hostile faces turned immediately toward him, and he felt the surge of renewed energy and anger from his men.

Only one of them, Santos, was seated at the table, but Santos was the team medic, and he was usually the calmest of the bunch. Ensign Peter "Rocky" Greenberg, second in command of the team and a controlled, detail-oriented kind of guy, leaned against the bulkhead with his arms crossed and murder in his narrowed brown eyes. Antonio Withrock, nicknamed Bunny because he never ran out of energy, was prowling the confines of the room like a mean, hungry cat, his dark skin pulled tight across his high cheekbones. Paul Drexler, the team sniper, sat cross-legged on top of the table while he wiped an oiled cloth lovingly over the disassembled parts of his beloved Remington bolt-action 7.62 rifle. Zane didn't even lift his eyebrows at the sight. His men were supposed to be unarmed, and they had been during the security exercise that had gone so damn sour, but *keeping* Drexler unarmed was another story.

"Planning on taking over the ship?" Zane inquired mildly of the sniper.

His blue eyes cold, Drexler cocked his head as if considering the idea. "I might."

Winstead "Spooky" Jones had been sitting on the deck, his back resting against the bulkhead, but at Zane's entrance he rose effortlessly to his feet. He didn't say anything, but his gaze fastened on Zane's face, and a spark of interest replaced some of the anger in his eyes.

Spook never missed much, and the other team members had gotten in the habit of watching him, picking up cues from his body language. No more than three seconds passed before all five men were watching Zane with complete concentration.

Greenberg was the one who finally spoke. "How's Bobcat doing, boss?"

They had read Spooky's tension, but misread the cause, Zane realized. They thought Higgins had died from his wounds. Drexler began assembling his rifle with sharp, economical motions. "He's stabilized," Zane reassured them. He knew his men, knew how tight they were. A SEAL team had to be tight. Their trust in each other had to be absolute, and if something happened to one of them, they all felt it. "They're transferring him now. It's touchy, but I'll put my money on Bobcat. Odie's gonna be okay, too." He hitched one hip on the edge of the table, his pale eyes glittering with the intensity that had caught Spooky's attention. "Listen up, children. An ambassador's daughter was snatched a few hours ago, and we're going into Libya to get her."

Six black-clad figures slipped silently along the narrow, deserted street in Benghazi, Libya. They communicated by hand signals, or by whispers into the Motorola headsets they all wore under their black knit balaclava hoods. Zane was in his battle mode; he was utterly calm as they worked their way toward the four-story stone building where Barrie Lovejoy was being held on the top floor, if their intelligence was good, and if she hadn't been moved within the past few hours.

Action always affected him this way, as if every cell in his body had settled into its true purpose of existence. He had missed this, missed it to the point that he knew he wouldn't be able to stay in the Navy without it. On a mission, all his senses became more acute, even as a deep center of calm radiated outward. The more intense the action, the calmer he became, as time stretched out into slow motion. At those times he could see and hear every detail, analyze and predict the outcome, then make his decision and act—all within a split second that felt like minutes. Adrenaline would flood his body—he would feel the blood racing through his veins—but his mind would remain detached and calm. He had been told that the look on his face during those times was frighteningly remote, jarring in its total lack of expression.

The team moved forward in well-orchestrated silence. They each knew what to do, and what the others would do. That was the purpose of the trust and teamwork that had been drilled into them through the twenty-six weeks of hell that was formally known as BUD/S training. The bond between them enabled them to do more together than could be accomplished if each worked on his own. Teamwork wasn't just a word to the SEALs, it was their center.

Spooky Jones was point man. Zane preferred using the wiry Southerner for that job because he had unfrayable nerves and could ghost around like a lynx. Bunny Withrock, who almost reverberated with nervous energy, was bringing up the rear. No one sneaked up on Bunny—except the Spook. Zane was right behind Jones, with Drexler, Greenberg and Santos ranging between him and Bunny. Green-

berg was quiet, steady, totally dependable. Drexler was uncanny with that rifle, and Santos, besides being a damn
good SEAL, also had the skill to patch them up and keep
them going, if they were patchable. Overall, Zane had never
worked with a better group of men.

Their presence in Benghazi was pure luck, and Zane
knew it. Good luck for them and, he hoped, for Miss
Lovejoy, but bad luck for the terrorists who had snatched
her off the street in Athens fifteen hours ago. If the
Montgomery hadn't been just south of Crete and in perfect
position for launching a rescue, if the SEALs hadn't been
on the carrier to practice special insertions as well as the
security exercise, then there would have been a delay of precious hours, perhaps even as long as a day, while another
team got supplied and into position. As it was, the special
insertion into hostile territory they had just accomplished
had been the real thing instead of just a practice.

Miss Lovejoy was not only the ambassador's daughter, she
was an employee at the embassy, as well. The ambassador
was apparently very strict and obsessive about his daughter, having lost his wife and son in a terrorist attack in
Rome fifteen years before, when Miss Lovejoy had been a
child of ten. After that, he had kept her secluded in private
schools, and since she had finished college, she had been
acting as his hostess as well as performing her "work" at the
embassy. Zane suspected her job was more window dressing
than anything else, something to keep her busy. She had
never really worked a day in her life, never been out from
under her father's protection—until today.

She and a friend had left the embassy to do some shopping. Three men had grabbed her, shoved her into a car and
driven off. The friend had immediately reported the abduction. Despite efforts to secure the airport and ports—cyni-

cally, Zane suspected deliberate foot-dragging by the Greek authorities—a private plane had taken off from Athens and flown straight to Benghazi.

Thanks to the friend's prompt action, sources on the ground in Benghazi had been alerted. It had been verified that a young woman of Miss Lovejoy's description had been taken off the plane and hustled into the city, into the very building Zane and his team were about to enter.

It had to be her; there weren't that many red-haired Western women in Benghazi. In fact, he would bet there was only one—Barrie Lovejoy.

They were betting her life on it.

Chapter 2

Barrie lay in almost total darkness, heavy curtains at the single window blocking out most of whatever light would have entered. She could tell that it was night; the level of street noise outside had slowly diminished, until now there was mostly silence. The men who had kidnapped her had finally gone away, probably to sleep. They had no worries about her being able to escape; she was naked, and tied tightly to the cot on which she lay. Her wrists were bound together, her arms drawn over her head and tied to the frame of the cot. Her ankles were also tied together, then secured to the frame. She could barely move; every muscle in her body ached, but those in her shoulders burned with agony. She would have screamed, she would have begged for someone to come and release the ropes that held her arms over her head, but she knew that the only people who would come would be the very ones who had tied her in this position, and she would do anything, give anything, to keep from ever seeing them again.

She was cold. They hadn't even bothered to throw a blanket over her naked body, and long, convulsive shivers kept shaking her, though she couldn't tell if she was chilled from the night air or from shock. She didn't suppose it mattered. Cold was cold.

She tried to think, tried to ignore the pain, tried not to give in to shock and terror. She didn't know where she was, didn't know how she could escape, but if the slightest opportunity presented itself, she would have to be ready to take it. She wouldn't be able to escape tonight; her bonds were too tight, her movements too restricted. But tomorrow—oh, God, tomorrow.

Terror tightened her throat, almost choking off her breath. Tomorrow they would be back, and there would be another one with them, the one for whom they waited. A violent shiver racked her as she thought of their rough hands on her bare body, the pinches and slaps and crude probings, and her stomach heaved. She would have vomited, if there had been anything to vomit, but they hadn't bothered to feed her.

She couldn't go through that again.

Somehow, she had to get away.

Desperately she fought down her panic. Her thoughts darted around like crazed squirrels as she tried to plan, to think of something, anything, that she could do to protect herself. But what *could* she do, lying there like a turkey all trussed up for Thanksgiving dinner?

Humiliation burned through her. They hadn't raped her, but they had done other things to her, things to shame and terrorize her and break her spirit. Tomorrow, when the leader arrived, she was sure her reprieve would be over. The threat of rape, and then the act of it, would shatter her and leave her malleable in their hands, desperate to do anything to avoid being violated again. At least that was what they planned, she thought. But she would be damned if she would go along with their plan.

She had been in a fog of terror and shock since they had grabbed her and thrown her into a car, but as she lay there in the darkness, cold and miserable and achingly vulnerable in her nakedness, she felt as if the fog was lifting, or maybe it was being burned away. No one who knew Barrie would ever have described her as hot-tempered, but then, what she felt building in her now wasn't as volatile and fleeting as mere temper. It was rage, as pure and forceful as lava forcing its way upward from the bowels of the earth until it exploded outward and swept away everything in its path.

Nothing in her life had prepared her for these past hours. After her mother and brother had died, she had been pampered and protected as few children ever were. She had seen some—most, actually—of her schoolmates as they struggled with the misery of broken parental promises, of rare, stressful visits, of being ignored and shunted out of the way, but she hadn't been like them. Her father adored her, and she knew it. He was intensely interested in her safety, her friends, her schoolwork. If he said he would call, then the call came exactly when he'd said it would. Every week had brought some small gift in the mail, inexpensive but thoughtful. She'd understood why he worried so much about her safety, why he wanted her to attend the exclusive girls' school in Switzerland, with its cloistered security, rather than a public school, with its attendant hurly-burly.

She was all he had left.

He was all she had left, too. When she'd been a child, after the incident that had halved the family, she had clung fearfully to her father for months, dogging his footsteps when she could, weeping inconsolably when his work took him away from her. Eventually the dread that he, too, would disappear from her life had faded, but the pattern of overprotectiveness had been set.

She was twenty-five now, a grown woman, and though

in the past few years his protectiveness had begun to chafe, she had enjoyed the even tenor of her life too much to really protest. She liked her job at the embassy, so much that she was considering a full-time career in the foreign service. She enjoyed being her father's hostess. She had the duties and protocol down cold, and there were more and more female ambassadors on the international scene. It was a moneyed and insular community, but by both temperament and pedigree she was suited to the task. She was calm, even serene, and blessed with a considerate and tactful nature.

But now, lying naked and helpless on a cot, with bruises mottling her pale skin, the rage that consumed her was so deep and primal she felt as if it had altered something basic inside her, a sea change of her very nature. She would *not* endure what they—nameless, malevolent "they"—had planned for her. If they killed her, so be it. She was prepared for death; no matter what, she would not submit.

The heavy curtains fluttered.

The movement caught her eye, and she glanced at the window, but the action was automatic, without curiosity. She was already so cold that even a wind strong enough to move those heavy curtains couldn't chill her more.

The wind was black, and had a shape.

Her breath stopped in her chest.

Mutely she watched the big black shape, as silent as a shadow, slip through the window. It couldn't be human; people made *some* sound when they moved. Surely, in the total silence of the room, she would have been able to hear the whisper of the curtains as the fabric moved, or the faint, rhythmic sigh of breathing. A shoe scraping on the floor, the rustle of clothing, anything—if it was human.

After the black shape had passed between them, the curtains didn't fall back into the perfect alignment that had blocked the light; there was a small opening in them, a slit that allowed a shaft of moonlight, starlight, street light—whatever it was—to relieve the thick darkness. Barrie strained to focus on the dark shape, her eyes burning as she watched it move silently across the floor. She didn't scream; whoever or whatever approached her, it couldn't be worse than the only men likely to come to her rescue.

Perhaps she was really asleep and this was only a dream. It certainly didn't feel real. But nothing in the long, horrible hours since she had been kidnapped had felt real, and she was too cold to be asleep. No, this was real, all right.

Noiselessly the black shape glided to a halt beside the cot. It towered over her, tall and powerful, and it seemed to be examining the naked feast she presented.

Then it moved once again, lifting its hand to its head, and it peeled off its face, pulling the dark skin up as if it was no more than the skin of a banana.

It was a mask. As exhausted as she was, it was a moment before she could find a logical explanation for the nightmarish image. She blinked up at him. A man wearing a mask. Neither an animal, nor a phantom, but a flesh-and-blood man. She could see the gleam of his eyes, make out the shape of his head and the relative paleness of his face, though there was an odd bulkiness to him that in no way affected the eerily silent grace of his movements.

Just another man.

She didn't panic. She had gone beyond fear, beyond everything but rage. She simply waited—waited to fight, waited to die. Her teeth were the only weapon she had, so she would use them, if she could. She would tear at her attacker's flesh, try to damage him as much as possible before she died. If she was lucky, she would be able to get him by the throat with her teeth and take at least one of these bastards with her into death.

He was taking his time, staring at her. Her bound hands clenched into fists. Damn him. Damn them all.

Then he squatted beside the cot and leaned forward, his head very close to hers. Startled, Barrie wondered if he meant to *kiss* her—odd that the notion struck her as so unbearable—and she braced herself, preparing to lunge upward when he got close enough that she had a good chance for his throat.

"Mackenzie, United States Navy," he said in a toneless whisper that barely reached her ear, only a few inches away.

He'd spoken in *English*, with a definitely American accent. She jerked, so stunned that it was a moment before the words made sense. *Navy. United States Navy.* She had been silent for hours, refusing to speak to her captors or respond in any way, but now a small, helpless sound spilled from her throat.

"Shh, don't make any noise," he cautioned, still in that toneless whisper. Even as he spoke he was reaching over her head, and the tension on her arms suddenly relaxed. The small movement sent agony screaming through her shoulder joints, and she sucked in her breath with a sharp, gasping cry.

She quickly choked off the sound, holding it inside as she ground her teeth against the pain. "Sorry," she whispered, when she was able to speak.

She hadn't seen the knife in his hand, but she felt the chill of the blade against her skin as he deftly inserted the blade under the cords and sliced upward, felt the slight tug that freed her hands. She tried to move her arms and found that she couldn't; they remained stretched above her head, unresponsive to her commands.

He knew, without being told. He slipped the knife into its scabbard and placed his gloved hands on her shoulders, firmly kneading for a moment before he clasped her forearms and gently drew her arms down. Fire burned in her joints; it felt as if her arms were being torn from her shoulders, even though he carefully drew them straight down, keeping them aligned with her body to lessen the pain. Barrie set her teeth again, refusing to let another sound break past the barrier. Cold sweat beaded her forehead, and nausea burned in her throat once more, but she rode the swell of pain in silence.

He dug his thumbs into the balls of her shoulders, massaging the sore, swollen ligaments and tendons, intensifying the agony. Her bare body drew into a taut, pale arch of suffering, lifting from the cot. He held her down, ruthlessly pushing her traumatized joints and muscles through the recovery process. She was so cold that the heat emanating from his hands, from the closeness of his body as he bent over her, was searingly hot on her bare skin. The pain rolled through her in great shudders, blurring her sight and thought, and through the haze she realized that now, when she definitely needed to stay conscious, she was finally going to faint.

She couldn't pass out. She refused to. Grimly she hung on, and in only a few moments, moments that felt much longer, the pain began to ebb. He continued the strong kneading, taking her through the agony and into relief. She went limp, relaxing on the cot as she breathed through her mouth in the long, deep drafts of someone who has just run a race.

"Good girl," he whispered as he released her. The brief praise felt like balm to her lacerated emotions. He straightened and drew the knife again, then bent over the foot of the cot. Again there was the chill of the blade, this time against her ankles, and another small tug, then her feet were free, and involuntarily she curled into a protective ball, her body moving without direction from her brain in a belated, useless effort at modesty and self-protection. Her thighs squeezed tightly together, her arms crossed over and hid her breasts, and she buried her face against the musty ticking of the bare mattress. She couldn't look up at him, she couldn't. Tears burned her eyes, clogged her throat.

"Have you been injured?" he asked, the ghostly whisper rasping over her bare skin like an actual touch. "Can you walk?"

Now wasn't the time to let her raw nerves take over. They still had to get out undetected, and a fit of hysteria would ruin everything. She gulped twice, fighting for control of her emotions as grimly as she had fought to control the pain. The tears spilled over, but she forced herself to straighten from the defensive curl, to swing her legs over the edge of the cot. Shakily she sat up and forced herself to look at him. She hadn't done anything to be ashamed of; she would get through this. "I'm okay," she replied, and was grateful that the obligatory whisper disguised the weakness of her voice.

He crouched in front of her and silently began removing the web gear that held and secured all his equipment. The room was too dark for her to make out exactly what each item was, but she recognized the shape of an automatic weapon as he placed it on the floor between them. She watched him, uncomprehending, until he began shrugging out of his shirt. Sick terror hit her then, slamming into her like a sledgehammer. My God, surely *he* wasn't—

Gently he put the shirt around her, tucking her arms into the sleeves as if she was a child, then buttoning each button, taking care to hold the fabric away from her body so his fingers wouldn't brush against her breasts. The cloth still held his body heat; it wrapped around her like a blanket, warming her, covering her. The sudden feeling of security unnerved her almost as much as being stripped naked. Her heart lurched inside her chest, and the bottom dropped out of her stomach. Hesitantly she reached out her hand in an apology, and a plea. Tears dripped slowly down her face, leaving salty tracks in their wake. She had been the recipient of so much male brutality in the past day that his gentleness almost destroyed her control, where their blows and crudeness had only made her more determined to resist them. She had expected the same from him and instead had received a tender care that shattered her with its simplicity.

A second ticked past, two: then, with great care, he folded his gloved fingers around her hand.

His hand was much bigger than hers. She felt the size and heat of it engulf her cold fingers and sensed the control of a man who exactly knew his own strength. He squeezed gently, then released her.

She stared at him, trying to pierce the veil of darkness and see his features, but his face was barely distinguishable and blurred even more by her tears. She could make out some details, though, and discern his movements. He wore a black T-shirt, and as silently as he had removed his gear, he now put it on again. He peeled back a flap on his wrist, and she caught the faint gleam of a luminous watch. "We have exactly two and a half minutes to get out of here," he murmured. "Do *what* I say, *when* I say it."

Before, she couldn't have done it, but that brief moment of understanding, of connection, had buoyed her. Barrie nodded and got to her feet. Her knees wobbled. She stiffened them and shoved her hair out of her face. "I'm ready."

She had taken exactly two steps when, below them, a staccato burst of gunfire shattered the night.

He spun instantly, silently, slipping away from her so fast that she blinked, unable to follow him. Behind her, the door opened. A harsh, piercing flood of light blinded her, and an ominous form loomed in the doorway. The guard—of course there was a guard. Then there was a blur of movement, a grunt, and the guard sagged into supporting arms. As silently as her rescuer seemed to do everything else, he dragged the guard inside and lowered him to the floor. Her rescuer stepped over the body, snagged her wrist in an unbreakable grip and towed her from the room.

The hallway was narrow, dirty and cluttered. The light that had seemed so bright came from a single naked bulb. More gunfire was erupting downstairs and out in the street. From the left came the sound of pounding feet. To the right was a closed door, and past it she could see the first step of an unlit stairway.

He closed the door of the room they had just left and lifted her off her feet, slinging her under his left arm as if she was no more than a sack of flour. Barrie clutched dizzily at his leg as he strode swiftly to the next room and slipped into the sheltering darkness. He had barely shut the door when a barrage of shouts and curses in the hallway made her bury her face against the black material of his pants leg.

He righted her and set her on her feet, pushing her behind him as he unslung the weapon from his shoulder. They stood at the door, unmoving, listening to the commotion just on the other side of the wooden panel. She could discern three different voices and recognized them all. There were more shouts and curses, in the language she had heard off and on all day long but couldn't understand. The curses turned vicious as the guard's body, and her absence, were discovered. Something thudded against the wall as one of her kidnappers gave vent to his temper.

"This is One. Go to B."

That toneless whisper startled her. Confused, she stared at him, trying to make sense of the words. She was so tired that it took her a moment to realize he must be speaking a coded message into a radio. Of course he wasn't alone; there would be an entire team of rescuers. All they had to do was get out of the building, and there would be a helicopter waiting somewhere, or a truck, or a ship. She didn't care if they'd infiltrated on bicycles; she would gladly walk out— barefoot, if necessary.

But first they had to get out of the building. Obviously the plan had been to spirit her out the window without her kidnappers being any the wiser until morning, but something had gone wrong, and the others had been spotted. Now they were trapped in this room, with no way of rejoining the rest of his team.

Her body began to revolt against the stress it had endured for so many long hours, the terror and pain, the hunger, the effort. With a sort of distant interest she felt each muscle begin quivering, the shudders working their way up her legs, her torso, until she was shaking uncontrollably.

She wanted to lean against him but was afraid she would hinder his movements. Her life—and his—depended completely on his expertise. She couldn't help him, so the least she could do was stay out of his way. But she was desperately in need of support, so she fumbled her way a couple of steps to the wall. She was careful not to make any noise, but he sensed her movement and half turned, reaching behind himself with his left hand and catching her. Without speaking he pulled her up against his back, keeping her within reach should he have to change locations in a hurry.

His closeness was oddly, fundamentally reassuring. Her captors had filled her with such fear and disgust that every feminine instinct had been outraged, and after they had finally left her alone in the cold and the dark, she had wondered with a sort of grief if she would ever again be able to trust a man. The answer, at least with *this* man, was yes.

She leaned gratefully against his back, so tired and weak that, just for a moment, she had to rest her head on him. The heat of his body penetrated the rough fabric of the web vest, warming her cheek. He even smelled hot, she noticed through a sort of haze; his scent was a mixture of clean, fresh sweat and musky maleness, exertion and tension heating it to an aroma as heady as that of the finest whiskey. *Mackenzie*. He'd said his name was Mackenzie, whispered it to her when he crouched to identify himself.

Oh, God, he was so warm, and she was still cold. The gritty stone floor beneath her bare feet seemed to be wafting cold waves of air up her legs. His shirt was so big it dwarfed her, hanging almost to her knees, but still she was naked beneath it. Her entire body was shaking.

They stood motionless in the silent darkness of the empty room for an eternity, listening to the gunfire as it tapered off in the distance, listening to the shouts and curses as they, too, diminished, listened for so long that Barrie drifted into a light doze, leaning against him with her head resting on his back. He was like a rock, unmoving, his patience beyond anything she had ever imagined. There were no nervous little adjustments of position, no hint that his muscles got tired. The slow, even rhythm of his breathing was the only movement she could discern, and resting against him as she was, the sensation was like being on a raft in a pool, gently rising, falling….

She woke when he reached back and lightly shook her. "They think we got away," he whispered. "Don't move or make any sound while I check things out."

Obediently she straightened away from him, though she almost cried at the loss of his body heat. He switched on a flashlight that gave off only a slender beam; black tape had been placed across most of the lens. He flicked the light around the room, revealing that it was empty except for some old boxes piled along one wall. Cobwebs festooned all of the corners, and the floor was covered with a thick layer of dust. She could make out a single window in the far wall, but he was careful not to let the thin beam of light get close to it and possibly betray their presence. The room seemed to have been unused for a very long time.

He leaned close and put his mouth against her ear. His warm breath washed across her flesh with every word. "We have to get out of this building. My men have made it look as if we escaped, but we probably won't be able to hook up with them again until tomorrow night. We need someplace safe to wait. What do you know about the interior layout?"

She shook her head and followed his example, lifting herself on tiptoe to put her lips to his ear. "Nothing," she whispered. "I was blindfolded when they brought me here."

He gave a brief nod and straightened away from her. Once again Barrie felt bereft, abandoned, without his physical nearness. She knew it was just a temporary weakness, this urge to cling to him and the security he represented, but she needed him now with an urgency that was close to pain in its intensity. She wanted nothing more than to press close to him again, to feel the animal heat that told her she wasn't alone; she wanted to be in touch with the steely strength that stood between her and those bastards who had kidnapped her.

Temporary or not, Barrie hated this neediness on her part; it reminded her too sharply of the way she had clung to her father when her mother and brother had died. Granted, she had been just a child then, and the closeness that had developed between her and her father had, for the most part, been good. But she had seen how stifling it could be, too, and quietly, as was her way, she had begun placing increments of distance between them. Now this had happened, and her first instinct was to cling. Was she going to turn into a vine every time there was some trauma in her life? She didn't want to be like that, didn't want to be a weakling. This nightmare had shown her too vividly that all security, no matter how solid it seemed, had its weak points. Instead of depending on others, she would do better to develop her own strengths, strengths she knew were there but that had lain dormant for most of her life. From now on, though, things were going to change.

Perhaps they already had. The incandescent anger that had taken hold of her when she'd lain naked and trussed on that bare cot still burned within her, a small, white-hot core that even her mind-numbing fatigue couldn't extinguish. Because of it, she refused to give in to her weakness, refused to do anything that might hinder Mackenzie in any way. Instead she braced herself, forcing her knees to lock and her shoulders to square. "What are we going to do?" she whispered. "What can I do to help?"

Because there were no heavy blackout curtains on this grimy window, she was able to see part of his features as he looked at her. Half his face was in shadow, but the scant light gleamed on the slant of one high, chiseled cheekbone, revealed the strong cut of his jaw, played along a mouth that was as clearly defined as that of an ancient Greek statue.

"I'll have to leave you here alone for a little while," he said. "Will you be all right?"

Panic exploded in her stomach, her chest. She barely choked back the scream of protest that would have betrayed them. Grinding her teeth together and electing not to speak, because the scream would escape if she did, she nodded her head.

He hesitated, and Barrie could feel his attention focusing on her, as if he sensed her distress and was trying to decide whether or not it was safe to leave her. After a few moments he gave a curt nod that acknowledged her determination, or at least gave her the benefit of the doubt. "I'll be back in half an hour," he said. "I promise."

He pulled something from a pocket on his vest. He unfolded it, revealing a thin blanket of sorts. Barrie stood still as he snugly wrapped it around her. Though it was very thin, the blanket immediately began reflecting her meager body heat. When he let go of the edges they fell open, and Barrie clutched frantically at them in an effort to retain that fragile warmth. By the time she had managed to pull the blanket around her, he was gone, opening the door a narrow crack and slipping through as silently as he had come through the window in the room where she had been held. Then the door closed, and once again she was alone in the darkness.

Her nerves shrieked in protest, but she ignored them. Instead she concentrated on being as quiet as she could, listening for any sounds in the building that could tell her what was going on. There was still some noise from the street, the result of the gunfire that had alarmed the nearby citizenry, but that, too, was fading. The thick stone walls of the building dulled any sound, anyway. From within the building, there was only silence. Had her captors abandoned the site after her supposed escape? Were they in pursuit of Mackenzie's team, thinking she was with them?

She swayed on her feet, and only then did she realize that she could sit down on the floor and wrap the blanket around her, conserving even more warmth. Her feet and legs were almost numb with cold. Carefully she eased down onto the floor, terrified she would inadvertently make some noise. She sat on the thin blanket and pulled it around herself as best she could. Whatever fabric it was made from, the blanket blocked the chill of the stone floor. Drawing up her legs, Barrie hugged her knees and rested her head on them. She was more comfortable now than she had been in many long hours of terror and, inevitably, her eyelids began to droop heavily. Sitting there alone in the dark, dirty, empty room, she went to sleep.

Chapter 3

Pistol in hand, Zane moved silently through the decrepit old building, avoiding the piles of debris and crumbled stone. They were already on the top floor, so, except for the roof, the only way he could go was down. He already knew where the exits were, but what he didn't know was the location of the bad guys. Had they chosen this building as only a temporary hiding place and abandoned it when their victim seemingly escaped? Or was this their regular meeting place? If so, how many were there, and *where* were they? He had to know all that before he risked moving Miss Lovejoy. There was only another hour or so until dawn; he had to get her to a secure location before then.

He stopped at a turn in the corridor, flattening himself against the wall and easing his head around the corner just enough that he could see. Empty. Noiselessly, he moved down the hallway, just as cautiously checking the few rooms that opened off it.

He had pulled the black balaclava into place and smeared dust over his bare arms to dull the sheen of his skin and decrease his visibility. Giving his shirt to Miss Lovejoy and leaving his arms bare had increased his visibility somewhat, but he judged that his darkly tanned arms weren't nearly as likely to be spotted as her naked body. Even in the darkness of the room where they had been keeping her, he had been able to clearly make out the pale shimmer of her skin. Since none of her clothes had been in evidence, giving her his shirt was the only thing he could have done. She'd been shaking with cold—evidence of shock because the night was warm—and she likely would have gone into hysterics if he'd tried to take her out of there while she was stark naked. He had been prepared, if necessary, to knock her out. But she'd been a little trooper so far, not even screaming when he had suddenly loomed over her in the darkness. With his senses so acute, though, Zane could feel how fragile her control was, how tightly she was strung.

It was understandable. She had likely been raped, not once but many times, since she had been kidnapped. She might fall apart when the crisis was over and she was safe, but for now she was holding together. Her gutsiness made his heart clench with a mixture of tenderness and a lethal determination to protect her. His first priority was to get her out of Libya, not wreak vengeance on her kidnappers—but if any of the bastards happened to get in his way, so be it.

The dark maw of a stairwell yawned before him. The darkness was reassuring; it not only signaled the absence of a guard, it would shield him. Humans still clung to the primitive instincts of cave dwellers. If they were awake, they wanted the comfort of light around them, so they could see the approach of any enemies. Darkness was a weapon that torturers used to break the spirit of their captives, because it emphasized their helplessness, grated on their nerves. But he was a SEAL, and darkness was merely a circumstance he could use. He stepped carefully into the stairwell, keeping his back to the wall to avoid any crumbling edges of the stone. He was fairly certain the stairs were safe, otherwise the kidnappers wouldn't have been using them, but he didn't take chances. Like idiots, people stacked things on stair steps, blocking their own escape routes.

A faint lessening of the darkness just ahead told him that he was nearing the bottom of the steps. He paused while he was still within the protective shadow, listening for the slightest sound. There. He heard what he'd been searching for, the distant sound of voices, angry voices tripping over each other with curses and excuses. Though Zane spoke Arabic, he was too far away to make out what they were saying. It didn't matter; he'd wanted to know their location, and now he did. Grimly he stifled the urge to exact revenge on Miss Lovejoy's behalf. His mission was to rescue her, not endanger her further.

There was a stairwell at each end of the building. Knowing now that the kidnappers were on the ground floor at the east end, Zane began making his way to the west staircase. He didn't meet up with any guards; as he had hoped, they thought the rescue had been effected, so they didn't see any point now in posting guards.

In his experience, perfect missions were few and far between, so rare that he could count on one hand the number of missions he'd been on where everything had gone like clockwork. He tried to be prepared for mechanical breakdowns, accidents, forces of nature, but there was no way to plan for the human factor. He didn't know how the kidnappers had been alerted to the SEALs' presence, but he had considered that possibility from the beginning and made an alternate plan in case something went wrong. Something had—exactly what, he would find out later: except for that brief communication with his men, telling them to withdraw and switch to the alternate plan, they had maintained radio silence.

Probably it was pure bad luck, some late-night citizen unexpectedly stumbling over one of his men. Things happened. So he had formulated Plan B, his just-in-case plan, because as they had worked their way toward the building, he'd had an uneasy feeling. When his gut told him something, Zane listened. Bunny Withrock had once given him a narrow-eyed look and said, "Boss, you're even spookier than the Spook." But they trusted his instincts, to the point that mentally they had probably switched to Plan B as soon as he'd voiced it, before he had even gone into the building.

With Miss Lovejoy to consider, he'd opted for safety. That was why he had gone in alone, through the window, after Spook's reconnaissance had reported that the kidnappers had set guards at intervals throughout the first floor. There were no lights in any of the rooms on the fourth floor, where Miss Lovejoy was reportedly being held, so it was likely there was no guard actually in the room with her; a guard wouldn't want to sit in the darkness.

The kidnappers had inadvertently pinpointed the room for him: only one window had been covered with curtains. When Zane had reached that room, he had carefully parted the heavy curtains to make certain they hadn't shielded an interior light, but the room beyond had been totally dark. And Miss Lovejoy had been there, just as he had expected.

Now, ostensibly with nothing left to guard, the kidnappers all seemed to be grouped together. Zane cat-footed through the lower rooms until he reached the other staircase, then climbed silently upward. Thanks to Spooky, he knew of a fairly secure place to take Miss Lovejoy while they waited for another opportunity for extraction; all he had to do was get her there undetected. That meant he had to do it before dawn, because a half-naked, red-haired Western woman would definitely be noticeable in this Islamic country. He wouldn't exactly blend in himself, despite his black hair and tanned skin, because of his dark cammies, web gear and weaponry. Most people noticed a man with camouflage paint on his face and an automatic rifle slung over his shoulder.

He reached the room where he'd left Miss Lovejoy and entered as quietly as he'd left. The room was empty. Alarm roared through him, every muscle tightening, and then he saw the small, dark hump on the floor and realized that she had curled up with the thin survival blanket over her. She wasn't moving. Zane listened to the light, almost inaudible evenness of her breathing and realized she had gone to sleep. Again he felt that subtle inner clenching. She had been on edge and terrified for hours, obviously worn out but unable to sleep; the slight measure of security he'd been able to give her, consisting of his shirt, a blanket and a temporary, precarious hiding place, had been enough for her to rest. He hated to disturb her, but they had to move.

Gently he put his hand on her back, lightly rubbing, not shaking her awake but easing her into consciousness so she wouldn't be alarmed. After a moment she began stirring under his touch, and he felt the moment when she woke, felt her instant of panic, then her quietly determined reach for control.

"We're moving to someplace safer," he whispered, removing his hand as soon as he saw she was alert. After what she had been through, she wouldn't want to endure a man's touch any more than necessary. The thought infuriated him, because his instinct was to comfort her; the women in his family, mother, sister and sisters-in-law, were adored and treasured by the men. He wanted to cradle Barrie Lovejoy against him, whisper promises to her that he would personally dismember every bastard who had hurt her, but he didn't want to do anything that would undermine her fragile control. They didn't have time for any comforting, anyway.

She clambered to her feet, still clutching the blanket around her. Zane reached for it, and her fingers tightened on the fabric, then slowly loosened. She didn't have to explain her reluctance to release the protective cloth. Zane knew she was still both extrasensitive to cold and painfully embarrassed by her near nudity.

"Wear it this way," he whispered, wrapping the blanket around her waist sarong-style so that it draped to her feet. He tied the ends securely over her left hipbone, then bent down to check that the fabric wasn't too tight around her feet, so she would have sufficient freedom of movement if they had to run.

When he straightened, she touched his arm, then swiftly lifted her hand away, as if even that brief touch had been too much. "Thank you," she whispered.

"Watch me closely," he instructed. "Obey my hand signals." He explained the most basic signals to her, the raised clenched fist that meant "Stop!" and the open hand that meant merely "halt," the signal to proceed and the signal to hide. Considering her state of mind, plus her obvious fatigue, he doubted she would be able to absorb more than those four simple commands. They didn't have far to go, anyway; if he needed more commands than that, they were in deep ca-ca.

She followed him out of the room and down the west staircase, though he felt her reluctance to step into the Stygian depths. He showed her how to keep her back to the wall, how to feel with her foot for the edge of the step. He felt her stumble once, heard her sharply indrawn breath. He whirled to steady her; his pistol was in his right hand, but his left arm snaked out, wrapping around her hips to steady her as she teetered two steps above him. The action lifted her off her feet, hauling her against his left side. She felt soft in his grip, her hips narrow but nicely curved, and his nostrils flared as he scented the warm sweetness of her skin.

She was all but sitting on his encircling arm, her hands braced on his shoulders. Reluctantly he bent and set her on her feet, and she immediately straightened away from him. "Sorry," she whispered in the darkness.

Zane's admiration for her grew. She hadn't squealed in alarm, despite nearly falling, despite the way he'd grabbed her. She was holding herself together, narrowing her focus to the achievement of one goal: freedom.

She was even more cautious in her movements after that one misstep, letting more distance grow between them than he liked. On the last flight of steps he stopped, waiting for her to catch up with him. Knowing that she couldn't see him, he said, "Here," when she was near, so she wouldn't bump into him.

He eased his way down the last couple of steps into the faint light. There was no one in sight. With a brief wave of his hand he signaled her forward, and she slipped out of the darkness of the stairwell to stand beside him.

There was a set of huge wooden double doors that opened onto the street, but Zane was aware of increased noise outside as dawn neared, and it was too risky to use that exit. From their left came a raised voice, shouting in Arabic, and he felt her tense. Quickly, before the sound of one of her kidnappers unnerved her, he shepherded her into a cluttered storage room, where a small, single window shone high on the wall. "We'll go out this window," he murmured. "There'll be a drop of about four feet to the ground, nothing drastic. I'll boost you up. When you hit the ground, move away from the street but stay against the side of the building. Crouch down so you'll present the smallest possible silhouette. Okay?"

She nodded her understanding, and they picked their way over the jumbled boxes and debris until they were standing under the window. Zane stretched to reach the sill, hooked his fingers on the plaster and boosted himself up until he was balanced with one knee on the sill and one booted foot braced against a rickety stack of boxes. The window evidently hadn't been used in a long time; the glass was opaque with dust, the hinges rusty and stiff. He wrestled it open, wincing at the scraping noise, even though he knew it wouldn't carry to where the kidnappers were. Fresh air poured into the musty room. Like a cat he dropped to the floor, then turned to her.

"You can put your foot in my hand, or you can climb on my shoulders. Which do you prefer?"

With the window open, more light was coming through. He could see her doubtful expression as she stared at the window, and for the first time he appreciated the evenness of her features. He already knew how sweetly her body was shaped, but now he knew that Miss Lovejoy didn't hurt his eyes at all.

"Can you get through there?" she whispered, ignoring his question as she eyed first the expanse of his shoulders and then the narrowness of the window.

Zane had already made those mental measurements. "It'll be a tight fit, but I've been through tighter ones."

She gazed at his darkened face, then gave one of her sturdy nods, the one that said she was ready to go on. Now he could see her calculating the difficulty of maneuvering through the window with the blanket tied around her waist, and he saw the exact moment when she made her decision. Her shoulders squared and her chin came up as she untied the blanket and draped it around her like a long scarf, winding it around her neck and tossing the ends over her shoulders to dangle rakishly down her back.

"I think I'd better climb on your shoulders," she said. "I'll have more leverage that way."

He knelt on the floor and held his hands up for her to catch and brace herself. She went around behind him and daintily placed her right foot on his right shoulder, then lifted herself into a half crouch. As soon as her left foot had settled into place and her hands were securely in his, he rose steadily until he was standing erect. Her weight was negligible compared to what he handled during training. He moved closer to the wall, and she released his right hand to brace her hand against the sill. "Here I go," she whispered, and boosted herself through the window.

She went through it headfirst. It was the fastest way, but not the easiest, because she had no way of breaking her fall on the other side. He looked up and saw the gleam of pale, bare legs and the naked curves of her buttocks; then she vanished from sight, and there was a thump as she hit the ground.

Quickly Zane boosted himself up again. "Are you all right?" he whispered harshly.

There was silence for a moment, then a shaky, whispered answer. "I think so."

"Take the rifle." He handed the weapon to her, then dropped to the floor while he removed his web gear. That, too, went through the window. Then he followed, feet first, twisting his shoulders at an angle to fit through the narrow opening and landing in a crouch. Obediently, she had moved to the side and was sitting against the wall with the blanket once more clutched around her and his rifle cradled in her arms.

Dawn was coming fast, the remnants of darkness no more than a deep twilight. "Hurry," he said as he shrugged into the web vest and took the rifle from her. He slid it into position, then drew the pistol again. The heavy butt felt reassuring and infinitely familiar in his palm. With the weapon in his right hand and her hand clasped in his left, he pulled her into the nearest alley.

Benghazi was a modern city, fairly Westernized, and Libya's chief port. They were near the docks, and the smell of the sea was strong in his nostrils. Like the vast majority of waterfronts, it was one of the rougher areas of the city. From what he'd been able to tell, no authorities had shown up to investigate the gunfire, even supposing it had been reported. The Libyan government wasn't friendly—there were no diplomatic relations between the United States and Libya—but that didn't mean the government would necessarily turn a blind eye to the kidnapping of an ambassador's daughter. Of course, it was just as likely that it would, which was why diplomatic channels hadn't been considered. The best option had seemed to go in and get Miss Lovejoy out as quickly as possible.

There were plenty of ramshackle, abandoned buildings in the waterfront area. The rest of the team had withdrawn to one, drawing any pursuers away from Zane and Miss Lovejoy, while they holed up in another. They would rendezvous at oh-one-hundred hours the next morning.

Spooky had chosen the sites, so Zane trusted their relative safety. Now he and Miss Lovejoy wended their way through a rat's nest of alleyways. She made a stifled sound of disgust once, and he knew she'd stepped on something objectionable, but other than that she soldiered on in silence.

It took only a few minutes to reach the designated safe area. The building looked more down than up, but Spooky had investigated and reported an intact inner room. One outer wall was crumbled to little more than rubble. Zane straddled it, then caught Miss Lovejoy around the waist and effortlessly lifted her over the heap, twisting his torso to set her on the other side. Then he joined her, leading her under half-fallen timbers and around spiderwebs that he wanted left undisturbed. The fact that he could see those webs meant they had to get under cover, fast.

The door to the interior room hung haphazardly on one hinge, and the wood was rotting away at the top. He pulled her inside the protective walls. "Stay here while I take care of our tracks," he whispered, then dropped to a crouch and moved to where they had crossed the remnants of the outer wall. He worked backward from there, scattering dirt to hide the signs of their passage. There were dark, wet places on the broken pieces of stone that were all that remained of the floor. He frowned, knowing what those dark patches meant. Damn it, why hadn't she said something? Had she left a trail of blood straight to their hiding place?

Carefully he obliterated the marks. It wasn't completely her fault; he should have given more thought to her bare feet. The truth was, his mind had been more on her bare butt and the other details of her body that he'd already seen. He was far too aware of her sexually; the proof of it was heavy in his loins. After what she had been through that was the last thing she needed, so he would ignore his desire, but that didn't make it go away.

When he had worked his way to the room, he silently lifted the door and reset it in the frame, bracing it so it wouldn't sag again. Only then did he turn to face her. "Why didn't you tell me you'd cut your foot? When did it happen?" His voice was low and very even.

She was still standing where he'd left her, her face colorless in the half light coming through the open shutters of the window, her eyes so huge with fatigue and strain that she looked like a forlorn, bedraggled little owl. A puzzled frown knit her brows as she looked at her feet. "Oh," she said in dazed discovery as she examined the dark stains on her left foot. "I didn't realize it was cut. It must have happened when I stepped in that…whatever…in the alley. I remember that it hurt, but I thought there was just a sharp rock under the…stuff."

At least it hadn't happened any sooner than that. Their position should still be safe. He keyed the radio, giving the prearranged one click that told the team he was in the safe area and receiving two clicks in return, meaning his men were secure in their position, too. They would check in with each other at set intervals, but for the most part they would spend the day resting. Relieved, Zane turned his mind to other matters.

"Sit down and let me see your foot," he ordered. The last thing he needed was for her to be hobbled, though from what he'd seen of her so far, she wouldn't breathe a word of complaint, merely limp along as fast as she could.

There was nothing to sit on except the broken stones of the floor, so that was where she sat, carefully keeping the blanket wrapped around her waist. Her feet were filthy, caked with the same mess that caked his boots. Blood oozed sullenly from a cut on the instep of her left foot.

Zane shucked off his black hood and headset, took off his web vest and removed his gloves; then he unpacked his survival gear, which included a small and very basic first-aid kit. He sat cross-legged in front of her and lifted her foot to rest on his thigh. After tearing open a small packet containing a premoistened antiseptic pad, he thoroughly cleaned the cut and the area around it, pretending not to notice her involuntary flinches of pain, which she quickly tried to control.

The cut was deep enough that it probably needed a couple of stitches. He took out another antiseptic pad and pressed it hard over the wound until the bleeding stopped. "How long has it been since your last tetanus vaccination?" he asked.

Barrie thought that she had never heard anything as calm as his voice. She could see him clearly now; it was probably a good thing she hadn't been able to do so before, because her nerves likely couldn't have stood the pressure. She cleared her throat and managed to say, "I don't remember. Years," but her mind wasn't on what she was saying.

His thick black hair was matted with sweat, and his face was streaked with black and green paint. The black T-shirt he wore was grimy with mingled dust and sweat, not that the shirt she had on was in much better shape. The material strained over shoulders that looked a yard wide, clung to a broad chest and flat stomach, stretched over powerful biceps. His arms were corded with long, steely muscles, his wrists almost twice as thick as hers; his long-fingered hands were well-shaped, callused, harder than any human hands should be—and immensely gentle as he cleansed the wound on her foot.

His head was bent over the task. She saw the dense black eyelashes, the bold sweep of his eyebrows, the thin and arrogantly high bridge of his nose, the chiseled plane of his cheekbones. She saw his mouth, so clear-cut and stern, as if he seldom smiled. Beard stubble darkened his jaw beneath the camouflage paint. Then his gaze flicked up to her for a moment, cool and assessing, as if he was gauging her reaction to the sting of the antiseptic, and she was stunned by the clear, pale beauty of his blue gray eyes. He had silently and efficiently killed that guard, then stepped over the body as if it didn't exist. A wicked, ten-inch black blade rode in a scabbard strapped to his thigh, and he handled both pistol and rifle with an ease that bespoke a familiarity that went far beyond the normal. He was the most savage, dangerous, lethal thing, man or beast, that she had ever seen— and she felt utterly safe with him.

He had given her the shirt off his back, treating her with a courtesy and tenderness that had eased her shock, calmed her fears. He had seen her naked; she had been able to ignore that while they were still trapped in the same building with her kidnappers, but now they were relatively safe, and alone, and she was burningly aware of both his intense masculinity and of her nakedness beneath his shirt. Her skin felt unusually sensitive, as if it was too hot and tight, and the rasp of the fabric against her nipples was almost painfully acute.

Her foot looked small and fragile in his big hands. He frowned in concentration as he applied an antibiotic ointment to the cut, then fashioned a butterfly bandage to close the wound. He worked with a swift, sure dexterity, and it was only a moment before the bandaging was complete. Gently he lifted her foot off his leg. "There. You should be able to walk with no problem, but as soon as we get you to the ship, get the doc to put in a couple of stitches and give you an injection for tetanus."

"Yes, sir," she said softly.

He looked up with a swift, faint smile. "I'm Navy. That's, 'Aye, aye, sir.'"

The smile nearly took her breath. If he ever truly smiled, she thought, she might have heart failure. To hide her reaction, she held out her hand to him. "Barrie Lovejoy. I'm pleased to make your acquaintance."

He folded his fingers around hers and solemnly shook hands. "Lieutenant-Commander Zane Mackenzie, United States Navy SEALs."

A SEAL. Her heart jumped in her chest. That explained it, then. SEALs were known as the most dangerous men alive, men so skilled in the arts of warfare that they were in a class by themselves. He didn't just look lethal; he *was* lethal.

"Thank you," she whispered.

"My pleasure, ma'am."

Hot color flooded her face as she looked at her blanket-covered lap. "Please, call me Barrie. After all, your shirt is the only thing I…" Her voice trailed off, and she bit her lip. "I mean, formality at this point is—"

"I understand," he said gently, breaking into her stumbling explanation. "I don't want you to be embarrassed, so the circumstances are strictly between us, if you prefer. But I advise you to tell the ship's surgeon, or your own doctor, for the sake of your health."

Barrie blinked at him in confusion, wondering what on earth her health had to do with the fact that he'd seen her naked. Then comprehension dawned; if she hadn't been so tired, she would have realized immediately what conclusion he had drawn from the situation.

"They didn't rape me," she whispered. Her face flushed even hotter. "They—they touched me, they hurt me and did some…other things, but they didn't actually rape me. They were saving that for today. Some important guy in their organization was supposed to arrive, and I suppose they were planning a sort of p-party."

Zane's expression remained calm and grave, and she knew he didn't believe her. Why should he? He'd found her tied up and naked, and she'd already been in the kidnappers' hands for most of a day. Chivalry wasn't part of their code; they had refrained from rape only on orders from their leader, because he wanted to be there to enjoy her himself before the others had their turn on her.

He didn't say anything, and Barrie busied herself with the used antiseptic pads, which were still damp enough to clean the rest of the disgusting muck from her feet. She longed for a bath, but that was so far out of the question that she didn't even voice the wish.

While she busied herself with tidying up, he explored the small room, which didn't take long, because there was nothing in it. He closed the broken shutters over the window; the wooden slats were rotted away at the top, allowing some light through but preventing any passersby from seeing inside.

With the room mostly dark once more, it was like being in a snug, private cave. Barrie smothered a yawn, fighting the fatigue that dragged on her like lead weights. The only sleep she'd had was that brief nap while Zane had been finding a way out of the building, and she was so tired that even her hunger paled in comparison.

He noticed, of course; he didn't miss anything. "Why don't you go to sleep?" he suggested. "In a couple of hours, when more people are moving around and I won't be as noticeable, I'll go scrounge up something for us to eat and liberate some clothes for you."

Barrie eyed the paint streaking his face. "With makeup like that, I don't believe you're going to go unnoticed no matter how crowded the streets are."

That faint smile touched his lips again, then was gone. "I'll take it off first."

The smile almost kept her awake. Almost. She felt her muscles slowly loosening, as if his permission to sleep was all her body needed to hear. Her eyelids were too heavy for her to hold open anymore; it was like a veil of darkness descending. With her last fraction of consciousness, she was aware of his arms around her, gently lowering her to the floor.

Chapter 4

She had gone to sleep like a baby, Zane thought, watching her. He'd seen it often enough in his ten nephews, the way little children had of dropping off so abruptly, their bodies looking almost boneless as they toppled over into waiting arms. His gaze drifted over her face. Now that dawn was here, even with the shutters closed, he could plainly see the exhaustion etched on her face; the wonder was that she had held up so well, rather than that she'd gone to sleep now.

He could use some rest himself. He stretched out beside her, keeping a slight distance between them; not touching, but close enough that he could reach her immediately if their hiding place was discovered. He was still wired, too full of adrenaline to sleep yet, but it felt good to relax and let himself wind down while he waited for the city to come completely awake.

Now he could also see the fire in her hair, the dark auburn shade that, when she stood in the sun, would glint with gold and bronze. Her eyes were a deep, soft green, her brows and lashes like brown mink. He wouldn't have been surprised by freckles, but her skin was clear and creamy, except for the bruise that mottled one cheek. There were bruises on her arms, and though he couldn't see them, he knew the shirt covered other marks left by brutal men. She'd insisted they hadn't raped her, but probably she was ashamed for anyone else to know, as if she'd had any choice in the matter. Maybe she wanted to keep it quiet for her father's sake. Zane didn't care about her reasons; he just hoped she would get the proper medical care.

He thought dispassionately about slipping to the building where they'd held her and killing any and all of the bastards who were still there. God knew they deserved it, and he wouldn't lose a minute's worth of sleep over any of them. But his mission was to rescue Miss Lovejoy—Barrie—and he hadn't accomplished that yet. If he went back, there was the chance that he would be killed, and that would endanger her, as well as his men. He'd long ago learned how to divorce his emotions from the action so he could think clearly, and he wasn't about to compromise a mission now... But *damn*, he wanted to kill them.

He liked the way she looked. She wasn't drop-dead gorgeous or anything like that, but her features were regular, and asleep, with her woes put aside for the moment, her expression was sweetly serene. She was a pretty little thing, as finely made as an expensive porcelain figurine. Oh, he supposed she was probably of middle height for a woman, about five feet five, but he was six-three and outweighed her by at least a hundred pounds, so to him she was little. Not as little as his mother and sister, but they were truly slight, as delicate as fairies. Barrie Lovejoy, for all her aristocratic bloodlines, had the sturdiness of a pioneer. Most women, with good reason, would have broken down long before now.

He was surprised to feel himself getting a little drowsy. Despite their situation, there was something calming about lying here beside her, watching her sleep. Though he was solitary by nature and had always preferred sleeping alone after his sexual appetite had been satisfied, it felt elementally right, somehow, to guard her with his body as they slept. Had cavemen done this, putting themselves between the mouth of the cave and the sleeping forms of their women and children, drowsily watching the gentle movements of their breathing as the fires died down and night claimed the land? If it was an ancient instinct, Zane mused, he sure as hell hadn't felt it before now.

But he wanted to touch her, to feel the softness of her flesh beneath his hand. He wanted to fold her within the warm protection of his body, tuck her in close, curl around her and keep her there with an arm draped around her waist. Only the knowledge that the last thing in the world she would want now was a man's touch kept him from doing just that.

He wanted to hold her. He ached to hold her.

She was dwarfed by his shirt, but he'd seen the body hidden by the folds of cloth. His night vision was very good; he'd been able to discern her high, round breasts, not very big, but definitely mouth-watering, and tipped with small, tight nipples. She was curvy, womanly, with a small waist and rounded hips and a neat little triangle of pubic hair. He'd seen her buttocks. Just thinking about it made him feel hollowed out with desire; her butt was fine indeed. He would like to feel it snuggled up against his thighs.

He wasn't going to be able to sleep, after all. He was fully aroused, desire pulsing through his swollen and rigid flesh. Wincing, he turned onto his back and adjusted himself to a more comfortable position, but the comfort was relative. The only way he would truly find ease was within the soft, hot clasp of her body, and that wasn't likely to happen.

The small room grew brighter and warmer as dawn developed into full morning. The stone walls would protect them from most of the day's heat, but soon they would need water. Water, food, and clothes for her. A robe would be better than Western-style clothing, because the traditional Muslim attire would cover her hair, and there were enough traditionalists in Benghazi that a robe wouldn't draw a second glance.

The streets were noisy now, the waterfront humming with activity. Zane figured it was time for him to do some foraging. He wiped the camouflage paint from his skin as best he could and disguised what was left by smearing dirt on his face. He wasn't about to go unarmed, so he pulled the tail of his T-shirt free from his pants and tucked the pistol into the waistband at the small of his back, then let the shirt fall over it. Anyone who paid attention would know the bulge for what it was, but what the hell, it wasn't unusual for people to go armed in this part of the world. Thanks to his one-quarter Comanche heritage, his skin had a rich bronze hue, and in addition he was darkly tanned from countless hours of training in the sun and sea and wind. There was nothing about his appearance that would attract undue notice, not even his eyes, because there were plenty of Libyans with a European parent.

He checked Barrie, reassuring himself that she was still sleeping soundly. He'd told her that he would be slipping out for a while, so she shouldn't be alarmed if she woke while he was gone. He left their crumbling sanctuary as silently as he had entered it.

It was over two hours before he returned, almost time for the designated check-in time with his men. He had a definite talent for scavenging, he thought, though outright thievery would probably be a better term. He carried a woman's black robe and head covering, and wrapped up in

it was a selection of fruit, cheese and bread, as well as a pair
of slippers he hoped would fit Barrie. The water had been
the hardest to come by, because he'd lacked a container.
He'd solved that by stealing a stoppered gallon jug of wine,
forbidden by the Koran but readily available anyway. He
had poured out the cheap, sour wine and filled the jug with
water. The water would have a definite wine taste to it, but
it would be wet, and that was all they required.

While he had the opportunity, he disguised the entrance
to their lair a bit, piling some stones in front of it, arranging a rotted timber so that it looked as if it blocked the door.
The door was still visible, but looked much less accessible.
He tested his handiwork to make certain they could still get
out easily enough, then slipped inside and once again
braced the door in its sagging frame.

He turned to check on Barrie. She was still asleep. The
room was considerably warmer, and she had kicked the
blanket aside. His shirt was up around her waist.

The kick of desire was like taking a blow to the chest.
He almost staggered from it, his heart racing, his breath
strangling in his throat. Sweat beaded on his forehead, ran
down his temple. *God.*

He should turn away. He should put the blanket over her.
He should put sex completely out of his mind. There were
any number of things he should do, but instead he stared
at her with a hunger so intense he ached with it, quivered
with it. Greedily his gaze moved over every female inch of
her. His sex was throbbing like a toothache. He wanted her
more intensely than he'd ever wanted a woman before. His
famous cool remoteness had failed him—there wasn't a
cool inch on him, and his desire was so damn strong and
immediate, he was shaking from the effort of resisting it.

Moving slowly, stiffly, he set his purloined goodies on the

floor. His breath hissed between his clenched teeth. He hadn't known sexual frustration could be this painful. He'd never had any trouble getting a woman whenever he'd wanted one. This woman was off-limits, though, from even an attempt at seduction. She'd been through enough without having to fend off her rescuer, too.

As warm as the room was now, if he spread the blanket over her she would only kick it off again. Gingerly he went down on one knee beside her and with shaking hands pulled the shirt tail down to cover her. With slight disbelief he eyed the fine tremor of his fingers. He never trembled. He was rock steady during the most tense and dangerous situations, icily controlled in combat. He had parachuted out of a burning plane, swum with sharks and sewn up his own flesh. He had ridden unbroken horses and even bulls a time or two. He had killed. He had done all of that with perfect control, but this sleeping, red-haired woman made him shake.

Grimly he forced himself to turn aside and pick up the radio headset. Holding the earpiece in place, he clicked once and immediately heard two clicks in response. Everything was okay.

Maybe some water would cool him down. At least thinking about it was better than thinking about Barrie. He dropped a couple of purification tablets into the jug, in case the small amount of wine that had remained in it wasn't enough to kill all the invisible little critters. The tablets didn't improve the taste any—just the opposite—but they were better than a case of the runs.

He drank just enough to relieve his thirst, then settled down with his back to a wall. There was nothing to do but wait and contemplate the walls, because he sure as hell didn't trust himself to look at Barrie.

* * *

Voices woke her. They were loud, and close by. Barrie bolted upright, her eyes huge with alarm. Hard arms grabbed her, and an even harder hand clamped itself over her mouth, stifling any sound she might have made. Confused, disoriented, in sheer terror she began to fight as much as she could. Teeth. She should use her teeth. But his fingers were biting hard into her jaw, and she couldn't open her mouth. Desperately she tried to shake her head, and he merely gathered her in tighter, tucking her against him in a way that was oddly protective.

"Shh" came that toneless whisper, and the familiarity of it cut through the panic and fog of sleep. Zane.

Instantly she relaxed, weak with relief. Feeling the tension leave her muscles, he tilted her face, still keeping his hand over her mouth. Their eyes met in the shadowed light, and he gave a brief nod as he saw that she was awake now, and aware. He released her jaw, his hard fingers trailing briefly over her skin in apology for the tightness of his grip. The barely there caress went through her like lightning. She shivered as it seared a path along nerve endings throughout her body and instinctively turned her face into the warm hollow created by the curve of his shoulder.

The arm around her had loosened immediately when she shivered, but at her action she felt him hesitate a fraction of a second, then gather her snugly against him once more.

The voices were closer, and added to them were some thuds and the sound of crumbling rock. She listened to the rapid, rolling syllables of Arabic, straining to concentrate on the voices. Were they the same voices she had heard through yesterday's long nightmare? It was difficult to tell.

She didn't understand the language; hers had been a finishing-school education, suited to an ambassador's daughter. She spoke French and Italian fluently, Spanish a little less so. After her father's posting in Athens she had made it a point to study Greek, too, and had learned enough that she could carry on a simple conversation, though she understood more than she spoke.

Fiercely she wished she had insisted on lessons in Arabic, too. She had hated every moment she'd spent in the kidnappers' hands, but not speaking the language had made her feel even more helpless, more isolated.

She would rather die than let them get their hands on her again.

She must have tensed, because Zane gave her a light squeeze of reassurance. Swiftly she glanced at his face. He wasn't looking at her; instead he was concentrating on the fragile, half-rotted door that protected the entrance to their sanctuary, and on the voices beyond. His expression was utterly calm and distant. Abruptly she realized that he *did* understand Arabic, and whatever was being said by the people picking through the ruins of the building, he wasn't alarmed by it. He was alert, because their hiding place could be compromised at any moment, but evidently he felt confident of being able to handle that problem.

With reason, no doubt. From what she'd seen, she thought he was capable of handling just about any situation. She would trust him with her life—and had.

The voices went on for a long time, sometimes coming so close to their hiding place that Zane palmed that big pistol and held it aimed unwaveringly at the door. Barrie stared at that hand, so lean and powerful and capable. There wasn't the slightest tremor visible; it was almost unreal, almost inhuman, for any man to be that calm and have such perfect control over his body.

They sat silently in the warm, shadowy little room, their

breathing for the most part their only movements. Barrie noticed that the blanket no longer covered her legs, but the shirt, thank God, kept her reasonably decent. It was too hot to lie under the blanket, anyway.

Time crept by at a sloth's pace. The warmth and silence were hypnotic, lulling her into a half dream state of both awareness and distance. She was ferociously hungry, but unaffected by it, as if she was merely aware of someone else's hunger. After a while her muscles began to ache from being in one position for so long, but that didn't matter, either. Thirst, though, was different. In the increasing heat, her need for water began to gnaw at her. The kidnappers had given her some water a couple of times, but she'd had nothing to drink in hours— since she had learned they expected her to relieve herself in their presence, in fact. She had chosen to do without water rather than provide them with such amusement again.

Sweat streaked down Zane's face and dampened his shirt. She was perfectly content to remain where she was, nestled against his side. The arm around her made her feel safer than if their hiding place had been constructed of steel, rather than crumbling stone and plaster, and rotting wood.

She had never been exposed to a man like him before. Her only contact with the military had been with the senior officers who attended functions at the embassy, colonels and generals, admirals, the upper brass; there were also the Marine guards at the embassy, with their perfect uniforms and perfect manners. Though she supposed the Marine guards had to be exemplary soldiers or they wouldn't have been chosen as embassy guards, still, they were nothing like the man who held her so protectively. They were soldiers; he was a warrior. He was as different from them as the lethal, ten-inch black blade strapped to his thigh was from a pocketknife. He was a finely honed weapon.

For all that, he wasn't immortal, and they weren't safe. Their hiding place could be discovered. He could be killed; she could be recaptured. The hard reality of that was something she couldn't ignore as she could hunger and cramped muscles.

After a long, long time, the voices went away. Zane released her and walked noiselessly to the door to look out. She had never before seen anyone move with such silent grace, like a big jungle cat on velvet paws instead of a battle-hardened warrior in boots.

She didn't move until he turned around, the faint relaxation of his expression telling her the danger was past. "What were they doing?" she asked, taking care to keep her voice low.

"Scavenging building materials, picking up blocks, any pieces of wood that hadn't rotted. If they'd had a sledgehammer, they probably would have dismantled these walls. They carted the stuff off in a wheelbarrow. If they need more, they'll probably be back."

"What will we do?"

"The same thing we did this time—hunker down and keep quiet."

"But if they come in here—"

"I'll handle it." He cut her worry short before she could completely voice it, but he did it with a tone of reassurance. "I brought some food and water. Interested?"

Barrie scrambled to her knees, eagerness in every line of her body. "Water! I'm so thirsty!" Then she halted, her recent experience fresh in her mind. "But if I drink anything, where will I go to…you know."

He regarded her with faint bemusement, and she blushed

a little as she realized that wasn't a problem he normally encountered. When he and his men were on a mission, they would relieve themselves wherever and whenever they needed.

"I'll find a place for you to go," he finally said. "Don't let that stop you from drinking the water you need. I also found some clothes for you, but as hot as it's getting in here, you'll probably want to wait until night before you put them on."

He indicated the black bundle beside his gear, and she realized it was a robe. She thought of the modesty it would provide, and gratitude flooded her; at least she wouldn't have to face his men wearing nothing more than his shirt. But he was right; in the heat of day, and in the privacy of this small room, she would prefer wearing his shirt. They both knew she was bare beneath it; he'd already seen her stark naked, and demonstrated his decency by giving her the shirt and ignoring her nakedness, so there was no point now in swathing herself in an ankle-length robe.

He produced a big jug and unstoppered it. "It'll taste funny," he warned as he passed the jug to her. "Purification tablets."

It did taste funny—warm, with a chemical flavor. But it was wonderful. She drank a few swallows, not wanting to make her stomach cramp after being empty for so long. While she was drinking, he unwrapped the bits of food he'd procured—a loaf of hard bread, a hunk of cheese and several oranges, plums and dates. It looked like a feast.

He straightened the blanket for her to sit on, then took out his knife and cut small portions of both the loaf and cheese and gave them to her. She started to protest that she was hungry enough to eat much more than that, but realized that what he had would have to last them all day, and perhaps longer than that. She wasn't about to complain about the amount of food she *did* have.

She had never been particularly fond of cheese, and she suspected that if she hadn't been so hungry she wouldn't have been fond of this cheese, either, but at the moment it was delicious. She nibbled at both bread and cheese, finding satisfaction in the simple act of chewing. As it happened, she had overestimated her appetite. The small portion he had given her was more than enough.

He ate more heartily, and polished off one of the oranges. He insisted that she eat a couple of the juicy slices and drink a bit more water. Feeling replete, Barrie yawned and refused the offer of another orange slice.

"No, thanks, I'm full."

"Would you like to freshen up now?"

Her head whipped around, sending her red hair flying. Amusement twinkled in his pale eyes at her eager, pleading expression. "There's enough water?"

"Enough to dampen a bandana."

She didn't have a bandana, of course, but he did. Carefully he poured just enough water from the jug to wet the square cloth, then politely turned his back and busied himself with his gear.

Slowly Barrie smoothed the wet cloth over her face, sighing in pleasure at the freshness of the sensation. She hadn't realized how grimy she felt until now, when she was able to rectify the situation. She found a sore place on her cheek, where one of the men had hit her, and other tender bruises on her arms. Glancing at Zane's broad back, she quickly unbuttoned the shirt just enough that she could slide the handkerchief inside and rub it over her torso and under her arms. After she fastened the garment, her dusty legs got the same attention. The dampness was wonderfully cooling, almost voluptuous in the sensual delight it gave her.

"I'm finished," she said, and returned the dark bandana to him when he turned around. "It felt wonderful. Thank you."

Then her heart leaped in her chest, because he evidently felt the same need to cool off as she had, but unlike her, he didn't keep his shirt on. He peeled the snug black T-shirt off over his head and dropped it on the blanket, then sat on his heels while he moistened the bandana and began scrubbing it over his face.

Oh, my. Helplessly she stared at the rippling muscles of his chest and stomach, the way they flexed and relaxed with the flow of his movements. The dim light caught the deep bronze of his skin, gleamed on the smooth, powerful curve of his shoulder. Her fascinated gaze wandered over the slant of his shoulder blades, the diamond of black hair that stretched from nipple to nipple on his chest. He twisted around to reach for something, and she found his back equally fascinating, with the deep furrow of his spine bisecting two muscular planes.

There was an inch-long scar on his left cheekbone. She hadn't noticed it before because his face had been so dirty, but now she could plainly see the silvery line of it. It wasn't a disfiguring scar at all, just a straight little slash, as precise as a surgeon's cut. The scar along his rib cage was different, easily eight or nine inches in length, jagged, the scar tissue thick and ridged. Then there were the two round, puckered scars, one just above his waist, the other just below his right shoulder blade. Bullet wounds. She'd never seen one before, but she recognized them for what they were. There was another slash running along his right bicep, and God only knew how many other scars there were on the rest of his body. The warrior hadn't led a charmed life; his body bore the signs of battle.

He squatted half-naked, unconcernedly rubbing the damp handkerchief across his sweaty chest, lifting his arms to wash under them, exposing the smooth undersides and intriguing patches of hair. He was so fundamentally, elementally male, and so purely a warrior, that her breath strangled in her lungs as she watched him.

The rush of warmth through her body told her that she was more female than she'd ever imagined.

A little dazed, she sat back, resting against the wall. Absently she made certain the shirt tail preserved her modesty, but thoughts were tumbling through her mind, dizzyingly fast yet very clear.

They weren't out of danger yet.

During the past twenty-four horrific hours, she hadn't spent a lot of time wondering about the motive behind her kidnapping. She'd had too much to deal with as it was, the sheer terror, the confusion, the pain of the blows they'd given her.

She'd been blindfolded much of the time, and disoriented. She'd been humiliated, stripped naked and roughly fondled, taunted with the prospect of rape, and yet they had stopped short of rape—for a reason. Sheer psychological torture had undoubtedly played a role, but most of all they'd had orders to save her for the man who was to arrive today.

Who was he? He was the one behind her kidnapping; he had to be. But why?

Ransom? When she thought about it now, coolly and clearly, she didn't think so. Yes, her father was rich. Many a diplomat came from a moneyed background; it wasn't unusual. But if money had been the motive, there were others who were richer, though perhaps she had been chosen specifically because it was well known that her father would beggar himself to keep her safe. Perhaps.

But why would they have taken her out of the country? Wouldn't they have wanted to keep her close by, to make the exchange for money easier? No, the very fact that they'd taken her out of the country meant they'd kidnapped her for another reason. Maybe they would have asked for money anyway; since they already had her, why not? But money wasn't the primary object. So what was?

She didn't know, and since she didn't know who the leader was, she had no way of guessing what he truly wanted.

Not herself. She dismissed that notion out of hand. She wasn't the object of obsession, because no man so obsessed with a woman that he was driven to such lengths would let his men maul her. Nor was she the type to inspire obsession, she thought wryly. Certainly none of the men she'd dated had shown any signs of obsessive behavior.

So…there was something else, some piece of puzzle she was missing. Was it someone she knew? Something she'd read or seen?

Nothing came to mind. She wasn't involved in intrigue, though of course she knew which employees at the embassy were employed by the CIA. That was standard, nothing unusual. Her father often spoke privately with Art Sandefer and, lately, Mack Prewett, too. She'd often thought that Art was more bureaucrat than spy, though the intelligence in his tired gaze said he'd done his time in the field, too. She didn't know about Mack Prewett. There was something restless and hard about him, something that made her uneasy.

Her father said Mack was a good man. She wasn't certain about that, but neither did he seem like a villain. Still, there had been that time a couple of weeks ago when she hadn't known anyone was with her father and had breezily walked in without knocking. Her father had been handing a thick manila envelope to Mack; both of them had looked startled and uncomfortable, but her father wasn't a diplomat for nothing. He'd efficiently smoothed over the slight awkwardness, and Mack had left the office almost immediately, taking the envelope with him. Barrie hadn't asked any questions about it, because if it was CIA business, then it wasn't her business.

Now she wondered what had been in that envelope.

That small incident was the only thing the slightest bit untoward that she could remember. Art Sandefer had once said that there was no such thing as coincidence, but could that moment be linked to her kidnapping? Could it be the *cause* of it? That was a reach.

She didn't know what was in the envelope, hadn't shown any interest in it. But she had seen her father giving it to Mack Prewett. That meant…what?

She felt as if she was feeling her way through a mental maze, taking wrong turns, stumbling into dead ends, then groping her way back to logic. Her father would never, in any way, do anything that would harm her. Therefore, that envelope had no significance—unless he was involved in something dangerous and wanted out. Her kidnapping made sense only if someone was using her as a weapon to make her father do something he didn't want to do.

She couldn't accept the idea of her father doing anything traitorous—at least, not voluntarily. She wasn't blind to his weaknesses. He was a bit of a snob, he didn't at all like even the idea that someday she might fall in love and get married, he was protective to the point of smothering her. But he was an honorable man, and a truly patriotic man. It could be that the kidnappers were trying to force her father to do something, give them some information, perhaps, and he had resisted; she could be the means they were using to force him to do what they wanted.

That felt logical. The envelope probably had nothing at all to do with her kidnapping, and Art Sandefer was wrong about coincidence.

But what if he wasn't?

Then, despite her instincts about him, her father was involved in something he shouldn't be. The thought made her sick to her stomach, but she had to face the possibility, had to think of every angle. She had to face it, then put it aside, because there was nothing she could do about it now.

If the kidnappers had been going to use her as a weapon against her father, then they wouldn't give up. If it had just been ransom, they would have thrown up their hands at her supposed escape and said the Arabic equivalent of, "Ah, to hell with it."

The leader hadn't been here. She didn't even know where "here" was; she'd had too much on her mind to ask questions about her geographic location.

"Where are we?" she murmured, thinking she really should know.

Zane lifted his eyebrows. He was sitting down, lounging against the wall at a right angle to her, having finished cleaning up, and she wondered how long she'd been lost in thought. "The waterfront district," he said. "It's a rough section of town."

"I meant, what town?" she clarified.

Realization dawned in his crystal clear eyes. "Benghazi," he said softly. "Libya."

Libya. Stunned, she absorbed the news, then went back to the mental path she'd been following.

The leader had been flying in today. From where? Athens? If he'd been in contact with his men, he would know she'd somehow escaped. But if he had access to the embassy, and to her father, then he would also know that she hadn't been returned to the embassy. Therefore, she would logically still be in Libya. Also logically, they would be actively searching for her.

She looked at Zane again. His eyes were half-closed, he looked almost asleep. Because of the heat, he hadn't put his T-shirt back on. But despite the drowsy look on his face, she sensed that he was vitally aware of everything going on around them, that he was merely letting his body rest while his mind remained on guard.

After the humiliation and pain her guards had dealt her, Zane's concern and consideration had been like a balm, soothing her, helping to heal her bruised emotions before she even had time to know how deep the damage went. Almost before she knew it, she had been responding to him as a woman does to a man, and somehow that was all right.

He was the exact opposite of the thugs who had so delighted in humiliating her. Those thugs were probably searching all over the city for her, and until she was out of this country, the possibility existed that they would recapture her. And if they did, this time there would be no respite.

No. It was intolerable. But if the unthinkable happened, she would be damned if she would give them the satisfaction they'd been anticipating. She would be damned if she would let them take her virginity.

She had never thought of her virginity as anything other than a lack of experience and inclination. At school in Switzerland there had been precious few opportunities for meeting boys, and she hadn't been particularly interested in those she had met. After she left school, her father's protective possessiveness, as well as her duties at the embassy, had restricted any social life she might have developed. The men she met hadn't seemed any more interesting than the few boys she had met while in school. With AIDS added in as a threat, it simply hadn't seemed worth the risk to have sex simply for the experience.

But she had dreamed. She had dreamed of meeting a man, growing to love him, making love with him. Simple, universal dreams.

The kidnappers had almost taken all that from her, almost wrecked her dream of loving a man by abusing her so severely that, if she had remained in their hands much longer, she knew she would have been so severely traumatized that she might never have been able to love a man or tolerate his touch. If Zane hadn't taken her out of there, her first sexual experience would have been one of rape.

No. A thousand times no.

Even if they managed to recapture her, she wouldn't let them murder that dream.

Scrambling to her feet, Barrie took the few steps to where Zane lounged against the wall. She saw his muscled body come to alertness at her action, though he didn't move. She stood over him, staring at him with green eyes burning in the dim light. The look he gave her was hooded, unreadable.

"Make love to me," she said in a raw voice.

Chapter 5

"Barrie…" he began, his tone kind, and she knew he was going to refuse.

"No!" she said fiercely. "Don't tell me I should think about it, or that I really don't want to do it. I know what I went through with those bastards. I know you don't believe it, but they *didn't* rape me. But they looked at me, they touched me, and I couldn't stop them." She stopped and drew a deep breath, steadying herself. "I'm not stupid. I know we're still in danger, that you and your men could be wounded or even killed trying to rescue me and that I could end up back in their hands anyway. I've never made love before, with anyone. I don't want my first time to be rape, do you understand? I don't want them to have that satisfaction. *I want the first time to be with you.*"

She had surprised him, she saw, and she had already noticed that Zane Mackenzie wasn't a man whose expression revealed much of what he was thinking. He sat up straight, his pale eyes narrowed as he examined her with a piercing gaze.

He was still going to refuse, and she didn't think she could bear it. "I promise," she blurted desperately. "They didn't do that to me. I can't have any disease, if that's what you're worried about."

"No," he said, his voice suddenly sounding strained. "That isn't what I'm worried about."

"Don't make me beg," she pleaded, wringing her hands together, aware that she was already doing exactly that.

Then the expression in those pale eyes softened, grew warmer. "I won't," he said softly, and rose to his feet with that powerful, feline grace of his. He towered over her, and for a moment Barrie felt the difference in their sizes so sharply that she wondered wildly what she thought she was doing. Then he moved past her to the blanket; he knelt and smoothed it, then dropped down on it, stretching out on his back, and watched her with a world of knowledge in his slightly remote, too-old eyes.

He knew. And until she read that knowledge in his eyes, she hadn't even been aware of what she really needed. But watching him lie down and put himself at her service, something inside her shattered. *He knew.* He understood the emotions roiling deep inside her, understood what had brought her to him with her fierce, startling demand. It wasn't just that she wanted her first time to be of her own volition, with the man of her choice; the kidnappers had taken something from her, and he was giving it back. They had tied her down, stripped her, humiliated her, and she had been helpless to stop them. Zane was giving control back to her, reassuring her and at the same time subtly letting her exact her vengeance against the male of the species.

She didn't want to lie helpless beneath him. She wanted to control this giving of her body, wanted things to move at her pace instead of his, wanted to be the one who decided how much, how far, how fast.

And he was going to let her do it.

He was giving control of his body to her.

She could barely breathe as she sank to her knees beside him. The warm, bare, richly tanned flesh lured her hands closer, closer, until the urge overcame her nervousness and her fingers lightly skimmed over his stomach, his chest. Her heart hammered wildly. It was like petting a tiger, knowing how dangerous the animal was but fascinated beyond resistance by the rich pelt. She wanted to feel all of that power under her hands. Carefully she flattened her hands along his ribs, molding his flesh beneath her palms, feeling the resilience of skin over the powerful bands of muscle and, beneath that, the strong solidity of bone. She could feel the rhythmic thud of his heartbeat, the expansion of his ribs as he breathed.

Both heartbeat and breathing seemed fast. Swiftly she glanced at his face and blushed at what she saw there, the heat in his heavy-lidded eyes, the deepened color of his lips. She knew what lust looked like; she'd seen the cruel side of it on the faces of her captors, and now she saw the pleasurable side of it in Zane. It startled her, because somehow she hadn't considered lust in the proposition she'd made to him, and her hands fell away from his body.

His lips parted in a curl of amusement that revealed the gleam of white teeth, and she felt her heart almost stop. His smile was even more potent than she'd expected. "Yeah, I'm turned on," he said softly. "I have to be, or this won't work."

He was right, of course, and her blush deepened. That was the trouble with inexperience. Though she knew the mechanics of lovemaking, and once or twice her escort for the evening had kissed her with unexpected ardor and held her close enough for her to tell that he was aroused, still, she'd never had to deal directly with an erection—until now.

This particular one was there for her bidding. Furtively she glanced at the front of his pants, at the ridge pushing against the cloth.

"We don't have to do this," he offered once again, and Barrie flared from hesitance to determination.

"Yes, I do."

He moved his hands to his belt. "Then I'd better—"

Instantly she stopped him, pushing his hands up and away, forcing them down on each side of his head. "I'll do it," she said, more fiercely than she'd intended. This was her show.

"All right," he murmured, and again she knew that he understood. Her show, her control, every step of the way. He relaxed against the blanket, closing his eyes as if he was going to take a nap.

It was easier, knowing he wasn't watching her, which of course had been his intention. Barrie didn't want to fumble, didn't want to underline her inexperience any more than she already had, so before she reached for his belt she studied the release mechanism for a moment to make certain she understood it. She didn't give herself time to lose her nerve. She simply reached out, opened the belt and unfastened his pants. Under the pants were black swim trunks. Puzzled, Barrie stared at them. Swim trunks?

Then she understood. He was a SEAL; the acronym stood for SEa, Air and Land. He was at home in all three elements, capable of swimming for miles. Since Benghazi was a seaport, that was probably how his team had infiltrated, from the sea. Maybe they'd used some sort of boat to reach land, but it was possible they'd been dropped off some distance from the port and had swum the rest of the way.

He had risked his life to save her, was still doing so, and now he was giving her his body. Everything inside her squeezed tight, and she trembled from the rush of emotion. Oh, God. She had learned more about herself in the past twenty-four hours than in the entire past twenty-five years of her life. Perhaps the experience had changed her. Either way, something had happened inside her, something momentous, and she was learning how to deal with it.

She had let her father wrap her in a suffocating blanket of protection for fifteen years; she couldn't blame him for it, because she'd *needed* that blanket. But that time was past. Fate had pitched her headlong into life, ripped her out of her protective cocoon, and like a butterfly, she couldn't draw the silken threads back around her. All she could do was reach out for the unknown.

She slipped her hands under the waistband of the swim trunks and began working them, and his pants, down his hips. He levered his pelvis off the ground to aid her. "Don't take them all the way off," he murmured, still keeping his eyes closed and his hands resting beside his head. "I can handle things if I get caught with my pants down, but if they're completely off, it would slow me down some."

Despite her nervousness, Barrie smiled at that supreme self-confidence, the wry humor. If he wasn't so controlled, he could be described as cocky. He had no doubt whatsoever about his fighting ability.

Her hands stroked down his buttocks as she slipped her hands inside his garments. An unexpected frisson of pleasure rippled through her at the feel of his butt, cool and smooth, hard with muscle. Tush connoisseurs would envy her the moment, and she wished she had the nerve to linger, to fully appreciate this male perfection. Instead she tugged at his clothes, pulling them down to the middle of his thighs. He relaxed, letting his hips settle on the blanket again, and Barrie studied the startling reality of a naked man. She'd read books that described sexual arousal, but seeing it firsthand, and at close range, was far more impressive and wondrous.

Blindly she reached out, her hand drawn as if by a magnet. She touched him, stroking one fingertip down the length of his swollen sex. It pulsed and jerked upward, as if following the caress. He inhaled sharply. His reaction warmed her, and the tightness in her chest, her body, clenched once more, then began to loosen with that rush of warmth. Bolder now, she folded her fingers around him, gently sighing with pleasure as she felt the heat beneath the coolness, iron beneath silk, the urgent throbbing.

And she felt her own desire, rushing like a heated river through her flesh, turning angry determination into lovemaking. *This is how it should be,* she thought with relief; they should come together in pleasure, not in anger. And she didn't want to wait, didn't want to give herself time to reconsider, or she would lose her nerve.

Swiftly she straddled him, mounted him. No longer in anger at other men, no longer in desperation. *Pleasure,* warm and sweet. With her knees clasping his hips, acting on instinct, she held the thick shaft in position and slowly sank down on him, guiding their bodies together.

The first brush of his flesh against hers was hot, startling, and she instinctively jerked herself upright, away from the alien touch. Zane quivered, the barest ripple of reaction, then once more lay motionless between her legs, his eyes still closed, letting her proceed at her own pace.

Her chest was so constricted she could barely breathe; she sucked in air in quick little gasps. That contact, brief as it had been, had touched off an insistent throbbing between her legs, as if her body, after its initial startled rejection, had paused in instinctive recognition of female for male. Her breasts felt tight and feverish beneath the black fabric of his shirt. Alien, yes…but infinitely exciting. Desire wound through her, the river rising.

She told herself that she was prepared for the sudden acute sense of vulnerability, for her body's panic at the threat of penetration, even though desire was urging her on to that very conclusion. More gingerly, she settled onto him again, holding herself steady as she placed him against the entrance to her body and let her weight begin to impale her on the throbbing column of flesh.

The discomfort began immediately and was worse than she'd expected. She halted her movement, gulping as she tried to control her instinctive flinching away from the source of pain. He was breathing deeply, too, she noticed, though that was the only motion he made. She pushed harder, gritting her teeth against the burning sensation of being stretched, and then she couldn't bear any more and jerked herself off him. This time the discomfort between her legs didn't go away but continued to burn.

It wasn't going to get any better, she told herself. She might as well go ahead and do it. Breathing raggedly, once more she lowered herself onto him. Tears burned in her eyes as she struggled to complete the act. Why wouldn't it just go *in*? The pressure between her legs was enormous, intolerable, and a sob caught in her throat as she surged upward.

"Help me," she begged, her voice almost inaudible.

Slowly his eyes opened, and she almost flinched at the pale fire that burned there. He moved just one hand, the right one. Gently he touched her cheek, his callused fingertips rough and infinitely tender; then he trailed them down her throat and lightly over the shirt to her left breast, where they lingered for a heart-stopping moment at her nipple, then finally down to the juncture of her legs.

The caress was as light as a whisper. It lingered between her legs, teasing, brushing, stroking. She went very still, her body poised as she concentrated on this new sensation. Her eyes closed as all her senses focused on his hand and what it was doing, the way he was touching her. It was delicious, but not...quite... enough. He tantalized her with the promise of something more, something that was richer, more powerful, and yet that lightly stroking finger never quite touched her where she wanted. Barrie inhaled deeply, her nipples rising in response. Her entire body hung in suspense. She waited, waited for the gentle touch to brush her with ecstasy, waited.... Her hips moved, her body instinctively seeking, following his finger.

Ah. There. Just for a moment, *there*. A low moan bubbled up in her throat as pleasure shot through her. She waited for him to repeat the caress, but instead his fingers moved maddeningly close, teasing and retreating. Again her hips followed, and again she was rewarded by that lightning flash of pure sensation.

A subtle, sensual dance began. He led, and she followed. The just-right touches came more often, the pleasure became more shattering as the intensity built with each repetition. Between her legs, his male shaft still probed for entrance, and somehow each movement of her hips seemed to ease him a bit closer to that goal. Her body rocked, swaying in the ancient rhythm of desire, surging and retreating like the tides. She could feel him stretching her, feel the discomfort sharpened by her movements...and yet the desire lured her onward like a Lorelei, and somehow she began to need him inside her, need him to the point that the pain no longer mattered. She braced her hands on his chest, and her movements changed, lifting and falling rather than swaying side to side. His touch changed, too, suddenly pressing directly on the place where she most wanted it.

She bit her lip to keep from crying out. His thumb rubbed insistently, releasing a torrent, turning the warm river into something wild and totally beyond her control. She was so hot that she was burning up with desire, aching with emptiness. The pain no longer mattered; she had to have what his body promised, what hers needed. With a low moan she pressed downward, forcing her soft flesh to admit the intruder. She felt the resistance, the inner giving; then suddenly his hot, swollen sex pushed up inside her.

It hurt. It hurt a lot. She froze in place, and her eyes flew open, huge with distress. Their gazes locked, hers dark with pain, his burning with ruthlessly restrained desire. Suddenly she became aware of how taut the muscled body beneath her was, how much his control was costing him. But he had promised to let her set the pace, and he had kept that promise, moving only when she had asked for help.

Part of her wanted to stop, but a deeper, more powerful instinct kept her astride him. She could feel him throbbing inside her, feel the answering tightening of her body, as if the flesh knew more than the mind, and perhaps it did. He tensed even more. His skin gleamed with sweat, his heartbeat hammered beneath her palm. She felt a jolt of excitement at having this supremely male, incredibly dangerous warrior as hers to command, just for this time suspended from reality. They had met only hours ago; they had only hours left before they would likely never see each other again. But for now he was hers, embedded inside her, and she wasn't going to forgo a moment of the experience.

"What do I do now?" she whispered.

"Just keep moving," he whispered in return, and she did. Rising. Falling. Lifting herself almost off him, then sink-ing down. Over and over, until she forgot about the pain and lost herself in the primeval joy. His hand remained between her legs, continuing the caress that urged her onward, even though she no longer needed to be urged. She moved on him, faster and faster, taking him deeper and deeper. His powerful body flexed between her thighs, arching, and a growl rumbled in his throat. Immediately he forced himself to lie flat again, chained by his promise.

Up. Down. Again. And again, the crescendo building inside her, the heat rising to an unbearable fever, the tension coiling tighter and tighter, until she felt as if she would shatter if she moved another muscle. She froze in place over him, whimpering, unable to push herself over the final hurdle.

The growl rumbled in his throat again. No, deeper than a growl; it was the sound of a human volcano exploding from the forces pent up inside. His control broke, and he moved, fiercely clamping both hands on her hips and pulling her down hard even as he arched once more and thrust himself in her to the hilt. He hadn't gone so deep before; she hadn't taken that much of him. The sensation was electric. She stifled a scream as he convulsed beneath her, heaving upward between her thighs, lifting her so that her knees left the ground. His head was thrown back, his neck corded with the force of his release, his teeth bared. Barrie felt the hot spurting of his release, felt him so deep inside her that he was touching the very center of her being, and it was enough to push her over the edge.

Pure lightning speared through her. She heard herself cry out, a thin cry of ecstasy that nothing could stifle. All her inner muscles contracted around him, relaxed, squeezed again, over and over, as if her body was drinking from his.

Finally the storm subsided, leaving her weak and shak-

ing. Her bones had turned to jelly, and she could no longer
sit upright. Helplessly she collapsed forward, folding on
him like a house of cards caught in an earthquake. He
caught her, easing her down so that she lay on his chest, and
he wrapped his arms around her as she lay there gasping and
sobbing. She hadn't meant to cry, didn't understand why
the tears kept streaming down her face. "Zane," she whispered, and couldn't say anything more.

His big, hard hands stroked soothingly up and down her
back. "Are you okay?" he murmured, and there was something infinitely male and intimate in his deep voice, an undertone of satisfaction and possessiveness.

Barrie gulped back the tears, forcing herself to coherency.
"Yes," she said in a thin, waterlogged tone. "I didn't know
it would hurt so much. Or feel so good," she added, because
she was crying for both reasons. Odd, that she should have
been as unprepared for the pleasure as she had been for the
pain. She felt overwhelmed, unbalanced. Had she truly
been so foolish as to think she could perform such an intimate act and remain untouched emotionally? If she had
been capable of that kind of mental distance she wouldn't
have remained a virgin until now. She would have found a
way around her father's obsessive protectiveness if she had
wanted to, if any man had ever elicited one-tenth the response in her this warrior had aroused within two minutes
of their meeting. If her rescuer had been any other man, she
wouldn't have asked such an intimate favor of him.

Their lovemaking had forged a link between them, a
bond of the flesh that was far stronger and went far deeper
than she'd imagined. Despite her chastity, had she believed
the modern, permissive notion that making love could have
no more lasting meaning than simple fun, like riding a
roller coaster? Maybe, for some people, *sex* could be as triv-

ial as a carnival ride, but she would never again think of lovemaking as anything that shallow. True lovemaking was deep and elemental, and she knew she would never be the same. She hadn't been from the moment he had given her his shirt and she had fallen in love with him. Without even seeing his face, she had fallen in love with the essence of the man, his strength and decency. It wouldn't have mattered if, when morning came, his features had been ugly or twisted with scars. In the darkness of that barren room, and the darkness of her heart, she had already seen beneath whatever lay on the surface, and she had loved him. It was that simple, and that difficult.

Just because she felt that way didn't mean he did. Barrie knew what a psychologist would say. It was the white-knight syndrome, the projection of larger-than-life characteristics onto a person because of the circumstances. Patients fell in love with their doctors and nurses all the time. Zane had simply been doing his job in rescuing her, while to her it had meant her life, because she hadn't for a moment supposed that her captors would let her live. She owed him her life, would have been grateful to him for the rest of that life—but she didn't think she would have loved just any man who had crawled through that window. She loved *Zane*.

She lay silently on him, her head nestled against his throat, their bodies still linked. She could feel the strong rhythm of his heartbeat thudding against her breasts, could feel his chest expand with each breath. His hot, musky scent excited her more than the most expensive cologne. She felt more at home here, lying with him on a blanket in the midst of a shattered building, than she ever had in the most luxurious and protected environment.

She knew none of the details of his life. She didn't know

how old he was, where he was from, what he liked to eat or read or what programs he watched on television. She didn't know if he'd ever been married.

Married. My God, she hadn't even asked. She felt suddenly sick to her stomach. If he was married, then he wouldn't be the man she had thought he was, and she had just made the biggest mistake of her life.

But neither would the fault be entirely his. She had begged him, and he had given her more than one chance to change her mind. She didn't think she could bear it if he'd made love to her out of pity.

She drew a deep breath, knowing she had to ask. Ignorance might be bliss, but she couldn't allow herself that comfort. If she had done something so monumentally wrong, she wanted to know.

"Are you married?" she blurted.

He didn't even tense but lay utterly relaxed beneath her. One hand slid up her back and curled itself around her neck. "No," he said in that low voice of his. "You can take your claws out of me now." The words were lazily amused.

She realized she was digging her fingernails into his chest and hastily relaxed her fingers. Distressed, she said, "I'm sorry, I didn't mean to hurt you."

"There's pain, and there's pain," he said comfortably. "Bullets and knives hurt like hell. In comparison, a little she-cat's scratching doesn't do much damage."

"She-cat?" Barrie didn't know if she should be affronted or amused. After a brief struggle, amusement won. None of her friends or associates would ever have described her in such terms. She'd heard herself described as ladylike, calm, circumspect, conscientious, but certainly never as a she-cat.

"Mmm." The sound was almost like a purr in his throat. His hard fingers lazily massaged her neck, while his other hand slipped down her back to burrow under the shirt and curl possessively over her bottom. His palm burned her flesh like a brand. "Dainty. And you like being stroked."

She couldn't deny that, not when he was the one doing the stroking. The feel of his hand on her bottom was startlingly erotic. She couldn't help wiggling a little, and then gasped as she felt the surge of his flesh inside her. His breath caught, too, and his fingers dug into the cleft of her buttocks.

"I need to ask you a couple of questions," he said, and his voice sounded strained.

Barrie closed her eyes, once again feeling the warm loosening deep inside that signaled the return of desire. That had been a remarkable sensation, when his sex had expanded inside her, both lengthening and getting thicker. Oh, dear. She wanted to do it again, but she didn't think she had the strength. "What?" she murmured, distracted by what was happening between her legs.

"Did you get rid of the ghosts?"

Ghosts. He meant her lingering horror at the way those men had touched her. She thought about it and realized, with some surprise, that she had. She was still angry at the way she'd been treated, and she would dearly love to have Zane's pistol in her hands and those men in her sights, even though she'd never held a pistol before in her life. But the wounded, feminine part of her had triumphed by finding pleasure in making love with Zane, and in doing so she had healed herself. Pleasure… somehow the word fell far short of what she had experienced. Even ecstasy didn't quite describe the intensity, the sensation of imploding, melting, becoming utterly lost in her physical self.

"Yes," she whispered. "The ghosts are gone."

"Okay." His voice still sounded strained. "Second question. Will that damn shirt have to be surgically removed?"

She was startled into sitting upright. The action drove him deeper inside her and wrenched a sharp gasp from her, a groan from him. Panting, she stared at him. They had just made love—were, in fact, *still* making love—but the shirt she wore was what had kept her from going to pieces when he'd first found her, had given her the nerve to run barefoot down dark alleys, had become the symbol of a lot more than just modesty. Maybe she wasn't as recovered as she'd thought. The kidnappers had stripped her, forced her to be naked in front of them, and when Zane had first entered the room and seen her that way, she had been mortified. She didn't know if she could be naked with him now, if she could let him see the body that had been pinched and bruised by other men.

His crystal clear gaze was calm, patient. Again he understood. He knew what he was asking of her. He could have left things as they were, but he wanted more. He wanted her trust, her openness, with no dark secrets between them.

He wanted them to become lovers.

The realization was sharp, almost painful. They had loved each other physically, but with restraint like a wall between them. He had done what she had asked of him, had held himself back until the last moment, when his climax had shattered his control. Now he was asking something of her, asking her to give as he had given.

Almost desperately she clutched the front of the shirt. "I—they left marks on me."

"I've seen bruises before." He reached up and gently touched her cheek. "You have one right here, as a matter of fact."

Instinctively she reached up to the cheek he'd touched, feeling the tenderness. As soon as she released the front of the shirt, he moved his hands to the buttons and slowly began unfastening them, giving her time to protest. She bit her lip, fighting the urge to grab the widening edges of the cloth and hold them together.

When the garment was open all the way down, he slid his hands inside and cupped her breasts, his palms hot as they covered the cool mounds. Her nipples tingled as they hardened, reaching out for the contact. "The bruises shame *them*," he murmured. "Not you."

She closed her eyes as she sat astride him, feeling him hard and hot inside her, his hands just as hard and hot on her breasts. She didn't protest when his hands left her breasts, left them feeling oddly tight and aching, while he pushed the black shirt off her shoulders. The fabric puddled around her arms, and he lifted each in turn, slipping them free.

She was naked. The warm air brushed against her bare skin with the lightest of touches, and then she felt his fingertips doing the same, trailing so gently over each of the dark marks on her shoulders, her arms and breasts, her stomach, that she barely felt him. "Lean down," he said.

Slowly she obeyed, guided by his hands, down, down— and he lifted his head, meeting her mouth with his.

Their first kiss...and they'd already made love. Barrie was shocked at how she could have been so foolish as to forgo the pleasure of his kisses. His lips were firm, warm, hungry. She sank against him with a little sound of mingled surprise and delight humming in her throat. Her breasts flattened against him, the crisp hair on his chest rasping her ultrasensitive nipples, another joy she had unknowingly skipped.

Oh, this was delicious. His tongue probed for entrance, and she immediately gave it.

Several minutes later he let his head drop to the blanket. He was panting slightly, his eyes heavy-lidded. "I have another question."

"What?" She didn't want to give up the delights of his mouth. She'd never enjoyed kissing so much before, but he was diabolically good at it. She followed him down, nipping at his lower lip, depositing hot little kisses.

He chuckled beneath her mouth. The deep, rusty sound charmed her. She sensed that his laughter was even rarer than his smiles, therefore doubly precious.

"Will you let me be on top this time?"

The question surprised her into laughter. She stifled it as best she could, burying her head against his neck, but her body shook with giggles. He slipped out of her, making her laugh even harder. She was still laughing when he wrapped one strong arm around her and rolled, lifting her so they didn't roll off the blanket, efficiently tucking her beneath him and settling between her legs. Her laughter caught on a gasp as he surged heavily into her.

Her senses swam as she was bombarded by new feelings, when she had already experienced so much. She'd known he was a big man, but lying beneath him sharply brought home the difference in their sizes. Though he propped his weight on his forearms to keep from crushing her, she still felt the heaviness of that iron-muscled body. His shoulders were so broad that he dwarfed her, wrapped around her, shielded her. When she had been on top, she had controlled the depth of his penetration. The control was his now, her thighs spread wide by his hips. He felt bigger, harder than he had before.

He waited a moment to see how she would accept the vulnerability of her position. But she didn't feel vulnerable, she realized. She felt utterly secure, buffered by his strength.

Tremulously she smiled at him and lifted her arms to wind them around his neck.

He smiled in return. And then Zane Mackenzie made love to her.

Chapter 6

There seemed to be scarcely a moment for the rest of the day when they weren't making love, resting from making love or about to make love. The sounds of the waterfront surrounded them, the low bellow of ships, truck horns, the sounds of chains and cranes, but inside that small, dim room there seemed to be nothing else in the world but each other. Barrie lost herself in the force of his unbridled sensuality and discovered within herself a passion that matched his. The need to be quiet only added to the intensity.

He kissed the bruises on her breasts and sucked her nipples until they throbbed with pleasure. His beard-stubbled chin rasped against her breasts, her belly, but he was always careful not to cause her pain as he searched for all the other bruises on her body and paid them the same tender homage.

"Tell me how they hurt you," he murmured, "and I'll make it better."

At first Barrie shied away from divulging the details, even to him, but as the hot afternoon wore on and he pleasured her so often she was drunk with the overload on her senses, it began to seem pointless to keep anything from him. Haltingly she began to whisper things to him.

"Like this?" he asked, repeating the action that had so upset her—except it wasn't the same. What had been meant to punish at the hands of the kidnappers became purest pleasure in Zane Mackenzie's hands. He caressed her until her body forgot those other touches, until it remembered only him.

She whispered another detail, and he wiped out that memory, too, replacing the bad with caresses that lifted her to peak after sensual peak. She couldn't imagine being handled more tenderly than he handled her, or with such delight. He didn't try to hide how much he enjoyed looking at her, touching her, making love to her. He reveled in her body, in the contrast between her soft curves and his hard muscularity. It aroused her to be the focus of such intense masculine pleasure, to feel his absorption with the texture of her skin, the curve of her breast, the snug sheathing between her legs. He explored her; he petted her, he drowned her in sexuality. The area around them was still so busy they didn't dare converse much, so they communicated with their bodies.

Three times, while they were lying drowsily in the aftermath of loving, he checked his watch and reached for the headset radio. He would click it once, listen, then put it aside.

"Your men?" she asked, after the first time.

He nodded. "They're hiding out, waiting until it's safe to rendezvous."

Then the chatter of voices outside became louder as some people approached, and they fell silent.

The afternoon wore on, and the light began to dim. She wasn't particularly hungry, but Zane insisted that she eat. He pulled up his pants; she once more donned his shirt. More formally attired now, they sat close together on the blanket and finished off the bread and fruit, but neither of

them wanted any of the cheese. The water was warm and
still tasted of chemicals. Barrie sat within the curve of his
arm and dreaded leaving.

She wanted to be safe and comfortable again, but she
hated to lose this closeness with Zane, this utter reliance
and companionship and intimacy. She wouldn't push him
to continue their relationship; under the circumstances, he
might feel responsible and think he would have to let her
down gradually, and she didn't want to put him in that position. If he indicated that he wanted to see her afterward,
then…why, then her heart would fly.

But even if he did, it would be difficult for them to see
each other regularly. He was more than just a military man;
he was a SEAL. Much of what he did couldn't be discussed.
He would have a home base, duties, missions. If they escaped safely, the danger to him didn't end there. A chill settled around her heart when she thought of the times in the
future when, because it was his job, he would calmly and
deliberately walk into a deadly situation. While they were
hidden in this small room might be the only time she could
ever be certain he was safe and unharmed.

The fear and uncertainty would almost drive her mad,
but she would endure them, she would endure anything, for
the opportunity to see him, to grow closer to him. Their relationship, if there was to be one, would have to grow in
reverse. Usually people came to know each other, grew to
trust and care, and then became lovers; they had become
lovers almost immediately, and now they would have to get
to know each other, find out all the quirks and personal history and tastes that made them individuals.

When she got back, she would have to deal with her father. He must be frantic, and once she was safely home, he
would be even more paranoid and obsessive. But if Zane

wanted her, she would have to deliberately hurt her father's feelings for the first time in her life; he would be supplanted as number one in her life. Most parents handled the change in their offsprings' lives with happiness, assuming the chosen mate was decent, but Barrie knew it wouldn't matter who she fell in love with, her father would be opposed to him. No man, to him, was good enough for her. Even more, he would bitterly resent anything that would take her out of his protection. She was all he had left of his family, and it didn't help that she greatly resembled her mother. As ambassador, her father had a very active social life, but he'd only ever loved one woman, and that was her mother.

She would never turn her back on her father, because she loved him dearly, but if the chance for a relationship, possibly a lifetime, with Zane was in the balance, she would put as much distance between herself and her father as necessary until he accepted the situation.

She was planning her life around dreams, she thought wryly as she brushed the bread crumbs from the blanket. She would do better to let the future take care of itself and concern herself with how they were going to get out of Benghazi.

"What time do we leave?"

"After midnight. We'll give most people time to get settled down for the night." He turned to her with the heavy-lidded gaze she had already learned signaled arousal and, reaching out, he began to unbutton her shirt. "Hours," he whispered.

Afterward they lay close together, despite the heat, and dozed. She didn't know how long it was before she woke, but when she did it was to almost total darkness. Unlike the night before, though, when she had lain in cold, lonely terror, now she was pressed against Zane's side, and his arms securely held her. Her head was pillowed on his shoulder, one bare leg was hooked over his hips. She stretched a bit and yawned, and his arms tightened, letting her know that he was awake. Perhaps he had never slept at all, but had held her and safeguarded her. The noise beyond the ruined building had died down; even the sounds from the docks were muted, as if the darkness smothered them.

"How much longer?" she asked, sitting up to fumble for the jug of water. She found it and drank; the taste wasn't too bad, she decided. Maybe she was becoming used to the chemicals, whatever they were.

He peeled the cover from his watch so he could see the luminous dial. "Another few hours. I need to check in with the guys in a couple of minutes."

She passed the water jug to him, and he drank. They lay back down, and she cuddled close. She put her right hand on his chest and felt the strong, healthy thudding of his heart. Idly she twirled her fingers in the crisp hairs, delighting in the textures of his body.

"What happens then? When we leave, I mean."

"We get out of the city, make our rendezvous point just at sunrise, and we're picked up."

He made it sound so simple, so easy. She remembered the swim trunks he wore and lifted her head to frown at him, even though she knew he couldn't see her. "Is our rendezvous point on dry land?"

"Not exactly."

"I see. I hope you have a boat?" It was a question, not a statement.

"Not exactly."

She caught his chest hairs and gave them a tug. "*Exactly* what *do* you have?"

"Ouch!" Snagging her hand, he disentangled it and lifted

it to his mouth, lightly brushing his lips across her knuckles. "*Exactly*, we have a Zodiac, a seven-man, motorized inflatable craft. My team came in short two men, so there are only six of us. We'll be able to fit you in."

"I'm so glad." She yawned and snuggled her head more securely into the hollow of his shoulder. "Did you leave someone behind so there would be room for me?"

"No," he said shortly. "We're undermanned because of a problem I'll have to take care of when we get back. If there had been any other team available, we wouldn't be here, but we were the closest, and we needed to get you out in a hurry, before they moved you."

His tone dissuaded her from asking about the problem that put him in such a black mood, but she'd seen him in action; she knew she wouldn't want to be on the receiving end of his anger when he got back. She waited while he picked up the headset and checked in with his men, then returned to her questions.

"Where do we go in the Zodiac?"

"Out to sea," he said simply. "We radio ahead, and we'll be picked up by a helicopter from the *Montgomery*, an aircraft carrier. You'll be flown home from the carrier."

"What about you?" she whispered. "Where will you go?" That was as close as she would allow herself to get to asking him about his future plans.

"I don't know. My team was performing exercises on the *Montgomery*, but that's blown to hell now, with two of them injured. I'll have to clean up that mess, and I don't know how long it will take."

He didn't know where he would be, or if he did, he wasn't saying. Neither was he saying that he would call her, though he *did* know where *she* would be. Barrie closed her eyes and listened painfully to all that he wasn't saying. The hurt was worse than she'd anticipated, but she closed it off in a place deep inside. Later it would come out, but if she only had a few hours left with him, she didn't intend to waste them crying about what might have been. Few women would have a chance to even know a man like Zane Mackenzie, much less love him. She was greedy; she wanted it all, wanted everything, but even this little bit was more than a lot of people experienced, and she would have to be grateful for that.

Whatever happened, she could never return to the safe little cocoon her father had fashioned for her. She couldn't let herself forget the kidnapping and the unknown *why* of it. Of course, her father would know why; the kidnapper would already have made his demands. But Barrie wanted to know the reason, too; after all, she had been more directly affected than anyone else.

Lightly Zane touched her nipple, circling it with his callused fingertips and bringing it erect. "I know you have to be sore," he said, sliding his hand down her belly to nestle it between her legs. "But can you take me again?" With the utmost care he eased one long finger into her; Barrie winced, but didn't flinch away from him. Yes, she was sore; she had been sore since the first time. She had discovered that the discomfort was easily discounted when the rewards were so great.

"I could be persuaded," she whispered, sliding her hand down his belly to measure his immediate seriousness. She found that he was very serious. Granted, she had no experience against which to compare this, but she had read magazine articles and knew that usually only teenage boys and very young men could maintain this pace. Maybe it was because he was in such superb physical condition. Maybe she was just lucky, though twenty-four hours before she hadn't thought so. But circumstances had changed, and so had she.

Fate had given her this man for now, and for a few more hours, she thought as he leaned over her and his mouth captured hers. She would make the most of it.

Once more he led her through the maze of alleys, but this time she was clad in the enveloping black robe, and a chador covered her hair. Her feet were protected by slippers, which were a little too big and kept slipping up and down on her heels, but at least she wasn't barefoot. It felt strange to have on clothes, especially so many, even though she was bare underneath the robe.

Zane was once more rigged out with his gear and weaponry, and with the donning of those things he had become subtly more remote, almost icily controlled, the way he'd been the night before when he'd first found her. Barrie sensed his acute alertness and guessed that he was concentrating totally on the job at hand. She silently followed him, keeping her head a little bowed as a traditional Muslim woman would do.

He halted at the corner of a building and sank to his haunches, motioning for her to do the same. Barrie copied him and took the extra precaution of drawing the chador across her face.

"Two, this is One. How's it looking?" Once more he was speaking in that toneless whisper that barely carried to her, though she was right behind him. After a moment he said, "See you in ten."

He glanced around at Barrie. "It's a go. We don't have to shift to Plan C."

"What was Plan C?" she whispered.

"Run like hell for Egypt," he said calmly. "It's about two hundred miles due east."

He would do it, too, she realized. He would steal some

kind of vehicle and go for it. His nerves must be made of solid iron. Hers weren't; she was shaking inside with nervousness, but she was holding up. Or maybe it wasn't nervousness; maybe it was exhilaration at the danger and excitement of action, of *escaping*. As long as they were still in Benghazi, in Libya, they hadn't really gotten free.

Ten minutes later he stopped in the shadow of a dilapidated warehouse. Perhaps he clicked his radio; in the dark, she couldn't tell. But suddenly five black shapes materialized out of the darkness, and they were surrounded before she could blink.

"Gentlemen, this is Miss Lovejoy," Zane said. "Now let's get the hell out of Dodge."

"With pleasure, boss." One of the men bowed to Barrie and held out his hand. "This way, Miss Lovejoy."

There was a certain rough élan about them that she found charming, though they didn't let it interfere with the business at hand. The six men immediately began moving out in choreographed order, and Barrie smiled at the man who'd spoken as she took the place he had indicated in line. She was behind Zane, who was second in line behind a man who moved so silently, and blended so well into the shadows, that even knowing he was there, sometimes she couldn't see him. The other four men ranged behind her at varying distances, and she realized that she couldn't hear them, either. In fact, she was the only one of the group who was making any noise, and she tried to place her slippered feet more carefully.

They wound their way through the alleys and finally stopped beside a battered minibus. Even in the darkness Barrie could see the huge dents and dark patches of rust that decorated the vehicle. They stopped beside it, and Zane opened the sliding side door for her. "Your chariot," he murmured.

Barrie almost laughed as he handed her into the little bus: if she hadn't had experience navigating long evening gowns, she would have found the ankle-length robe awkward, but she managed it as if she was a nineteenth-century lady being handed into a carriage. The men climbed in around her. There were only two bench seats; if there had ever been a third one in the back, it had long since been removed, perhaps to make room for cargo. A wiry young black man got behind the steering wheel, and Zane took the other seat in front. The eerily silent man who had been on point squeezed in on her left side, and another SEAL sat on her right, carefully placing her in a human security box. The other two SEALs knelt on the floorboard behind them, their muscular bodies and their gear filling the limited space.

"Let's go, Bunny Rabbit," Zane said, and the young black man grinned as he started the engine. The minibus looked as though it was on its last wheels, but the motor purred.

"You shoulda been there last night," the black guy said. "It was tight for a minute, real tight." He sounded as enthusiastic as if he was describing the best party he'd ever attended.

"What happened?" Zane asked.

"Just one of those things, boss," the man on Barrie's right said with a shrug evident in his voice. "A bad guy stepped on Spook, and the situation went straight into fubar."

Barrie had been around enough military men to know what fubar meant. She sat very still and didn't comment.

"Stepped right *on* me," the SEAL on her left said in an aggrieved tone. "He started squalling like a scalded cat, shooting at everything that moved and most things that didn't. Aggravated me some." He paused. "I'm not staying for the funeral."

"When we got your signal we pulled back and ran like

hell," the man on her right continued. "You must've already had her out, because they came after us like hound dogs. We laid low, but a couple of times I thought we were going to have to fight our way out. Man, they were walking all over us, and they kept hunting all night long."

"No, we were still inside," Zane said calmly. "We just stepped into the next room. They never thought to check it."

The men snorted with mirth; even the eerie guy on her left managed a chuckle, though it didn't sound as if he did it often enough to be good at it.

Zane turned around in the seat and gave Barrie that brief twitch of a smile. "Would you like some introductions, or would you rather not know these raunchy-smelling bums?"

The atmosphere in the bus *did* smell like a locker room, only worse. "The introductions, please," she said, and her smile was plain in her voice.

He indicated the driver. "Antonio Withrock, Seaman Second Class. He's driving because he grew up wrecking cars on dirt tracks down South, so we figure he can handle any situation."

"Ma'am," said Seaman Withrock politely.

"On your right is Ensign Rocky Greenberg, second in command."

"Ma'am," said Ensign Greenberg.

"On your left is Seaman Second Class Winstead Jones."

Seaman Winstead Jones growled something unintelligible. "Call him Spooky or Spook, not Winstead," Zane added.

"Ma'am," said Seaman Jones.

"Behind you are Seamen First Class Eddie Santos, our medic, and Paul Drexler, the team sniper."

"Ma'am," said two voices behind her.

"I'm glad to meet you all," Barrie said, her sincerity plain. She had trained her memory at countless official functions, so she had their names down cold. She hadn't yet put a face to Santos or Drexler, but from his name she figured Santos would be Hispanic, so that would be an easy distinction to make.

Greenberg began to tell Zane the details of everything that had happened. Barrie listened and didn't intrude. The fact was, this midnight drive through Benghazi felt a little surreal. She was surrounded by men armed to their eyeteeth, but they were traveling through an area that was still fairly active for so late at night. There were other vehicles in the streets, pedestrians on the sidewalks. They even stopped at a traffic light, with other vehicles around them. The driver, Withrock, hummed under his breath. No one else seemed concerned. The traffic light changed, the battered little minibus moved forward, and no one paid them any attention at all.

Several minutes later they left the city. Occasionally she could see the gleam of the Mediterranean on their right, which meant they were traveling west, toward the center of Libya's coast. As the lights faded behind them, she began to feel lightheaded with fatigue. The sleep she had gotten during the day, between bouts of lovemaking, hadn't been enough to offset the toll stress had taken on her. She couldn't see herself leaning on either of the men beside her, however, so she forced herself to sit upright and keep her eyes open.

She suspected that she was more than a little punch-drunk.

After a while Zane said, "Red goggles."

She was tired enough that she wondered if that was some kind of code, or if she'd misunderstood him. Neither, evidently. Each man took a pair of goggles from his pack and donned them. Zane glanced at her and said in explanation, "Red protects your night vision. We're going to let our vision adjust now, before Bunny kills the headlights."

She nodded, and closed her eyes to help her own vision adjust. She realized at once that, if she wanted to stay awake, closing her eyes for whatever reason wasn't the smartest thing to do, but her eyelids were so heavy that she couldn't manage to open them again. The next thing she knew, the minibus was lurching heavily from side to side, throwing her against first Greenberg, then Spooky. Dazed with sleep, she tried to hold herself erect, but she couldn't seem to find her balance or anything to hold on to. She was about to slide to the floorboard when Spooky's forearm shot out in front of her like an iron bar, anchoring her in the seat.

"Thank you," she said groggily.

"Anytime, ma'am."

Sometime while she had been asleep, Bunny had indeed killed the headlights, and they were plunging down an embankment in the dark. She blinked at something shiny looming in front of them; she had a split second of panic and confusion before she recognized the sea, gleaming in the starlight.

The minibus lurched to a halt. "End of the line," Bunny cheerfully announced. "We have now reached the hidey-hole for one IBS. That's military talk for inflatable boat, small," he said over his shoulder to Barrie. "These things are too fancy to be called plain old rafts."

Zane snorted. Barrie remembered that he'd described it as exactly that, a raft.

Watching them exit the minibus was like watching quicksilver slip through cracks. If there had been a working overhead light when the SEALs had commandeered the vehicle, they had taken care of that detail, because no light came on when the doors were cracked open. Spooky slipped past her, no mean feat given the equipment he was carrying, and when Greenberg slid the side door open a few inches, Spooky wiggled on his stomach through the small opening. One second he was there, the next he was gone. Barrie stared at the door with widened eyes in full appreciation of how he'd acquired his nickname. He was definitely spooky.

The others exited the minibus in the same manner; it was as if they were made of water, and when the doors opened they simply leaked out. They were that fluid, that silent. Only Bunny, the driver, remained behind with Barrie. He sat in absolute silence, pistol in hand, as he methodically surveyed the night-shrouded coast. Because he was silent, she was too. The best way not to be any trouble to them, she thought, was to follow their example.

There was one quick little tap on the window, and Bunny whispered, "It's clear. Let's go, Miss Lovejoy."

She scooted over the seat to the door while Bunny eeled out on the driver's side. Zane was there, opening the door wider, reaching in to steady her as she slid out onto the ground. "Are you holding up okay?" he asked quietly.

She nodded, not trusting herself to speak, because she was so tired her speech was bound to be slurred.

As usual, he seemed to understand without being told. "Just hold on for another hour or so, and we'll have you safe on board the carrier. You can sleep then."

Without him, though; that fact didn't need stating. Even if he intended to continue their relationship, and he hadn't given any indication of it, he wouldn't do so on board the ship. She would put off sleeping forever if it would postpone the moment when she had to admit, once and for all, that their relationship had been a temporary thing for him, prompted by both the hothouse of intimacy in which they'd spent the day, and her own demands.

She wouldn't cry; she wouldn't even protest, she told herself. She'd had him for a day, for one incredibly sensual day.

He led her down to the small, rocky strip of beach, where the dark bulk of the IBS had been positioned. The other five men were gathered around it in specific positions, each standing with his back to the raft while he held his weapon at the ready, edgily surveying the surroundings.

Zane lifted her into the IBS and showed her where to sit. The IBS bobbed in the water as the men eased it away from the shore. When the water was chest deep on Santos, the shortest one, they all swung aboard in a maneuver they had practiced so many times it looked effortless. Spooky started the almost soundless motor and aimed the IBS for the open sea.

Then a roar erupted behind them, and all hell broke loose.

She recognized the sharp *rat-tat-tat* of automatic weapons and half turned to look behind them. Zane put his hand on her head and shoved her down to the bottom of the boat, whirling, already bringing his automatic rifle around as he did so. The IBS shot forward as Spooky gave it full throttle. The SEALs returned fire, lightning flashing from the weapons, spent cartridges splattering down on her as she curled into a ball and drew the chador over her face to keep the hot brass from burning her.

"Drexler!" Zane roared. "Hit those bastards with explosives!"

"Got it, boss!"

Barrie heard a grunt, and something heavy and human fell across her. One of the men had been hit. Desperately she tried to wriggle out from under the crushing weight so she could help him, but she was effectively pinned, and he groaned every time she moved.

She knew that groan.

Terror such as she had never felt before raced through her veins. With a hoarse cry she heaved at the heavy weight, managing to roll him to the side. She fought her way free of the enveloping chador and didn't even notice the hot cartridge shell that immediately skimmed her right cheek.

An explosion shattered the night, lighting up the sea like fireworks, the percussion knocking her to the bottom of the boat again. She scrambled to her knees, reaching for Zane. "No," she said hoarsely. "No!"

The light from the explosion had sharply delineated every detail in stark white. Zane lay sprawled half on his side, writhing in pain as he pressed his hands to his abdomen. His face was a colorless blur, his eyes closed, his teeth exposed in a grimace. A huge wet patch glistened on the left side of his black shirt, and more blood was pooling beneath him.

Barrie grabbed the chador and wadded it up, pressing it hard to the wound. A low animal howl rattled in his throat, and he arched in pain. "Santos!" she screamed, trying to hold him down while still holding the chador in place. "*Santos!*"

With a muttered curse the stocky medic shouldered her aside. He lifted the chador for a second, then quickly pressed it into place and grabbed her hand, guiding it into position. "Hold it," he rapped out. "Press down—hard."

There was no more gunfire, only the hum of the motor. Salt spray lashed her face as the boat shot through the waves. The team maintained their discipline, holding their assigned positions. "How bad is it?" Greenberg yelled.

Santos was working feverishly. "I need light!"

Almost instantly Greenberg had a flashlight shining down on them. Barrie bit her lip as she saw how much blood had puddled around them. Zane's face was pasty white, his eyes half-shut as he gasped for breath.

"He's losing blood fast," Santos said. "Looks like the bullet got a kidney, or maybe his spleen. Get that damn helicopter on the way. We don't have time to get into international waters." He popped the cap off a syringe, straightened Zane's arm and deftly jabbed the needle into a vein. "Hang on, boss. We're gonna get you airlifted outta here."

Zane didn't reply. He was breathing noisily through his clenched teeth, but when Barrie glanced at him she could see the gleam of his eyes. His hand lifted briefly, touched her arm, then fell heavily to his side.

"Damn you, Zane Mackenzie," she said fiercely. "Don't you *dare*—" She broke off. She couldn't say the word, couldn't even admit to the possibility that he might die.

Santos was checking Zane's pulse. His eyes met hers, and she knew it was too fast, too weak. Zane was going into shock, despite the injection Santos had given him.

"I don't give a damn how close in we still are!" Greenberg was yelling into the radio. "We need a helo *now*. Just get the boss out of here and we'll wait for another ride!"

Despite the pitching of the boat, Santos got an IV line started and began squeezing a bag of clear plasma into Zane's veins. "Don't let up on the pressure," he muttered to Barrie.

"I won't." She didn't take her gaze off Zane's face. He was still aware, still looking at her. As long as that connection was maintained, he would be all right. He had to be.

The nightmare ride in the speeding boat seemed to take forever. Santos emptied the first bag of plasma and connected a second one to the IV. He was cursing under his breath, his invectives varied and explicit.

Zane lay quietly, though she knew he was in terrible pain. His eyes were dull with pain and shock, but she could sense his concentration, his determination. Perhaps the only way he could remain conscious was by focusing so intently on her face, but he managed it.

But if that helicopter didn't get there soon, not even his superhuman determination would be able to hold out against continued blood loss. She wanted to curse, too, wanted to glare at the night sky as if she could conjure a helicopter out of thin air, but she didn't dare look away from Zane. As long as their gazes held, he would hold on.

She heard the distinctive *whap-whap-whap* only a moment before the Sea King helicopter roared over them, blinding lights picking them out. Spooky throttled back, and the boat settled gently onto the water. The helicopter circled to them and hovered directly overhead, the powerful rotors whipping the sea into a frenzy. A basket dropped almost on their heads. Working swiftly, Santos and Greenberg lifted Zane into the basket and strapped him in, maneuvering around Barrie as she maintained pressure on the wound.

Santos hesitated, then indicated for her to let go and move back. Reluctantly she did. He lifted the chador, then immediately jammed it back into place. Without a word he straddled the basket, leaning hard on the wound. "Let's go!" he yelled. Greenberg stepped back and gave the thumbs-up to the winch operator in the helicopter. The basket rose toward the hovering monster, with Santos perched precariously on top of Zane. As the basket drew even with the open bay, several pairs of hands reached out and drew them inward. The helicopter immediately lifted away, banking hard, roaring toward the carrier.

There was an eerie silence left behind. Barrie slumped against one of the seats, her face rigid with the effort of maintaining control. No one said a word. Spooky started the motor again, and the little craft shot through the darkness, following the rapidly disappearing lights of the helicopter.

It was over an hour before the second helicopter settled onto the deck of the huge carrier. The remaining four members of the team leaped to the deck almost before the helicopter had touched down. Barrie clambered after them, ran with them. Greenberg had one hand clamped on her arm to make certain she didn't get left behind.

Someone in a uniform stepped in front of them. "Miss Lovejoy, are you all right?"

Barrie gave him a distracted glance and dodged around him. Another uniform popped up, but this one was subtly different, as if the wearer belonged on board this gigantic ship. The first man had worn a dress uniform, marking him as a non-crew member. Greenberg skidded to a halt. "Captain—"

"Lieutenant-Commander Mackenzie is in surgery," the captain said. "Doc didn't think he'd make it to a base with such a high rate of blood loss. If they can't get the bleeding stopped, they'll have to remove his spleen."

The first uniformed officer had reached them. "Miss Lovejoy," he said firmly, taking her arm. "I'm Major Hodson. I'll escort you home."

The military moved at its own pace, to its own rules. She was to be taken home immediately; the ambassador wanted his daughter back. Barrie protested. She yelled, she cried, she even swore at the harried major. None of it did any good. She was hustled aboard another aircraft, this time a cargo transport plane. Her last glimpse of the *Montgomery* was as the sun's first rays glistened on the blue waters of the Mediterranean, and the sight was blurred by her tears.

Chapter 7

By the time the transport touched down in Athens, Barrie had cried so hard and for so long that her eyes were swollen almost shut. Major Hodson had tried everything to pacify her, then to console her; he assured her that he was just following orders, and that she would be able to find out how the SEAL was doing later. It was understandable that she was upset. She'd been through a lot, but she would have the best medical care—

At that, Barrie shot out of the uncomfortable web seat, which was all the transport plane afforded. "*I'm* not the one who was shot!" she yelled furiously. "I don't need medical care, best, worst or mediocre! I want to be taken to wherever Zane Mackenzie is taken. I don't care what your orders are!"

Major Hodson looked acutely uncomfortable. He tugged at the collar of his uniform. "Miss Lovejoy, I'm sorry. I can't do anything about this situation. After we're on the ground and your father is satisfied that you're okay, then where you go is up to you."

His expression plainly said that as far as he was concerned, she could go to hell. Barrie sat down, breathing hard and wiping away tears. She'd never acted like that before in her life. She'd always been such a lady, a perfect hostess for her father.

She didn't feel at all ladylike now; she felt like a ferocious tigress, ready to shred anyone who got in her way. Zane was severely wounded, perhaps dying, and these *fools* wouldn't let her be with him. Damn military procedure, and damn her father's influence, for they had both wrenched her away from him.

As much as she loved her father, she knew she would never forgive him if Zane died and she wasn't there. It didn't matter that he didn't know about Zane; nothing mattered compared to the enormous horror that loomed before her. *God, don't let him die!* She couldn't bear it. She would rather have died herself at her kidnappers' hands than for Zane to be killed while rescuing her.

The flight took less than an hour and a half. The transport landed with a hard thump that jerked her in the web seat, then taxied for what seemed like an interminable length of time. Finally it rolled to a stop, and Major Hodson stood, plainly relieved to be free of his unpleasant burden.

A door was slid open, and a flight of steps rolled up to it. Clutching the black robe around her, Barrie stepped out into the bright Athens sunlight. It was full morning now, the heat already building. She blinked and lifted a hand to shield her eyes. It felt like forever since she'd been in the sunshine.

A gray limousine with darkly tinted windows was waiting on the tarmac. The door was shoved open, and her father bounded out, dignity forgotten as he ran forward. "Barrie!" Two days of worry and fear lined his face, but there was an almost desperate relief in his expression as he hurried up the steps to fold her in his arms.

She started crying again, or maybe she had never stopped.

She buried her face against his suit, clutching him with desperate hands. "I've got to go back," she sobbed, the words barely intelligible.

He tightened his arms around her. "There, there, baby," he breathed. "You're safe now, and I won't let anything else happen to you, I swear. I'll take you home—"

Wildly she shook her head, trying to pull away from him. "No," she choked out. "I've got to get back to the *Montgomery*. Zane—he was shot. He might die. Oh, God, I've got to go back *now!*"

"Everything will be all right," he crooned, hustling her down the steps with an arm locked around her shoulders. "I have a doctor waiting—"

"I don't need a doctor!" she said fiercely, jerking away from him. She'd never done that before, and his face went blank with shock. She shoved her hair out of her face. The tangled mass hadn't been combed in two days, and it was matted with sweat and sea spray. "Listen to me! The man who rescued me was shot. *He might die*. He was still in surgery when Major Hodson forced me on board this plane. I want to go back to the ship. I want to make sure Zane is okay."

William Lovejoy firmly took hold of his daughter's shoulders again, leading her across the tarmac to the waiting limo. "You don't have to go back to the ship, sweetheart," he said soothingly. "I'll ask Admiral Lindley to find out how his man is doing. He *is* one of the SEAL team, I presume?"

Numbly she nodded.

"There wouldn't be any point in going back to the ship, I'm sure you can see that. If he survived surgery, he'll be airlifted to a military hospital."

If he survived surgery. The words were like a knife, hot and slicing, going through her. She balled her hands into fists, every cell in her body screaming for her to ignore logic, ignore the attempts to soothe her. She needed to get to Zane.

Three days later, she stood in her father's office with her chin high and her eyes colder than he'd ever seen them. "You told Admiral Lindley to block my requests," she accused.

The ambassador sighed. He removed his reading glasses and carefully placed them on the inlaid walnut desk. "Barrie, you know I've denied you very little that you've asked for, but you're being unreasonable about this man. You know that he's recovering, and that's all you need to know. What point would there be in rushing to his bedside? Some tabloid might find out about it, and then your ordeal would be plastered in sleazy newspapers all over the world. Is that what you want?"

"My ordeal?" she echoed. "My ordeal? What about his? He nearly died! That's assuming Admiral Lindley told me the truth, and he really is still alive!"

"Of course he is. I only asked Joshua to block any inquiries you made about his location." He unfolded his tall form from the chair and came around to lean against the desk and take her resistant hands in his. "Barrie, give yourself time to get over the trauma. I know you've invested this…this guerrilla fighter with all sorts of heroic characteristics, and that's only normal. After a while, when you've regained your perspective, you'll be glad you didn't embarrass yourself by chasing after him."

It was almost impossible to contain the volcanic fury rising in her. Nobody was listening; no one wanted to listen. They kept going on and on about her ordeal, how she would heal in time, until she wanted to pull her hair out. She had insisted over and over that she hadn't been raped, but she had fiercely refused to be examined by a doctor, which of course had only fueled speculation that the kidnappers had indeed raped her. But she'd known her body bore the marks of Zane's lovemaking, marks and traces that were precious and private, for no one else's eyes. Everyone was treating her as if she was made of crystal, carefully not mentioning the kidnapping, until she thought she would go mad.

She wanted to see Zane. That was all. Just see him, assure herself that he would be all right. But when she'd asked one of the Marine officers stationed at the embassy to make some inquiries about Zane, it was Admiral Lindley who had gotten back to her instead of the captain.

The dignified, distinguished admiral had come to the ambassador's private quarters less than an hour before. Barrie hadn't yet returned to her minor job in the embassy, feeling that she couldn't keep her mind on paperwork, so she had received the admiral in the beautifully appointed parlor.

After polite conversation about her health and the weather, the admiral came to the point of his visit. "You've been making some inquiries about Zane Mackenzie," he said kindly. "I've kept abreast of his condition, and I can tell you now with complete confidence that he'll fully recover. The ship's surgeon was able to stop the bleeding, and it wasn't necessary to remove his spleen. His condition was stabilized, and he was transferred to a hospital. When he's able, he'll be sent Stateside for the remainder of his convalescence."

"Where is he?" Barrie had demanded, her eyes burning. She'd scarcely slept in three days. Though she was once more impeccably clothed and coifed, the strain she'd been under had left huge dark circles under her eyes, and she was losing weight fast, because her nerves wouldn't let her eat.

Admiral Lindley sighed. "William asked me to keep that information from you, Barrie, and I have to say, I think he's right. I've known Zane a long time. He's an extraordinary warrior. But SEALs are a breed apart, and the characteristics that make them such great warriors don't, as a whole, make them model citizens. They're trained weapons, to put it bluntly. They don't keep high profiles, and most information about them is restricted."

"I don't want to know about his training," she said, her voice strained. "I don't want to know about his missions. I just want to see him."

The admiral shook his head. "I'm sorry."

Nothing she said budged him. He refused to give her even one more iota of information. Still, Zane was alive; he would be all right. Just knowing that made her feel weak inside, as the unbearable tension finally relaxed.

That didn't mean she would forgive her father for interfering.

"I love him," she now said deliberately. "You have no right to keep me from seeing him."

"Love?" Her father gave her a pitying look. "Barrie, what you feel isn't love, it's hero-worship. It will fade, I promise you."

"Do you think I haven't considered that?" she fired back. "I'm not a teenager with a crush on a rock star. Yes, I met him under dangerous, stressful circumstances. Yes, he saved my life—and he nearly died doing it. I know what infatuation is, and I know what love is, but even if I didn't, the decision isn't yours to make."

"You've always been reasonable," he argued. "At least concede that your judgment may not be at its sharpest right now. What if you acted impulsively, married this man—I'm sure he'd jump at the chance—and then realized that you really didn't love him? Think what a mess it would be. I know it sounds snobbish, but he isn't our kind. He's a sailor, and a trained killer. You've dined with kings and danced with princes. What could the two of you have in common?"

"First, that doesn't just *sound* snobbish, it *is* snobbish. Second, you must not think much of me as a person if you consider your money my only attraction."

"You know that isn't what I meant," he said, genuinely shocked. "You're a wonderful person. But how could someone like that appreciate the life you live? How do you know he wouldn't have his eye on the main chance?"

"Because I know him," she declared. "I know him in a way I never would have if I'd met him at an embassy party. According to you, a SEAL couldn't be kind and considerate, but he was. They all were, for that matter. Dad, I've told you over and over that I wasn't raped. I know you don't believe me, and I know you've suffered, worrying about me. But I swear to you—I *swear*—that I wasn't. They were planning to, the next day, but they were waiting for someone. So, though I was terrified and upset, I haven't been through the trauma of a gang rape the way you keep thinking. Seeing Zane lying in a pool of blood was a hell of a lot more traumatic than anything those kidnappers did!"

"Barrie!" It was the first time her father had ever heard her curse. Come to think of it, she had never cursed at all, until rough men had grabbed her off the street and subjected her to hours of terror. She had cursed them, and meant it. She had cursed Major Hodson, and meant that, too.

With an effort, she regulated her tone. "You know that the first attempt to get me out didn't quite work."

He gave an abrupt nod. He'd suffered agonies, thinking their only hope of rescuing her had failed and imagining what she must be suffering. That was when he'd given up hope of ever seeing her alive again. Admiral Lindley hadn't been as pessimistic; the SEALs hadn't checked in, and though there were reports of gunfire in Benghazi, if a team of SEALs had been killed or captured, the Libyan government would have trumpeted it all over the world. That meant they were still there, still working to free her. Until they heard from the team that the rescue had failed, there was still hope.

"Well, it did work, in a way. Zane came in alone to get me, while the rest of the team was a diversion, I guess, in case things went wrong. He had a backup plan, what to do if they were spotted, because you can't control the human factor." She realized she was repeating things Zane had said to her during those long hours when they had lain drowsily together, and she missed him so much that pain knotted her insides. "The team was so well-hidden that one of the guards didn't see Spooky until he actually stepped on him. That's what gave the alarm and started the shooting. A guard had been posted in the corridor outside the room where they had me tied up, and he ran in. Zane killed him," she said simply. "Then, while the others were chasing the team, he got me out of the building. We were separated from the team and had to hide for a day, but I was safe."

The ambassador listened gravely, soaking up these details of how she had been returned to him. They hadn't talked before, not about the actual rescue. She had been too distraught about Zane, almost violent in her despair. Now that she knew he was alive, even though she was still so angry she could barely contain it, she was able to tell her father how she had been returned to him alive.

"While I stayed in our hiding place, Zane risked his life by going out and stealing food and water for us, as well as the robe and chador for me. He took care of the cut on my foot. When scavengers were practically dismantling the place around us, he kept himself between me and any danger. That's the man I fell in love with, that's the man you say isn't 'our kind.' He may not be yours, but he's definitely mine!"

The expression in her father's eyes was stunned, almost panicked. Too late, Barrie saw that she had chosen the wrong tack in her argument. If she had presented her concern for Zane as merely for someone who had done so much for her, if she had insisted that it was only right she thank him in person, her father could have been convinced. He was very big on preserving the niceties, on behaving properly. Instead, she had convinced him that she truly loved Zane Mackenzie, and too late she saw how much he had feared exactly that. He didn't want to lose her, and now Zane presented a far bigger threat than before.

"Barrie, I…" He fumbled to a stop, her urbane, sophisticated father who was never at a loss for words. He swallowed hard. It was true that he'd seldom denied her anything, and those times he had refused had been because he thought the activity she planned or the object she wanted—once it had been a motorcycle—wasn't safe. Keeping her safe was his obsession, that and holding tightly to his only remaining family, his beloved child, who so closely resembled the wife he'd lost.

She saw it in his eyes as his instinct to pamper her with anything she desired warred with the knowledge that this time, if he did, he would probably lose her from his life. He didn't want occasional visits from her; they had both endured that kind of separation during her school years. He wanted her *there*, in his everyday life. She knew part of his obsession was selfish, because she made domestic matters very easy for him, but she had never doubted his love for her.

Pure panic flashed in his expression. He said stiffly, "I still think you need to give yourself time for your emotions to calm. And surely you realize that the conditions you describe are what that man is *used* to. How could he ever fit into your life?"

"That's a moot question, since marriage or even a relationship was never discussed. I want to see him. I don't want him to think that I didn't care enough even to check on his condition."

"If any sort of relationship was never discussed, why would he expect you to visit him? It was a mission for him, nothing more."

Barrie's shoulders were military straight, her jaw set, her green eyes dark with emotion. "It was more," she said flatly, and that was as much of what had happened between her and Zane as she was willing to discuss. She took a deep breath and pulled out the heavy artillery. "You owe it to me," she said, her gaze locked with his. "I haven't asked any details about what happened here, but I'm an intelligent, logical person—"

"Of course you are," he interrupted, "but I don't see—"

"Was there a ransom demanded?" She cut across his interruption.

He was a trained diplomat; he seldom lost control of his expression. But now, startled, the look he gave her was blank with puzzlement. "A ransom?" he echoed.

A new despair knotted itself in her stomach, etched itself in her face. "Yes, ransom," she said softly. "There wasn't one, was there? Because money wasn't what *he* wanted. He wants something from you, doesn't he? Information. He's either trying to force you to give it to him, or you're already in it up to your eyebrows and you've had a falling out with him. Which is it?"

Again his training failed him; for a split second his face revealed panicked guilt and consternation before his expression smoothed into diplomatic blandness. "What a ridiculous charge," he said calmly.

She stood there, sick with knowledge. If the kidnapper had been using her as a weapon to force her father into betraying his country, the ambassador most likely would have denied it, because he wouldn't want her to be worried, but that wasn't what she'd read in his face. It was guilt.

She didn't bother responding to his denial. "You owe me," she repeated. "You owe Zane."

He flinched at the condemnation in her eyes. "I don't see it that way at all."

"You're the reason I was kidnapped."

"You know there are things I can't tell you," he said, releasing her hands and walking around the desk to resume his seat, symbolically leaving the role of father and entering that of ambassador. "But your supposition is wrong, and, of course, an indication of how off-balance you still are."

She started to ask if Art Sandefer would think her supposition was so wrong, but she couldn't bring herself to threaten her father. Feeling sick, she wondered if that made her a traitor, too. She loved her country; living in Europe as much as she had, she had seen and appreciated the dramatic differences between the United States and every other country on earth. Though she liked Europe and had a fondness for French wine, German architecture, English orderliness, Spanish music and Italy in general, whenever she set foot in the States she was struck by the energy, the richness of life where even people who were considered poor lived well compared to everywhere else. The United States wasn't perfect, far from it, but it had something special, and she loved it.

By her silence, she could be betraying it.

By staying here, she remained in danger. Kidnapping her

had failed once, but that didn't mean *he*, the unknown, faceless enemy, wouldn't try again. Her father knew who *he* was, she was certain of it. Immediately she saw how it would be. She would be confined to the embassy grounds, or allowed out only with an armed escort. She would be a prisoner of her father's fear.

There was really no place she would be entirely safe, but remaining here only made the danger more acute. And once she was away from the enclave of the embassy, she would have a better chance of locating Zane, because Admiral Lindley's influence couldn't cover every nook and cranny of the globe. The farther away from Athens she was, the thinner that influence would be.

She faced her father, knowing that she was deliberately breaking the close ties that had bound them together for the past fifteen years. "I'm going home," she said calmly. "To Virginia."

Two weeks later, Zane sat on the front porch of his parents' house, perched on top of Mackenzie's Mountain, just outside Ruth, Wyoming. The view was breathtaking, an endless vista of majestic mountains and green valleys. Everything here was as familiar to him as his own hands. Saddles, boots, some cattle but mostly horses. Books in every room of the sprawling house, cats prowling through the barns and stables, his mother's sweet, bossy coddling, his father's concern and understanding.

He'd been shot before; he'd been sliced up in a knife fight. He'd had his collarbone broken, ribs cracked, a lung punctured. He had been seriously injured before, but this was the closest he'd ever come to dying. He'd been bleeding to death, lying there in the bottom of the raft with Barrie crouched over him, pressing the chador over the wound

with every ounce of her weight. Her quickness, her determination, had made the difference. Santos squeezing the
plasma from the bags into his veins had made the difference.
He had been so close that he could pick out a dozen details
that had made the difference; if any one of them hadn't happened, he would have died.

He'd been unusually quiet since leaving the naval hospital and returning home for convalescence. It wasn't that
he was in low spirits, but rather that he had a lot of thinking to do, something that hadn't been easy when practically
the entire family had felt compelled to visit and reassure
themselves of his relative well-being. Joe had flown in from
Washington for a quick check on his baby brother; Michael
and Shea had visited several times, bringing their two rap-
scallion sons with them; Josh and Loren and their three had
descended for a weekend visit, which was all the time
Loren's job at the hospital in Seattle had allowed. Maris had
driven all night to be there when he was brought home. At
least he'd been able to walk on his own by then, even if very
slowly, or likely she would still be here. She had pulled up
a chair directly in front of him and sat for hours, her black
eyes locked on his face as if she was willing vitality from her
body into his. Maybe she had been. His little sister was fey,
magical; she operated on a different level than other people did.

Hell, even Chance had shown up. He'd done so warily,
eyeing their mother and sister as if they were bombs that
might go off in his face, but he was here, sitting beside Zane
on the porch.

"You're thinking of resigning."

Zane didn't have to wonder how Chance had known
what was on his mind. After nearly battering each other to
death when they were fourteen, they had reached an un-

usual communion. Maybe it was because they'd shared so much, from classes to girls to military training. Even after all this time, Chance was as wary as a wounded wolf and didn't like people to get close to him, but even though he resisted, he was helpless against family. Chance had never in his life been loved until Mary had brought him home with her and the sprawling, brawling Mackenzies had knocked him flat. It was fun to watch him still struggle against the family intimacy each time he was drawn into the circle, because within an hour he always surrendered. Mary wouldn't let him do anything else; nor would Maris. After accepting him as a brother, Zane had never even acknowledged Chance's wariness. Only Wolf was willing to give his adopted son time to adjust—but there was still a limit on how much time he would allow.

"Yeah," he finally said.

"Because you nearly bought it this time?"

Zane snorted. "When has that ever made any difference to either of us?" He alone of the family knew the exact details of Chance's work. It was a toss-up which of them was in the most danger.

"Then it's this last promotion that did it."

"It took me out of the field," Zane said quietly. Carefully he leaned back in the chair and propped his booted feet on the porch railing. Though he was a fast healer, two and a half weeks wasn't quite long enough to let him ignore the wound. "If two of my men hadn't been wounded in that screwup on the *Montgomery*, I wouldn't have been able to go on this last mission."

Chance knew about the screwup. Zane had told him about it, and screwup was the most polite description he'd used. As soon as he'd regained consciousness in the naval hospital, he'd been on the phone, starting and directing the investigation. Though Odessa would fully recover, it was likely Higgins would have to retire on disability. The guards who had shot the two SEALs might escape court-martial if their counsel was really slick, but at the very least they would be cashiered out of the service. The extent of the damage to the careers of Captain Udaka and Executive Officer Boyd remained to be seen; Zane had targeted the shooters, but the ripple effect would go all the way up to the captain.

"I'm thirty-one," Zane said. "That's just about the upper limit for active missions. I'm too damn good at my job, too. The Navy keeps promoting me for it, then they say I'm too highly ranked to go on missions."

"You want to throw in with me?" Chance asked casually.

He'd considered it. Very seriously. But something kept nagging at him, something he couldn't quite bring into focus.

"I want to. If things were different, I would, but…"

"What things?"

Zane shrugged. At least part of his uneasy feeling could be nailed down. "A woman," he said.

"Oh, hell." Chance kicked back and surveyed the world over the toes of his boots. "If it's a woman, you won't be able to concentrate on anything until you've gotten her out of your system. Damn their sweet little hides," he said fondly. Chance generally had women crawling all over him. It didn't hurt that he was drop-dead handsome, but he had a raffish, daredevil quality to him that brought them out of the woodwork.

Zane wasn't certain he could get Barrie out of his system. He wasn't certain he wanted to. He didn't wonder why she had disappeared without even saying goodbye, hope you're feeling better. Bunny and Spook had told him how she'd been dragged, kicking and yelling and swearing, aboard a plane and taken back to Athens. He figured her father, combined with the Navy's policy of secrecy concerning the SEALs, had prevented her from finding out to which hospital they'd taken him.

He missed her. He missed her courage, her sturdy willingness to do whatever needed doing. He missed the serenity of her expression, and the heat of her lovemaking.

God, yes.

The one memory, more than any of the others, that was branded in his brain was the moment when she had reached for his belt and said in that fierce whisper, "I'll do it!"

He'd understood. Not just why she needed to be in control, but the courage it took her to wipe out the bad memories and replace them with good ones. She'd been a virgin; she had told the truth about that. She hadn't known what to do, and she hadn't expected the pain. But she had taken him anyway, sweetly, hotly, sliding her tight little body down on him and shattering his control the way no other woman had ever done.

She could have been a spoiled, helpless little socialite; she *should* have been exactly that. Instead she had made the best of a tense, dangerous situation, done what she could to help and hadn't voiced a single complaint.

He liked being with her, liked talking to her. He was too much of a loner to easily accept the word love in connection with anyone other than family, but with Barrie…maybe. He wanted to spend more time with her, get to know her better, let whatever would develop get to developing.

He wanted her.

First things first, though. He had to get his strength back; right now he could walk from room to room without aid, but he would think twice about heading down to the stables by himself. He had to decide whether or not he was going to stay in the Navy; it felt like time to be moving on, since the reason he'd joined in the first place was being taken away from him as he moved up the ranks. If he wasn't going to remain a SEAL, then what would he do for a living? He had to decide, had to get his life settled.

Barrie might not be interested in any kind of relationship with him, though from the way Spook and Bunny had described her departure, he didn't think that was the case. The day of lovemaking they had shared had been more than propinquity for both of them.

Getting in touch with her could take some doing, though. That morning he had placed a call to the embassy in Athens. He'd given his name and asked to speak to Barrie Lovejoy. It had been Ambassador William Lovejoy who had come on the line, however, and the conversation hadn't been cordial.

"It isn't that Barrie doesn't appreciate what you did, but I'm sure you understand that she wants to put all of that behind her. Talking with you would bring it all back and needlessly upset her," the ambassador had said in a cool, well-bred voice, his diction the best money could buy.

"Is that her opinion, or yours?" Zane had asked, his tone arctic.

"I don't see that it matters," the ambassador had replied, and hung up.

Zane decided he would let it rest for now. He wasn't in any shape to do much about it, so he would wait. When he had his mind made up about what he was going to do, there would be plenty of time to get in touch with Barrie, and now that he knew the ambassador had given orders for his calls not to be routed to her, the next time he would be prepared to do an end run around her father.

"Zane," his mother called from inside the house, pulling his thoughts to the present. "Are you getting tired?"

"I feel fine," he called back. It was an exaggeration, but he wasn't unduly tired. He glanced at Chance and saw the smirk on his brother's face.

"With all the worry about you, she forgot about my cracked ribs," Chance whispered.

"Glad to be of service," Zane drawled. "Just don't expect me to get shot every time you bang yourself up a little." The entire family thought it was hilarious the way Chance reacted to Mary's coddling and fussing, as if the attention terrified him, even though he was never able to resist her. Chance was putty in Mary's hands, but then, they all were. They'd grown up with the fine example of their father to emulate, and Wolf Mackenzie might growl and stomp, but Mary usually got her way.

"Chance?"

Zane controlled a grin as Chance stiffened, the smirk disappearing from his face as if it had never been.

"Ma'am?" he answered cautiously.

"Are you still keeping a pressure wrap on your ribs?"

That familiar panicked expression was in his eyes now. "Ah…no, ma'am." He could have lied; Mary would have believed him. But none of them ever lied to her, even when it was in their best interests. It would hurt the little tyrant's feelings too much if she ever discovered any of her kids had lied to her.

"You know you're supposed to wrap them for another week," said the voice from inside the house. It was almost like hearing God speak, except this voice was light and sweet and liquidly Southern.

"Yes, ma'am."

"Come inside and let me take care of that."

"Yes, ma'am," Chance said again, resignation in his voice. He got up from his rocking chair and went into the house. As he passed Zane, he muttered, "Getting shot didn't work. Try something else."

Chapter 8

Two months later, Sheriff Zane Mackenzie stood naked at the window of the pleasant two-bedroom Spanish-style house he had bought in southern Arizona. He was staring out over the moonlit desert, something wild and hot running through him at the sight. His SEAL training had taught him how to adapt to any environment, and the hot, dry climate didn't bother him.

Once he'd made up his mind to resign his commission, things had rapidly fallen into place. Upon hearing that he was leaving the Navy, a former SEAL team member who was now on the governor's staff in Phoenix had called and asked if he would be interested in serving the remaining two years of the term of a sheriff who had died in office.

At first Zane had been taken aback; he'd never considered going into law enforcement. Moreover, he didn't know anything about Arizona state laws.

"Don't worry about it," his friend had said breezily. "Sheriff is a political position, and most of the time it's more administrative than anything else. The situation you'd be going into is more hands-on, though. A couple of the deputies have quit, so you'd be shorthanded until some more can be hired, and the ones still there will resent the hell out of you because one of them wasn't appointed to finish out the sheriff's term."

"Why not?" Zane asked bluntly. "What's wrong with the chief deputy?"

"She's one of the ones who quit. She left a couple of months before the sheriff died, took a job on the force in Prescott."

"None of the others are qualified?"

"I wouldn't say that."

"Then what would you say?"

"You gotta understand, there's not a lot of selection here. A couple of the young deputies are good, real good, but they're *too* young, not enough experience. The one twenty-year guy isn't interested. A fifteen-year guy is a jerk, and the rest of the deputies hate his guts."

Sheriff. Zane thought about it, growing more intrigued with the idea. He had no illusions about it being a cake-walk. He would have difficulties with the fifteen-year veteran, at least, and likely all the other deputies would have some reservations and resistance about someone from the outside being brought in. Hell, he liked it better that way. Cakewalks didn't interest him. He'd rather have a challenging job any day. "Okay, I'm interested. What does it involve?"

"A lot of headache, mostly. The pay's decent, the hours are lousy. A reservation sits on part of the county, so you'll have to deal with the BIA. There's a big problem with illegal immigrants, but that's for the INS to worry about. Generally, this isn't a high crime area. Not enough people."

So here he was, his strength back, the owner of a house and a hundred acres of land, newly sworn in as sheriff. He'd brought in a few of his horses from his parents' place in Wyoming. It was a hell of a change from the Navy.

It was time to see about Barrie. He'd thought about her a lot over the past few months, but lately he couldn't think about anything else. The uneasy feeling was persisting, growing stronger. He'd put his resources to work, and to his surprise found that she'd left Athens within a week of being returned there. She was currently living at the Lovejoy private residence in Arlington, Virginia. Moreover, last month the ambassador had abruptly asked to be replaced, and he, too, had returned to Virginia. Zane wished Mr. Lovejoy had remained in Athens, but his presence was a problem that could be handled.

No matter what her father did or said, Zane was determined to see Barrie. There was unfinished business between them, a connection that had been abruptly cut when he'd been shot and she had been forced aboard a flight to Athens. He knew the hot intimacy of those long hours together could have been a product of stress and propinquity, but at this point, he didn't give a damn. There were other considerations, ones he couldn't ignore. That was why he had a flight out of Tucson to Washington in the morning. He needed to be sleeping, but one thought kept going around and around in his head. She was pregnant.

He couldn't say why he was so convinced of it. It was a gut feeling, an intuition, even a logical conclusion. There hadn't been any means of birth control available; they had made love several times. Put the two facts together, and the possibility of pregnancy existed. He didn't think it was a mere possibility, though; he thought it was a fact.

Barrie was going to have his baby.

The rush of fierce possessiveness he felt was like a tidal wave, sweeping away all his cautious plans. There wouldn't be any gradual getting-to-know-each-other stage, no easing into the idea of a serious relationship. If she was pregnant, they would get married immediately. If she didn't like the idea, he would convince her. It was as simple as that.

She was pregnant. Barrie hugged the precious knowledge to herself, not ready yet to let anyone else know, certainly not her father. The kidnapping and the aftermath had driven a wedge between them that neither of them could remove. He was desperate to restore their former relationship; nothing else could have induced him to resign from a post, an action that could have had serious repercussions for his career if it hadn't generally been thought that he had resigned because she had been so traumatized by the kidnapping that she couldn't remain in Athens and he wanted to be with her.

She tried not to think about whatever he might be involved in, because it hurt. It hurt horribly that he might be a traitor. Part of her simply couldn't believe it; he was an old-fashioned man, a man to whom honor wasn't just a word but a way of life. She had no proof, only logic and her own deductions…that, and the expression he hadn't quite been able to hide when she had asked him directly if he was involved in anything that might have resulted in her being kidnapped.

It also hurt horribly that he had kept her from Zane. She had made inquiries once she reached Virginia, but once again she had collided with a stone wall. No one would give her any information at all about him. She had even contacted SEAL headquarters and been politely stonewalled again. At least with the SEALs it was probably policy to safeguard the team members' identities and location, given the sensitive nature of the antiterrorism unit.

She was having his baby. She wanted him to know about it. She wouldn't expect anything of him that he didn't want to give, but she wanted him to know about his child. And she desperately wanted to see him again. She was adrift and lonely and frightened, her emotions in turmoil, and she needed some security in that part of her life, at least. He wasn't the kind of man who would blithely walk away from his offspring and ignore their existence. This baby would be a permanent link between them, something she could count on.

She doubted her father would relent concerning Zane even if he knew about the baby; his possessiveness would probably extend to a grandchild, even an illegitimate one. He would take steps to keep her pregnancy quiet, and even when the news got around, as it inevitably would, people would assume it was a child of rape, and they would look at her pityingly and talk about how brave she was.

She thought she would go mad. She had escaped to Virginia only to have her father follow. He panicked if she went anywhere unescorted. She had her own car, but he didn't want her driving it; he wanted his driver to take her wherever she wanted to go. She had had to sneak to a pharmacy to buy a home pregnancy test, though she had been sure fairly early on that she was pregnant. The test had merely confirmed what her body had already told her.

Barrie knew she should be worried and upset about this unplanned pregnancy, but it was the only thing in her life right now that made her happy. She was intensely lonely; the kidnapping and the long hours alone with Zane had set her apart from the other people in her life. She had memories they couldn't share, thoughts and needs no one could understand. Zane had been there with her; he would have understood her occasional pensiveness, her reticence in talking about it. It wasn't that she was secretive, for she would have liked to talk to someone who understood. But what she had shared with Zane was like a combat experience, forming a unique bond between the people who had lived it.

She wouldn't be able to keep her pregnancy secret much longer; she had to arrange prenatal care, and all telephone calls were now recorded. She supposed she could sneak out again and set up a doctor's appointment from a pay phone, but she would be damned if she would.

Enough was enough. She was an adult, and soon to be a mother. She hated the fact that her relationship with her father had deteriorated to the point where they barely spoke, but she couldn't find a way to mend it. As long as the possibility of his involvement in treasonous activities remained, she was helpless. She wanted him to explain, to give her a plausible reason why she had been kidnapped. She wanted to stop looking over her shoulder every time she went out; she didn't want to feel as if she truly *needed* to be guarded. She wanted to live a normal life. She didn't want to raise her baby in an atmosphere of fear.

But that was exactly the atmosphere that permeated the house. It was stifling her. She had to get away, had to remove herself from the haunting fear that, as long as her father was involved in whatever had given him such a guilty expression, she could be kidnapped again. The very thought made her want to vomit, and she didn't have just herself to worry about now. She had her baby to protect.

The fatigue of early pregnancy had gotten her into the habit of sleeping late, but one morning she woke early, disturbed by a pair of raucous birds fighting for territory in the tree outside her window. Once she was awake, nausea soon followed, and she made her usual morning dash to the bathroom. Also as usual, when the bout of morning sickness had passed, she felt fine. She looked out the window at the bright morning and realized she was inordinately hungry, the first time in weeks that the idea of food was appealing.

It was barely six o'clock, too early for Adele, the cook, to have arrived. Breakfast was normally at eight, and she had been sleeping past that. Her stomach growled. She couldn't wait another two hours for something to eat.

She put on her robe and slippers and quietly left her room; her father's bedroom was at the top of the stairs, and she didn't want to disturb him. Even more, she didn't want him to join her for an awkward tête-à-tête. He tried so hard to carry on as if nothing had happened, and she couldn't respond as she had before.

He should still be asleep, she thought, but when she reached the top of the stairs she heard him saying something she couldn't understand. She paused, wondering if he'd heard her after all and had been calling out to her. Then she heard him say *Mack* in a sharp tone, and she froze.

A chill roughened her entire body, and the bottom dropped out of her stomach. The only Mack she knew was Mack Prewett, but why would her father be talking to him? Mack Prewett was still stationed in Athens, as far as she knew, and since her father had resigned, he shouldn't have had any reason to be talking to him.

Then her heart leaped wildly as another possibility occurred to her. Perhaps he had been saying *Mackenzie* and she'd heard only the first syllable. Maybe he was talking about Zane. If she listened, she might find out where he was, or at least *how* he was. With no additional information about his condition, it had been hard to believe Admiral Lindley's assurance that he would fully recover. Belief required trust, and she no longer trusted the admiral, or her father.

She crept closer to his door and put her ear against it.

"—finished soon," he was saying sharply, then he was silent for a moment. "I didn't bargain on this. Barrie wasn't supposed to be involved. Get it wrapped up, Mack."

Barrie closed her eyes in despair. The chill was back, even colder than before. She shook with it, and swallowed hard against the return of nausea. So he *was* involved, he and Mack Prewett both. Mack was CIA. Was he a double agent, and if so, for whom? The world situation wasn't like it had been back in the old days of the Cold War, when the lines had been clearly drawn. Nations had died since then, and new ones taken their place. Religion or money seemed to be the driving force behind most differences these days; how would her father and Mack Prewett fit into that? What information would her father have that Mack wouldn't?

The answer eluded her. It could be anything. Her father had friends in every country in Europe, and any variety of confidential information could come his way. What didn't make sense was why he would sell that information; he was already a wealthy man. But money, to some people, was as addictive as a narcotic. No amount was ever enough; they had to have more, then still more, always looking for the next hit in the form of cash and the power that went with it.

Could she have been so wrong in her judgment of him? Had she still been looking at him with a child's eyes, seeing only her father, the man who had been the security in her life, instead of a man whose ambitions had tainted his honor?

Blindly she stumbled to her bedroom, not caring if he heard her. He must still have been engrossed in his conversation, though, or she didn't make as much noise as she thought she had, because his door remained closed.

She curled up on the bed, protectively folding herself around the tiny embryo in her womb.

What was it he hadn't bargained on? The kidnapping?

That was over two months in the past. Had there been a new threat to use her as a means of ensuring he did something?

She was helplessly fumbling around in the dark with these wild conjectures, and she hated it. It was like being in alien territory, with no signs to guide her. What was she supposed to do? Take her suspicions to the FBI? She had nothing concrete to go on, and over the years her father had made a lot of contacts in the FBI; who could she trust there?

Even more important, if she stayed here, was she in danger? Maybe her wild conjectures weren't wild at all. She had seen a lot during her father's years in foreign service and noticed even more when she had started working at the embassy. Things happened, skulduggery went on, dangerous situations developed. Given the kidnapping, her father's reaction and now his unreasonable attitude about her safety, she didn't think she could afford to assume everything would be okay.

She had to leave.

Feverishly she began trying to think of someplace she could go where it wouldn't be easy to find her, and how she could get there without leaving a paper trail that would lead a halfway competent terrorist straight to her. Meanwhile, Mack Prewett wasn't a halfway competent bureaucrat, he was frighteningly efficient; he was like a spider, with webs of contacts spreading out in all directions. If she booked a flight using her real name, or paid for it with a credit card, he would know.

To truly hide, she had to have cash, a lot of it. That meant emptying her bank account, but how could she get there without her father knowing? It had reached the point where she would have to climb out the window and walk to the nearest pay phone to call a cab.

Maybe the house was already being watched.

She moaned and covered her face with her hands. Oh, God, this was making her paranoid, but did she dare *not* suspect anything? As some wit had observed, even paranoids had enemies.

She had to think of the baby. No matter how paranoid an action seemed, she had to err on the side of safety. If she had to dress in dark clothing, slither out a window in the wee hours of the morning and crawl across the ground until she was well away from this house...as ridiculous as it sounded, she would do it. Tonight? The sooner she got away, the better.

Tonight.

That decision made, she took a deep breath and tried to think of the details. She would have to carry some clothing. She would take her checkbook and bank book, so she could close out both her checking and savings accounts. She would take her credit cards and get as much cash as she could on them; everything together would give her a hefty amount, close to half a million dollars. How would she carry that much money? She would need an empty bag.

This was beginning to sound ludicrous, even to her. How was she supposed to crawl across the lawn in the darkness, dragging two suitcases behind her?

Think! she fiercely admonished herself. Okay, she wouldn't have to carry either clothes or suitcases with her. All she would need to carry was her available cash, which was several hundred dollars, her checkbook and savings account book, and her credit cards, which she would destroy after they had served their purpose. She could buy new clothes and makeup, as well as what luggage she would immediately need, as soon as a discount store opened. She could buy do-it-yourself hair coloring and dye her red hair brown, though not until after she had been to the bank. She didn't want the teller to be able to describe her disguise.

With cash in her possession, she would have several options. She could hop on Amtrak and go in any direction, then get off the train before her ticketed destination. Then she could buy a cheap used car, pay cash for it, and no one would know where she went from there. To be on the safe side, she would drive that car for only one day, then trade it in on a better car, again paying cash.

These were drastic measures, but doable. She still wasn't certain she wasn't being ridiculous, but did she dare bet that way, when her life, and that of her child, could hang in the balance? *Desperate times call for desperate measures.* Who had said that? Perhaps an eighteenth-century revolutionary; if so, she knew how he had felt. She had to disappear as completely as possible. She would mail her father a postcard before she left town, letting him know that she was all right but that she thought it would be better to get away for a while, otherwise he would think she had indeed been kidnapped again, and he would go mad with grief and terror. She couldn't do that to him. She still loved him very much, even after all he had done. Again a wave of disbelief and uncertainty hit her. It seemed so impossible that he would sell information to terrorists, so opposite to the man she had always known him to be. She was aware that he wasn't universally well liked, but the worst accusation she had ever heard leveled against him was that he was a snob, which even she admitted was accurate. He was very effective as a diplomat and ambassador, working with the CIA, which was of course set up in every embassy, using his social standing and contacts to smooth the way whenever a problem cropped up. He had personally been acquainted with the last six presidents, and prime ministers called him a friend. This man was a traitor?

It couldn't be. If she had only herself to consider, she would give him the benefit of the doubt.

But there was the baby, the tiny presence undetectable to any but herself. She could feel it in her breasts, which had become so tender she was always aware of them, and in the increased sensitivity and pressure low down in her abdomen, as her womb began to swell with amniotic fluid and increased blood flow. It was almost a hot feeling, as if the new life forming within her was generating heat with the effort of development.

Zane's baby.

She would do anything, no matter how Draconian, to keep it safe. She had to find some secure place where she could get the prenatal care she needed. She would have to change her name, get a new driver's license and a new social security card; she didn't know how these last two would be accomplished, but she would find out. There were always shady characters who could tell her. The driver's license could be forged, but the social security card would have to come through the regular administration. Even though social security was being phased out, until it was completely gone, everyone still had to have a number in order to get a legitimate job.

There was something else to consider. It would be stupid of her to live off her cash until it was all gone. She would need a job, anything that paid enough to keep a roof over their heads and food in their stomachs. She had degrees in art and history, but she wouldn't be able to use her own name, so she wouldn't be able to use those degrees to get a teaching job.

She didn't know what the job situation would be wherever she settled; she would simply have to wait and see. It didn't matter what she did, waiting tables or office work, she would take whatever was available.

She glanced at the clock: seven-thirty. Nerves notwithstanding, she was acutely hungry now, to the point of being sick with it. Her pregnant body had its own agenda, ignoring upset emotions and concentrating only on the business at hand.

The thought brought a smile to her face. It was almost as if the baby was already stomping a tiny foot and demanding what it wanted.

Tenderly she pressed her hand over her belly, feeling a slight firmness that surely hadn't been there before. "All right," she whispered to it. "I'll feed you."

She showered and dressed, mentally preparing herself to face her father without giving anything away. When she entered the breakfast room, he looked up with an expression of delight, quickly tempered by caution. "Well, it's a pleasure to have your company," he said, folding the newspaper and laying it aside.

"Some birds woke me up," she said, going to the buffet to help herself to toast and eggs. She fought a brief spell of nausea at the sight of sausage and changed her mind about the eggs, settling on toast and fruit. She hoped that would be enough to satisfy the demanding little creature.

"Coffee?" her father asked as she sat down. He already had the silver carafe in his hand, poised to pour.

"No, not today," she said hastily, as her stomach again clenched warningly. "I've been drinking too much caffeine lately, so I'm trying to cut down." That was a direct lie. She had stopped drinking anything with caffeine in it as soon as she suspected she might be pregnant, but it was as if her system was still warning her against it. "I'll drink orange juice." So far, that hadn't turned her stomach.

She applied herself to her food, replying civilly to his conversational gambits, but she couldn't bring herself to wholeheartedly enter into a discussion with him the way she once would have done. She could barely look at him, afraid her feelings would be plain on her face. She didn't want him any more alert than he already was.

"I'm having lunch with Congressman Garth," he told her. "What are your plans for the day?"

"None," she replied. Her plans were all for the night.

He looked relieved. "I'll see you this afternoon, then. I'll drive myself, so Poole will be available to drive you if you do decide to go anywhere."

"All right," she said, agreeing with him because she wasn't going anywhere.

Once he'd left the house, she spent the day reading and occasionally napping. Now that she had made up her mind to go, she felt more peaceful. Tomorrow would be an exhausting day, so she needed to rest while she could.

Her father returned in the middle of the afternoon. Barrie was sitting in the living room, curled up with a book. She looked up as he entered and immediately noticed how the drawn look of worry eased when he saw her. "Did you have a nice lunch?" she asked, because that was what she would have done before.

"You know how these political things are," he said. Once he would have sat down and told her all about it, but this time he smoothly evaded talking specifics. Senator Garth was on several important committees concerning national security and foreign affairs. Before she could ask any more questions, he went into his study, closing the door behind him. Before, he had always kept it open as an invitation to her to visit whenever she wanted. Sadly Barrie looked at the closed door, then returned to her book.

The doorbell startled her. She put the book aside and went to answer it, cautiously looking through the peephole before opening the door. A tall, black-haired man was standing there.

Her heart jumped wildly, and a wave of dizziness swept over her. Behind her, she heard her father coming out of his study. "Who is it?" he asked sharply. "Let me get it."

Barrie didn't reply. She jerked the door open and stared up into Zane's cool, blue gray eyes. Her heart was pounding so hard she could barely breathe.

That sharp gaze swept down her body, then came up to her face. "Are you pregnant?" he asked quietly, his voice pitched low so her father couldn't hear, even though he was rapidly approaching.

"Yes," she whispered.

He nodded, a terse movement of his head as if that settled that. "Then we'll get married."

Chapter 9

Her father reached them then, and shouldered Barrie aside. "Who are you?" he demanded, still in that sharp tone.

Zane coolly surveyed the man who would be his father-in-law. "Zane Mackenzie," he finally replied, when he had finished his appraisal. His darkly tanned face was impassive, but there was a piercing quality to his pale eyes that made Barrie suddenly aware of how dangerous this man could be. It didn't frighten her; under the circumstances, this quality was exactly what she needed.

William Lovejoy had been alarmed, but now his complexion turned pasty, and his expression froze. He said stiffly, "I'm sure you realize it isn't good for Barrie to see you again. She's trying to put that episode behind her—"

Zane looked past Lovejoy to where Barrie stood, visibly trembling as she stared at him with pleading green eyes. He hadn't realized how green her eyes were, a deep forest green, or how expressive. He got the impression that she wasn't pleading for him to be nice to her father, but rather that she was asking for help in some way, with some thing. His battle instincts stirred, his senses lifting to the next level of acuity. He didn't know exactly what she was asking of him, but he would find out, as soon as he dealt with the present situation. It was time to let the former ambassador know exactly where he stood.

"We're getting married," he said, still looking at Barrie, as he cut through the ambassador's continuing explanation on why it would be best if he left immediately. His steely voice, which had instantly commanded the attention of the deadliest guerrilla fighters in the world, cut through Lovejoy's stuffy, patronizing explanation.

The ambassador broke off, and a look of panic flashed across his face. Then he said, "Don't be ridiculous," in a strained tone. "Barrie isn't going to marry a sailor who thinks he's something special because he's a trained assassin."

Zane's cool gaze switched from Barrie to her father and went arctic cold, the blue fading to a gray that glinted like shards of ice. Lovejoy took an involuntary step back, his complexion going from pasty to white.

"Barrie, will you marry me?" Zane asked deliberately, keeping his gaze focused on Lovejoy.

She glanced from him to her father, who tensed as he waited for her answer.

"Yes," she said, her mind racing. Zane. She wouldn't question the miracle that had brought him here, but she was so desperate that she would have married him even if she hadn't loved him. Zane was a SEAL; if anyone could keep her safe from the unknown enemy who had her father so on edge, he could. She was carrying his child, and evidently that possibility was what had brought him to Virginia in search of her. He was a man who took his responsibilities seriously. She would have preferred that he cared for her as deeply as she did for him, but she would take what she could get. She knew he was attracted to her; if he wasn't, she wouldn't be pregnant.

She would marry him, and perhaps with time he would come to love her.

Her father flinched at her answer. Half turning to her, he said imploringly, "Baby, you don't want to marry someone like him. You've always had the best, and he can't give it to you."

Squaring her shoulders, she said, "I'm going to marry him—as soon as possible."

Seeing the intractability in her expression, her father looked at Zane. "You won't get a penny of her inheritance," he said with real venom.

"Dad!" she cried, shocked. She had her own money, inheritances from her mother and grandparents, so she wasn't worried about being destitute even if he carried through on his threat; it was the fact that he'd made the threat at all, that he would try to sabotage her future with Zane in such a blatant, hurtful manner, that hurt.

Zane shrugged. "Fine," he said with deceptive mildness. Barrie heard the pure iron underlying the calm, even tone. "Do what you want with your money, I don't give a damn. But you're a fool if you thought you could keep her with you for the rest of your life. You can act like an ass and cheat yourself out of your grandchildren if you want, but nothing you say is going to change a damn thing."

Lovejoy hung there, his face drawn with pain. Anguish darkened his eyes as he looked at his daughter. "Don't do it," he pleaded, his voice shaking.

Now it was her turn to wince, because in spite of everything, she hated to hurt him. "I'm pregnant," she whispered, straightening her shoulders against any other hurtful thing he might say. "And we're getting married."

He swayed on his feet, stunned by her announcement. She hadn't thought it possible he could turn any whiter, but he did. "What?" he croaked. "But—but you said you weren't raped!"

"She wasn't," Zane said. There was a soft, drawling, very masculine undertone in his voice.

Their eyes met. Barrie gave him a soft, wry smile. "I wasn't," she verified, and despite everything, a sudden, subtle glow lit her face.

Her father couldn't think of anything else to say. He gaped at them for a moment, unable to handle this turn of events. Then a red tide of anger ran up his face, chasing away the pallor. "You bastard!" he choked out. "You took advantage of her when she was vulnerable—"

Barrie grabbed his arm and jerked him around. "Stop it!" she yelled, her slender body tense with fury. Her nerves had been shredded since that morning, and this confrontation was only making them worse. Zane's sudden appearance, though it made her almost giddy with happiness, was another shock to her system, and she'd had enough. "If anyone took advantage, *I* did. If you want the details I'll give them to you, but I don't think you really want to know!"

It was on the tip of her tongue to ask him if he'd thought he could keep her a virgin forever, but she bit the bitter words off unspoken. That would be too hurtful, and once said, she would never be able to take the words back. He loved her, perhaps too much; his fear of losing her was why he was lashing out. And, despite everything, she loved him, too. Pain congealed inside her as she stared starkly at him, all pretense gone. "I know," she whispered. "Do you understand? I *know.* I know why you've been so paranoid every time I've left the house. *I have to leave.*"

He inhaled sharply, shock ripping away his last vestige of control. He couldn't sustain her burning gaze, and he looked away. "Keep her safe," he said to Zane in a stifled voice, then walked stiffly toward his study.

"I intend to." That difficulty solved, he spared no more than a glance for his departing foe. His gaze switched to Barrie, and a slow, heart-stopping smile touched his lips. "Go get packed," he said.

They were on their way within the hour.

She hurried up to her bedroom and filled her suitcases, bypassing the evening gowns and designer suits in favor of more practical clothing. The ankle-length cotton skirt she was already wearing was comfortable enough for travel; she pulled on a silk shirt over the sleeveless blouse she wore and let it go at that. Every instinct she had was screaming at her to hurry.

She dragged the bags to the top of the stairs. It didn't require a lot of effort, they all had wheeled bottoms, but when Zane saw her, he left his post by the door and took the stairs two at a time. "Don't lift those," he ordered, taking the bags from her hands. "You should have called me."

His tone was the same one he had used in commanding his men, but Barrie was too nervous to fight that battle with him right now. He lifted all three cases with an ease that made her blink and started down the stairs with them. She rushed after him. "Where are we going? Are we flying or driving?"

"Las Vegas. Flying."

"You already have the tickets?" she asked in surprise.

He paused and glanced over his shoulder at her, the dark wings of his eyebrows lifting fractionally. "Of course," he said, and resumed his trip down the stairs.

Such certainty and self-assurance were daunting. Briefly she wondered what on earth she was getting herself into.

More and more she was becoming aware of just how much in control Zane Mackenzie was, of himself and everything around him. She might never be able to break through that barrier. *Except in bed.* The memory zinged through her, bringing a flush to her cheeks that wasn't caused by rushing around. He had lost control there, and it had been… breathtaking.

"What time is the flight?" Once more she hurried to catch up to him. "Will we have time to go to my bank? I need to close out my accounts—"

"You can transfer them to a local bank when we get home."

While he carried her bags out to the rental car he was driving, Barrie went to the study and knocked softly on the door. There was no answer; after a moment she opened the door anyway. Her father was sitting at the desk, his elbows propped on top of it and his face buried in his hands.

"Bye, Dad," she said softly.

He didn't answer, but she saw his Adam's apple bob as he swallowed.

"I'll let you know where I am."

"No," he said, his voice strangled. "Don't." He lifted his head. His eyes were anguished. "Not yet. Wait…wait a while."

"All right," she whispered, understanding slicing through her. It was safer for her that way. He must suspect the phone line was tapped.

"Baby, I—" He broke off and swallowed hard again. "I only want you to be happy—and safe."

"I know." She felt dampness on her cheeks and wiped away the tears that were wetting them.

"He isn't the kind of man I wanted for you. The SEALs are—well, never mind." He sighed. "Maybe he *can* keep you safe. I hope so. I love you, baby. You've been the center of my life. You know I never meant—" He halted, unable to go on.

"I know," she said again. "I love you, too."

She quietly closed the door and stood with her head bowed. She didn't hear him approach, but suddenly Zane was there, his arm hard around her waist as he drew her with him out to the car. He didn't ask any questions, just opened the door for her and helped her inside, then closed the door with a finality that was unmistakable.

She sat tensely during the drive to the airport, watching the traffic buzz around them.

"This is the most privacy we'll have for a while," Zane said as he competently threaded the car through the insanity of rush hour. "Why don't you tell me what's going on?" He had slipped on a pair of sunglasses, and his eyes were hidden from her view, but she didn't have to see them to know how cool and remote the expression in them was.

She lifted her chin and stared straight ahead, considering the way his suggestions sounded like orders. This wasn't going to be easy, but he had to know everything. She needed his protection, at least while she still carried his child. He wouldn't be on guard unless he knew there was a threat. She had to be honest with him. "I want you to know—one of the reasons I agreed to marry you is that I need protection, and you're a SEAL. If anything…dangerous…happens, you'll know how to handle it."

"Dangerous, how?" He sounded very matter-of-fact, almost disinterested. She supposed that, given his job, danger was so common to him that it was more the rule than the exception.

"I think the kidnappers may try again. And now I have more than just myself to worry about." Briefly, unconsciously, her hand moved to her lower belly in the instinctive way a pregnant woman touched the growing child within, as if reassuring it of its safety.

He glanced in the rearview mirror, calmly studying the traffic behind and around them. After a moment of consideration, he went straight to the heart of the matter. "Have you notified the FBI? The police?"

"No."

"Why not?"

"Because I think Dad may be involved," she said, almost strangling on the words.

Once again he checked the rearview mirror. "In what way?"

He sounded so damn remote. She clenched her hands into fists, determined to hold on to her control. If he could be self-contained, then so could she. She forced her voice to evenness. "The reason for the kidnapping wasn't ransom, so they must want information from him. I can't think of anything else it *could* be."

He was silent for a moment, deftly weaving in and out of the tangle of vehicles. She could almost hear that cool, logical brain sorting through the ramifications. Finally he said, "Your father must be in it up to his neck, or he'd have gone to the FBI himself. You would have been taken to a safe place and surrounded by a wall of agents."

He'd reached exactly the same conclusion she had. That didn't make her feel any better. "Since we've been back in Virginia, he's been impossible. He doesn't want me to leave the house by myself, and he's monitoring all telephone calls. He was always protective, but not like this. At first I thought he was overreacting because of what happened in Athens, but when I thought it through, I realized the threat still existed." She swallowed. "I'd made up my mind to sneak out tonight and disappear for a while."

If Zane had waited another day, she would have been gone. He wouldn't have had any idea where to find her, and she had no way of contacting him. Tears burned her eyes at the thought. Dear God, it had been so close.

"Hold on," he said, then jerked the steering wheel to the right, cutting across a lane of traffic and throwing the car into a sharp turn into another street. The tires squealed, and horns blared. Even with his warning, she barely had time to brace herself, and the seat belt tightened with a jerk.

"What's wrong?" she cried, struggling to right herself and ease the strangling grip of the seat belt.

"There's a possibility we had company. I didn't want to take any chances."

Alarmed, Barrie twisted around in the seat, staring at the cars passing through the intersection behind them, vainly trying to see anyone who looked familiar or any vehicle making an obvious effort to cut across traffic and follow them. The traffic pattern looked normal.

"Two Caucasian men, in their thirties or forties, both wearing sunglasses," Zane said with no more emphasis than if he'd been observing the clouds in the sky. She remembered this almost supernatural calmness from before. In Benghazi, the more tense the situation, the cooler he had become, totally devoid of emotion. For him to take the action he had, he'd been certain they were being followed. The bottom dropped out of her stomach, and she fought a sudden rise of nausea. To suspect she was in danger was one thing, having it confirmed was something else entirely.

Then what he'd said registered in her brain. "Caucasian?" she echoed. "But—" She stopped, because of course it made sense. While she had subconsciously been looking for Libyans, she had to remember that this Gordian knot of intrigue involved both Libyans and Mack Prewett's cohorts; given his resources, she had to be suspicious of everyone, not just Middle Easterners. Black, white or Oriental, she couldn't trust anyone—except Zane.

"Since they know what I'm driving, we're going to ditch the car." Zane took another turn, this time without the dramatics, but also without signaling or slowing down more than was necessary. "I'll make a phone call and have the car taken care of. We'll get a ride to the airport."

She didn't ask who he would call; the area was crawling with military personnel from all the branches of service. Someone in dress whites would collect the car and return it to the rental company, and that would be that. By then, she and Zane would be on their way to Las Vegas.

"They'll be able to find me anyway," she said suddenly, thinking of the airline ticket in her name.

"Eventually. It'll take a while, though. We have a substantial grace period."

"Maybe not." She bit her lip. "I overheard Dad talking to Mack Prewett this morning. Mack's CIA, deputy station chief in Athens. Dad told him that he wanted this finished, that he never meant for me to be involved."

Zane lifted his eyebrows. "I see."

She supposed he did. If her father was working with the CIA in anything legitimate, he would have been able to protect her through legal channels. Mack Prewett's involvement changed the rules. He would have access to records that ordinary people wouldn't have. Even though the CIA didn't operate within the United States, the tentacles of influence were far-reaching. If Mack wanted to know if she'd taken a flight out of either of the major area airports, he would have that information within minutes.

"If they were sharp enough to get the license plate number on the car, they'll have my name very shortly," he said.

"If they didn't get the number, then they won't have a clue about my identity. Either way, it's too late to worry about it now. They either have it or they don't, and there's no need to change our immediate plans. We'll take the flight to Las Vegas and lose them there, at least for a while."

"How will we lose them? If Mack can get access to your records…"

"I resigned my commission. I'm not a SEAL anymore."

"Oh," she said blankly. She struggled to adjust to yet another change. She had already been imagining and mentally preparing for life as the wife of a military officer, with the frequent moves, the politics of rank. It wouldn't have been much different from life in the embassy, just on a different level. Now she realized she had no idea what kind of life they would have.

"What will we do, then?" she asked.

"I've taken the job of sheriff in a county in southern Arizona. The sheriff died in office, so the governor appointed me to complete his term. There are two years left until new elections, so we'll be in Arizona for at least two years, maybe more."

A sheriff! That was a definite surprise, and the offhand manner with which he had announced it only deepened her sense of unreality. She struggled to focus on the important things. "What your job is doesn't matter," she said as evenly as possible. "It's your training that counts."

He shrugged and wheeled the car into the entrance of a parking garage. "I understand." His voice was flat, emotionless. "You agreed to marry me because you think I'll be able to protect you." He let down the window and leaned out to get the ticket from the automatic dispenser. The red barrier lifted, and he drove through.

Barrie wound her fingers together. Her initial flush of

happiness had given way to worry. Zane had come after her, yes, and asked her to marry him, but perhaps she'd been wrong about the attraction between them. She felt uprooted and off-balance. Zane didn't seem particularly happy to see her, but then, she had certainly tossed a huge problem into his lap. He would become a husband and a father in very short order, and on top of that, he had to protect them from an unknown enemy. He hadn't even kissed her, she thought, feeling close to tears, and she was a little surprised at herself for even thinking of such a thing right now. If he was right and someone had been following them, then the danger had been more immediate than she had feared. How could she worry about his reasons for marrying her? After all, the baby's safety was one of the reasons she was marrying *him*. "I want you to protect our baby," she said quietly. "There are other reasons, but that's the main one." Her feelings for him were something she could have handled on her own; she wouldn't take that chance with her baby's safety.

"A damn important one. You're right, too." He gave her a brief glance as he pulled the car into a parking slot on the third level. "I won't let anything hurt you or the baby."

He pulled off his sunglasses and got out of the car with a brief "Wait here," and strode off toward a pay phone. When he reached it, he punched in a series of numbers, then turned so he could watch her and the car while he talked.

Barrie felt her nerves jolt and her stomach muscles tighten as she stared across the parking deck at him. She was actually marrying this man. He looked taller than she remembered, a little leaner, though his shoulders were so wide they strained the seams of his white cotton shirt. His black hair was a bit longer, she thought, but his tan was just as dark. Except for the slight weight loss, he didn't show any sign of having been shot only a little over two months earlier. His physical toughness was intimidating; *he* was intimidating. How could she have forgotten? She had remembered only his consideration, his passion, the tender care he'd given her, but he'd used no weapon other than his bare hands to kill that guard. While she had remembered his lethal competency and planned to use it on her own behalf, she had somehow forgotten that it was a prominent part of him, not a quality she could call up when she needed it and tuck away into a corner when the need was over. She would have to deal with this part of him on a regular basis and accept the man he was. He wasn't, and never would be, a tame house cat.

She liked house cats, but she didn't want him to be one, she realized.

She felt another jolt, this time of self-discovery. She needed to be safe now, because of the baby, but she didn't want to be permanently cossetted and protected. The grueling episode in Benghazi had taught her that she was tougher and more competent than she'd ever thought, in ways she hadn't realized. Her father would have approved if she'd married some up-and-coming ambassador-to-be, but that wasn't what she wanted. She wanted some wildness in her life, and Zane Mackenzie was it. For all that maddening control of his, he was fierce and untamed. He didn't have a streak of wildness; he had a core of it.

The strain between them unnerved her. She had dreamed of him finding her and holding out his arms, of falling into them, and when she had opened the door to him today she had expected, like a fool, for her dream to be enacted. Reality was much more complicated than dreams.

The truth was, they had known each other for about twenty-four hours total, and most of those hours had been over two months earlier. In those hours they had made love with raw, scorching passion, and he had made her pregnant, but the amount of time remained the same.

Perhaps he had been involved with someone else, but a sense of responsibility had driven him to locate her and find out if their lovemaking had had any consequences. He would do that, she thought; he would turn his back on a girl-friend, perhaps even a fiancée, to assume the responsibility for his child.

Again she was crashing into the brick wall of ignorance; she didn't know anything about his personal life. If she had known anything about his family, where he was from, she would have been able to find him. Instead, he must think she hadn't cared enough even to ask about his condition, to find out if he had lived or died.

He was coming back to the car now, his stride as smooth and effortlessly powerful as she remembered, the silent walk of a predator. His dark face was as impassive as before, de-fying her efforts to read his expression.

He opened the door and slid behind the wheel. "Trans-port will be here in a few minutes."

She nodded, but her mind was still occupied with their personal tangle. Before she lost her nerve, she said evenly, "I tried to find you. They took me back to Athens imme-diately, while you were still in surgery. I tried to get in touch with you, find out if you were still alive, how you were doing, what hospital you were in—anything. Dad had Admiral Lindley block every inquiry I made. He did tell me you were going to be okay, but that's all I was able to find out."

"I guessed as much. I tried to call you at the embassy a couple of weeks after the mission. The call was routed to your father."

"He didn't tell me you'd called," she said, the familiar anger and pain twisting her insides. Since she'd been forced off the *Montgomery*, those had been her two main emotions. So he *had* tried to contact her. Her heart lifted a little. "After I came home, I tried again to find you, but the Navy wouldn't tell me anything."

"The antiterrorism unit is classified." His tone was absent; he was watching in the mirrors as another car drove slowly past them, looking for an empty slot.

She sat quietly, nerves quivering, until the car had disappeared up the ramp to the next level.

"I'm sorry," she said, after several minutes of silence. "I know this is a lot to dump in your lap."

He gave her an unreadable glance, his eyes very clear and blue. "I wouldn't be here if I didn't want to be."

"Do you have a girlfriend?"

This time the look he gave her was so long that she blushed and concentrated her attention on her hands, which were twisting together in her lap.

"If I did, I wouldn't have made love to you," he finally said.

Oh, dear. She bit her lip. This was going from bad to worse. He was getting more and more remote, as if the fleeting moment of silent communication between them when he'd asked her to marry him had never existed. Her stomach clenched, and suddenly a familiar sensation of being too hot washed over her.

She swallowed hard, praying that the nausea that had so far confined itself to the mornings wasn't about to put in an unexpected appearance. A second later she was scrambling out of the car and frantically looking around for a bathroom. God, did parking decks *have* bathrooms?

"Barrie!" Zane was out of the car, striding toward her, his dark face alert. She had the impression that he intended to head her off, though she hadn't yet chosen a direction in which to dash.

The stairwell? The elevator? She thought of the people who would use them and discarded both options. The most sensible place was right there on the concrete, and everything fastidious in her rebelled at the idea. Her stomach had different ideas, however, and she clamped a desperate hand over her mouth just as Zane reached her.

Those sharp, pale eyes softened with comprehension. "Here," he said, putting a supporting arm around her. The outside barriers of the parking deck were waist-high concrete walls, and that was where he swiftly guided her. She resisted momentarily, appalled at the possibility of throwing up on some unsuspecting passerby below, but his grip was inexorable, and her stomach wasn't waiting any longer. He held her as she leaned over the wall and helplessly gave in to the spasm of nausea.

She was shaking when it was over. The only comfort she could find was that, when she opened her eyes, she saw there was nothing three stories below but an alley. Zane held her, leaning her against his supporting body while he blotted her perspiring face with his handkerchief, then gave it to her so she could wipe her mouth. She felt scorched with humiliation. The strict teachings of her school in Switzerland hadn't covered what a lady should do after vomiting in public.

And then she realized he was crooning to her, his deep voice an almost inaudible murmur as he brushed his lips against her temple, her hair. One strong hand was splayed over her lower belly, spanning her from hipbone to hipbone, covering his child. Her knees felt like noodles, so she let herself continue leaning against him, let her head fall into the curve of his shoulder.

"Easy, sweetheart," he whispered, once again pressing his lips to her temple. "Can you make it back to the car, or do you want me to carry you?"

She couldn't gather her thoughts enough to give him a coherent answer. After no more than a second, he evidently thought he'd given her enough time to decide, so he made the decision for her by scooping her up into his arms. A few quick strides brought them to the car. He bent down and carefully placed her on the seat, lifting her legs into the car, arranging her skirt over them. "Do you want something to drink? A soft drink?"

Something cold and tart sounded wonderful. "No caffeine," she managed to say.

"You won't be out of my sight for more than twenty seconds, but keep an eye out for passing cars, and blow the horn if anything scares you."

She nodded, and he hit the door lock, then closed the door, shutting her inside a cocoon of silence. She preferred the fresh air but understood why she shouldn't be standing outside the car, exposed to view—and an easy target. She leaned her head against the headrest and closed her eyes. The nausea was gone as swiftly as it had come, though her insides felt like jelly. She was weak, and sleepy, and a bit bemused by his sudden tenderness.

Though she shouldn't be surprised, she thought. She was pregnant with his child, and the possibility of exactly that was what had brought him in search of her. As soon as he'd realized she was nauseated, a condition directly related to her condition, so to speak, he'd shown nothing but tender concern and demonstrated once again his ability to make snap decisions in urgent situations.

His tap on the window startled her, because in her sleepy state she hadn't thought he'd been gone nearly long enough to accomplish his mission. But a green can, frosty with condensation, was in his hand, and suddenly she ferociously wanted that drink. She unlocked the door and all but snatched the can from him before he could slide into the seat. She had it popped open and was drinking greedily by the time he closed the door.

When the can was empty, she leaned back with a sigh of contentment. She heard a low, strained laugh and turned her head to find Zane looking at her with both amusement and something hot and feral mingled in his gaze. "That's the first time watching a woman drink a soft drink has made me hard. Do you want another? I'll try to control myself, but a second one might be more than I can stand."

Barrie's eyes widened. A blush warmed her cheeks, but that didn't stop her from looking at his lap. He was telling the truth. Good heavens, was he ever telling the truth! Her hand clenched with the sudden need to reach out and stroke him. "I'm not thirsty now," she said, her voice huskier than usual. "But I'm willing to go for a second one if you are."

The amusement faded out of his eyes, leaving only the heat behind. He was reaching out for her when his head suddenly snapped around, his attention caught by an approaching vehicle. "Here's our ride," he said, and once again his voice was cool and emotionless.

Chapter 10

She was marrying him because she wanted his protection. The thought gnawed at Zane during the long flight to Las Vegas. She sat quietly beside him, sometimes dozing, talking only if he asked her a question. She had the drained look of someone who had been under a lot of pressure, and now that it had eased, her body was giving in to fatigue. Finally she fell soundly asleep, her head resting against his shoulder.

The pregnancy would be taking a toll on her, too. He couldn't see any physical change in her yet, but his three older brothers had produced enough children that he knew how tired women always got the first few months—at least, how tired Shea and Loren had been. Nothing ever slowed Caroline down, not even five sons.

At the thought of the baby, fierce possessiveness jolted through him again. His baby was inside her. He wanted to scoop her onto his lap and hold her, but a crowded plane wasn't the place for what he had in mind. That would have to wait until after the marriage ceremony, when they were in a private hotel room.

He wanted her even more than he had before.

When she had opened the door and he'd looked down

into her stunned green eyes, his arousal had been so strong and immediate that he'd had to restrain himself from reaching for her. Only the sight of her father bearing down on them had held him back.

He shouldn't have waited as long as he had. As soon as he'd been able to get around okay, he should have come after her. She had been living in fear, and handling it the same way she had in Benghazi, with calm determination.

He didn't want her ever to be afraid again.

Bunny's and Spooky's arrival at the parking deck, in Bunny's personally customized 1969 Oldsmobile 442, had been like a reunion. Barrie had tumbled out of the rental car with a happy cry and been enthusiastically hugged and twirled around by both SEALs. They were both discreetly armed, he'd noticed approvingly. They were wearing civilian clothes, with their shirts left loose outside their pants to conceal the firepower tucked under their arms and in the smalls of their backs. Normally, when they were off-duty, they didn't carry firearms, but Zane had explained the situation to them and left their preparations to their own discretion, since he wasn't their commanding officer any longer. In typical fashion, they had prepared for anything. His own weapon was still resting in a holster under his left armpit, covered by a lightweight summer jacket.

"Don't you worry none, ma'am," Spooky had reassuringly told Barrie. "We'll get you and the boss to the airport safe and sound. There's nothing outside of NASCAR that can keep up with Bunny's wheels."

"I'm sure there isn't," she'd replied, eyeing the car. It looked unremarkable enough; Bunny had painted it a light gray, and there wasn't any more chrome than would be on a factory job. But the deep-throated rumble from the idling engine didn't sound like any sound a factory engine would make, and the tires were wide, with a soft-looking tread.

"Bulletproof glass, reinforced metal," Bunny said proudly as he helped Zane transfer her luggage to the trunk of his car. "Plate steel would be too heavy for the speed I want, so I went with the new generation of body armor material, lighter and stronger than Kevlar. I'm still working on the fireproofing."

"I'll feel perfectly safe," she assured him.

As she and Zane crawled into the back seat of the two-door car, she whispered to him, "Where's Nascar?"

Spooky could hear a pin drop at forty paces. Slowly he turned around in the front seat, his face mirroring his incredulity. "Not where, ma'am," he said, struggling with shock. "*What*. NASCAR. Stock car racing." A good Southerner, he'd grown up with stock car racing and was always stunned when he encountered someone who hadn't enjoyed the same contact with the sport.

"Oh," Barrie said, giving him an apologetic smile. "I've spent a lot of time in Europe. I don't know anything about racing except for the Grand Prix races."

Bunny snorted in derision. "Play cars," he said dismissively. "You can't run them on the streets. Stock car racing, now that's real racing." As he was speaking, he was wheeling his deceptive monster out of the parking deck, his restless gaze touching on every surrounding detail.

"I've been to horse races," Barrie offered, evidently in an attempt to redeem herself.

Zane controlled a smile at the earnestness of her tone. "Do you ride?" he asked.

Her attention swung to him. "Why, yes. I love horses."

"You'll make a good Mackenzie, then," Spooky drawled. "Boss raises horses in his spare time." There was a bit of irony in his tone, because SEALs had about as much spare time as albinos had color.

"Do you really?" Barrie asked, her eyes shining.

"I own a few. Thirty or so."

"Thirty!" She sat back, a slight look of confusion on her face. He knew what she was thinking: one horse was expensive to own and keep, let alone thirty. Horses needed a lot of land and care, not something she associated with an ex-Naval officer who had been a member of an elite antiterrorism group.

"It's a family business," he explained, swiveling his head to examine the traffic around them.

"Everything's clear, boss," Bunny said. "Unless they've tagged us with a relay, but I don't see how that's possible."

Zane didn't, either, so he relaxed. A moving relay surveillance took a lot of time and coordination to set up, and the route had to be known. Bunny was taking such a circuitous route to the airport that any tail would long since have been revealed or shaken. Things were under control—for now.

They made it to National without incident, though to be on the safe side Bunny and Spooky had escorted them as far as the security check. While Zane quietly handled his own armed passage through security, his two former team members had taken themselves off to collect the rental car and turn it in, though to the agency office at Dulles, not National, where he had rented it. Just another little twist to delay anyone who was looking for them.

Now that they were safely on the plane, he began planning what he would do to put an end to the situation.

The first part of it was easy. He would put Chance on the job of finding out what kind of mess her father was involved in; for her sake, he hoped it wasn't anything treasonous, but whatever was going on, he intended to put a

stop to it. Chance had access to information that put national security agencies to shame. If William Lovejoy was
selling out his country, then he would go down. There was
no other option. Zane had spent his adult years offering his
life in protection of his country, and now he was a peace
officer sworn to uphold the law; it was impossible for him
to look the other way, even for Barrie. He didn't want her
to be hurt, but he damn sure wanted her to be safe.

Barrie slept until the airliner's wheels bounced on the
pavement. She sat upright, pushing her hair away from her
face, looking about with a slight sense of disorientation. She
had never before been able to sleep on a plane; this sleepiness was just one more of the many changes her pregnancy
was making in her body, and her lack of control over the
process was disconcerting, even frightening.

On the other hand, the rest had given her additional energy, something she needed to face the immense change she
was about to make in her life. This change was deliberate,
but no less frightening.

"I want to shower and change clothes first," she said
firmly. This marriage might be hasty, without any resemblance to the type of wedding ceremony she had always en-
visioned for herself, but while she was willing to forgo the
pomp and expensive trappings, she wasn't willing—outside of a life-and-death situation—to get married wearing
wrinkled clothes and still blinking sleep from her eyes.

"Okay. We'll check in to a hotel first." He rubbed his jaw,
his callused fingers rasping over his beard stubble. "I need
to have a shave anyway."

He had needed to shave that day in Benghazi, too. In a
flash of memory she felt again the scrape of his rough chin
against her naked breasts, and a wave of heat washed over

her, leaving her weak and flushed. The cool air blowing from the tiny vent overhead was suddenly not cool enough.

She hoped he wouldn't notice, but it was a faint hope, because he was trained to take note of every detail around him. She imagined he could describe every passenger within ten rows of them in either direction, and when she'd been awake she had noticed that he'd shown an uncanny awareness of anyone approaching them from the rear on the way to the lavatories.

"Are you feeling sick?" he asked, eyeing the color in her cheeks.

"No, I'm just a little warm," she said with perfect truth, while her blush deepened.

He continued to watch her, and the concern in his eyes changed to a heated awareness. She couldn't even hide that from him, damn it. From the beginning it had been as if he could see beneath her skin; he sensed her reactions almost as soon as she felt them.

Slowly his heavy-lidded gaze moved down to her breasts, studying the slope and thrust of them. She inhaled sharply as her nipples tightened in response to his blatant interest, a response that shot all the way to her loins.

"Are they more sensitive?" he murmured.

Oh, God, he shouldn't do this to her, she thought wildly. They were in the middle of a plane full of people, taxiing toward an empty gate, and he was asking questions about her breasts and looking as if he would start undressing her any minute now.

"Are they?"

"Yes," she whispered. Her entire body felt more sensitive, from both her pregnancy and her acute awareness of him. Soon he would be her husband, and once again she would be lying in his arms.

"Ceremony first," he said, his thoughts echoing hers in that eerie way he had. "Otherwise we won't get out of the hotel until tomorrow."

"Are you psychic?" she accused under her breath.

A slow smile curved his beautiful mouth. "It doesn't take a psychic to know what those puckered nipples mean."

She glanced down and saw her nipples plainly beaded under the lace and silk of her bra and blouse. Her face red, she hastily drew her shirt over the betraying little nubs, and he gave a low laugh. At least no one else was likely to have heard him, she thought with scant comfort. He'd pitched his voice low, and the noise on board made it difficult to overhear conversations, anyway.

The flight attendants were telling them to remain in their seats until the plane was secured and the doors opened, and as usual the instructions were ignored as passengers surged into the aisles, opening the overhead bins and dragging down their carry-on luggage or hauling it out from under the seats. Zane stepped deftly into the aisle, and the movement briefly pulled his jacket open. She saw the holster under his left arm and the polished metal butt of the pistol tucked snugly inside it. Then he automatically shrugged one shoulder, and the jacket fell into place, a movement he'd performed so many times he didn't have to think about it.

She'd known he was armed, of course, because he'd informed the airport and airline security before they'd boarded the plane. During the boredom and enforced inactivity of the flight, however, she had managed to push the recent events from her mind, but the sight of that big automatic brought them all back.

He extended his hand to steady her as she stepped into the aisle ahead of him. Standing pressed like sardines in the line, she felt him like a warm and solid wall at her back, his arms slightly extended so that his hands rested on the seat backs, enveloping her in security. His breath stirred the hair on top of her head, making her realize anew exactly how big he was. She was of average height, but if she leaned back, her head would fit perfectly into the curve of his shoulder.

The man in front of her shifted, forcing her backward, and Zane curved one arm around her as he gathered her against his body, his big hand settling protectively over her lower belly. Barrie bit her lip as her mind bounced from worry to the pleasure of his touch. This couldn't go on much longer—either this exquisite frustration or the sharp darts of terror—or she would lose her mind.

The line of passengers began to shuffle forward as the doors were opened and they were released from the plane. Zane's hand dropped from her belly. As she began to move forward, Barrie caught the eye of an older woman who had chosen to remain in her seat until the stampede was over, and the woman gave her a knowing smile, her gaze flicking to Zane.

"Ma'am," Zane said smoothly in acknowledgment, and Barrie knew he'd caught the little byplay. His acute awareness of his surroundings was beginning to spook her. What if she didn't want him to notice everything? Most women would be thrilled to death with a husband who actually took note of details, but probably not to the extent that Zane Mackenzie did.

On the other hand, if the alternative was living without him, she would learn how to cope, she thought wryly. She'd spent over two months pining for him, and now that she had him, she wasn't about to get cold feet because he was alert. He was a trained warrior—an assassin, her father had called him. He wouldn't have survived if he hadn't been aware of everything going on around him, and neither would she.

That alertness was evident as they followed the signs to the baggage claim area. The airport was a shifting, flowing beehive, and Zane's cool gaze was constantly assessing the people around them. As he had more than once before, he kept himself between her and everybody else, steering her close to the wall and protecting her other side with his body. He'd already taken one bullet while doing that, she thought, and had to fight the sudden terrified impulse to grab him and shove *him* against the wall.

Before they reached the baggage claim, however, he pulled her to a halt. "Let's wait here a minute," he said.

She strove for calm, for mastery over the butterflies that suddenly took flight in her stomach. "Did you see anything suspicious?" she asked.

"No, we're waiting for someone." He looked at her, his cool gaze warming as he studied her face. "You're a gutsy little broad, Miss Lovejoy. No matter what, you hold it together and try to do the best you can. Not bad for a pampered society babe."

Barrie was taken aback. She'd never been called a broad before, or a society babe. If it hadn't been for the teasing glint in his eyes, she might have taken exception to the terms. Instead, she considered them for a moment, then gave a brief nod of agreement. "You're right," she said serenely. "I *am* gutsy for a pampered society babe."

He was surprised into a chuckle, a deliciously rich sound that was cut short when they were approached by a middle-aged man who wore a suit and carried a radio set in his hand. "Sheriff Mackenzie?" he asked.

"Yes."

"Travis Hulsey, airport security." Mr. Hulsey flashed his identification. "We have your luggage waiting for you in a secure area, as requested. This way, please."

So he'd even thought of that, Barrie marveled as they followed Mr. Hulsey through an unmarked door. An attempt to grab her inside the airport would be tricky, given the security, so the most logical thing to do would be to wait at the ground transportation area, where everyone went after collecting luggage, then follow them to their destination and wait for a better opportunity. Zane had thwarted that; he must have made the arrangements when he'd gone forward to the lavatory.

The dry desert heat slapped them in the face as soon as they stepped through the door. Her three suitcases and his one garment bag, which he had collected from a locker at National, were waiting for them at a discreet entrance well away from the main ground transportation area. Also waiting for them was a car, beside which stood a young man with the distinctive austere military haircut, even though he wore civilian clothes.

The young man all but snapped to attention. "Sir," he said. "Airman Zaharias at your service, sir."

Zane's dark face lit with amusement. "At ease," he said. "I'm not my brother."

Airman Zaharias relaxed with a grin. "When I first saw you, sir, I wasn't sure."

"If he pulled rank and this is messing up your leave time, I'll get other transport."

"I volunteered, sir. The general did me a personal favor when I was fresh out of basic. Giving his brother a ride downtown is the least I can do."

Brother? *General?* Barrie raised some mental eyebrows. First horses, now this. She realized she didn't know anything about her soon-to-be husband's background, but the details she'd gleaned so far were startling, to say the least.

Zane introduced her with grave courtesy. "Barrie, Airman Zaharias is our safe transport, and he has donated his personal vehicle and time off for the service. Airman Zaharias, my fiancée, Barrie Lovejoy."

She solemnly shook hands with the young airman, who was almost beside himself in his eagerness to please.

"Glad to meet you, ma'am." He unlocked the trunk and swiftly began loading their luggage, protesting when Zane lifted two of the bags and stowed them himself. "Let me do that, sir!"

"I'm a civilian now," Zane said, amusement still bright in his eyes. "And I was Navy, anyway."

Airman Zaharias shrugged. "Yes, sir, but you're still the general's brother." He paused, then asked, "Were you really a SEAL?"

"Guilty."

"Damn," Airman Zaharias breathed.

They climbed into the air-conditioned relief of the airman's Chevrolet and were off. Their young driver evidently knew Las Vegas well, and without asking for instructions he ignored the main routes. Instead he circled around and took Paradise Road north out of the airport. He chattered cheerfully the entire time, but Barrie noticed that he didn't mention the exact nature of the favor Zane's general brother had done for him, nor did he venture into personal realms. He talked about the weather, the traffic, the tourists, the hotels. Zane directed him to a hotel off the main drag, and soon Airman Zaharias was on his way and they were checking in to the hotel.

Barrie bided her time, standing quietly to one side while Zane arranged for them to be listed in the hotel's computer as Glen and Alice Temple—how he arrived at those names she had no idea—and ignoring the clerk's knowing smirk. He probably thought they were adulterous lovers on a tryst, which suited her just fine; it would keep him from being curious about them.

They weren't alone in the elevator, so she held her tongue then, too. She held it until they were in the suite Zane had booked, and the bellman had been properly tipped and dismissed. The suite was as luxurious as any she had stayed in in Europe. A few hours before, she might have worried that the cost was more than Zane could afford, that he'd chosen it because he thought she would expect it. Now, however, she had no such illusion. As soon as he had closed and locked the door behind the bellman, she crossed her arms and stared levelly at him. "Horses?" she inquired politely. "Family business? A brother who happens to be an Air Force general?"

He shrugged out of his jacket, then his shoulder holster. "All of that," he said.

"I don't know you at all, do I?" She was calm, even a little bemused, as she watched him wrap the straps around the holster and deposit the weapon on the bedside table.

He unzipped his garment bag and removed a suit from it, then began unpacking other items. His pale glance flashed briefly at her. "You know *me*," he said. "You just don't know all the details of my family yet, but we haven't had much time for casual chatting. I'm not deliberately hiding anything from you. Ask any question you want."

"I don't want to conduct a catechism," she said, though she needed to do exactly that. "It's just…" She spread her hands in frustration, because she was marrying him and she didn't already know all this.

He began unbuttoning his shirt. "I promise I'll give you

a complete briefing when we have time. Right now, sweetheart, I'd rather you got your sweet little butt in one shower while I get in the other, so we can get married and into this bed as fast as possible. About an hour after *that*, we'll talk."

She looked at the bed, a bigger-than-king-size. Priorities, priorities, she mused. "Are we safe here?"

"Safe enough for me to concentrate on other things."

She didn't have to ask what those other things were. She looked at the bed again and took a deep breath. "We could rearrange the order of these things," she proposed. "What do you think about bed, talk and then wedding? Say, tomorrow morning?"

He froze in the act of removing his shirt. She saw his eyes darken, saw the sexual tension harden his face. After a moment he pulled the garment free and dropped it to the floor, his movements deliberate. "I haven't kissed you yet," he said.

She swallowed. "I noticed. I've wondered—"

"Don't," he said harshly. "Don't wonder. The reason I haven't kissed you is that, once I start, I won't stop. I know we're doing things out of order—hell, everything's been out of order from the beginning, when you were naked the first time I saw you. I wanted you then, sweetheart, and I want you now, so damn bad I'm aching with it. But trouble is still following you around, and my job is to make damn sure it doesn't get close to you and our baby. I might get killed—"

She made a choked sound of protest, but he cut her off. "It's a possibility, one I accept. I've accepted it for years. I want us married as soon as possible, because I don't know what might happen tomorrow. In case I miscalculate or get unlucky, I want our baby to be legitimate, to be born with the Mackenzie name. A certain amount of protection goes with that name, and I want you to have it. Now."

Tears swam in her eyes as she stared at him, at this man who had already taken one bullet for her and was prepared to take another. He was right—she knew *him*, knew the man he was, even if she didn't know what his favorite color was or what kind of grades he'd made in school. She knew the basics, and it was the basics she had so swiftly and fiercely learned to love. So he wasn't as forthcoming as she might have wished; she would deal with it. So what if he was so controlled it was scary, and so what if those uncanny eyes noticed everything, which would make it difficult to surprise him on Christmas and his birthday? She would deal with that, too, very happily.

If he was willing to die for her, the least she could do was be completely honest with him.

"There's another reason I agreed to marry you," she said.

His dark brows lifted in silent question.

"I love you."

Chapter 11

He wore a dark gray suit with black boots and a black hat. Barrie wore white. It was a simple dress, ankle length and sleeveless, classic in its lines and lack of adornment. She loosely twisted up her dark auburn hair, leaving a few wisps hanging about her face to soften the effect. Her only jewelry was a pair of pearl studs in her ears. She got ready in the bath off the bedroom, he showered in the bath off the parlor. They met at the door between the two rooms, ready to take the step that would make them husband and wife.

At her blunt declaration of love, an equally blunt expression of satisfaction had crossed his face, and for once he didn't hide anything he was feeling. "I don't know about love," he'd said, his voice so even she wanted to shake him. "But I do know I've never wanted another woman the way I want you. I know this marriage is forever. I'll take care of you and our children, I'll come home to you every night, and I'll try my damnedest to make you happy."

It wasn't a declaration of love, but it was certainly one of devotion, and the tears that came so easily to her these days swam in her eyes. Her self-contained warrior *would* love her, when he lowered his guard enough to let himself. He had spent years with his emotions locked down, while he operated in tense, life-and-death situations that demanded cool, precise thoughts and decisions. Love was neither cool nor concise; it was turbulent, unpredictable, and it left one vulnerable. He would approach love as cautiously as if it was a bomb.

"Don't cry," he said softly. "I swear I'll be a good husband."

"I know," she replied, and then they had both gone to their separate bathrooms to prepare for their wedding.

They took a taxi to a chapel, one of the smaller ones that didn't get as much business and didn't have a drive-through service. Getting married in Las Vegas didn't take a great deal of effort, though Zane took steps to make it special. He bought her a small bouquet of flowers and gave her a bracelet of dainty gold links, which he fastened around her right wrist. Her heart beat heavily as they stood before the justice of the peace, and the bracelet seemed to burn around her wrist. Zane held her left hand securely in his right, his grip warm and gentle, but unbreakable.

Outwardly it was all very civilized, but from the first moment they'd met, Barrie had been acutely attuned to him, and she sensed the primal possessiveness of his actions. He had already claimed her physically, and now he was doing it legally. She already carried his child inside her. His air of masculine satisfaction was almost visible, it was so strong. She felt it, too, as she calmly spoke her vows, this linkage of their lives. During a long, hot day in Benghazi they had forged a bond that still held, despite the events that had forced them apart.

He had one more surprise for her. She hadn't expected a ring, not on such short notice, but at the proper moment he reached into the inside pocket of his jacket and produced two plain gold bands, one for her and one for him. Hers was a little loose when he slipped it over her knuckle, but their eyes met in a moment of perfect understanding. She would be gaining weight, and soon the ring would fit. She took the bigger, wider band and slid it onto the ring finger of his left hand, and she felt her own thrill of primal satisfaction. He was hers, by God!

Their marriage duly registered, the certificate signed and witnessed, they took another taxi to the hotel. "Supper," he said, steering her toward one of the hotel's dining rooms. "You didn't eat anything on the plane, and it's after midnight eastern time."

"We could order room service," she suggested.

His eyes took on that heavy-lidded look. "No, we couldn't." His tone was definite, a little strained. His hand was warm and heavy on the small of her back. "You need to eat, and I don't trust my self-control to last that long unless we're in a public place."

Perhaps feeding her was his only concern, or perhaps he knew more about seduction than most men, she thought as they watched each other over a progression of courses. Knowing that he was going to make love to her as soon as they reached the suite, anticipating the heaviness of his weight on her, the hard thrust of his turgid length into her…the frustration readied her for him as surely as if he was stroking her flesh. Her breasts lifted hard and swollen against the bodice of her dress. Her insides tightened with desire, so that she had to press her legs together to ease the throbbing. His gaze kept dropping to her breasts, and as before, she couldn't temper her response. She could feel her own moisture, feel the heaviness in her womb.

She was scarcely aware of what she ate—something bland, to reduce the chances of early-pregnancy nausea. She drank only water. But turnabout was fair play, so she lingered over each bite while she stared at his mouth, or in the direction of his lap. She delicately licked her lips, shivering with delight as his face darkened and his jaw set. She stroked the rim of her water glass with one fingertip, drawing his gaze, making his breath come harder and faster. Beneath the table, she rubbed her foot against the muscled calf of his leg.

He turned to snare their waiter with a laser glare. "Check!" he barked, and the waiter hurried to obey that voice of command. Zane scribbled their room number and his fictitious name on the check, and Barrie stared at him in amazement. It was hard to believe he could remember something like that when she could barely manage to walk.

For revenge, when he pulled her chair back so she could stand, she allowed the knuckles of one hand to brush, oh, so very lightly, against his crotch. He went absolutely rigid for a moment, and his breath hissed out between his teeth. All innocence, Barrie turned to give him a sweetly inquiring What's-wrong? look.

His darkly tanned face was even darker with the flush running under the browned skin. His expression was set, giving away little, but his eyes were glittering like shards of diamond. His big hand closed firmly around her elbow. "Let's go," he said in the soundless whisper she'd first heard in a dark room in Benghazi. "And don't do that again, or I swear I'll have you in the elevator."

"Really." She smiled at him over her shoulder. "How… uplifting."

A faint but visible shudder racked him, and the look he gave her promised retribution. "Here I've been thinking you were so sweet."

"I am sweet," she declared as they marched toward the elevator. "But I'm not a pushover."

"We'll see about that. I'm going to push you over." They

reached the bank of elevators, and he jabbed the call button with more force than necessary.

"You won't have to push hard. As a matter of fact, you can just blow me over." She gave him another sweet smile and pursed her lips, blowing a tiny puff of air against his chest to demonstrate.

The bell chimed, the doors opened, and they stood back to allow the car's passengers to exit. They stepped inside alone, and even though people were hurrying toward them to catch that car, Zane ruthlessly punched their floor number and then the door close button. When the car began to rise, he turned on her like a tiger on fresh meat.

She stepped gracefully out of his reach, staring at the numbers flashing on the digital display. "We're almost there."

"You're damn right about that," he growled, coming after her. In the small confines of the elevator she didn't have a chance of evading him, not that she wanted to. What she wanted was to drive him as crazy as he was driving her. His hard hands closed around her waist and lifted her; his muscled body pinned her to the wall. His hips pushed insistently at hers, and she gasped at how hard he was. Automatically her legs opened, allowing him access to the tender recesses of her body. He thrust against her, his hips moving rhythmically, and his mouth came down on hers, smothering, fiercely hungry.

The bell chimed softly, and the elevator gave a slight lurch as it stopped. Zane didn't release her. He simply turned with her still in his grasp and left the elevator, striding rapidly down the hall to their suite. Barrie twined her arms around his neck and her legs around his hips, biting back little moans as each stride he took rubbed his swollen sex against the aching softness of her loins. Pleasure arced through her like lightning with every step, and helplessly she felt her hips undulate against him in a mindless search for a deeper pleasure. A low curse hissed out from between his clenched teeth.

She didn't know if they passed anyone in the hall. She buried her face against his neck and gave in to the soaring hunger. She had needed him for so long, missed him, worried herself sick about him. Now he was here, vitally alive, about to take her with the same uncomplicated fierceness as before, and she didn't care about anything else.

He pushed her against a wall, and for one terrified, delirious moment she thought she had tempted him too much. Instead he unhooked her legs from around his waist and let her slide to the floor. He was breathing hard, his eyes dilated with a sexual hunger that wouldn't be denied much longer, but on one level he was still very much in control. Lifting one finger to his lips to indicate silence, he slipped his right hand inside his jacket. When his hand emerged, it was filled with the butt of that big automatic. He thumbed off the safety, dealt with the electronic lock on the door to their suite, depressed the door handle and slipped noiselessly inside. The door closed as silently as it had opened.

Barrie stood frozen in the hallway, sudden terror chasing away her desire as she waited with her eyes closed and her hands clenched into fists, all her concentration focused on trying to hear anything from inside the suite. She heard nothing. Absolutely nothing. Zane moved like a cat, but so did other men, men like him, men who worked best under cover of night and who could kill as silently as he had dispatched that guard in Benghazi. Her kidnappers hadn't possessed the same expertise, but whoever was behind her abduction wouldn't use Middle Eastern men here in the middle of the glitter and flash of Las Vegas. Perhaps this time he would hire someone more deadly, someone more interested in getting the job done than in terrifying a bound and helpless woman. Any thump, any whisper, might signal the end of Zane's life, and she thought she would shatter under the strain.

She didn't hear the door open again. All she heard was Zane saying, "All clear," in a calm, normal tone, and then she was in his arms again. She didn't think she moved; she thought he simply gathered her in, pulling her into the security of his embrace.

"I'm sorry," he murmured against her hair as he carried her inside. He paused to lock and chain the door. "But I won't take chances with your safety."

Fury roared through her like a brushfire. She lifted her head from the sanctuary of his shoulder and glared at him. "What about yours?" she demanded violently. "Do you have any idea what it does to me when you do things like that? Do you think I don't notice when you put yourself between me and other people, so if anyone shoots at me, you'll be the one with the bullet hole?" She hit him on the chest with a clenched fist, amazing even herself; she had never struck anyone before. She hit him again. "Damn it, I want you healthy and whole! I want our baby to have its daddy! I want to have more of your babies, so that means you have to stay alive, do you hear me?"

"I hear," he rumbled, his tone soothing as he caught her pounding fists and pressed them against his chest, stilling them. "I'd like the same things myself. That means I have to do whatever's necessary to keep you and Junior safe."

She relaxed against him, her lips trembling as she fought back tears. She wasn't a weepy person; it was just the hormonal roller coaster of pregnancy that was making her so, but still, she didn't want to cry all over him. He had enough to handle without having to deal with a sobbing wife every time he turned around.

When she could manage a steady tone, she said in a small voice, "Junior, is it?"

She saw the flash of his grin as he lifted her in his arms. "I'm afraid so," he said as he carried her to the bed. "My sister Maris is the only female the Mackenzies have managed to produce, and that was twenty-nine years and ten boys ago."

He bent and gently placed her on the bed and sat down beside her. His dark face was intent as he reached beneath her for the zipper of her dress. "Now let's see if I can get you back to where you were before you got scared, and we'll introduce Junior to his daddy," he whispered.

Barrie was seized by a mixture of shyness and uneasiness as he stripped the dress down her hips and legs, then tossed it aside. Since her kidnappers had stripped her in a deliberate attempt to terrorize her, to break her spirit, she hadn't been comfortable with being naked. Except for those hours hidden in the ruins in Benghazi, when Zane had finally coaxed her out of his shirt and she had lost herself in his lovemaking, she had hurried through any times of necessary nudity, such as when she showered, pulling on clothes or a robe as soon as possible. Once upon a time she had lingered after her bath, enjoying the wash of air over her damp skin as she pampered herself with perfumed oils and lotions, but for the past two months that luxury had fallen beneath her urgent need to be covered.

Zane wanted her naked.

Her dress was already gone, and the silk and lace of her matching bra and underpants weren't much protection. Deftly he thumbed open the front fastening of her bra, and the cups loosened, sliding apart to reveal the inner curves of her breasts. Barrie couldn't help herself; she protectively crossed her arms over her breasts, holding the bra in place.

Zane paused, his face still as his pale gaze lifted to her face, examining the helpless, embarrassed expression she wore. She didn't have to explain. He'd been there; he knew. "Still having problems with that shirt?" he asked gently, referring to the way she'd clung so desperately to his garment.

He'd switched on a single lamp. She lay exposed in the small circle of light, while his face was shadowed. She moistened her lips and nodded once, a slight acknowledgment that was all he needed.

"We can't undo things," he said, his face and tone serious. Using one finger, he lightly stroked the upper curves of her breasts, where they plumped above the protection of her crossed arms. "We can put them behind us and move on, but we can't undo them. They stay part of us, they change us inside, but as other things happen, we change still more. I remember the face of the first man I killed. I don't regret doing it, because he was a bomb-happy piece of scum who had left his calling card on a cruise ship, killing nine old people who were just trying to enjoy their retirement. Right then he was trying like hell to kill *me*...but I always carry his face with me, deep inside."

He paused, thinking, remembering. "He's a part of me now, because killing him changed me. He made me stronger. I know that I can do whatever has to be done, and I know how to go on. I've killed others," he said, as calmly as if he was discussing the weather, "but I don't remember their faces. Only his. And I'm glad I won."

Barrie stared at him, the shadows emphasizing the planes and hollows of his somber face, deepening the oldness in his eyes. Deep inside she understood, the realization going past thought into the center of instinct. Being kidnapped had changed her; she'd faced that before Zane had rescued her. She *was* stronger, more decisive, more willing to take action. When he'd shown up that afternoon, she had been preparing to take extraordinary measures to protect herself and the child she carried by disappearing from the comfortable life she'd always known. She'd been naked with Zane before—and enjoyed it. She would again.

Slowly she lifted one hand and stroked the precise line of the small scar on his left cheekbone. He turned his head a little, rubbing his cheek against her fingers.

"Take off *your* clothes," she suggested softly. Balance. If her nudity was balanced by his, she would be more comfortable.

His eyebrows quirked upward. "All right."

She didn't have to explain, but then, she'd known she wouldn't. She lay on the bed and watched him peel out of his jacket, then remove the shoulder holster, which once more carried its lethal cargo. This last was carefully placed on the bedside table, where it would be within reach. Then his shirt came off, and he dropped it on the floor, along with her dress and his jacket.

The new scar on his upper abdomen was red and puckered, and bisected by a long surgical scar where the ship's surgeon had sliced into him to stop the bleeding and save his life. She had seen the scar before, when he had removed his shirt before showering, but she had been under orders not to touch him then lest she make him forget his priorities. There was no such restriction now.

Her fingers moved over the scar, feeling the heat and vitality of the man, and she thought how easily all of that could have been snuffed out. She had come so close to losing him….

"Don't think about it," he murmured, catching her hand and lifting it to his lips. "It didn't happen."

"It could have."

"It didn't." His tone was final as he bent over to tug off his boots. They dropped to the floor with twin thuds, then he stood to unfasten his pants.

He was right. It hadn't happened. Pick yourself up, learn something, and go on. It was in the past. The future was their marriage, their child. The present was *now*, and as Zane swiftly stripped off his remaining clothes, a lot more urgent.

He sat beside her again, comfortable in his own skin. It was such wonderful skin, she thought a little dreamily, reaching out to stroke his gleaming shoulders and furry chest and rub the tiny nipples hidden among the hair until they stood stiffly erect. She knew she was inviting him to reciprocate, and her breath caught in her chest as she waited for him to accept.

He wasn't slow about it. His hands went to the parted cups of her bra, and his gaze lifted to hers. "Ready?" he asked with a slight smile.

She didn't reply, just shrugged one shoulder so that her breast slid free of the cup, and that was answer enough.

He glanced downward as he pushed the other cup aside, and she saw his pupils flare with arousal as he looked at her. His breath hissed out through parted lips. "I see our baby here," he whispered, gently touching one nipple with a single fingertip. "You haven't gained any weight, your stomach's still flat, but he's changed you here. Your nipples are darker, and swollen." Ever so lightly, his touch circled the aureola, making it pucker and stand upright. Barrie whimpered with the rush of desire, the familiar lightning strike from breast to loin.

He rubbed his thumb over the tip, then gently curved his hand beneath her breast, lifting it so that it plumped in his palm. "How much more sensitive are they?" he asked, never looking up from his absorption with these new details in her body.

"Some—sometimes I can't bear the touch of my bra." she breathed.

"Your veins are bluer, too," he murmured. "They look like rivers running under a layer of white satin." He leaned down and kissed her, taking possession of her mouth while he continued to fondle her breasts with exquisite care. She melted with a purring little hum of pleasure, lifting herself so she could taste him more deeply. His lips were as hot and forceful as she remembered, as delicious. He took his time; the kiss was slow and deep, his tongue probing. Her pregnancy-sensitive breasts hardened into almost painful arousal, her loins becoming warm and liquid.

He bore her down onto the pillows, his hands slipping over her body, completely removing the bra and then disposing of her underpants. His eyes glittered hotly as he leaned over her. "I'm going to do everything to you I couldn't do before," he whispered. "We don't have to worry about being on guard, or making noise, or what time it is. I'm going to eat you up, Little Red."

She should have been alarmed, because his expression was so fierce and hungry she could almost take him literally. Instead, she reached out for him, almost frantic with the need to feel him covering her, taking her.

He had other ideas. He caught her hands and pressed them to the bed, as she had once done to him. He had trusted her with control, and now she returned the gift, arching her body up for whatever was his pleasure.

His pleasure was her breasts, with their fascinating changes. He took one distended nipple into his mouth, carefully, lightly. That was enough to make her moan, though not with pain; the prickles of sensation were incredibly intense. His tongue batted at her nipple, swirled around it, then pushed it hard against the roof of his mouth as he began suckling.

Her cry was thin, wild. Her breath exploded out of her lungs, and she couldn't seem to draw in any replacement air. Oh, God, she hadn't realized her breasts were *that* sensitive, or that he would so abruptly push her past both pleasure and pain into a realm so raw and powerful she couldn't bear it. She surged upward, and he controlled the motion, holding her down, transferring his mouth to her other nipple, which received the same tender care and enticement, then the sudden, deliberate pressure that made her cry out again.

He wouldn't stop. She screamed for him to, begged him, but he wouldn't stop. She heard her voice, frantic, pleading: "Zane—please. Oh, God, please. Don't—more. *More.*" And then, sobbing, *"Harder!"* And she realized she wasn't begging him to stop, but to continue. She writhed in his arms as he pushed her higher and higher, harder and harder, his mouth voracious on her breasts, and suddenly all her senses coalesced into a huge single throb that centered in her loins, and she came apart with pleasure.

When she could breathe again, think again, her limbs were weak and useless in the aftermath. She lay limply on the bed, her eyes closed, and wondered how she had survived the implosion.

"Just from sucking your breasts?" he murmured incredulously as he kissed his way down her stomach. "Oh, damn, are we going to have fun for the next seven months!"

"Zane...wait," she whispered, lifting one hand to his head. It was the only movement she had enough energy to make. "I can't—I need to rest."

He slid down between her legs and lifted her thighs onto his shoulders. "You don't have to move," he promised her in a deep, rich voice. "All you have to do is lie there." Then he kissed her, slowly, deeply, and her body arched as it began all over again, and he showed her all the things he hadn't been able to do to her before.

He brought her to completion once more before finally crawling forward and settling his hips between her thighs. She moaned when he filled her with a smooth, powerful thrust. She quivered beneath him, shocked by the thickness and depth of his penetration. How could she have forgotten? The discomfort took her by surprise, and she clung to him as she tried to adjust, to accept. He soothed her, whispering hot, soft words in her ear, stroking her flesh, which was already so sensitive that even the smooth sheet beneath her felt abrasive.

But, oh, how she had wanted this. *This*. Not just pleasure, but the sense of being joined together, the deep and intimate linkage of their bodies. This fed a craving within her that the climaxes he'd given her hadn't begun to touch. Her hips lifted. She wanted all of him, wanted him so deep that he touched her womb, ripening with his seed. He tried to moderate the thrusts that were rapidly pushing her toward yet another climax, but she dug her nails into his back, insisting without words on everything he had to give.

He shuddered, and with a deep-throated groan, gave her what she asked.

She slept then. It was long after midnight on the east coast, and she was exhausted. She was disturbed by the presence of the big, muscled man beside her in the bed, though, his body radiating heat like a furnace, and she kept waking from a restless doze.

He must sleep like a cat, she thought, because every time

she woke and changed positions, he woke up, too. Finally he pulled her on top of him, settling her with her face tucked against his neck and her legs straddling his hips. "Maybe now you can rest," he murmured, kissing her hair. "You slept this way in Benghazi."

She remembered that, remembered the long day of making love, how he had sometimes been on top when they dozed, and sometimes she had. Or perhaps she had been the only one who dozed while he had remained alert.

"I've never slept with a man before," she murmured in sleepy explanation, nestling against him. "*Slept* slept, that is."

"I know. I'm your first in both cases."

The room was dark; at some time he had turned off the lamp, though she didn't remember when. The heavy curtains were drawn against the neon of the Las Vegas night, with only thin strips of light penetrating around the edges. It reminded her briefly of that horrible room in Benghazi, before Zane had taken her away, but then she shut out the memory. That no longer had the power to frighten her. Zane was her husband now, and the pleasant ache in her body told her that the marriage had been well and truly consummated.

"Tell me about your family," she said, and yawned against his neck.

"Now?"

"Mmm. We're both awake, so you might as well."

There was a twitch of flesh against her inner thigh. "I can think of other things to do," he muttered.

"I'm not ruling anything out." She wriggled her hips and was rewarded by a more insistent movement. "But you can talk, too. Tell me about the Mackenzie clan."

She could feel his slight shrug. "My dad is a half-breed American Indian, my mom is a schoolteacher. They live on a mountain just outside Ruth, Wyoming. Dad raises and trains horses. He's the best I've ever seen, except for my sister. Maris is magic with horses."

"So the horses really are a family business."

"Yep. We were all raised on horseback, but Maris is the only one who went into the training aspect. Joe went to the Air Force Academy and became a jet jockey, Mike became a cattle rancher, Josh rode jets for the Navy, and Chance and I went to the Naval Academy and got our water wings. We can both fly various types of aircraft, but flying is just a means of getting us to where we're needed, nothing else. Chance got out of Naval Intelligence a couple of years ago."

Barrie's talent with names kicked in. She lifted her head, all sleepiness gone as she ran that list of names through her head. She settled on one, put the details together and gasped. "Your brother is General Joe Mackenzie on the Joint Chiefs of Staff?" Of course. How many Joe Mackenzies were Air Force generals?

"The one and only."

"Why, I've met him and his wife. I think it was the year before last, at a charity function in Washington. Her name is Caroline."

"You're right on target." He shifted a little, and she felt a nudging between her legs. She inhaled as he slipped inside her. Talk about right on target.

"Joe and Caroline have five sons, Michael and Shea have two boys, and Josh and Loren have three," Zane murmured, gently thrusting. "Junior will be the eleventh grandchild."

Barrie sank against him, her attention splintered by the pleasure building with each movement of his hips. "Don't talk," she said, and heard his quiet laughter as he rolled over and placed her beneath him…just where she wanted to be.

Chapter 12

Barrie awoke to nausea, sharp and urgent. She bolted out of bed and into the bathroom, barely reaching it in time. When the bout of vomiting was over, she sank weakly to the floor and closed her eyes, unable to work up enough energy to care that she was curled naked on the floor of a hotel bathroom, or that her husband of less than twelve hours was witness to it all. She heard Zane running water; then a wonderfully cool, wet washcloth was placed on her heated forehead. He flushed the toilet, something she hadn't been able to manage, and said, "I'll be right back."

As usual, she rapidly began to feel better after she had thrown up. Embarrassed, she got up and washed out her mouth and was standing in front of the mirror surveying her tousled appearance with some astonishment when Zane appeared with a familiar green can in his hand.

He had already popped the top. She snatched the can from him and began greedily drinking, tilting the can up like some college freshman guzzling beer. When it was empty, she sighed with repletion and slammed the can down on the countertop as if it was indeed an empty soldier of spirits. Then she looked at Zane, and her eyes widened.

"I hope you didn't go out to the drink machine like that,"

she said faintly. He was still naked. Wonderfully, impressively naked. And very aroused.

He looked amused. "I got it out of the minibar in the parlor." He glanced down at himself, and the amusement deepened. "There's another can. Want to go for it?"

Barrie drew herself up and folded a bold hand around his thrusting sex. "I'm not the kind of woman who loses her inhibitions after a couple of Seven-Ups," she informed him with careful dignity. She paused, then winked at him. "One will do."

Somehow she had expected they would make it back to the bed. They didn't. His hunger was particularly strong in the mornings, and after a tempestuous few moments she found herself on her knees, half bent over the edge of the bathtub while he crouched behind her. Their lovemaking was raw and fast and powerful, and left her once again lying weakly on the floor. She found some satisfaction in the fact that he was sprawled beside her, his long legs stretched under the vanity top.

After a long time he said lazily, "I'd thought I could wait until we were in the shower. I underestimated the effect of a soft drink on you, sweetheart...and what watching you drink it does to me."

"I think we're on to something," she reflected, curling nakedly against him and ignoring the chill of the floor. "We need to buy stock in the company."

"Good idea." He turned his head and began kissing her, and for a moment she wondered if the bathroom floor was going to get another workout. But he released her and rose lithely to his feet, then helped her up. "Do you want to have room service, or go down to a restaurant for breakfast?"

"Room service." She was already hungry, and with room service their breakfast should be there by the time she showered and dressed. She gave Zane her order, then, while he called it in, she selected the clothes she wanted. The silk dress was badly wrinkled, so she carried it into the bathroom with her to let the steam from her shower repair the damage.

She took her time in the shower, but even so, some wrinkles remained in the dress by the time she finished. She left the water running and turned it on hot to increase the amount of steam. On a hook behind the door hung a thick terry-cloth bathrobe with the hotel's logo stitched on the breast pocket. She pulled it on and belted it around her, smiling at the weight and size of the garment, and went out to see how long it would be before their breakfast arrived.

Zane wasn't in the bedroom; she could hear him talking in the parlor, and wondered if room service had been unusually quick. But she heard only his voice as she walked to the open door.

He was on the phone, half-turned away from her as he sat on the arm of the couch. She had the impression that he was listening to the shower running even as he carried on his conversation.

"Keep the tail on her father, as well as on *his* tail," he was saying. "I want to catch them all at one time, so I don't have to worry about any loose ends. When the dust settles, Justice and State can sort it out between them."

Barrie gasped, all the color washing out of her face. Zane's head jerked around, and he stared at her, the blue mostly gone from his eyes, leaving them as sharp and gray as frost.

"Yeah," he said into the receiver, his gaze never wavering from hers. "Everything's under control here. Keep the pressure on." He hung up and turned fully to face her.

He hadn't showered yet, she noticed dully. His hair wasn't wet; there was no betraying dampness to his skin. He must have gotten on the phone as soon as she had begun her shower, setting in motion the betrayal that could send her father to jail.

"What have you done?" she whispered, barely holding herself together against the pain that racked her. "Zane, *what have you done?*"

Coolly he stood and came toward her. Barrie backed up, clutching the lapels of the thick robe as if it could protect her.

He flicked a curious glance toward the bathroom, where billows of steam were escaping from the half-open door. "Why is the shower still running?"

"I'm steaming the wrinkles out of my dress," she answered automatically.

His eyebrows lifted wryly. Though she didn't find the pun amusing, she had the thought that this was evidently a wrinkle he hadn't anticipated.

"Who were you talking to?" she asked, her voice stiff with hurt and betrayal and the strain of holding it all under control.

"My brother Chance."

"What does he have to do with my father?"

Zane watched her steadily. "Chance does intelligence work for a government agency; not the FBI or CIA."

Barrie swallowed against the constriction in her throat. Maybe Zane hadn't betrayed her father; maybe he'd already been under surveillance. "How long has he been following my father?"

"Chance is directing the tails, not doing them himself," Zane corrected.

"How long?"

"Since last night. I called him while you were showering then, too."

At least he didn't try to lie or evade. "How could you?" she whispered, her eyes wide and stark.

"Very easily," he replied, his voice sharp. "I'm an officer of the law. Before that, I was an officer in the Navy, in service to this country. Did you think I would ignore a traitor, even if it's your father? You asked me to protect you and our baby, and that's exactly what I'm doing. When you clean out a nest of snakes, you don't pick out a few of them to kill and leave the others. You wipe them out."

The edges of her vision blurred, and she felt herself sway. Oh, God, how could she ever forgive him if her father went to prison? How could she ever forgive herself? She was the cause of this. She had known the kind of man Zane was, but she had allowed herself to ignore it because she'd wanted him so desperately. Of course he'd turned her father in; if she'd been thinking clearly, instead of with her emotions, her hormones, she would have known exactly what he would do, what he had done. It didn't take a genius to predict the actions of a man who had spent his life upholding the laws of his country, and only a fool would ignore the obvious conclusion.

She hadn't even thought about it, so she guessed that made her the biggest fool alive.

She heard him say her name, his tone insistent, and then her vision was blocked by his big body as he gripped her arms.

Desperately she hung on to consciousness, gulping in air and refusing to let herself faint. "Let go of me," she protested, and was shocked at how far away her voice sounded.

"Like hell I will." Instead he swung her off her feet and carried her to the bed, then bent to place her on the tumbled sheets.

As he had the night before, he sat beside her. Now that

she was lying down, her head cleared rapidly. He was leaning over her, one arm braced on the other side of her hip, enclosing her in the iron circle of his embrace. His gaze never left her face.

Barrie wished she could find refuge in anger, but there was none. She understood Zane's motives, and his actions. All she could feel was a huge whirlpool of pain, sucking her down. Her father! As much as she loved Zane, she didn't know if she could bear it if he caused her father to be arrested. This wasn't anything like theft or drunken driving. Treason was heinous, unthinkable. No matter what conclusion her logic drew, she simply couldn't see her father doing anything like that, unless he was somehow being forced to do it. She knew *she* wasn't the weapon being used against him, although she had been drawn into it, probably when he had balked at something. No, she and Zane had both realized immediately that if she was being threatened and her father had nothing to hide, he would have had her whisked away by the FBI before she knew what was happening.

"Please," she begged, clutching his arm. "Can't you warn him somehow, get him out of it? I know you didn't like him, but you don't know him the way I do. He's always done what he thought was best for me. He was always there when I needed him, and b-before I left he gave me his blessing." Her voice broke on a sob, and she quickly controlled it. "I know he's a snob, but he isn't a bad person! If he's gotten involved in something he shouldn't, it was by accident, and now he doesn't know how to get out without endangering me! That *has* to be it. Zane, please!"

He caught her hand, folding it warmly within his. "I can't do that," he said quietly. "If he hasn't done anything wrong, he'll be all right. If he's a traitor—" He shrugged, indicating the lack of options. He wouldn't lift a finger to help a traitor, period. "I didn't want you to know anything about it because I didn't want you to be upset any more than necessary. I knew I wouldn't be able to protect you from worry if he's arrested, but I didn't want you to find out about it beforehand. You've had enough to deal with these past couple of months. My first priority is keeping you and the baby safe, and I'll do that, Barrie, no matter what."

She stared at him through tear-blurred eyes, knowing she had collided with the steel wall of his convictions. Honor wasn't just a concept to him, but a way of life. Still, there was one way she might reach him. "What if it was *your* father?" she asked.

A brief spasm touched his face, telling her that she'd struck a nerve. "I don't know," he admitted. "I hope I'd be able to do what's right…but I don't know."

There was nothing more she could say.

The only thing she could do was warn her father herself.

She moved away from him, sliding off the bed. He lifted his arm and let her go, though he watched her closely, as if waiting for her to faint or throw up or slap him in the face. Considering her pregnancy and her state of mind, she realized, all three were possible, if she relaxed her control just a fraction. But she wasn't going to do any of them, because she couldn't afford to waste the time.

She hugged the oversize robe about her, as she had once hugged his shirt. "What exactly is your brother doing?" She needed as much information as possible if she was going to help her father. Maybe it was wrong, but she would worry about that, and face the consequences, later. She knew she was operating on love and blind trust, but that was all she had to go on. When she thought of her father as the man she knew him to be, she knew she had to trust both that knowledge and his honor. Despite their enormous differences, in that respect he was very like Zane, the man he'd scorned as a son-in-law: honor was a part of his code, his life, his very being.

Zane stood. "You don't need to know, exactly."

For the first time she felt the flush of anger redden her cheeks. "Don't throw my words back at me," she snapped. "You can say no without being sarcastic."

He studied her, then gave a curt nod. "You're right. I'm sorry."

She stalked into the bathroom and slammed the door. The small room was hot and damp with steam, the air thick with it. Barrie turned off the shower and turned on the exhaust fan. There wasn't a wrinkle left in the silk dress. Hurriedly she shed the robe and pulled on the underwear she'd carried into the bathroom, then pulled the dress on over her head. The silk stuck to her damp skin; she had to jerk the fabric to get it into place. The need to hurry beat through her like wings. How much time did she have before room service arrived with their breakfast?

The mirror was fogged over. She grabbed a towel and rubbed a clear spot on the glass, then swiftly combed her hair and began applying a minimum of makeup. The air was so steamy that it would be a wasted effort to apply very much, but she wanted to appear as normal as possible.

Oh, God, the exhaust fan was making so much noise she might not have heard their breakfast arriving. Hastily she cut it off. Zane would have knocked if their food was here, she assured herself. It hadn't arrived yet.

She tried to remember where her purse was, and think how she could get it and get out the door without Zane knowing. His hearing was acute, and he would be watching for her. But the room service waiter would bring their breakfast to the parlor, and Zane, being as cautious as he was, would watch the man's every move. That was the only time he would be distracted, and the only chance she would have to get out of the room undetected. Her window of opportunity would be brief, because he would call her as soon as the waiter left. If she had to wait for an elevator, she was sunk. She could always try the stairs, but all Zane would have to do was take the elevator down to the lobby and wait for her there. With his hearing, he probably heard the elevator every time it chimed, and that would give him an idea of whether she had been able to get one of the cars or had taken the stairs.

She opened the bathroom door a little, so he wouldn't be able to catch the click of the latch.

"What are you doing?" he called. It sounded as if he was standing just inside the double doors that connected the bedroom to the parlor, waiting for her.

"Putting on makeup," she snapped, with perfect truth. She blotted the sweat off her forehead and began again with the powder. Her brief flash of anger was over, but she didn't want him to know it. Let him think she was furious; a woman who was both pregnant and angry deserved a lot of space.

There was a brief knock on the parlor door, and a Spanish-accented voice called out, "Room service."

Quickly Barrie switched on the faucet, so the sound of running water would once again mask her movements. Peering through the small opening by the door, she saw Zane cross her field of vision, going to answer the knock. He was wearing his shoulder holster, which meant, as she had hoped, that he was on guard.

She slipped out of the bathroom, carefully pulled the door back to leave the same small opening, then darted to the other side of the bedroom, out of his line of sight if he glanced inside when he passed by the double doors. Her purse was lying on one of the chairs, and she snatched it up, then slipped her feet into her shoes.

The room service cart clattered as it was rolled into the room. Through the open parlor doors she could hear the waiter casually chatting as he set up the table. Zane's pistol made the waiter nervous; she could hear it in his voice. And his nervousness made Zane that much more wary of him. Zane was probably watching him like a hawk, those pale eyes remote and glacier-cold.

Now was the tricky part. She eased up to the open double doors, peeking through the crack to locate her husband. Relief made her knees wobble; he was standing with his back to the doors while he watched the waiter. The running faucet was doing its job; he was listening to it, rather than positioning himself on the other side of the table so he could watch both the waiter and the bathroom door. He probably did it deliberately, dividing his senses rather than diluting the visual attention he was paying to the waiter.

Her husband was not an ordinary man. Escaping him, even for five minutes, wouldn't be easy.

Taking a deep breath, she silently crossed the open expanse, every nerve in her body drawn tight as she waited for his hard hand to clamp down on her shoulder. She reached the bedroom door to the hallway and held the chain so it wouldn't clink when she slipped it free. That done, her next obstacle was the lock. She moved her body as close to the door as possible, using her flesh to muffle the sound, and slowly turned the latch. The dead bolt slid open with smooth precision and a snick that was barely audible even to her.

She closed her eyes and turned the handle then, concentrating on keeping the movement smooth and silent. If it made any noise, she was caught. If anyone was walking by in the hallway and talking, the change in noise level would alert Zane, and she was caught. If the elevator was slow, she was caught. Everything had to be perfect, or she didn't have a chance.

How much longer did she have? It felt as if she had already taken ten minutes, but it was probably no more than one. Crockery was still rattling in the parlor as the waiter arranged their plates and saucers and water glasses. The door opened, and she slipped through, then spent the same agonizing amount of time making sure it closed as silently as it opened. She released the handle and ran.

She reached the elevators without hearing him shout her name and jabbed the down button. It obediently lit, and remained lit. There was no welcoming chime to signal the arrival of the elevator. Barrie restrained herself from punching the button over and over again in a futile attempt to convey her urgency to a piece of machinery.

"Please," she whispered under her breath. "*Hurry.*"

She would have tried calling her father from the hotel room, but she knew Zane would stop her if he heard her on the phone. She also knew her father's phone was tapped, which meant that incoming calls were automatically recorded. She would try to protect her father, but she refused to do anything that might endanger either Zane or their baby by leading the kidnappers straight to the hotel. She would have to call her father from a pay phone on the street, and a different street, at that.

Down the hall, she heard the room service cart clatter again as the waiter left their suite. Her heart pounding, she stared at the closed elevator doors, willing them to open. Her time was down to mere seconds.

The melodic chime sounded overhead.

The doors slid open.

She looked back as she stepped inside, and her heart nearly stopped. Zane hadn't yelled, hadn't called her name. He was running full speed down the hall, his motion as fluid and powerful as a linebacker's, and pure fury was blazing in his eyes.

He was almost there.

Panicked, she simultaneously pushed the buttons for the lobby and for the door to close. She stepped back from the closing gap as Zane lunged forward, trying to get his hand in the door, which would trigger the automatic opening sensor.

He didn't quite make it. The doors slid shut, and the box began to move downward. "God *damn* it," he roared in frustration, and Barrie flinched as his fist thudded against the doors.

Weakly she leaned against the wall and covered her face with her hands while she shook with reaction. Dear God, she'd never imagined anyone could be so angry. He'd been almost incandescent with it, his eyes all but glowing.

He was probably racing down the stairs, but he had twenty-one floors to cover, and he was no match for the elevator—unless it stopped to pick up passengers on other floors. This possibility nearly brought her to her knees. She watched the numbers change, unable to breathe. If it stopped even once, he might catch her in the street. If it stopped twice, he would catch her in the lobby. Three times, and he would be waiting for her at the elevator.

She would have to face that rage, and she'd never dreaded anything more. Leaving Zane had never been her intention. After she'd warned her father, she would go back to the suite. She didn't fear Zane physically; she knew instinctively that he would never hit her, but somehow that wasn't much comfort.

She had wanted to see him lose control, outside of that final moment in lovemaking when his body took charge and he gave himself over to orgasm. Nausea roiled in her stomach, and she shuddered. Why had she ever wished for such a stupid thing? Oh, God, she never wanted to see him lose his temper again.

He might never forgive her. She might be forsaking forever any chance that he could love her. The full knowledge of what she was risking to warn her father rode her shoulders all the way to the lobby, one long, smooth descent, without any stops.

The rattle and clink of the slot machines never stopped, no matter how early or how late. The din surrounded her as she hurried through the lobby and out to the street. The desert sun was blindingly white, the temperature already edging past ninety, though the morning was only half gone. Barrie joined the tourists thronging the sidewalk, walking quickly despite the heat. She reached the corner, crossed the street and kept walking, not daring to look back. Her red hair would be fairly easy to spot at a distance, even in a crowd, unless she was hidden by someone taller. Zane would have reached the lobby by now. He would quickly scan the slot machine crowd, then erupt onto the street.

Her chest ached, and she realized she was holding her breath again. She gulped in air and hurried to put a building between herself and the hotel entrance. She was afraid to look back, afraid she would see her big, black-haired husband bearing down on her like a thunderstorm, and she knew she would never be able to outrun him.

She crossed one more street and began looking for a pay phone. They were easy to find, but getting an available one was something else again. Why were so many tourists using pay phones at this time of the morning?

Barrie stood patiently, the hot sun beating down on her head, while a blue-haired elderly lady in support stockings gave detailed instructions to someone on when to feed her cat, when to feed her fish and when to feed her plants. Finally she hung up with a cheerful, "Bye-bye, dearie," and she gave Barrie a sweet smile as she hobbled past. The smile was so unexpected that Barrie almost burst into tears. Instead she managed a smile of her own and stepped up to the phone before anyone could squeeze ahead of her.

She used her calling card number because it was faster, and since she was calling from a pay phone, it didn't matter how she placed the call. *Please, God, let him be there*, she silently prayed as she listened to the tones, then the ringing. It was lunchtime on the east coast; he could be having lunch with someone, or playing golf—he could be anywhere. She tried to remember his schedule, but nothing came to mind. Their relationship had been so strained for the past two months that she had disassociated herself from his social and political appointments.

"Hello?"

The answer was so cautious, so wary sounding, that at first she didn't recognize her father's voice.

"Hello?" he said again, sounding even more wary, if possible.

Barrie pressed the handset hard to her ear, trying to keep her hand from shaking. "Daddy," she said, her voice strangled. She hadn't called him Daddy in years, but the old name slipped out past the barrier of her adulthood.

"Barrie? Sweetheart?" Life zinged into his voice, and she could picture him in her mind, sitting up straighter at his desk.

"Daddy, I can't say much." She fought to keep her voice even, so he would be able to understand her. "You have to be careful. You have to protect yourself. People *know*. Do you hear me?"

He was silent a moment, then he said with a calmness that was beyond her, "I understand. Are you safe?"

"Yes," she said, though she wasn't sure. She still had to face her husband.

"Then take care, sweetheart, and I'll talk to you soon."

"Bye," she whispered, then carefully hung the receiver in its cradle and turned to go to the hotel. She had taken about ten steps when she was captured in the hard grip she had been dreading. She didn't see him coming, so she couldn't brace herself. One second he wasn't there, the next second he was, surfacing out of the crowd like a shark.

Despite everything, she was glad to see him, glad to get it over with instead of dreading the first meeting during every dragging step to the hotel. The tension and effort had drained her. She leaned weakly against him, and he clamped his arm around her waist to support her. "You shouldn't be out in the sun without something on your head," was all he said. "Especially since you haven't eaten anything today."

He was in control, that incandescent fury cooled and conquered. She wasn't foolish enough to believe it was gone, however. "I had to warn him," she said tiredly. "And I didn't want the call traced to the hotel."

"I know." The words were brief to the point of curtness. "It might not make any difference. Las Vegas is crawling with a certain group of people this morning, and you may have been spotted. Your hair." Those two words were enough. Redheads were always distinctive, because there were so few of them. She felt like apologizing for the deep, rich luster of her hair.

"They're here?" she asked in a small voice. "The kidnappers?"

"Not the original ones. There's a deep game going on, baby, and I'm afraid you just jumped into the middle of it."

The sun beat down on her unprotected head, the heat increasing by the minute. Every step seemed more and more of an effort. Her thoughts scattered. She might have plunged Zane and herself into the very danger she'd wanted to avoid. "Maybe I *am* a pampered society babe with more hair than brains," she said aloud. "I didn't mean—"

"I know," he said again, and unbelievably, he squeezed her waist. "And I never said you have more hair than brains. If anything, you're too damn smart, and it seems you have a natural talent for sneaking around. Not many people could have gotten out of that suite without me hearing them. Spook, maybe. And Chance. No one else."

Barrie leaned more of her weight against him. She was on his left side, and she felt the hard lump of the holster beneath his jacket. When he'd grabbed her, he'd instinctively kept his right hand free, in case he needed his pistol. What he *didn't* need, she thought tiredly, was having to support her weight and keep his balance in a firefight. She forced herself to straighten away from him, despite the way his arm tightened around her waist. He gave her a questioning look.

"I don't want to impede you," she explained.

His mouth curved wryly. "See what I mean? Now you're thinking of combat stuff. If you weren't so sweet, Mrs. Mackenzie, you'd be a dangerous woman."

Why wasn't he lambasting her? She couldn't imagine he'd gotten over his fury so fast; Zane struck her as the type of man who seldom lost his temper, but when he did, it was undoubtedly a memorable occasion—one that could last for years. Maybe he was saving it for when they were in the privacy of the suite, remaining on guard while they were in the street. He could do that, compartmentalize his anger, shove it aside until it was safe to bring it out.

She found herself studying the surging, milling, strolling crowd of tourists that surrounded them, looking for any betraying sign of interest. It helped take her mind off how incredibly weak she felt. This pregnancy was making itself felt with increasing force; though it had been foolish of her to come out into the sun without eating breakfast, and without a hat, normally she wouldn't have had any problem with the heat in this short amount of time.

How much farther was it to the hotel? She concentrated on her steps, on the faces around her. Zane maintained a slow, steady pace, and when he could, he put himself between her and the sun. The human shade helped, marginally.

"Here we are," he said, ushering her into the cool, dim cavern of the lobby. She closed her eyes to help them adjust from the bright sunlight and sighed with relief as the blast of air-conditioning washed over her.

The elevator was crowded on the ride up. Zane pulled her against the back wall, so he would have one less side to protect, and also to set up a human wall of protection between them and the open doors. She felt a faint spurt of surprise as she realized she knew what he was thinking, the motives behind his actions. He would do what he could to keep anything from happening, and to protect these people, but if push came to shove, he would ruthlessly sacrifice the other people in this elevator to keep her safe.

They got off on the twenty-first floor, the ride uneventful. A man and woman got off at the same time, a middle-aged couple with Rochester accents. They turned down the hallway leading away from the suite. Zane guided Barrie after them, following the couple until they reached their room around the corner. As they walked past, Barrie glanced inside the room as the couple entered it; it was untidy, piled with shopping bags and the dirty clothes they'd worn the day before.

"Safe," Zane murmured as they wound their way to the suite.

"They wouldn't have had all the tourist stuff if they'd just arrived?"

He slanted an unreadable look at her. "Yeah."

The suite was blessedly cool. She stumbled inside, and Zane locked and chained the door. Their breakfast still sat on the table, untouched and cold. He all but pushed her into a chair anyway. "Eat," he ordered. "Just the toast, if nothing else. Put jelly on it. And drink all the water." He sat down on the arm of the couch, picked up the phone and began dialing.

Just to be safe, she ate half a slice of dry toast first, eschewing the balls of butter, which wouldn't melt on the cold toast anyway. Her stomach was peaceful at the moment, but she didn't want to do anything to upset it. She smeared the second half slice with jelly.

As she methodically ate and drank, she began to feel better. Zane was making no effort to keep her from hearing his conversation, and she gathered he was talking to his brother Chance again.

"If she was spotted, we have maybe half an hour," he was saying. "Get everyone on alert." He listened a moment, then said, "Yeah, I know. I'm slipping." He said goodbye with a cryptic, "Keep it cool."

"Keep what cool?" Barrie asked, turning in her chair to face him.

A flicker of amusement lightened his remote eyes. "Chance has a habit of sticking his nose, along with another part of his anatomy, into hot spots. He gets burned occasionally."

"And you don't, I suppose?"

He shrugged. "Occasionally," he admitted.

He was very calm, unusually so, even for him. It was like waiting for a storm to break. Barrie took a deep breath and braced herself. "All right, I'm feeling better," she said, more evenly than she felt. "Let me have it."

He regarded her for a moment, then shook his head—regretfully, she thought. "It'll have to wait. Chance said there's a lot of activity going on all of a sudden. It's all about to hit the fan."

Chapter 13

They didn't have even the half hour Zane had hoped for.

The phone rang, and he picked it up. "Roger," he said, and placed the receiver into its cradle. He stood and strode over to Barrie. "They're moving in," he said, lifting her from the chair with an implacable hand. "And you're going to a different floor."

He was shoving her out of harm's way. She stiffened against the pressure of his hand, digging in her heels. He stopped and turned to face her, then placed his hand over her belly. "You have to go," he said, without a flicker of emotion. He was in combat mode, his face impassive, his eyes cold and distant.

He was right. Because of the baby, she had to go. She put her hand over his. "All right. But do you have an extra pistol I could have—just in case?"

He hesitated briefly, then strode into the bedroom to his garment bag. The weapon he removed was a compact, five-shot revolver. "Do you know how to use it?"

She folded her hand around the butt, feeling the smoothness of the wood. "I've shot skeet, but I've never used a handgun. I'll manage."

"There's no empty chamber, and no safety," he said as

he escorted her out the door. "You can pull the hammer back before you fire, or you can use a little more effort and just pull the trigger. Nothing to it but aiming and firing. It's a thirty-eight caliber, so it has stopping power." He was walking swiftly toward the stairs as he talked. He opened the stairwell door and began pushing her up the stairs, their steps echoing in the concrete silo. "I'm going to put you in an empty room on the twenty-third floor, and I want you to stay there until either Chance or I come for you. If anyone else opens the door, shoot them."

"I don't know what Chance looks like," she blurted.

"Black hair, hazel eyes. Tall. So good-looking you start drooling when you see him. That's what he says women do, anyway."

They reached the twenty-third floor. Barrie was only slightly winded, Zane not at all. As they stepped into the carpeted silence of the hallway, she asked, "How do you know which rooms are empty?"

He produced one of the electronic cards from his pocket. "Because one of Chance's people booked the room last night and slipped me the key card while we were eating supper. Just in case."

He always had an alternate plan—just in case. She should have guessed.

He opened the door to room 2334 and ushered her inside, but he didn't enter himself. "Lock and chain the door, and stay put," he said, then turned and walked swiftly toward the stairwell. Barrie stood in the doorway and watched him. He stopped and looked at her over his shoulder. "I'm waiting to hear the door being locked," he said softly.

She stepped back, turned the lock and slid the chain into place.

Then she stood in the middle of the neat, silent room and quietly went to pieces.

She couldn't stand it. Zane was deliberately walking into danger—*on her account*—and she couldn't join him. She couldn't be there with him, couldn't guard his back. Because of the baby growing inside her, she was relegated to this safe niche while the man she loved faced bullets for her.

She sat on the floor and rocked back and forth, her arms folded over her stomach, keening softly as tears rolled down her face. This terror for Zane's safety was worse than anything she'd ever felt before, far worse than what she'd known at the hands of her kidnappers, worse even than when he'd been shot. At least she'd *been* there then. She'd been able to help, able to touch him.

She couldn't do anything now.

A sharp, deep report that sounded like thunder made her jump. Except it wasn't thunder; the desert sky was bright and cloudless. She buried her face against her knees, weeping harder. More shots. Some lighter, flatter in tone. A peculiar cough. Another deep thundering, then several in quick succession.

Then silence.

She pulled herself together and scrambled to the far corner of the room, behind the bed. She sat with her back against the wall and her arms braced on her knees, the pistol steady as she held it trained on the door. She didn't see how anyone other than Zane or Chance could know where she was, but she wouldn't gamble on it. She didn't know what any of this was about, or who her enemies were, except for Mack Prewett, probably.

Time crawled past. She didn't have her wristwatch on, and the clock radio on the bedside table was turned away from her. She didn't get up to check the time. She simply sat there with the pistol in her hand and waited, and died a little more with each passing minute of Zane's absence.

He didn't come. She felt the coldness of despair grow in her heart, spreading until it filled her chest, the pressure of it almost stopping her lungs. Her heartbeat slowed to a heavy, painful rhythm. *Zane.* He would have come, if he'd been able. He'd been shot again. Wounded. She wouldn't let herself even think the word *dead*, but it was there, in her heart, her chest, and she didn't know how she could go on.

There was a brief knock on the door. "Barrie?" came a soft call, a voice that sounded tired and familiar. "It's Art Sandefer. It's over. Mack's in custody, and you can come out now."

Only Zane and Chance were supposed to know where she was. Zane had said that if anyone else opened the door, to shoot them. But she'd known Art Sandefer for years, known and respected both the man and the job he did. If Mack Prewett had been dirty, Art would have been on top of it. His presence here made sense.

"Barrie?" The door handle rattled.

She started to get up and let him in, then sank back to the floor. No. He wasn't Zane and he wasn't Chance. If she had lost Zane, the least she could do was follow his last instructions to the letter. His objective had been her safety, and she trusted him more than she had ever trusted anyone else in her life, including her father. She definitely trusted him more than she did Art Sandefer.

She was unprepared for the peculiar little coughing sound. Then the lock on the door exploded, and Art Sandefer pushed the door open and stepped inside. In his hand was a pistol with a thick silencer fitted onto the end of the barrel. Their eyes met across the room, his weary and cynical and acutely intelligent. And she knew.

Barrie pulled the trigger.

* * *

Zane was there only moments, seconds, later. Art had slumped to a sitting position against the open door, his hand pressed to the hole in his chest as his eyes glazed with shock. Zane kicked the weapon from Art's outstretched hand, but that was all the attention he paid to the wounded man. He stepped over him as if he wasn't there, rapidly crossing the room to where Barrie sat huddled in the corner, her face drawn and gray. Her gaze was oddly distant and unfocused. Panic roared through him, but a swift inspection didn't reveal any blood. She looked unharmed.

He hunkered down beside her, gently brushing her hair from her face. "Sweetheart?" he asked in a soft tone. "It's over now. Are you all right?"

She didn't answer. He sat down on the floor beside her and pulled her onto his lap, holding her close and tight against the warmth of his body. He kept up a reassuring murmur, a gentle sound of reassurance. He could feel the thud of her heartbeat against him, the rhythm hard and alarmingly slow. He held her tighter, his face buried against the richness of her hair.

"Is she all right?" Chance asked as he, too, stepped over Art Sandefer and approached his brother and new sister-in-law. Other people were coming into the room, people who tended to the wounded man. Mack Prewett was one of them, his eyes sharp and hard as he watched his former superior.

"She'll be fine," Zane murmured, lifting his head. "She shot Sandefer."

The brothers' eyes met in a moment of understanding. The first one was tough. With luck and good care, Sandefer would survive, but Barrie would always be one of those who knew what it was like to pull that trigger.

"How did he know which room?" Zane asked, keeping his voice calm.

Chance sat down on the bed and leaned forward, his forearms braced on his knees. His expression was pleasant enough, his eyes cool and thoughtful. "I must have a leak in my group," he said matter-of-factly. "And I know who it is, because only one person knew this room number. I'll take care of it."

"You do that."

Barrie stirred in Zane's grip, her arms lifting to twine around his neck. "Zane," she said, her voice faint and choked, shaking.

Because he'd felt the same way, he heard the panic in her voice, the despair. "I'm okay," he whispered, kissing her temple. "I'm okay."

A sob shook her, then was quickly controlled. She was soldiering on. Emotion swelled in his chest, a huge golden bubble of such force that it threatened to stop his breathing, his heartbeat. He closed his eyes to hold back the tears that burned his lids. "Oh, God," he said shakily. "I thought I was too late. I saw Sandefer walk in before I could get off a round at him, and then I heard the shot."

Her arms tightened convulsively around his neck, but she didn't say anything.

Zane put his hand on her belly, gulping in air as he fought for control. He was trembling, he noticed with distant surprise. Only Barrie could make mincemeat of his nerves. "I want the baby," he said, his voice still shaking. "But I didn't even think about it then. All I could think was that if I lost you—" He broke off, unable to continue.

"Baby?" Chance asked, politely inquiring.

Barrie nodded, her head moving against Zane's chest. Her face was still buried against him, and she didn't look up.

"Barrie, this is my brother Chance," Zane said. His tone was still rough, uneven.

Blindly Barrie held out her hand. Amused, Chance gently shook it, then returned it to Zane's neck. He had yet to see her face. "Glad to meet you," he said. "I'm happy about the baby, too. That should deflect Mom's attention for a while."

The room was filled to overflowing: hotel security, Las Vegas police, medics, not to mention Mack Prewett and the FBI, who were quietly controlling everything. Chance's people had pulled back, melting into the shadows where they belonged, where they operated best. Chance picked up the phone, made one brief call, then said to Zane, "It's taken care of."

Mack Prewett came over and sat down on the bed beside Chance. His face was troubled as he looked at Barrie, clutched so tightly in Zane's arms. "Is she all right?"

"Yes," she said, answering for herself.

"Art's critical, but he might make it. It would save us a lot of trouble if he didn't." Mack's voice was flat, emotionless.

Barrie shuddered.

"You were never meant to be involved, Barrie," Mack said. "I began to think Art was playing both sides, so I asked your father to help me set him up. The information had to be legitimate, and the ambassador knows more people, has access to more inside information, than can be believed. Art went for the bait like a hungry carp. But then he asked for something really critical, the ambassador stalled, and the next thing we knew, you'd been snatched. Your dad nearly came unglued."

"Then those bastards in Benghazi knew we were coming in," Zane said, his eyes going cold.

"Yeah. I managed to shuffle the time frame a little when

I gave the information to Art, but that was the most I could do to help. They weren't expecting you as early as you got there."

"I couldn't believe it of him. Art Sandefer, of all people," Barrie said, lifting her head to look at Mack. "Until I saw his eyes. I thought *you* were the dirty one."

Mack smiled crookedly. "It rocked me that you figured out anything was going on at all."

"Dad tipped me off. He acted so frightened every time I left the house."

"Art wanted you," Mack explained. "He was playing it cool for a while, or we would have had this wrapped up weeks ago. But it wasn't just the information. Art wanted *you*."

Barrie was stunned by what Mack was saying. She glanced at Zane and saw his jaw tighten. So that was why she hadn't been raped in Benghazi; Art had been saving her for himself. He could never have released her, of course, if she had seen his face. Perhaps he would have drugged her, but more likely he would simply have raped her, kept her for himself for a while, then killed her. She shuddered, turning her face once more against Zane's throat. She was still having trouble believing he was safe and unharmed; it was difficult to drag herself out of the black pit of despair, even though she knew the worst hadn't happened. She felt numb, sick.

But then a thought occurred to her, one she would have had sooner if concern for Zane hadn't wiped everything else from her mind. She looked at Mack again. "Then my father's in the clear."

"Absolutely. He was working with me from the get-go." He met her gaze and shrugged. "Your dad can be a pain in the rear, but his loyalty was never in question."

"When I called him this morning—"

Mack grimaced. "He was relieved to know you loved him enough to call, despite the evidence against him. Your leaving the hotel stirred up a hornet's nest, though. I thought we had everything under control."

"How?"

"Me," Chance interjected, and for the first time Barrie looked at her brother-in-law. She didn't drool, but she had to admit that his good looks were startling. Viewed objectively, he was the most handsome man she'd ever seen. However, she far preferred Zane's scarred, somber face, with its ancient eyes.

"I checked into another hotel under Zane's name," Chance explained. "You weren't listed at all, but Art knew you were with Zane, because he'd checked the license plate on that rental car and traced the rental to Zane's credit card. We didn't want to make it too obvious for him, we wanted him to have to work to find us, so he wouldn't be suspicious. When he found out you'd married Zane, though, he stopped being so cautious." Chance grinned. "Then you went for a walk this morning, and fubar happened. The pay phone you chose was right across the street from the hotel where I'd checked in, and Art's people spotted you immediately."

Across the room, the medics finally had Art Sandefer ready for transport to a hospital. Zane watched the man being carried out, then cut his narrowed gaze to Mack. "If I'd known about you a little sooner, most of this could have been avoided."

Mack didn't back down from that glacial stare. "As far as that goes, Commander, I didn't expect you to have the contacts you have—" he glanced at Chance "—or to move as fast as you did. I'd been working on Art for months. You made things happen in one day."

Zane stood, effortlessly lifting Barrie in his arms as he did so. "It's over now," he said with finality. "If you gentlemen will excuse me, I need to take care of my wife."

Taking care of her involved getting a third room, because the suite was in bad shape and he didn't want her to see it. He placed her on the bed, locked the door, then stripped both her and himself and got into bed with her, holding their naked bodies as close together as possible. They both needed the reassurance of bare skin, no barriers between them. He got hard immediately, but now wasn't the time for lovemaking.

Barrie couldn't seem to stop trembling, and, to her astonishment, neither could Zane. They clung together, touching each other's faces, absorbing the smell and feel of each other in an effort to dispel the terror.

"I love you," he whispered, holding her so close her ribs ached from the pressure. "God, I was so scared! I can't keep it together where you're concerned, sweetheart. For the sake of my sanity, I hope the rest of our lives are as dull as dishwater."

"They will be," she promised, kissing his chest. "We'll work on it." And tears blurred her eyes, because she hadn't expected so much, so fast.

Then, finally, it was time for more. Gently he entered her, and they lay entwined, not moving, as if their nerves couldn't stand a sharp assault now, even one of pleasure. That, too, came in its own time…her pleasure, and his.

Epilogue

"Twins," Barrie said, her voice still full of stunned bewilderment as she and Zane drove along the road that wound up the side of Mackenzie's Mountain. "Boys."

"I told you how it would be," Zane said, glancing at the mound of her stomach, which was much too big for five months of pregnancy. "Boys."

She gave him a glassy stare of shock. "You didn't," she said carefully, "say they would come in pairs."

"There haven't been twins in our family before," Zane said, just as carefully. In truth, he felt as shaky as Barrie did. "This is a first."

She stared out the window, her gaze passing blindly over the breathtaking vista of craggy blue mountains. They lived in Wyoming now; with Zane's two-year tenure as sheriff in Arizona over, he had declined to run for election, and they had moved closer to the rest of the family. Chance had been after him for those two years to join his organization—though Barrie still wasn't certain exactly what that organization *was*—and Zane had finally relented. He wouldn't be doing fieldwork, because he didn't want to risk the life he had with Barrie and Nick and now these two new babies who were growing inside her, but he had a rare knack for planning for the unexpected, and that was the talent he was using.

The entire family, including her father, was gathered on the mountain to celebrate the Fourth of July, which was the next day. Zane, Barrie and Nick had driven up two days before for an extended visit, but today had been her scheduled checkup, and he'd driven her into town to the doctor's office. Given the way her waistline had been expanding, they should have expected the news, but Zane had simply figured she was further along in her pregnancy than they'd thought. Seeing those two little fetuses on the ultrasound had been quite a shock, but there hadn't been any doubt about it. Two heads, two tails, four arms and hands, four legs and feet—and both babies definitely male. Very definitely.

"I can't think of two names," Barrie said, sounding very near tears.

Zane reached over to pat her knee. "We have four more months to think of names."

She sniffed. "There's no way," she said, "that I can carry them for four more months. We'll have to come up with names before then."

They *were* big babies, both of them, much bigger than Nick had been at this stage.

"After Nick, it took a lot of courage just to think of having another baby," she continued. "I'd geared myself up for one. *One*. Zane, what if *they're both like Nick?*"

He blanched. Nick was a hellion. Nick had a good shot at turning the entire family gray-haired within another year. For a very short person with a limited vocabulary,

their offspring could cause an unbelievable uproar in a remarkably short period of time.

They reached the crest of the mountain, and Zane slowed
the car as they neared the large, sprawling ranch house. A
variety of vehicles were parked around the yard—Wolf's
truck, Mary's car, Mike and Shea's Suburban, Josh and
Loren's rental, Ambassador Lovejoy's rental, Maris's snazzy
truck, Chance's motorcycle. Joe and Caroline and their
five hooligans had arrived by helicopter. Boys seemed to be
everywhere, from Josh's youngest, age five, to John, who was
Joe's oldest and was now in college and here with his current girlfriend.

They were adding two more to the gang.

They got out and walked up the steps to the porch. Zane
put his arm around her and hugged her close, tilting her face
up for a kiss that quickly grew heated. Barrie glowed with
a special sexuality when she was pregnant, and the plain
truth was he couldn't resist her. Their love play was often
extended these days, now that pregnancy had once again
made her breasts as sensitive as they had been when she'd
carried Nick.

"Stop that!" Josh called cheerfully from inside the house.
"That's what got her in that condition in the first place!"

Reluctantly Zane released his wife, and together they
went into the house. "That isn't exactly right," he told
Josh, who laughed.

The big television was on, and Maris, Josh and Chance
were watching some show-jumping event. Wolf and Joe
were discussing cattle with Mike. Caroline was arguing politics with the ambassador. Mary and Shea were organizing
a game for the younger kids. Loren, who was often an oasis

of calm in the middle of the Mackenzie hurricane, gave Barrie's rounded stomach a knowing look. "How did the checkup go?" she asked.

"Twins," Barrie said, still in that numb tone. She gave Zane a helpless, how-did-this-happen look.

The whirlwind of activity came to a sudden stop. Heads lifted and turned. Her father gasped. Mary's face suddenly glowed with radiance.

"Both boys," Zane announced, before anyone could ask.

A sigh almost of relief went around the room. "Thank God," Josh said weakly. "What if it was another one—or *two*—like Nick!"

Barrie's head swiveled around as she began searching for a particular little head. "Where *is* Nick?" she asked.

Chance bolted upright from his sprawled position on the couch. The adults looked around with growing panic. "She was right here," Chance said. "She was dragging one of Dad's boots around."

Zane and Barrie both began a rapid search of the house. "How long ago?" Barrie called.

"Two minutes, no more. Just before you drove up." Maris was on her knees, peering under beds.

"Two minutes!" Barrie almost moaned. In two minutes, Nick could almost single-handedly wreck the house. It was amazing how such a tiny little girl with such an angelic face could be such a demon. "Nick!" she called. "Mary Nicole, come out, come out, wherever you are!" Sometimes that worked. Most times it didn't.

Everyone joined in the search, but their black-haired little terror was nowhere to be found. The entire family had been ecstatic at her birth, and she had been utterly doted on, with even the rough-and-tumble cousins fascinated by the daintiness and beauty of the newest Mackenzie. She really did look angelic, like Pebbles on the old *Flintstones* cartoons. She was adorable. She had Zane's black hair; slanted, deceptively innocent blue eyes; and dimples on each side of her rosebud mouth. She had sat up by herself at four months, crawled at six, walked at eight, and the entire family had been on guard ever since.

They found Wolf's boot beneath Mary's glassed-in collection of angels. From the scuff marks on the wall, Zane deduced his little darling had been trying to knock the collection down by heaving the boot at it. Luckily the boot had been too heavy for her to handle. Her throwing arm wasn't well developed yet, thank God.

She had a frightful temper for such a little thing, and an outsize will, too. Keeping her from doing something she was determined to do was like trying to hold back the tide with a bucket. She had also inherited her father's knack for planning, something that was eerie in a two-year-old. Nick was capable of plotting the downfall of anyone who crossed her.

Once, when Alex, Joe's second oldest, had seen her with a knife in her hand and swiftly snatched it away before she could harm anyone or anything, Nick had thrown a howling temper tantrum that had been halted only when Zane swatted her rear end. Discipline from her adored daddy made her sob so heartbrokenly that everyone else got a lump in their throats. That, and making her sit down in her punishment chair, were so far the only two things they'd discovered that could reduce her to tears.

When she had stopped sobbing, she had pouted in a corner for a while, all the time giving Alex threatening looks over one tiny shoulder. Then she had gone to Barrie for comfort, crawling into her mother's lap to be rocked. Her next stop had been Zane's lap, to show him that she forgave him. She'd wound her little arms around his neck and rubbed her chubby little cheek against his rough one. She'd even taken a brief nap, lying limply against his broad shoulder. She'd woken, climbed down and darted off to the kitchen, where she'd implored Mary, whom she called Gamma, for a "dink." She was allowed to have soft drinks without caffeine, so Mary had given her one of the green bottles they always kept in store especially for Nick. Zane and Barrie always shared a look of intimate amusement at their daughter's love for Seven-Up, but there was nothing unusual about seeing her clutching the familiar bottle in her tiny hands. She would take a few sips, then with great concentration screw the top onto the bottle and lug it around with her until it was finally empty, which usually took a couple of hours.

On this occasion, Zane had happened to be watching her, smiling at her blissful expression as her little hands closed on the bottle. She had strutted out of the kitchen without letting Mary open the bottle for her and stopped in the hallway, where she vigorously shook the bottle with so much vigor that her entire little body had been bouncing up and down. Then, with a meltingly sweet smile on her face, she had all but danced into the living room and handed the bottle to Alex with a flirtatious tilt of her head. "Ope' it, pees," she'd said in her adorable small voice... and then she'd backed up a few steps.

"No!" Zane had yelled, leaping up from his chair, but it was too late. Alex had already twisted the cap and broken the seal. The bottle spewed and spurted, the sticky liquid spraying the wall, the floor, the chair. It hit Alex full blast in the face. By the time he'd managed to get the cap securely back on the bottle, he was soaked.

Nick had clapped her hands and said, "Hee, hee, hee," and Zane wasn't certain if it was a laugh or a taunt. It didn't matter. He had collapsed on the floor in laughter, and there was an unbreakable law written in stone somewhere that you couldn't punish youngsters if you'd laughed at what they'd done.

"Nick!" he called now. "Do you want a Popsicle?" Next to Seven-Ups, Popsicles were her favorite treat.

There was no answer.

Sam tore into the house. He was ten, Josh and Loren's middle son. His blue eyes were wide. "Uncle Zane!" he cried. "Nick's on top of the house!"

"Oh, my God," Barrie gasped, and rushed out of the house as fast as she could. Zane tore past her, his heart in his throat, every instinct screaming for him to get to his child as fast as possible.

Everyone spilled into the yard, their faces pale with alarm, and looked up. Nick was sitting cross-legged on the edge of the roof, her little face blissful as she stared down at them. "Hi," she chirped.

Barrie's knees wobbled, and Mary put a supporting, protective arm around her.

It was no mystery how Nick had gotten on the roof—a ladder was leaning against the house, and Nick was as agile as a young goat. The ladder shouldn't have been there; in fact, Zane would have sworn it hadn't been when he and Barrie had arrived, no more than five minutes earlier.

He started up the ladder, his gaze glued on his daughter. A scowl screwed her small features together, and she scrambled to her feet, perilously close to the edge of the roof. "No!" she shrieked. "No, Daddy!"

He froze in place. She didn't want to come down, and she was absolutely fearless. She paid no more heed to her danger than if she'd been in her bed.

"Zane," Barrie whispered, her voice choked.

He was shaking. Nick stomped one little foot and pointed a dimpled finger at him. "Daddy down," she demanded.

He couldn't get to her in time. No matter how fast he moved, his baby was going to fall. There was only one thing to do. "Chance!" he barked.

Chance knew immediately. He ambled forward, not making any swift movements that would startle her. When he was directly below her, he grinned at his cherubic niece, and she grinned at him. He was her favorite uncle.

"Dance," she crowed, showing all her tiny white teeth.

"You little Antichrist," he said fondly. "I'm really going to miss you when you're in prison. I give you...oh, maybe to the age of six."

Benjy, Josh's youngest, piped up behind them, "Why did Uncle Chance call her Dannychrist? Her name's Nick."

Nick spread her arms wide, bouncing up and down on her tiptoes. Chance held up his arms. "Come on, cupcake," he said, and laughed. "Jump!"

She did.

He deftly snagged her in midair, and hugged the precious little body to his chest. Barrie burst into tears of relief.

LINDA HOWARD

Then Zane was there, taking his daughter in his arms, pressing his lips to her round little head, and Barrie rushed over to be enveloped in his embrace, too.

Caroline looked at Joe. "I forgive you for not having any female sperm," she announced, and Joe laughed.

Josh was frowning sternly at Sam. "How did the ladder get there?" he demanded.

Sam looked at his feet.

Mike and Joe began to frown at their boys.

"Whose bright idea was it to play on top of the house?" Mike asked of the seven boys who hadn't been inside, and thus absolved of blame.

Seven boys scuffed their shoes on the ground, unable to look up at the three fathers confronting them.

Josh took down the ladder, which was supposed to be in the barn. He pointed to the structure in question. "March," he said sternly, and two boys began their reluctant walk to the barn—and their retribution. Benjy clung to Loren's leg, blinking at his two older brothers.

Mike pointed to the barn. His two boys went.

Joe raised an eyebrow at his three youngest. They went.

The three tall, broad-shouldered brothers followed their sons to the barn.

Nick patted Barrie's face. "Mommy cwy?" she asked, and her lower lip quivered as she looked at Zane. "Fix, Daddy."

"I'll fix, all right," he muttered. "I'll fix some glue to your little butt and stick you on a chair."

Barrie giggled through her tears. "Everyone wished for a girl," she said, hiccuping as she laughed and cried at the same time. "Well, we got our wish!"

Wolf reached out and plucked his only granddaughter

from his son's brawny arms. She beamed at him, and he said ruefully, "With luck, it'll be thirty years before there's another one. Unless…" His dark eyes narrowed as he looked at Chance.

"No way," Chance said firmly. "You can turn that look on Maris. I'm not getting married. I'm not reproducing. They're starting to come by the bunches now, so it's time to call a halt. I'm not getting into this daddy business."

Mary gave him her sweet smile. "We'll see," she said.

A GAME OF CHANCE

For the readers

The Beginning

Coming back to Wyoming—coming home—always evoked in Chance Mackenzie such an intense mixture of emotions that he could never decide which was strongest, the pleasure or the acute discomfort. He was, by nature and nurture—not that there had been any nurturing in the first fourteen or so years of his life—a man who was more comfortable alone. If he was alone, then he could operate without having to worry about anyone but himself, and, conversely, there was no one to make him uncomfortable with concern about his own well-being. The type of work he had chosen only reinforced his own inclinations, because covert operations and anti-terrorist activities predicated he be both secretive and wary, trusting no one, letting no one close to him.

And yet... And yet, there was his family. Sprawling, brawling, ferociously overachieving, refusing to let him withdraw, not that he was at all certain he could even if they would allow it. It was always jolting, alarming, to step back into that all-enveloping embrace, to be teased and questioned—*teased*, him, whom some of the most deadly people on earth justifiably feared—hugged and kissed, fussed

over and yelled at and…loved, just as if he were like everyone else. He knew he wasn't; the knowledge was always
there, in the back of his mind, that he was *not* like them.
But he was drawn back, again and again, by something deep
inside hungering for the very things that so alarmed him.
Love was scary; he had learned early and hard how little he
could depend on anyone but himself.

The fact that he had survived at all was a testament to
his toughness and intelligence. He didn't know how old he
was, or where he had been born, what he was named as a
child, or if he even had a name—nothing. He had no memory of a mother, a father, anyone who had taken care of him.
A lot of people simply didn't remember their childhoods,
but Chance couldn't comfort himself with that possibility,
that there had been someone who had loved him and taken
care of him, because he remembered too damn many other
details.

He remembered stealing food when he was so small he
had to stand on tiptoe to reach apples in a bin in a small-
town supermarket. He had been around so many kids now
that, by comparing what he remembered to the sizes they
were at certain ages, he could estimate he had been no more
than three years old at the time, perhaps not even that.

He remembered sleeping in ditches when it was warm,
hiding in barns, stores, sheds, whatever was handy, when it
was cold or raining. He remembered stealing clothes to
wear, sometimes by the simple means of catching a boy
playing alone in a yard, overpowering him and taking the
clothes off his back. Chance had always been much stronger
physically than other boys his size, because of the sheer
physical difficulty of staying alive—and he had known how
to fight, for the same reason.

He remembered a dog taking up with him once, a black-and-white mutt that tagged along and curled up next to him to sleep, and Chance remembered being grateful for the warmth. He also remembered that when he reached for a piece of steak he had stolen from the scraps in back of a restaurant, the dog bit him and stole the steak. Chance still had two scars on his left hand from the dog's teeth. The dog had gotten the meat, and Chance had gone one more day without food. He didn't blame the dog; it had been hungry, too. But Chance ran it off after that, because stealing enough food to keep himself alive was difficult enough, without having to steal for the dog, too. Besides, he had learned that when it came to survival, it was every dog for himself.

He might have been five years old when he learned that particular lesson, but he had learned it well.

Of course, learning how to survive in both rural and urban areas, in all conditions, was what made him so good at his job now, so he supposed his early childhood had its benefits. Even considering that, though, he wouldn't wish his childhood on a dog, not even the damn mutt that had bitten him.

His real life had begun the day Mary Mackenzie found him lying beside a road, deathly ill with a severe case of flu that had turned into pneumonia. He didn't remember much of the next few days—he had been too ill—but he had known he was in a hospital, and he had been wild with fear, because that meant he had fallen into the hands of the system, and he was now, in effect, a prisoner. He was obviously a minor, without identification, and the circumstances would warrant the child welfare services being notified. He had spent his entire life avoiding just such an event, and he had tried to make plans to escape, but his thoughts were vague, hard to get ordered, and his body was too weak to respond to his demands.

But through it all he could remember being soothed by an angel with soft blue-gray eyes and light, silvery brown hair, cool hands and a loving voice. There had also been a big, dark man, a half-breed, who calmly and repeatedly addressed his deepest fear. "We won't let them take you," the big man had said whenever Chance briefly surfaced from his fever-induced stupor.

He didn't trust them, didn't believe the big half-breed's reassurances. Chance had figured out that he himself was part American Indian, but big deal, that didn't mean he could trust these people any more than he could trust that damn thieving, ungrateful mutt. But he was too sick, too weak, to escape or even struggle, and while he was so helpless Mary Mackenzie had somehow hog-tied him with devotion, and he had never managed to break free.

He hated being touched; if someone was close enough to touch him, then they were close enough to attack him. He couldn't fight off the nurses and doctors who poked and prodded and moved him around as if he were nothing more than a mindless piece of meat. He had endured it, gritting his teeth, struggling with both his own panic and the almost overpowering urge to fight, because he knew if he fought them he would be restrained. He had to stay free, so he could run when he recovered enough to move under his own power.

But *she* had been there for what seemed like the entire time, though logically he knew she had to have left the hospital sometimes. When he burned with fever, she washed his face with a cold cloth and fed him slivers of ice. She brushed his hair, stroked his forehead when his head ached so bad he thought his skull would crack; and took over bathing him when she saw how alarmed he became when the nurses did it. Somehow he could bear it better when she bathed him, though even in his illness he had been puzzled by his own reaction.

She touched him constantly, anticipating his needs so that his pillows were fluffed before he was aware of any discomfort, the heat adjusted before he became too hot or too cold, his legs and back massaged when the fever made him ache from head to toe. He was swamped by maternal fussing, enveloped by it. It terrified him, but Mary took advantage of his weakened state and ruthlessly overwhelmed him with her mothering, as if she were determined to pack enough loving care into those few days to make up for a lifetime of nothing.

Sometime during those fever-fogged days, he began to like the feel of her cool hand on his forehead, to listen for that sweet voice even when he couldn't drag his heavy eyelids open, and the sound of it reassured him on some deep, primitive level. Once he dreamed, he didn't know what, but he woke in a panic to find her arms around him, his head pillowed on her narrow shoulder as if he were a baby, her hand gently stroking his hair while she murmured reassuringly to him—and he drifted back to sleep feeling comforted and somehow...safe.

He was always startled, even now, by how small she was. Someone so relentlessly iron-willed should have been seven feet tall and weighed three hundred pounds; at least then it would have made sense that she could bulldoze the hospital staff, even the doctors, into doing what she wanted. She had estimated his age at fourteen, but even then he was over a full head taller than the dainty woman who took over his life, but in this case size didn't matter; he was as helpless against her as was the hospital staff.

There was nothing at all he could do to fight off his growing addiction to Mary Mackenzie's mothering, even though he knew he was developing a weakness, a vulnerability, that terrified him. He had never before cared for anyone or anything, instinctively knowing that to do so would expose his emotional underbelly. But knowledge and wariness couldn't protect him now; by the time he was well enough to leave the hospital, he loved the woman who had decided she was going to be his mother, loved her with all the blind helplessness of a small child.

When he left the hospital it had been with Mary and the big man, Wolf. Because he couldn't bear to leave her just yet, he braced himself to endure her family. Just for a little while, he had promised himself, just until he was stronger.

They had taken him to Mackenzie's Mountain, into their home, their arms, their hearts. A nameless boy had died that day beside the road, and Chance Mackenzie had been born in his place. When Chance had chosen a birthday— at his new sister Maris's insistence—he chose the day Mary found him, rather than the perhaps more logical date that his adoption was final.

He had never had anything, but after that day he had been flooded with…everything. He had always been hungry, but now there was food. He had been starved, too, for learning, and now there were books everywhere, because Mary was a teacher down to her fragile bones, and she had force-fed him knowledge as fast as he could gulp it down. He was accustomed to bedding down wherever and whenever he could, but now he had his own room, his own bed, a routine. He had clothes, new ones, bought specifically for him. No one else had ever worn them, and he hadn't had to steal them.

But most of all, he had always been alone, and abruptly he was surrounded by family. Now he had a mother and a father, *four* brothers, a little sister, a sister-in-law, an infant nephew, and all of them treated him as if he had been there from the beginning. He could still barely tolerate being touched, but the Mackenzie family touched *a lot*. Mary—Mom—was constantly hugging him, tousling his hair, kissing him good-night, fussing over him. Maris, his new sister, pestered the living hell out of him just the way she did her other brothers, then would throw her skinny arms around his waist and fiercely hug him, saying, "I'm so glad you're ours!"

He was always taken aback on those occasions, and would dart a wary glance at Wolf, the big man who was the head of the Mackenzie pack and who was now Chance's dad, too. What did he think, seeing his innocent little daughter hug someone like Chance? Wolf Mackenzie was no innocent; if he didn't know exactly what experiences had molded Chance, he still recognized the dangerous vein in the half-wild boy. Chance always wondered if those knowing eyes could see clear through him, see the blood on his hands, find in his mind the memory of the man he had killed when he was about ten.

Yes, the big half-breed had known very well the type of wild animal he had taken into his family and called son, had known and, like Mary, had loved him, anyway.

His early years had taught Chance how risky life was, taught him not to trust anyone, taught him that love would only make him vulnerable and that vulnerability could cost him his life. He had known all that, and still he hadn't been able to stop himself from loving the Mackenzies. It never stopped scaring him, this weakness in his armor, and yet when he was in the family bosom was the only time he was completely relaxed, because he knew he was safe with them. He couldn't stay away, couldn't distance himself now that he was a man who was more than capable of taking care of himself, because their love for him, and his for them, fed his soul.

He had stopped even trying to limit their access to his heart and instead turned his considerable talents to doing everything he could to make their world, their lives, as safe as possible. They kept making it tougher for him; the Mackenzies constantly assaulted him with expansions: his brothers married, giving him sisters-in-law to love, because his brothers loved them and they were part of the family now. Then there were the babies. When he first came into the family there was only John, Joe and Caroline's first son, newly born. But nephew had followed nephew, and somehow Chance, along with everyone else in the Mackenzie family, found himself rocking infants, changing diapers, holding bottles, letting a dimpled little hand clutch one of his fingers while tottering first steps were made…and each one of those dimpled hands had clutched his heart, too. He had no defense against them. There were twelve nephews now, and one niece against whom he was particularly helpless, much to everyone else's amusement.

Going home was always nerve-racking, and yet he yearned for his family. He was afraid for them, afraid for himself, because he didn't know if he could live now without the warmth the Mackenzies folded about him. His mind told him he would be better off if he gradually severed the ties and isolated himself from both the pleasure and the potential for pain, but his heart always led him home again.

Chapter 1

Chance loved motorcycles. The big beast between his legs throbbed with power as he roared along the narrow winding road, the wind in his hair, leaning his body into the curves with the beast so they were one, animal and machine. No other motorcycle in the world sounded like a Harley, with that deep, coughing rumble that vibrated through his entire body. Riding a motorcycle always gave him a hard-on, and his own visceral reaction to the speed and power never failed to amuse him.

Danger was sexy. Every warrior knew it, though it wasn't something people were going to read about in their Sunday newspaper magazines. His brother Josh freely admitted that landing a fighter on a carrier deck had always turned him on. "It falls just short of orgasm," was the way Josh put it. Joe, who could fly any jet built, refrained from commenting but always smiled a slow, knowing smile.

As for both Zane and himself, Chance knew there were times when each had emerged from certain tense situations, usually involving bullets, wanting nothing more than to have a woman beneath him. Chance's sexual need was ferocious at those times; his body was flooded with adrenaline and testosterone, he was *alive*, and he desperately needed a woman's soft body in which he could bury himself and release all the tension. Unfortunately, that need always had to wait: wait until he was in a secure position, maybe even in a different country entirely; wait until there was an available, willing woman at hand; and, most of all, wait until he had settled down enough that he could be relatively civilized in the sack.

But for now, there was only the Harley and himself, the rush of sweet mountain air on his face, and the inner mixture of joy and fear of going home. If Mom saw him riding the Harley without a helmet she would tear a strip off his hide, which was why he had the helmet with him, securely fastened behind the seat. He would put it on before sedately riding up the mountain to visit them. Dad wouldn't be fooled, but neither would he say anything, because Wolf Mackenzie knew what it was to fly high and wild.

He crested a ridge, and Zane's house came into view in the broad valley below. The house was large, with five bedrooms and four baths, but not ostentatious; Zane had instinctively built the house so it wouldn't attract undue attention. It didn't look as large as it was, because some of the rooms were underground. He had also built it to be as secure as possible, positioning it so he had an unrestricted view in all directions, but using natural formations of the land to block land access by all but the one road. The doors were steel, with state-of-the-art locks; the windows were shatterproof, and had cost a small fortune. Strategic walls had interior armor, and an emergency generator was installed in the basement. The basement also concealed another means of escape, if escape became necessary. Motion sensors were installed around the house, and as Chance wheeled the motorcycle into the driveway, he knew his arrival had already been signaled.

Zane didn't keep his family locked in a prison, but the security provisions were there if needed. Given their jobs, prudence demanded caution, and Zane had always prepared for emergencies, always had a backup plan.

Chance cut off the motor and sat for a minute, letting his senses return to normal while he ran a hand through his windswept hair. Then he kicked the stand down and leaned the Harley onto it, and dismounted much the way he would a horse. Taking a thin file from the storage compartment, he went up on the wide, shady porch.

It was a warm summer day, mid-August, and the sky was a cloudless clear blue. Horses grazed contentedly in the pasture, though a few of the more curious had come to the fence to watch with huge, liquid dark eyes as the noisy machine roared into the driveway. Bees buzzed around Barrie's flowers, and birds sang continuously in the trees. Wyoming. Home. It wasn't far away, Mackenzie's Mountain, with the sprawling house on the mountaintop where he had been given…life and everything else in this world that was important to him.

"The door's open." Zane's low, calm voice issued from the intercom beside the door. "I'm in the office."

Chance opened the door and went inside, his booted feet silent as he walked down the hall to Zane's office. With small clicks, the door locks automatically engaged behind him. The house was quiet, meaning Barrie and the kids weren't at home; if Nick was anywhere in the house she would have run squealing to him, hurling herself into his arms, chattering nonstop in her mangled English while holding his face clasped between both her little hands, making certain his attention didn't wander from her—as if he would dare look away. Nick was like a tiny package of unstable explosives; it was best to keep a weather eye on her.

The door to Zane's office was unexpectedly closed. Chance paused a moment, then opened it without knocking.

Zane was behind the desk, computer on, windows open to the warm, fresh air. He gave his brother one of his rare, warm smiles. "Watch where you step," he advised. "Munchkins on deck."

Automatically Chance looked down, checking out the floor, but he didn't see either of the twins. "Where?"

Zane leaned back in his chair a little, looking around for his offspring. Spotting them, he said, "Under the desk. When they heard me let you in, they hid."

Chance raised his eyebrows. To his knowledge, the ten-month-old twins weren't in the habit of hiding from anyone or anything. He looked more carefully and saw four plump, dimpled baby hands peeping from under the cover of Zane's desk. "They aren't very good at it," he observed. "I can see their hands."

"Give them a break, they're new at this stuff. They've only started doing it this week. They're playing Attack."

"Attack?" Fighting the urge to laugh, Chance said, "What am I supposed to do?"

"Just stand there. They'll burst from cover as fast as they can crawl and grab you by the ankles."

"Any biting involved?"

"Not yet."

"Okay. What are they going to do with me once they have me captured?"

"They haven't gotten to that part yet. For now, they just

pull themselves up and stand there giggling." Zane scratched his jaw, considering. "Maybe they'll sit on your feet to hold you down, but for the most part they like standing too much to settle for sitting."

The attack erupted. Even with Zane's warning, Chance was a little surprised. They were remarkably quiet, for babies. He had to admire their precision; they launched themselves from under the desk at a rapid crawl, plump little legs pumping, and with identical triumphant crows attached themselves to his ankles. Dimpled hands clutched his jeans. The one on the left plopped down on his foot for a second, then thought better of the tactic and twisted around to begin hauling himself to an upright position. Baby arms wrapped around his knees, and the two little conquerors squealed with delight, their bubbling chuckles eliciting laughter from both men.

"Cool," Chance said admiringly. "Predator babies." He tossed the file onto Zane's desk and leaned down to scoop the little warriors into his arms, settling each diapered bottom on a muscular forearm. Cameron and Zack grinned at him, six tiny white baby teeth shining in each identical dimpled face, and immediately they began patting his face with their fat little hands, pulling his ears, delving into his shirt pockets. It was like being attacked by two squirming, remarkably heavy marshmallows.

"Good God," he said in astonishment. "They weigh a ton." He hadn't expected them to have grown so much in the two months since he had seen them.

"They're almost as big as Nick. She still outweighs them, but I swear they feel heavier." The twins were sturdy and strongly built, the little boys already showing the size of the

Mackenzie males, while Nick was as dainty as her grand-mother Mary.

"Where are Barrie and Nick?" Chance asked, missing his pretty sister-in-law and exuberant, cheerfully diabolic niece.

"We had a shoe crisis. Don't ask."

"How do you have a shoe crisis?" Chance asked, unable to resist. He sat down in a big, comfortable chair across from Zane's desk, setting the babies more comfortably in his lap. They lost interest in pulling his ears and began babbling to each other, reaching out, entwining their arms and legs as if they sought the closeness they had known while forming in the womb. Chance unconsciously stroked them, enjoy-ing the softness of their skin, the feel of squirming babies in his arms. All the Mackenzie babies grew up accustomed to being constantly, lovingly touched by the entire ex-tended family.

Zane laced his hands behind his head, his big, powerful body relaxed. "First you have a three-year-old who loves her shiny, black, patent leather Sunday shoes. Then you make the severe tactical error of letting her watch *The Wizard of Oz*." His stern mouth twitched, and his pale eyes glittered with amusement.

Chance's agile mind immediately made the connection, and his acquaintance with the three-year-old in question allowed him to make a logical assumption: Nick had de-cided she had to have a pair of red shoes. "What did she use to try to dye them?"

Zane sighed. "Lipstick, what else?" Each and every young Mackenzie had had an incident with lipstick. It was a family tradition, one John had started when, at the age of two, he had used his mother's favorite lipstick to recolor the impressive rows of fruit salad on Joe's dress uniform.

Caroline had been impressively outraged, because the shade had been discontinued and finding a new tube had been much more difficult than replacing the small colored bars that represented medals Joe had earned and services he had performed.

"You couldn't just wipe it off?" The twins had discovered his belt buckle and zipper, and Chance moved the busy little hands that were trying to undress him. They began squirming to get down, and he leaned over to set them on the floor.

"Close the door," Zane instructed, "or they'll escape."

Leaning back, Chance stretched out a long arm and closed the door, just in time. The two diaper-clad escape artists had almost reached it. Deprived of freedom, they plopped down on their padded bottoms and considered the situation, then launched themselves in crawling patrol of the perimeters of the room.

"I *could* have wiped it off," Zane continued, his tone bland, "if I had known about it. Unfortunately, Nick cleaned the shoes herself. She put them in the dishwasher."

Chance threw back his head with a shout of laughter.

"Barrie bought her a new pair of shoes yesterday. Well, you know how Nick's always been so definite about what she wants to wear. She took one look at the shoes, said they were ugly, *even though they were just like the ones she ruined*, and refused to even try them on."

"To be accurate," Chance corrected, "what she said was that they were 'ugwy.'"

Zane conceded the point. "She's getting better with her Ls, though. She practices, saying the really important words, like lollipop, over and over to herself."

"Can she say 'Chance' yet, instead of 'Dance'?" Chance asked, because Nick stubbornly refused to even acknowledge she couldn't say his name. She insisted everyone else was saying it wrong.

Zane's expression was totally deadpan. "Not a chance."

Chance groaned at the pun, wishing he hadn't asked. "I gather Barrie has taken my little darling shopping, so she can pick out her own shoes."

"Exactly." Zane glanced over to check on his roaming offspring. As if they had been waiting for his parental notice, first Cam and then Zack plopped down on their butts and gave brief warning cries, all the while watching their father expectantly.

"Feeding time," Zane said, swiveling his chair around so he could fetch two bottles from a small cooler behind the desk. He handed one to Chance. "Grab a kid."

"You're prepared, as always," Chance commented as he went over to the twins and leaned down to lift one in his arms. Holding the baby up, he peered briefly at the scowling little face to make sure he had the one he thought he had. It was Zack, all right. Chance couldn't say exactly how he knew which twin was which, how anyone in the family knew, because the babies were so identical their pediatrician had suggested putting ID anklets on them. But they each had such definite personalities, which were reflected in their expressions, that no one in the family ever confused one twin for the other.

"I have to be prepared. Barrie weaned them last month, and they don't take kindly to having to wait for dinner."

Zack's round blue eyes were fiercely focused on the bottle in Chance's hand. "Why did she wean them so early?" Chance asked as he resumed his seat and settled the baby in the crook of his left arm. "She nursed Nick until she was a year old."

"You'll see," Zane said dryly, settling Cam on his lap.

As soon as Chance brought the bottle within reach of Zack's fat little hands the baby made a grab for it, guiding it to his rapacious, open mouth. He clamped down ferociously on the nipple. Evidently deciding to let his uncle hold the bottle, he nevertheless made certain the situation was stabilized by clutching Chance's wrist with both hands, and wrapping both chubby legs around Chance's forearm. Then he began to growl as he sucked, pausing only to swallow.

An identical growling noise came from Zane's lap. Chance looked over to see his brother's arm captured in the same manner as the two little savages held on to their meals.

Milk bubbled around Zack's rosebud mouth, and Chance blinked as six tiny white teeth gnawed on the plastic nipple.

"Hell, no wonder she weaned you!"

Zack didn't pause in his gnawing, sucking and growling, but he did flick an absurdly arrogant glance at his uncle before returning his full attention to filling his little belly.

Zane was laughing softly, and he lifted Cam enough that he could nuzzle one of the chubby legs so determinedly wrapped around his arm. Cam paused to scowl at the interruption, then changed his mind and instead favored his father with a dimpled, milky smile. The next second the smile was gone and he attacked the bottle again.

Zack's fuzzy black hair was as soft as silk against Chance's arm. Babies were a pure tactile pleasure, he thought, though he hadn't been of that opinion the first time he'd held one. The baby in question had been John, screaming his head off from the misery of teething.

Chance hadn't been with the Mackenzies long, only a few months, and he had still been extremely wary of all these people. He had managed—barely—to control his instinct to attack whenever someone touched him, but he still jumped like a startled wild animal. Joe and Caroline came to visit, and from the expressions on their faces when they entered the house, it had been a very long trip. Even Joe, normally so controlled and unflappable, was frustrated by his futile efforts to calm his son, and Caroline had been completely frazzled by a situation she couldn't handle with her usual impeccable logic. Her blond hair had been mussed, and her green eyes expressed an amazing mixture of concern and outrage.

As she had walked by Chance, she suddenly wheeled and deposited the screaming baby in his arms. Startled, alarmed, he tried to jerk back, but before he knew it he was in sole possession of the wiggling, howling little human. "Here," she said with relief and utmost confidence. "You get him calmed down."

Chance had panicked. It was a wonder he hadn't dropped the baby. He'd never held one before, and he didn't know what to do with it. Another part of him was astounded that Caroline would entrust her adored child to *him*, the mongrel stray Mary—Mom—had brought home with her. Why couldn't these people see what he was? Why couldn't they figure out he had lived wild in a kill-or-be-killed world, and that they would be safer if they kept their distance from him?

Instead, no one seemed to think it unusual or alarming that he was holding the baby, even though in his panic he held John almost at arm's length, clutched between his two strong young hands.

But blessed quiet fell in the house. John was startled out of his screaming. He stared interestedly at this new person and kicked his legs. Automatically Chance changed his grip on the baby, settling him in the cradle of one arm as he had seen the others do. The kid was drooling. A tiny bib was fastened around his neck, and Chance used it to wipe away most of the slobber. John saw this opportunity and grabbed Chance by the thumb, immediately carrying the digit to his mouth and chomping down. Chance had jumped at the force of the hard little gums, with two tiny, sharp teeth already breaking the surface. He grimaced at the pain, but hung in there, letting John use his thumb as a teething ring until Mom rescued him by bringing a cold wet washcloth for the baby to chew.

Chance had expected then to be relieved of baby duty, because Mom usually couldn't wait to get her hands on her grandson. But that day everyone had seemed content to leave John in his hands, even the kid himself, and after a while Chance calmed down enough to start walking around and pointing out things of interest to his little pal, all of which John obediently studied while gnawing on the relief-giving washcloth.

That had been his indoctrination to the ways of babies, and from that day on he had been a sucker for the parade of nephews his virile brothers and fertile sisters-in-law had produced on a regular basis. He seemed to be getting even worse, because with Zane's three he was total mush.

"By the way, Maris is pregnant."

Chance's head jerked up, and a wide grin lit his tanned face. His baby sister had been married nine whole months and had been fretting because she hadn't immediately gotten pregnant.

"When is it due?" He always ruthlessly arranged things so he could be home when a new Mackenzie arrived.

Technically, this one would be a MacNeil, but that was a minor point.

"March. She says she'll be crazy before then, because Mac won't let her out of his sight."

Chance chuckled. Other than her father and brothers, Mac was the only man Maris had ever met whom she couldn't intimidate, which was one of the reasons she loved him so much. If Mac had decided he was going to ride herd on Maris during her pregnancy, she had little hope of escaping on one of those long, hard rides she so loved.

Zane nodded toward the file on his desk. "You going to tell me about it?"

Chance knew Zane was asking about more than the contents of the file. He was asking why it hadn't been transmitted by computer, instead of Chance personally bringing a hard copy. Zane knew his brother's schedule; he was the only person, other than Chance himself, who did, so he knew Chance was currently supposed to be in France. He was also asking why he hadn't been notified of Chance's change in itinerary, why his brother hadn't made a simple phone call to let him know he was coming.

"I didn't want to risk even a hint of this leaking out."

Zane's eyebrows rose. "We have security problems?"

"Nothing that I know of," Chance said. "It's what I don't know about that worries me. But, like I said, no one else can hear even a whisper of this. It's between us."

"Now you've made me curious." Zane's cool blue eyes gleamed with interest.

"Crispin Hauer has a daughter."

Zane didn't straighten from his relaxed position, but his expression hardened. Crispin Hauer had been number one on their target list for years, but the terrorist was as elusive as he was vicious. They had yet to find any way to get close to him, any vulnerability they could exploit or bait they could use to lure him into a trap. There was a record of a marriage in London some thirty-five years ago, but Hauer's wife, formerly Pamela Vickery, had disappeared, and no trace of her had ever been found. Chance, along with everyone else, had assumed the woman died soon after the marriage, either by Hauer's hand or by his enemies'.

"Who is she?" Zane asked. "*Where* is she?"

"Her name is Sonia Miller, and she's here, in America."

"I know that name," Zane said, his gaze sharpening.

Chance nodded. "Specifically, she's the courier who was supposedly robbed of her package last week in Chicago."

Zane didn't miss the "supposedly," but then, he never missed anything. "You think it was a setup?"

"I think it's a damn good possibility. I found the link when I checked into her background."

"Hauer would have known she'd be investigated after losing a package, especially one containing aerospace documents. Why take the risk?"

"He might not have thought we would find anything. She was adopted. Hal and Eleanor Miller are listed as her parents, and they're clean as a whistle. I wouldn't have known she was adopted if I hadn't tried to pull up her birth certificate on the computer. Guess what—Hal and Eleanor never had any children. Little Sonia Miller didn't have a birth certificate. So I did some digging and found the adoption file—"

Zane's eyebrows rose. Open adoptions had caused so many problems that the trend had veered sharply back to closed files, which, coupled with electronic privacy laws and safeguards, had made it damn difficult to even locate those closed files, much less get into them. "Did you leave any fingerprints?"

"Nothing that will lead back to us. I went through a couple of relays, then hacked into the Internal Revenue and accessed the file from their system."

Zane grinned. If anyone did notice the electronic snooping, it likely wouldn't even be mentioned; no one messed with the tax people.

Zack had finished his bottle; his ferocious grip on it slackened, and his head lolled against Chance's arm as he briefly struggled against sleep. Automatically Chance lifted the baby to his shoulder and began patting his back. "Ms. Miller has been employed as a courier for a little over five years. She has an apartment in Chicago, but her neighbors say she's seldom there. I have to think this is a long-term setup, that she's been working with her father from the beginning."

Zane nodded. They had to assume the worst, because it was their job to do so. Only by anticipating the worst could they be prepared to handle it.

"Do you have anything in mind?" he asked, taking the bottle from Cam's slackened grip and gently lifting the sleeping baby to his own shoulder.

"Getting next to her. Getting her to trust me."

"She's not going to be the trusting sort."

"I have a plan," Chance said, and grinned, because that was usually Zane's line.

Zane grinned in return, then paused as a small security console in the wall dinged a soft alarm. He glanced at the security monitor. "Brace yourself," he advised. "Barrie and Nick are home."

Seconds later the front door opened and a shriek filled the house. "Unca *Dance*! UncaDanceUncaDanceUnca-

Dance!" The chant was punctuated by the sound of tiny feet running and jumping down the hall as Nick's celebration of his visit came closer. Chance leaned back in his chair and opened the office door a bare second before Nick barreled through it, her entire little body quivering with joy and eagerness.

She hurled herself at him, and he managed to catch her with his free arm, dragging her onto his lap. She paused to bestow a big-sisterly kiss and a pat on the back of Zack's head—never mind that he was almost as big as she was—then turned all her fierce attention to Chance.

"Are you staying dis time?" she demanded, even as she lifted her face for him to kiss. He did, nuzzling her soft cheek and neck and making her giggle, inhaling the faint sweet scent of baby that still clung to her.

"Just for a few days," he said, to her disappointment. She was old enough now to notice his long and frequent absences, and whenever she saw him she tried to convince him to stay.

She scowled; then, being Nick, she decided to move on to more important matters. Her face brightened. "Den can I wide your moborcycle?"

Alarm flared through him. "No," he said firmly. "You can't ride it, sit on it, lean on it, or put any of your toys on it *unless I'm with you.*" With Nick, it was best to close all the loopholes. She seldom disobeyed a direct order, but she was a genius at finding cracks to slip through. Another possibility occurred to him. "You can't put Cam or Zack on it, either." He doubted she could lift either of them, but he wasn't taking any risks.

"Thank you," Barrie said dryly, entering the office in time to catch his addendum. She leaned down to kiss him on the cheek, at the same time lifting Zack from his arms so he could protect himself from Nick's feet. All the Mackenzie males, at one time or another, had fallen victim to a tiny foot in the crotch.

"Mission accomplished?" Zane asked, leaning back in his chair and smiling at his wife with that lazy look in his pale eyes that said he liked what he was seeing.

"Not without some drama and convincing, but, yes, mission accomplished." She pushed a feather lock of red hair out of her eyes. As always, she looked stylish, though she was wearing nothing dressier than beige slacks and a white sleeveless blouse that set off her slim, lightly tanned arms. You could take the girl out of the finishing school, Chance thought admiringly, but you could never take the finishing school out of the girl, and Barrie had gone to the most exclusive one in the world.

Nick was still focused on negotiating riding rights on the motorcycle. She caught his face between her hands and leaned down so her nose practically touched his, insuring his complete attention. He nearly laughed aloud at the fierce intent in her expression. "I wet you wide my twicycle," she said, evidently deciding to cajole instead of demand.

"Somehow I missed that," Zane murmured in amusement, while Barrie laughed softly.

"You *offered* to let me ride your tricycle," Chance corrected. "But I'm too big to ride a tricycle, and you're too little to ride a motorcycle."

"Den when *can* I wide it?" She made her blue eyes wide and winsome.

"When you get your driver's license."

That stymied her. She had no idea what a driver's license was, or how to get it. She stuck a finger in her mouth while she pondered this situation, and Chance tried to divert her interest. "Hey! Aren't those new shoes you're wearing?"

Like magic, her face brightened again. She wriggled around so he could hold one foot up so close to his face she almost kicked him in the nose. "Dey're so *pwetty*," she crooned in delight.

He caught the little foot in his big hand, admiring the shine of the black patent leather. "Wow, that's so shiny I can see my face in it." He pretended to inspect his teeth, which set her to giggling.

Zane rose to his feet. "We'll put the boys down for their naps while you have her occupied."

Keeping Nick occupied wasn't a problem; she was never at a loss for something to say or do. He curled one silky black strand of her hair around his finger while she chattered about her new shoes, Grampa's new horses, and what Daddy had said when he hit his thumb with a hammer. She cheerfully repeated exactly what Daddy had said, making Chance choke.

"But I'm not 'posed to say dat," she said, giving him a solemn look. "Dat's a weally, weally bad word."

"Yeah," he said, his voice strained. "It is."

"I'm not 'posed to say 'damn,' or 'hell,' or 'ass,' or—"

"Then you shouldn't be saying them now." He managed to inject a note of firmness in his tone, though it was a struggle to keep from laughing.

She looked perplexed. "Den how can I tell you what dey are?"

"Does Daddy know what the bad words are?"

The little head nodded emphatically. "He knows dem *all*."

"I'll ask him to tell me, so I'll know which words not to say."

"Otay." She sighed. "But don't hit him too hard."

"Hit him?"

"Dat's de only time he says *dat* word, when he hits his dumb wid de hammer. He said so."

Chance managed to turn his laugh into a cough. Zane was an ex-SEAL; his language was as salty as the sea he was so at home in, and Chance had heard "dat word," and worse, many times from his brother. But Mom had also instilled strict courtesy in all her children, so their language was circumspect in front of women and children. Zane must not have known Nick was anywhere near him when he hit his thumb, or no amount of pain could have made him say that in her hearing. Chance only hoped she forgot it before she started kindergarten.

"Aunt Mawis is goin' to have a baby," Nick said, scrambling up to stand in his lap, her feet braced on his thighs. Chance put both hands around her to steady her, though his aid probably wasn't needed; Nick had the balance of an acrobat.

"I know. Your daddy told me."

Nick scowled at not being the first to impart the news. "She's goin' to foal in de spwing," she announced.

He couldn't hold back the laughter this time. He gathered the little darling close to him and stood, whirling her around and making her shriek with laughter as she clung to his neck. He laughed until his eyes were wet. God, he loved this child, who in the three short years of her life had taught them all to be on their toes at all times, because there was no telling what she was going to do or say. It took the entire Mackenzie family to ride herd on her.

Suddenly she heaved a sigh. "When's de spwing? Is it a wong, wong time away?"

"Very long," he said gravely. Seven months was an eternity to a three-year-old.

"Will I be old?"

He put on a sympathetic face and nodded. "You'll be four."

She looked both horrified and resigned. "Four," she said mournfully. "Whodadunkit?"

When he stopped laughing this time, he wiped his eyes and asked, "Who taught you to say *whodathunkit?*"

"John," she said promptly.

"Did he teach you anything else?"

She nodded.

"What? Can you remember it?"

She nodded.

"Will you tell me what they are?"

She rolled her eyes up and studied the ceiling for a moment, then gave him a narrow-eyed look. "Will you wet me wide your moborcycle?"

Damn, she was bargaining! He trembled with fear at the thought of what she would be like when she was sixteen. "No," he said firmly. "If you got hurt, your mommy and daddy would cry, Grampa and Gamma would cry, I would cry, Aunt Maris would cry, Mac would cry, Unca Mike would cry—"

She looked impressed at this litany of crying and interrupted before he could name everyone in the family. "I can wide a horse, Unca Dance, so why can't I wide your moborcycle?"

God, she was relentless. Where in the hell were Zane and Barrie? They'd had plenty of time to put the twins down for their naps. If he knew Zane, his brother was taking advantage of having a baby-sitter for Nick to get in some sexy time with his wife; Zane was always prepared to use a fluid situation to his advantage.

It was another ten minutes before Zane strolled back into the office, his eyes slightly heavy-lidded and his hard face subtly relaxed. Chance scowled at his brother. He'd spent the ten minutes trying to talk Nick into telling him what John had taught her, but she wasn't budging from her initial negotiation. "It's about time," he groused.

"Hey, I hurried," Zane protested mildly.

"Yeah, right."

"As much as possible," he added, smiling. He smoothed his big hand over his daughter's shining black hair. "Have you kept Uncle Chance entertained?"

She nodded. "I told him de weally, weally bad word you said when you hit your dumb."

Zane looked pained, then stern. "How did you tell him when you aren't supposed to say the word?"

She stuck her finger in her mouth and began studying the ceiling again.

"Nick." Zane plucked her from Chance's arms. "Did you say the word?"

Her lower lip stuck out a little, but she nodded, owning up to her transgression.

"Then you can't have a bedtime story tonight. You promised you wouldn't say it."

"I'm sowwy," she said, winding her arms around his neck and laying her head on his shoulder.

Gently he rubbed his hand up and down her back. "I know you are, sweetheart, but you have to keep your promises." He set her on her feet. "Go find Mommy."

When she was gone, out of curiosity Chance asked, "Why didn't you tell her that she couldn't watch television, instead of taking away the bedtime story?"

"We don't want to make television attractive by using it

as a treat or a privilege. Why? Are you taking notes on being a parent?"

Appalled, Chance said, "Not in this lifetime."

"Yeah? Fate has a way of jumping up and biting you on the ass when you least expect it."

"Well, my ass is currently bite-free, and I intend to keep it that way." He nodded at the file on Zane's desk. "We have some planning to do."

Chapter 2

This whole assignment was a tribute to Murphy's Law, Sunny Miller thought in disgust as she sat in the Salt Lake City airport, waiting for her flight to be called—if it were called at all, which she was beginning to doubt. This was her fifth airport of the day, and she was still almost a thousand miles from her destination, which was Seattle. She was *supposed* to have been on a direct flight from Atlanta to Seattle, but that flight had been canceled due to mechanical problems and the passengers routed on to other flights, none of which were direct.

From Atlanta she had gone to Cincinnati, from Cincinnati to Chicago, from Chicago to Denver, and from Denver to Salt Lake City. At least she was moving west instead of backtracking, and the flight from Salt Lake City, assuming it ever started boarding, was supposed to actually land in Seattle.

The way her day had gone, she expected it to crash instead.

She was tired, she had been fed nothing but peanuts all day, and she was afraid to go get anything to eat in case her flight was called and the plane got loaded and in the air in record time, leaving her behind. When Murphy was in control, anything was possible. She made a mental note to find this Murphy guy and punch him in the nose.

Her normal good humor restored by the whimsy, she re-settled herself in the plastic seat and took out the paperback book she had been reading. She was tired, she was hungry, but she wasn't going to let the stress get to her. If there was one thing she was good at, it was making the best of a situation. Some trips were smooth as silk, and some were a pain in the rear; so long as the good and the bad were balanced, she could cope.

Out of ingrained habit, she kept the strap of her soft leather briefcase looped around her neck, held across her body so it couldn't easily be jerked out of her grasp. Some couriers might handcuff the briefcase or satchel to their wrists, but her company was of the opinion that handcuffs drew unwanted attention; it was better to blend in with the horde of business travelers than to stand out. Handcuffs practically shouted "Important stuff inside!"

After what had happened in Chicago the month before, Sunny was doubly wary and also kept one hand on the briefcase. She had no idea what was in it, but that didn't matter; her job was to get the contents from point A to point B. When the briefcase had been jerked off her shoulder by a green-haired punk in Chicago last month, she had been both humiliated and furious. She was *always* careful, but evidently not careful enough, and now she had a big blotch on her record.

On a very basic level, she was alarmed that she had been caught off guard. She had been taught from the cradle to be both prepared and cautious, to be alert to what was going on around her; if a green-haired punk could get the best of her, then she was neither as prepared nor alert as she had thought. When one slip could mean the difference between life and death, there was no room for error.

Just remembering the incident made her uneasy. She returned the book to her carry-on bag, preferring to keep her attention on the people around her.

Her stomach growled. She had food in her carry-on, but that was for emergencies, and this didn't qualify. She watched the gate, where the two airline reps were patiently answering questions from impatient passengers. From the dissatisfied expressions on the passengers' faces as they returned to their seats, the news wasn't good; logically, she should have enough time to find something to eat.

She glanced at her watch: one-forty-five p.m., local time. She had to have the contents of the briefcase in Seattle by nine p.m. Pacific time tonight, which should have been a breeze, but the way things were going, she was losing faith the assignment could be completed on time. She hated the idea of calling the office to report another failure, even one that wasn't her fault. If the airline didn't get on the ball soon, though, she would have to do something. The customer needed to know if the packet wasn't going to arrive as scheduled.

If the news on the flight delay hadn't improved by the time she returned from eating, she would see about transferring to another airline, though she had already considered that option and none of the possibilities looked encouraging; she was in flight-connection hell. If she couldn't work out something, she would have to make that phone call.

Taking a firm grip on the briefcase with one hand and her carry-on bag with the other, she set off down the concourse in search of food that didn't come from a vending machine. Arriving passengers were pouring out of a gate to her left, and she moved farther to the right to avoid the crush. The maneuver didn't work; someone jostled her left shoulder, and she instinctively looked around to see who it was.

No one was there. A split-second reaction, honed by years of looking over her shoulder, saved her. She automatically tightened her grip on the briefcase just as she felt a tug on the strap, and the leather fell limply from her shoulder.

Damn it, not again!

She ducked and spun, swinging her heavy carry-on bag at her assailant. She caught a glimpse of feral dark eyes and a mean, unshaven face; then her attention locked on his hands. The knife he had used to slice the briefcase strap was in one hand, and he already had his other hand on the briefcase, trying to jerk it away from her. The carry-on bag hit him on the shoulder, staggering him, but he didn't release his grip.

Sunny didn't even think of screaming, or of being scared; she was too angry for either reaction, and both would have splintered her concentration. Instead, she wound up for another swing, aiming the bag for the hand holding the knife.

Around her she heard raised voices, full of confused alarm as people tried to dodge around the disturbance, and jostled others instead. Few, if any, of them would have any idea what the ruckus was about. Vision was hampered; things were happening too fast. She couldn't rely on anyone coming to help, so she ignored the noise, all her attention centered on the cretin whose dirty hand clutched her briefcase.

Whap! She hit him again, but still he held on to the knife.

"Bitch," he snarled, his knife-hand darting toward her.

She jumped back, and her fingers slipped on the leather. Triumphantly he jerked it away from her. Sunny grabbed for the dangling strap and caught it, but the knife made a silver flash as he sliced downward, separating the strap from the briefcase. The abrupt release of tension sent her staggering back.

The cretin whirled and ran. Catching her balance, Sunny shouted, "Stop him!" and ran in pursuit. Her long skirt had a slit up the left side that let her reach full stride, but the cretin not only had a head start, he had longer legs. Her carry-on bag banged against her legs, further hampering her, but she didn't dare leave it behind. Doggedly she kept running, even though she knew it was useless. Despair knotted her stomach. Her only prayer was that someone in the crowd would play hero and stop him.

Her prayer was abruptly answered.

Up ahead, a tall man standing with his back to the concourse turned and glanced almost negligently in the direction of the ruckus. The cretin was almost abreast of him. Sunny drew breath to yell out another "Stop him," even though she knew the cretin would be past before the man could react. She never got the words out of her mouth.

The tall man took in with one glance what was happening, and in a movement as smooth and graceful as a ballet pirouette, he shifted, pivoted and lashed out with one booted foot. The kick landed squarely on the cretin's right knee, taking his leg out from under him. He cart-wheeled once and landed flat on his back, his arms flung over his head. The briefcase skidded across the concourse before bouncing against the wall, then back into the path of a stream of passengers. One man hopped over the briefcase, while others stepped around it.

Sunny immediately swerved in that direction, snatching up the briefcase before any other quick-fingered thief could grab it, but she kept one eye on the action.

In another of those quick, graceful movements, the tall man bent and flipped the cretin onto his stomach, then wrenched both arms up high behind his back and held them with one big hand.

"Owww!" the cretin howled. "You bastard, you're breaking my arms!"

The name-calling got his arms roughly levered even higher. He howled again, this time wordlessly and at a much higher pitch.

"Watch your language," said his captor.

Sunny skidded to a halt beside him. "Be careful," she said breathlessly. "He had a knife."

"I saw it. It landed over there when he fell." The man didn't look up but jerked his chin to the left. As he spoke he efficiently stripped the cretin's belt from its loop and wound the leather in a simple but effective snare around his captive's wrists. "Pick it up before someone grabs it and disappears. Use two fingers, and touch only the blade."

He seemed to know what he was doing, so Sunny obeyed without question. She took a tissue out of her skirt pocket and gingerly picked up the knife as he had directed, being careful not to smear any fingerprints on the handle.

"What do I do with it?"

"Hold it until Security gets here." He angled his dark head toward the nearest airline employee, a transportation escort who was hovering nervously as if unsure what to do. "Security *has* been called, hasn't it?"

"Yes, sir," said the escort, his eyes round with excitement.

Sunny squatted beside her rescuer. "Thank you," she said. She indicated the briefcase, with the two dangling pieces of its strap. "He cut the strap and grabbed it away from me."

"Any time," he said, turning his head to smile at her and giving her her first good look at him.

Her first look was almost her last. Her stomach fluttered. Her heart leaped. Her lungs seized. *Wow*, she thought, and tried to take a deep breath without being obvious about it.

He was probably the best-looking man she had ever seen, without being pretty in any sense of the word. *Drop-dead handsome* was the phrase that came to mind. Slightly dazed, she took in the details: black hair, a little too long and a little too shaggy, brushing the collar at the back of his battered brown leather jacket; smooth, honey-tanned skin; eyes of such a clear, light brown that they looked golden, framed by thick black lashes. As if that wasn't enough, he had also been blessed with a thin, straight nose, high cheekbones, and such clearly delineated, well-shaped lips that she had the wild impulse to simply lean forward and kiss him.

She already knew he was tall, and now she had the time to notice the broad shoulders, flat belly and lean hips. Mother Nature had been in a *really* good mood when he was made. He should have been too perfect and pretty to be real, but there was a toughness in his expression that was purely masculine, and a thin, crescent-shaped scar on his left cheekbone only added to the impression. Looking down, she saw another scar slashing across the back of his right hand, a raised line that was white against his tanned skin.

The scars in no way detracted from his attractiveness; the evidence of rough living only accentuated it, stating unequivocally that this was a *man*.

She was so bemused that it took her several seconds to realize he was watching her with mingled amusement and interest. She felt her cheeks heat in embarrassment at being caught giving him a blatant once-over. Okay, twice-over.

But she didn't have time to waste in admiration, so she forced her attention back to more pressing concerns. The cretin was grunting and making noises designed to show he was in agony, but she doubted he was in any great pain, despite his bound hands and the way her hero had a knee pressed into the small of his back. She had the briefcase back, but the cretin still presented her with a dilemma: It was her civic duty to stay and press charges against him, but if her flight left any time soon, she might very well miss it while she was answering questions and filling out forms.

"Jerk," she muttered at him. "If I miss my flight…"

"When is it?" asked her hero.

"I don't know. It's been delayed, but they could begin boarding at any time. I'll check at the gate and be right back."

He nodded with approval. "I'll hold your friend here and deal with Security until you get back."

"I'll only be a minute," she said, and walked swiftly back to her gate. The counter was now jammed with angry or upset travelers, their mood far more agitated than when she had left just a few moments before. Swiftly she glanced at the board, where CANCELED had been posted in place of the DELAYED sign.

"Damn," she said, under her breath. "Damn, damn, damn." There went her last hope for getting to Seattle in time to complete her assignment, unless there was another miracle waiting for her. Two miracles in one day was probably too much to ask for, though.

She needed to call in, she thought wearily, but first she

could deal with the cretin and airport security. She retraced her steps and found that the little drama was now mobile; the cretin was on his feet, being frog-marched under the control of two airport policemen into an office where they would be out of the view of curious passersby.

Her hero was waiting for her, and when he spotted her, he said something to the security guys, then began walking to meet her.

Her heart gave a little flutter of purely feminine appreciation. My, he was good to look at. His clothes were nothing special: a black T-shirt under the old leather jacket, faded jeans and scuffed boots, but he wore them with a confidence and grace that said he was utterly comfortable. Sunny allowed herself a moment of regret that she would never see him again after this little contretemps was handled, but then she pushed it away. She couldn't take the chance of letting anything develop into a relationship—assuming there was anything there to develop—with him or anyone else. She never even let anything start, because it wouldn't be fair to the guy, and she didn't need the emotional wear and tear, either. Maybe one day she would be able to settle down, date, eventually find someone to love and marry and maybe have kids, but not now. It was too dangerous.

When he reached her, he took her arm with old-fashioned courtesy. "Everything okay with your flight?"

"In a way. It's been canceled," she said ruefully. "I have to be in Seattle tonight, but I don't think I'm going to make it. Every flight I've had today has either been delayed or rerouted, and now there's no other flight that would get me there in time."

"Charter a plane," he said as they walked toward the office where the cretin had been taken.

She chuckled. "I don't know if my boss will spring for that kind of money, but it's an idea. I have to call in, anyway, when we're finished here."

"If it makes any difference to him, I'm available right now. I was supposed to meet a customer on that last flight in from Dallas, but he wasn't on the plane, and he hasn't contacted me, so I'm free."

"You're a charter pilot?" She couldn't believe it. It—*he*—was too good to be true. Maybe she did qualify for two miracles in one day after all.

He looked down at her and smiled, making a tiny dimple dance in his cheek. God, he had a dimple, too! Talk about overkill! He held out his hand. "Chance McCall—pilot, thief-catcher, jack-of-all-trades—at your service, ma'am."

She laughed and shook his hand, noticing that he was careful not to grip her fingers too hard. Considering the strength she could feel in that tough hand, she was grateful for his restraint. Some men weren't as considerate. "Sunny Miller, tardy courier and target of thieves. It's nice to meet you, Mr. McCall."

"Chance," he said easily. "Let's get this little problem taken care of, then you can call your boss and see if he thinks a charter flight is just what the doctor ordered."

He opened the door of the unmarked office for her, and she stepped inside to find the two security officers, a woman dressed in a severe gray suit and the cretin, who had been handcuffed to his chair. The cretin glared at her when she came in, as if all this were her fault instead of his.

"You lyin' bitch—" the cretin began.

Chance McCall reached out and gripped the cretin's shoulder. "Maybe you didn't get the message before," he said in that easy way of his that in no way disguised the iron behind it, "but I don't care for your language. Clean it up." He didn't issue a threat, just an order—and his grip on the cretin's shoulder didn't look gentle.

The cretin flinched and gave him an uneasy look, perhaps remembering how effortlessly this man had manhandled him before. Then he looked at the two airport policemen, as if expecting them to step in. The two men crossed their arms and grinned. Deprived of allies, the cretin opted for silence.

The gray-suited woman looked as if she wanted to protest the rough treatment of her prisoner, but she evidently decided to get on with the business at hand. "I'm Margaret Fayne, director of airport security. I assume you're going to file charges?"

"Yes," Sunny said.

"Good," Ms. Fayne said in approval. "I'll need statements from both of you."

"Any idea how long this will take?" Chance asked. "Ms. Miller and I are pressed for time."

"We'll try to hurry things along," Ms. Fayne assured him.

Whether Ms. Fayne was super-efficient or yet another small miracle took place, the paperwork was completed in what Sunny considered to be record time. Not much more than half an hour passed before the cretin was taken away in handcuffs, all the paperwork was prepared and signed, and Sunny and Chance McCall were free to go, having done their civic duty.

He waited beside her while she called the office and explained the situation. The supervisor, Wayne Beesham, wasn't happy, but bowed to reality.

"What's this pilot's name again?" he asked.

"Chance McCall."

"Hold on, let me check him out."

Sunny waited. Their computers held a vast database of information on both commercial airlines and private charters. There were some unsavory characters in the charter business, dealing more in drugs than in passengers, and a courier company couldn't afford to be careless.

"Where's his home base?"

Sunny repeated the question to Chance.

"Phoenix," he said, and once again she relayed the information.

"Okay, got it. He looks okay. How much is his fee?" Sunny asked.

Mr. Beesham grunted at the reply. "That's a bit high."

"He's here, and he's ready to go."

"What kind of plane is it? I don't want to pay this price for a crop-duster that still won't get you there in time."

Sunny sighed. "Why don't I just put him on the line? It'll save time." She handed the receiver to Chance. "He wants to know about your plane."

Chance took the receiver. "McCall." He listened a moment. "It's a Cessna Skylane. The range is about eight hundred miles at seventy-five percent power, six hours flying time. I'll have to refuel, so I'd rather it be around the midway point, say at Roberts Field in Redmond, Oregon. I can radio ahead and have everything rolling so we won't spend much time on the ground." He glanced at his wristwatch. "With the hour we gain when we cross into the Pacific time zone, she can make it—barely."

He listened for another moment, then handed the receiver back to Sunny. "What's the verdict?" she asked.

"I'm authorizing it. For God's sake, get going."

She hung up and grinned at Chance, her blood pumping at the challenge. "It's a go! How long will it take to get airborne?"

"If you let me carry that bag, and we run...fifteen minutes."

Sunny never let the bag out of her possession. She hated to repay his courtesy with a refusal, but caution was so ingrained in her that she couldn't bring herself to take the risk. "It isn't heavy," she lied, tightening her grip on it. "You lead, I'll follow."

One dark eyebrow went up at her reply, but he didn't argue, just led the way through the busy concourse. The private planes were in a different area of the airport, away from the commercial traffic. After several turns and a flight of stairs, they left the terminal and walked across the concrete, the hot afternoon sun beating down on their heads and making her squint. Chance slipped on a pair of sunglasses, then shrugged out of the jacket and carried it in his left hand.

Sunny allowed herself a moment of appreciation at the way his broad shoulders and muscled back filled out the black T-shirt he wore. She might not indulge, but she could certainly admire. If only things were different—but they weren't, she thought, reining in her thoughts. She had to deal with reality, not wishful thinking.

He stopped beside a single-engine airplane, white with gray-and-red striping. After storing her bag and briefcase and securing them with a net, he helped her into the co-pilot's seat. Sunny buckled herself in and looked around with interest. She'd never been in a private plane before, or flown in anything this small. It was surprisingly comfortable. The seats were gray leather, and behind her was a bench seat with individual backs. Carpet covered the metal floor.

There were two sun visors, just like in a car. Amused, she flipped down the one in front of her and laughed aloud when she saw the small mirror attached to it.

Chance walked around the plane, checking details one last time before climbing into the seat to her left and buckling himself in. He put on a set of headphones and began flipping switches while he talked to the air traffic control tower. The engine coughed, then caught, and the propeller on the nose began to spin, slowly at first, then gaining speed until it was an almost invisible blur.

He pointed to another set of headphones, and Sunny put them on. "It's easier to talk using the headphones," came his voice in her ear, "but be quiet until we get airborne."

"Yes, sir," she said, amused, and he flashed a quick grin at her.

They were airborne within minutes, faster than she had ever experienced on a commercial carrier. Being in the small plane gave her a sense of speed that she had never before felt, and when the wheels left the ground the lift was incredible, as if she had sprouted wings and jumped into the air. The ground quickly fell away below, and the vast, glistening blue lake spread out before her, with the jagged mountains straight ahead.

"Wow," she breathed, and brought one hand up to shield her eyes from the sun.

"There's an extra pair of sunglasses in the glove box," he said, indicating the compartment in front of her. She opened it and dug out a pair of inexpensive but stylish Foster Grants with dark red frames. They were obviously some woman's sunglasses, and abruptly she wondered if he was married. He would have a girlfriend, of course; not only was he very nice to look at, he seemed to be a nice person.

It was a combination that was hard to find and impossible to beat.

"Your wife's?" she asked as she put on the glasses and breathed a sigh of relief as the uncomfortable glare disappeared.

"No, a passenger left them in the plane."

Well, that hadn't told her anything. She decided to be blunt, even while she wondered why she was bothering, since she would never see him again after they arrived in Seattle. "Are you married?"

Again she got that quick grin. "Nope." He glanced at her, and though she couldn't see his eyes through the dark glasses, she got the impression his gaze was intense. "Are you?"

"No."

"Good," he said.

Chapter 3

Chance watched her from behind the dark lenses of his sunglasses, gauging her reaction to his verbal opening. The plan was working better than he'd hoped; she was attracted to him and hadn't been trying very hard to hide it. All he had to do was take advantage of that attraction and win her trust, which normally might take some doing, but what he had planned would throw her into a situation that wasn't *normal* in any sense of the word. Her life and safety would depend on him.

To his faint surprise, she faced forward and pretended she hadn't heard him. Wryly, he wondered if he'd misread her and she wasn't attracted to him after all. No, she had been watching him pretty blatantly, and in his experience, a woman didn't stare at a man unless she found him attractive.

What was *really* surprising was how attractive he found *her*. He hadn't expected that, but sexual chemistry was an unruly demon that operated outside logic. He had known she was pretty, with brilliant gray eyes and golden-blond hair that swung smoothly to her shoulders, from the photographs in the file he had assembled on her. He just hadn't realized how damn *fetching* she was.

He slanted another glance at her, this time one of pure male assessment. She was of average height, maybe, though a little more slender than he liked, almost delicate. Almost. The muscles of her bare arms, revealed by a white sleeveless blouse, were well-toned and lightly tanned, as if she worked out. A good agent always stayed in good physical condition, so he had to expect her to be stronger than she looked. Her delicate appearance probably took a lot of people off guard.

She sure as hell had taken Wilkins off guard. Chance had to smother a smile. While Sunny had gone back to her gate to check on the status of her flight, which Chance had arranged to be cancelled, Wilkins had told him how she had swung her carry-on bag at him, one-armed, and that the damn thing had to weigh a ton, because it had almost knocked him off his feet.

By now, Wilkins and the other three, "Ms. Fayne" and the two security "policemen," would have vanished from the airport. The real airport security had been briefed to stay out of the way, and everything had worked like a charm, though Wilkins had groused at being taken down so roughly. "First that little witch damn near breaks my arm with that bag, then you try to break my back," he'd growled, while they all laughed at him.

Just what was in that bag, anyway? She had held on to it as if it contained the crown jewels, not letting him carry it even when she was right there with him, and only reluctantly letting him take it to stow in the luggage compartment behind them. He'd been surprised at how heavy it was, too heavy to contain the single change of clothes required by an overnight trip, even with a vast array of makeup and a hairdryer thrown in for good measure. The bag had to weigh a good fifty pounds, maybe more. Well, he would find out soon enough what was in it.

"What were you going to do with that guy if you'd caught him?" he asked in a lazy tone, partly to keep her talking, establishing a link between them, and partly because he was curious. She had been chasing after Wilkins with a fiercely determined expression on her face, so determined that, if Wilkins were still running, she would probably still be chasing him.

"I don't know," she said darkly. "I just knew I couldn't let it happen again."

"Again?" Damn, was she going to tell him about Chicago?

"Last month, a green-haired cretin snatched my briefcase in the airport in Chicago." She slapped the arm of the seat. "That's the first time anything like that has ever happened on one of my jobs, then to have it happen again just a month later—I'd have been fired. Heck, I would fire me, if I were the boss."

"You didn't catch the guy in Chicago?"

"No. I was in Baggage Claims, and he just grabbed the briefcase, zipped out the door and was gone."

"What about security? They didn't try to catch him?"

She peered at him over the top of the oversize sunglasses. "You're kidding, right?"

He laughed. "I guess I am."

"Losing another briefcase would have been a catastrophe, at least to me, and it wouldn't have done the company any good, either."

"Do you ever know what's in the briefcases?"

"No, and I don't want to. It doesn't matter. Someone could be sending a pound of salami to their dying uncle Fred, or it could be a billion dollars worth of diamonds—

not that I think anyone would ever ship diamonds by a courier service, but you get the idea."

"What happened when you lost the briefcase in Chicago?"

"My company was out a lot of money—rather, the insurance company was. The customer will probably never use us again, or recommend us."

"What happened to you? Any disciplinary action?" He knew there hadn't been.

"No. In a way, I would have felt better if they had at least fined me."

Damn, she was good, he thought in admiration—either that, or she was telling the truth and hadn't had anything to do with the incident in Chicago last month. It was possible, he supposed, but irrelevant. Whether or not she'd had anything to do with losing that briefcase, he was grateful it had happened, because otherwise she would never have come to his notice, and he wouldn't have this lead on Crispin Hauer.

But he didn't think she was innocent; he thought she was in this up to her pretty neck. She was better than he had expected, an actress worthy of an Oscar—so good he might have believed she didn't know anything about her father, if it wasn't for the mystery bag and her deceptive strength. He was trained to put together seemingly insignificant details and come up with a coherent picture, and experience had made him doubly cynical. Few people were as honest as they wanted you to believe, and the people who put on the best show were often the ones with the most to hide. He should know—he was an expert at hiding the black secrets of his soul.

He wondered briefly what it said about him that he was willing to sleep with her as part of his plan to gain her trust, but maybe it was better not to think about it. Someone had to be willing to work in the muck, to do things from which ordinary people would shrink, just to protect those ordinary people. Sex was…just sex. Part of the job. He could even divorce his emotions to the point that he actually looked forward to the task.

Task? Who was he kidding? He couldn't wait to slide into her. She intrigued him, with her toned, tight body and the twinkle that so often lit her clear gray eyes, as if she was often amused at both herself and the world around her. He was fascinated by her eyes, by the white striations that made her eyes look almost faceted, like the palest of blue diamonds. Most people thought of gray eyes as a pale blue, but when he was close to her, he could see that they were, very definitely, brilliantly gray. But most of all he was intrigued by her expression, which was so open and good-humored she could almost trademark the term "Miss Congeniality." How could she look like that, as sweet as apple pie, when she was working hand in glove with the most-wanted terrorist in his files?

Part of him, the biggest part, despised her for what she was. The animal core of him, however, was excited by the dangerous edge of the game he was playing, by the challenge of getting her into bed with him and convincing her to trust him. When he was inside her, he wouldn't be thinking about the hundreds of innocent people her father had killed, only about the linking of their bodies. He wouldn't let himself think of anything else, lest he give himself away with some nuance of expression that women were so good at reading. No, he would make love to her as if he had found his soul mate, because that was the only way he could be certain of fooling her.

But he was good at that, at making a woman feel as if he desired her more than anything else in the world. He knew just how to make her aware of him, how to push hard without panicking her—which brought him back to the fact that she had totally ignored his first opening. He smiled slightly to himself. Did she really think that would work?

"Will you have dinner with me tonight?"

She actually jumped, as if she had been lost in her thoughts. "What?"

"Dinner. Tonight. After you deliver your package."

"Oh. But—I'm supposed to deliver it at nine. It'll be late, and—"

"And you'll be alone, and I'll be alone, and you have to eat. I promise not to bite. I may lick, but I won't bite."

She surprised him by bursting into laughter.

Of all the reactions he had anticipated, laughter wasn't one of them. Still, her laugh was so free and genuine, her head tilted back against the seat, that he found himself smiling in response.

"'I may lick, but I won't bite.' That was good. I'll have to remember it," she said, chuckling.

After a moment, when she said nothing else, he realized that she was ignoring him again. He shook his head. "Does that work with most men?"

"Does what work?"

"Ignoring them when they ask you out. Do they slink away with their tails tucked between their legs?"

"Not that I've ever noticed." She grinned. "You make me sound like a femme fatale, breaking hearts left and right."

"You probably are. We guys are tough, though. We can be bleeding to death on the inside and we'll put up such a good front that no one ever knows." He smiled at her. "Have dinner with me."

"You're persistent, aren't you?"

"You still haven't answered me."

"All right—no. There, I've answered you."

"Wrong answer. Try again." More gently, he said, "I know you're tired, and with the time difference, nine o'clock is really midnight to you. It's just a meal, Sunny, not an evening of dancing. That can wait until our second date."

She laughed again. "Persistent *and* confident." She paused, made a wry little face. "The answer is still no. I don't date."

This time he was more than surprised, he was stunned. Of all the things he had expected to come out of her mouth, that particular statement had never crossed his mind. Damn, had he so badly miscalculated? "At all? Or just men?"

"At all." She gestured helplessly. "See, this is why I tried to ignore you, because I didn't want to go into an explanation that you wouldn't accept, anyway. No, I'm not gay, I like men very much, but I don't date. End of explanation."

His relief was so intense, he felt a little dizzy. "If you like men, why don't you date?"

"See?" she demanded on a frustrated rush of air. "You didn't accept it. You immediately started asking questions."

"Damn it, did you think I'd just let it drop? There's something between us, Sunny. I know it, and you know it. Or are you going to ignore that, too?"

"That's exactly what I'm going to do."

He wondered if she realized what she had just admitted. "Were you raped?"

"No!" she half shouted, goaded out of control. "I just… don't…date."

She was well on her way to losing her temper, he thought, amused. He grinned. "You're pretty when you're mad."

She sputtered, then began laughing. "How am I supposed to stay mad when you say things like that?"

"You aren't. That's the whole idea."

"Well, it worked. What it didn't do was change my mind. I'm sorry," she said gently, sobering. "It's just…I have my reasons. Let it drop. Please."

"Okay." He paused. "For now."

She gave an exaggerated groan that had him smiling again. "Why don't you try to take a nap?" he suggested. "You have to be tired, and we still have a long flight ahead of us."

"That's a good idea. You can't badger me if I'm asleep."

With that wry shot, she leaned her head back against the seat. Chance reached behind her seat and produced a folded blanket. "Here. Use this as a pillow, or you'll get a stiff neck."

"Thanks." She took off the headset and tucked the blanket between her head and shoulder, then shifted around in her seat to get more comfortable.

Chance let silence fall, occasionally glancing at her to see if she really fell asleep. About fifteen minutes later, her breathing deepened and evened out into a slow rhythm. He waited a few minutes longer, then eased the plane into a more westerly direction, straight into the setting sun.

Chapter 4

"Sunny." The voice was insistent, a little difficult to hear, and accompanied by a hand on her shoulder, shaking her. "Sunny, wake up."

She stirred and opened her eyes, stretching a little to relieve the kinks in her back and shoulders. "Are we there?"

Chance indicated the headset in her lap, and she slipped it on. "We have a problem," he said quietly.

The bottom dropped out of her stomach, and her heartbeat skittered. No other words, she thought, could be quite as terrifying when one was in an airplane. She took a deep breath, trying to control the surge of panic. "What's wrong?" Her voice was surprisingly steady. She looked around, trying to spot the problem in the cluster of dials in the cockpit, though she had no idea what any of them meant. Then she looked out of the window at the rugged landscape below them, painted in stark reds and blacks as the setting sun threw shadows over jagged rock. "Where are we?"

"Southeastern Oregon."

The engine coughed and sputtered. Her heart felt as if it did, too. As soon as she heard the break in the rhythm, she became aware that the steady background whine of the motor had been interrupted several times while she slept. Her subconscious had registered the change in sound but not put it in any context. Now the context was all too clear.

"I think it's the fuel pump," he added, in answer to her first question.

Calm. She had to stay calm. She pulled in a deep breath, though her lungs felt as if they had shrunk in size. "What do we do?"

He smiled grimly. "Find a place to set it down before it falls down."

"I'll take setting over falling any day." She looked out the side window, studying the ground below. Jagged mountain ridges, enormous boulders and sharp-cut arroyos slicing through the earth were all she could see. "Uh-oh."

"Yea. I've been looking for a place to land for the past half hour."

This was not good, not good at all. In the balance of good and bad, this weighed heavily on the bad side.

The engine sputtered again. The whole frame of the aircraft shook. So did her voice, when she said, "Have you radioed a Mayday?"

Again that grim smile. "We're in the middle of a great big empty area, between navigational beacons. I've tried a couple of times to raise someone, but there haven't been any answers."

The scale tipped even more out of balance. "I knew it," she muttered. "The way today has gone, I *knew* I'd crash if I got on another plane."

The grouchiness in her voice made him chuckle, despite the urgency of their situation. He reached over and gently squeezed the back of her neck, startling her with his touch, his big hand warm and hard on her sensitive nape. "We haven't crashed yet, and I'm going to try damn hard to make sure we don't. The landing may be rough, though."

She wasn't used to being touched. She had accustomed herself to doing without the physical contact that it was human nature to crave, to keep people at a certain distance. Chance McCall had touched her more in one afternoon than she had been touched in the past five years. The shock of pleasure almost distracted her from their situation—almost. She looked down at the unforgiving landscape again. "How rough does a landing have to get before it qualifies as a crash?"

"If we walk away from it, then it was a landing." He put his hand back on the controls, and she silently mourned that lost connection.

The vast mountain range spread out around them as far as she could see in any direction. Their chances of walking away from this weren't good. How long would it be before their bodies were found, if ever? Sunny clenched her hands, thinking of Margreta. Her sister, not knowing what had happened, would assume the worst—and dying in an airplane crash was *not* the worst. In her grief, she might well abandon her refuge and do something stupid that would get her killed, too.

She watched Chance's strong hands, so deft and sure on the controls. His clear, classic profile was limned against the pearl and vermillion sky, the sort of sunset one saw only in the western states, and likely the last sunset she would ever see. He would be the last person she ever saw, or touched, and she was suddenly, bitterly angry that she had never been able to live the life most women took for granted, that she hadn't been free to accept his offer of dinner and spend the trip in a glow of anticipation, free to flirt with him and maybe see the glow of desire in his golden-brown eyes.

She had been denied a lot, but most of all she had been denied opportunity, and she would never, never forgive her father for that.

The engine sputtered, caught, sputtered again. This time the reassuring rhythm didn't return. The bottom dropped out of her stomach. God, oh God, they were going to crash. Her nails dug into her palms as she fought to contain her panic. She had never before felt so small and helpless, so fragile, with soft flesh and slender bones that couldn't withstand such battering force. She was going to die, and she had yet to live.

The plane jerked and shuddered, bucking under the stress of spasmodic power. It pitched to the right, throwing Sunny against the door so hard her right arm went numb.

"That's it," Chance said between gritted teeth, his knuckles white as he fought to control the pitching aircraft. He brought the wings level again. "I have to take it down now, while I have a little control. Look for the best place."

Best place? There *was* no best place. They needed somewhere that was relatively flat and relatively clear; the last location she had seen that fit that description had been in Utah.

He raised the right wingtip, tilting the plane so he had a better side view.

"See anything?" Sunny asked, her voice shaking just a little.

"Nothing. Damn."

"Damn is the wrong word. Pilots are supposed to say something else just before they crash." Humor wasn't much of a weapon with which to face death, but it was how she had always gotten herself through the hard times.

Unbelievably, he grinned. "But I haven't crashed yet, sweetheart. Have a little faith. I promise I'll say the right word if I don't find a good-looking spot pretty soon."

"If you don't find a good-looking spot, I'll say it for you," she promised fervently.

They crossed a jagged, boulder-strewn ridge, and a long, narrow black pit yawned beneath them like a doorway to hell. "There!" Chance said, nosing the plane down.

"What? Where?" She sat erect, desperate hope flaring inside her, but all she could see was that black pit.

"The canyon. That's our best bet."

The black pit was a canyon? Weren't canyons supposed to be big? That looked like an arroyo. How on earth would the plane ever fit inside it? And what difference did it make, when this was their only chance? Her heart lodged itself in her throat, and she gripped the edge of the seat as Chance eased the pitching aircraft lower and lower.

The engine stopped.

For a moment all she heard was the awful silence, more deafening than any roar.

Then she became aware of the air rushing past the metal skin of the plane, air that no longer supported them. She heard her own heart beating, fast and heavy, heard the whisper of her breath. She heard everything except what she most wanted to hear, the sweet sound of an airplane engine.

Chance didn't say anything. He concentrated fiercely on keeping the plane level, riding the air currents down, down, aiming for that long, narrow slit in the earth. The plane spiraled like a leaf, coming so close to the jagged mountainside on the left that she could see the pits in the dark red rock.

Sunny bit her lip until blood welled in her mouth, fighting back the terror and panic that threatened to erupt in screams. She couldn't distract him now, no matter what. She wanted to close her eyes, but resolutely kept them open. If she died now, she didn't want to do it in craven fear. She couldn't help the fear, but she didn't have to be craven. She would watch death come at her, watch Chance as he fought to bring them down safely and cheat the grim horseman.

They slipped below the sunshine, into the black shadows, deeper and deeper. It was colder in the shadows, a chill that immediately seeped through the windows into her bones. She couldn't see a thing. Quickly she snatched off the sunglasses and saw that Chance had done the same. His eyes were narrowed, his expression hard and intent as he studied the terrain below.

The ground was rushing at them now, a ground that was pocked and scored with rivulets, and dotted with boulders. It was flat enough, but not a nice, clear landing spot at all. She braced her feet against the floor, her body rigid as if she could force the airplane to stay aloft.

"Hold on." His voice was cool. "I'm going to try to make it to the stream bed. The sand will help slow us down before we hit one of those rocks."

A stream bed? He was evidently much better at reading the ground than she was. She tried to see a ribbon of water, but finally realized the stream was dry; the bed was that thin, twisting line that looked about as wide as the average car.

She started to say "Good luck," but it didn't seem appropriate. Neither did "It was nice knowing you." In the end, all she could manage was "Okay."

It happened fast. Suddenly they were no longer skimming above the earth. The ground was *there*, and they hit it hard, so hard she pitched forward against the seat belt, then snapped back. They went briefly airborne again as the wheels bounced, then hit again even harder. She heard metal screeching in protest; then her head banged against the side window, and for a chaotic moment she didn't see or hear anything, just felt the tossing and bouncing of the plane. She was boneless, unable to hold on, flopping like a shirt in a clothes dryer.

Then there came the hardest bounce of all, jarring her teeth. The plane spun sideways in a sickening motion, then lurched to a stop. Time and reality splintered, broke apart, and for a long moment nothing made any sense; she had no grasp on where she was or what had happened.

She heard a voice, and the world jolted back into place.

"Sunny? Sunny, are you all right?" Chance was asking urgently.

She tried to gather her senses, tried to answer him. Dazed, battered, she realized that the force of the landing had turned her inside the confines of the seat belt, and she was facing the side window, her back to Chance. She felt his hands on her, heard his low swearing as he unclipped the seat belt and eased her back against his chest, supporting her with his body.

She swallowed, and managed to find her voice. "I'm okay." The words weren't much more than a croak, but if she could talk at all that meant she was alive. They were both alive. Joyful disbelief swelled in her chest. He had actually managed to land the plane!

"We have to get out. There may be a fuel leak." Even as he spoke, he shoved open the door and jumped out, dragging her with him as if she was a sack of flour. She felt rather sacklike, her limbs limp and trembling.

A fuel leak. The engine had been dead when they landed, but there was still the battery, and wiring that could short out and spark. If a spark got to any fuel, the plane and everything in it would go up in a fireball.

Everything in it. The words rattled in her brain, like marbles in a can, and with dawning horror she realized what that meant. Her bag was still in the plane.

"Wait!" she shrieked, panic sending a renewed surge of adrenaline through her system, restoring the bones to her legs, the strength to her muscles. She twisted in his grasp, grabbing the door handle and hanging on. "My bag!"

"Damn it, Sunny!" he roared, trying to break her grip on the handle. "Forget the damn bag!"

"No!"

She jerked away from him and began to climb back into the plane. With a smothered curse he grabbed her around the waist and bodily lifted her away from the plane. "I'll get the damn bag! Go on—get out of here! Run!"

She was appalled that he would risk his life retrieving her bag, while sending her to safety. "I'll get it," she said fiercely, grabbing him by the belt and tugging. "*You* run!"

For a split second he literally froze, staring at her in shock. Then he gave his head a little shake, reached in for the bag and effortlessly hefted it out. Wordlessly Sunny tried to take it, but he only gave her an incendiary look and she didn't have time to argue. Carrying the bag in his left hand and gripping her upper arm with his right, he towed her at a run away from the plane. Her shoes sank into the soft grit, and sand and scrub brush bit at her ankles, but she scrambled to stay upright and keep pace with him.

They were a good fifty yards away before he judged it safe. He dropped the bag and turned on her like a panther pouncing on fresh meat, gripping her upper arms with both hands as if he wanted to shake her. "What the hell are you thinking?" he began in a tone of barely leashed violence, then cut himself off, staring at her face. His expression altered, his golden-brown eyes darkening.

"You're bleeding," he said harshly. He grabbed his handkerchief out of his pocket and pressed it to her chin. Despite the roughness of his tone, his touch was incredibly gentle. "You said you weren't hurt."

"I'm not." She raised her trembling hand and took the handkerchief, dabbing it at her chin and mouth. There wasn't much blood, and the bleeding seemed to have stopped. "I bit my lip," she confessed. "Before you landed, I mean. To keep from screaming."

He stared down at her with an expression like flint. "Why didn't you just scream?"

"I didn't want to distract you." The trembling was growing worse by the second; she tried to hold herself steady, but every limb shook as if her bones had turned to gelatin.

He tilted up her face, staring down at her for a moment in the deepening twilight. He breathed a low, savage curse, then slowly leaned down and pressed his lips to her mouth. Despite the violence she sensed in him, the kiss was light, gentle, more of a salute than a kiss. She caught her breath, beguiled by the softness of his lips, the warm smell of his skin, the hint of his taste. She fisted her hands in his T-shirt, clinging to his strength, trying to sink into his warmth.

He lifted his head. "That's for being so brave," he murmured. "I couldn't have asked for a better partner in a plane crash."

"Landing," she corrected shakily. "It was a landing."

That earned her another soft kiss, this time on the temple. She made a strangled sound and leaned into him, a different sort of trembling beginning to take hold of her. He framed her face with his hands, his thumbs gently stroking the corners of her mouth as he studied her. She felt her lips tremble a little, but then, all of her was shaking. He touched the small sore spot her teeth had made in her lower lip; then he was kissing her again, and this time there was nothing gentle about it.

This kiss rocked her to her foundation. It was hungry, rough, deep. There were reasons why she shouldn't respond to him, but she couldn't think what they were. Instead, she gripped his wrists and went on tiptoe to slant her parted lips against his, opening her mouth for the thrust of his tongue. He tasted like man, and sex, a potent mixture that went to her head faster than hundred-proof whiskey. Heat bloomed in her loins and breasts, a desperate, needy heat that brought a low moan from her throat.

He wrapped one arm around her and pulled her against him, molding her to him from knee to breast while his kisses became even deeper, even harder. She locked her arms around his neck and arched into him, wanting the feel of his hard-muscled body against her with an urgency that swept away reason. Instinctively she pushed her hips against his, and the hard length of his erection bulged into the notch of her thighs. This time she cried out in want, in need, in a desire that burned through every cell of her body. His hand closed roughly around her breast, kneading, rubbing her nipple through the layers of blouse and bra, both easing and intensifying the ache that made them swell toward his touch.

Suddenly he jerked his head back. "I don't believe this," he muttered. Reaching up, he prised her arms from around his neck and set her away from him. He looked even more savage than he had a moment before, the veins standing out in his neck. "Stay here," he barked. "Don't move an inch. I have to check the plane."

He left her standing there in the sand, in the growing twilight, suddenly cold all the way down to the bone. Deprived of his warmth, his strength, her legs slowly collapsed, and she sank to the ground.

Chance swore to himself, steadily and with blistering heat, as he checked the plane for fuel leaks and other damage. He had deliberately made the landing rougher than necessary, and the plane had a reinforced landing gear as well as extra protection for the fuel lines and tank, but a smart pilot didn't take anything for granted. He had to check the plane, had to stay in character.

He didn't want to stay in character. He wanted to back her against one of those big boulders and lift her skirt. Damn! What was wrong with him? In the past fifteen years he'd held a lot of beautiful, deadly women in his arms, and even though he let his body respond, his mind had always remained cool. Sunny Miller wasn't the most beautiful, not by a long shot; she was more gamine than goddess, with bright eyes that invited laughter rather than seduction. So why was he so hot to get into her pants?

"Why" didn't matter, he angrily reminded himself. Okay, so his attraction to her was unexpected; it was an advantage, something to be used. He wouldn't have to fake anything, which meant there was even less chance of her sensing anything off-kilter.

Danger heightened the emotions, destroying inhibitions. They had lived through a life-threatening situation together, they were alone, and there was a definite physical attraction between them. He had arranged the first two circumstances; the third was a bonus. It was a textbook situation; studies in human nature had shown that, if a man and a woman were thrown together in a dangerous situation and they had only each other to rely on, they quickly formed both sexual and emotional bonds. Chance had the advantage, in that he knew the plane hadn't been in any danger of crashing, and that they weren't in a life-and-death situation. Sunny would think they were stranded, while he knew better. Whenever he signaled Zane, they would promptly be "rescued," but he wouldn't send that signal until Sunny took him into her confidence about her father.

Everything was under control. They weren't even in Oregon, as he'd told her. They were in Nevada, in a narrow box canyon he and Zane had scouted out and selected because it was possible to land a plane in it, and, unless one had the equipment to scale vertical rock walls, impossible to escape. They weren't close to any commercial flight pattern, he had disabled the transponder so no search plane would pick up a signal, and they were far off their route. They wouldn't be found.

Sunny was totally under his control; she just didn't know it.

The growing dusk made it impossible to see very much, and it was obvious that if the plane was going to explode in flames, it would already have done so. Chance strode back to where Sunny was sitting on the ground, her knees pulled up and her arms wrapped around her legs, and that damn bag close by her side. She scrambled to her feet as he approached. "All clear?"

"All clear. No fuel leaks."

"That's good." She managed a smile. "It wouldn't do us any good for you to fix the fuel pump if there wasn't any fuel left."

"Sunny…if it's a clogged line, I can fix it. If the fuel pump has gone out, I can't."

He decided to let her know right away that they might not be flying out of here in the morning.

She absorbed that in silence, rubbing her bare arms to ward off the chill of the desert air. The temperature dropped like a rock when the sun went down, which was one of the reasons he had chosen this site. They would have to share their body heat at night to survive.

He leaned down and hefted the bag, marveling anew at its weight, then took her arm to walk with her back to the plane. "I hope you have a coat in this damn bag, since you thought it was important enough to risk your life getting it," he growled.

"A sweater," she said absently, looking up at the crystal clear sky with its dusting of stars. The black walls of the canyon loomed on either side of them, making it obvious they were in a hole in the earth. A big hole, but still a hole. She shook herself, as if dragging her thoughts back to the problem at hand. "We'll be all right," she said. "I have some food, and—"

"Food? You're carrying food in here?" He indicated the bag.

"Just some emergency stuff."

Of all the things he'd expected, food was at the bottom of the list. Hell, food wasn't even *on* the list. Why would a woman on an overnight trip put food in her suitcase?

They reached the plane, and he set the bag down in the dirt. "Let me get some things, and we'll find a place to camp for the night. Can you get anything else in there, or is it full?"

"It's full," she said positively, but then, he hadn't expected her to open it so easily.

He shrugged and dragged out his own small duffel, packed with the things a man could be expected to take on a charter flight: toiletries, a change of clothes. The duffel was unimportant, but it wouldn't look right if he left it behind.

"Why can't we camp here?" she asked.

"This is a stream bed. It's dry now, but if it rains anywhere in the mountains, we could be caught in the runoff."

As he spoke, he got a flashlight out of the dash, the blanket from the back, and a pistol from the pocket in the pilot's side door. He stuck the pistol in his belt, and draped the blanket around her shoulders. "I have some water," he said, taking out a plastic gallon milk jug that he'd refilled with water. "We'll be all right tonight." Water had been the toughest thing to locate. He and Zane had found several box canyons in which he could have landed the plane, but this was the only one with water. The source wasn't much, just a thin trickle running out of the rock at the far end of the canyon, but it was enough. He would "find" the water tomorrow.

He handed her the flashlight and picked up both bags. "Lead the way," he instructed, and indicated the direction he wanted. The floor of the canyon sloped upward on one side; the stream bed was the only smooth ground. The going was rough, and Sunny carefully picked her way over rocks and gullies. She was conscientious about shining the light so he could see where he was going, since he was hampered by both bags.

Damn, he wished she had complained at least a little, or gotten upset. He wished she wasn't so easy to like. Most people would have been half-hysterical, or asking endless questions about their chances of being rescued if he couldn't get the plane repaired. Not Sunny. She coped, just as she had coped at the airport, with a minimum of fuss. Without *any* fuss, actually; she had bitten the blood out of her lip to keep from distracting him while he was bringing the plane down.

The canyon was so narrow it didn't take them long to reach the vertical wall. Chance chose a fairly flat section of sandy gray dirt, with a pile of huge boulders that formed a rough semi-circle. "This will give us some protection from the wind tonight."

"What about snakes?" she asked, eyeing the boulders.

"Possible," he said, as he set down the bags. Had he found a weakness he could use to bring her closer to him? "Are you afraid of them?"

"Only the human kind." She looked around as if taking stock of their situation, then kind of braced her shoulders. It was a minute movement, one he wouldn't have noticed if he hadn't been studying her so keenly. With an almost cheerful note she said, "Let's get this camp set up so we can eat. I'm hungry."

She squatted beside her bag and spun the combination dial of the rather substantial lock on her bag. With a quiet *snick* the lock opened, and she unzipped the bag. Chance was a bit taken aback at finding out what was in the bag this easily, but he squatted beside her. "What do you have? Candy bars?"

She chuckled. "Nothing so tasty."

He took the flashlight from her and shone it into the bag as she began taking out items. The bag was as neatly packed as a salesman's sample case, and she hadn't been lying about not having any room in there for anything else. She placed a sealed plastic bag on the ground between them. "Here we go. Nutrition bars." She slanted a look at him. "They taste like you'd expect a nutrition bar to taste, but they're concentrated. One bar a day will give us all we need to stay alive. I have a dozen of them."

The next item was a tiny cell phone. She stared at it, frozen, for a moment, then looked up at him with fragile hope in her eyes as she turned it on. Chance knew there wasn't a signal here, but he let her go through the motions, something inside him aching at the disappointment he knew she would feel.

Her shoulders slumped. "Nothing," she said, and turned the phone off. Without another word she returned to her unpacking.

A white plastic box with a familiar red cross on the top came out next. "First aid kit," she murmured, reaching back into the bag. "Water purification tablets. A couple of bottles of water, ditto orange juice. Light sticks. Matches." She listed each item as she set it on the ground. "Hairspray, deodorant, toothpaste, pre-moistened towelettes, hairbrush, curling iron, blow dryer, two space blankets—" she paused as she reached the bottom of the bag and began hauling on something bigger than any of the other items "—and a tent."

Chapter 5

A tent. Chance stared down at it, recognizing the type. This was survivalist stuff, what people stored in underground shelters in case of war or natural disaster—or what someone who expected to spend a lot of time in the wilderness would pack.

"It's small," she said apologetically. "Really just a one-man tent, but I had to get something light enough for me to carry. There will be enough room for both of us to sleep in it, though, if you don't mind being a little crowded."

Why would she carry a *tent* on board a plane, when she expected to spend one night in Seattle—in a hotel—then fly back to Atlanta? Why would anyone carry that heavy a bag around when she could have checked it? The answer was that she hadn't wanted it out of her possession, but he still wanted an explanation of why she was carrying it at all.

Something didn't add up here.

His silence was unnerving. Sunny looked down at her incongruous pile of possessions and automatically emptied out the bag, removing her sweater and slipping it on, sitting down to pull on a pair of socks, then stuffing her change of clothes and her grooming items back into the bag. Her mind was racing. There was something about his expression that made a chill go down her spine, a hardness that she hadn't glimpsed before. Belatedly, she remembered how easily he had caught the cretin in the airport, the deadly grace and speed with which he moved. This was no ordinary charter pilot, and she was marooned with him.

She had been attracted to him from the first moment she saw him, but she couldn't afford to let that blind her to the danger of letting down her guard. She was accustomed to living with danger, but this was a different sort of danger, and she had no idea what form it could, or would, take. Chance could simply be one of those men who packed more punch than others, a man very capable of taking care of himself.

Or he could be in her father's pay.

The thought chilled her even more, the cold going down to her bones before common sense reasserted itself. No, there was no way her father could have arranged for everything that had happened today, no way he could have known she would be in the Salt Lake City airport. Being there had been pure bad luck, the result of a fouled-up flight schedule. *She* hadn't known she would be in Salt Lake City. If her father had been involved, he would have tried to grab her in either Atlanta or Seattle. All the zig-zagging across the country she had done today had made it impossible for her father to be involved.

As her mind cleared of that silent panic, she remembered how Chance had dragged her bodily from the plane, the way he had draped the blanket around her, even the courtesy with which he had treated her in the airport. He was a strong man, accustomed to being in the lead and taking the risks. *Military training,* she thought with a sudden flash of clarity, and wondered how she had missed it before. Her life, and Margreta's, depended on how well she could read people, how prepared she was, how alert. With Chance, she had been so taken off guard by the strength of her attraction to him, and the shock of finding that interest returned, that she hadn't been thinking.

"What's this about?" he asked quietly, squatting down beside her and indicating the tent. "And don't tell me you were going to camp out in the hotel lobby."

She couldn't help it. The thought of setting up the tent in a hotel lobby was so ludicrous that she chuckled. Seeing the funny side of things was what had kept her sane all these years.

One big hand closed gently on the nape of her neck. "Sunny," he said warningly. "Tell me."

She shook her head, still smiling. "We're stranded here tonight, but essentially we're strangers. After we get out of here we'll never see each other again, so there's no point in spilling our guts to each other. You keep your secrets, and I'll keep mine."

The flashlight beam sharpened the angles of his face. He exhaled a long, exasperated breath. "Okay—for now. I don't know why it matters, anyway. Unless I can get the plane fixed, we're going to be here a long time, and the reason why you have the tent will be irrelevant."

She searched his face, trying to read his impassive expression. "That isn't reassuring."

"It's the truth."

"When we don't show up in Seattle, someone will search for us. The Civil Air Patrol, someone. Doesn't your plane have one of those beacon things?"

"We're in a canyon."

He didn't have to say more than that. Any signal would be blocked by the canyon walls, except for directly overhead. They were in a deep, narrow slit in the earth, the narrowness of the canyon limiting even more their chances of anyone picking up the signal.

"Well, darn," she said forcefully.

This time he was the one who laughed, and he shook his head as he released her neck and stood up. "Is that the worst you can say?"

"We're alive. That outcome is so good considering what *could* have happened that, in comparison, being stranded here only rates a 'darn.' You may be able to fix the plane." She shrugged. "No point in wasting the really nasty words until we know more."

He leaned down and helped her to her feet. "If I can't get us going again, I'll help you with those words. For now, let's get this tent set up before the temperature drops even more."

"What about a fire?"

"I'll look for firewood tomorrow—*if* we need it. We can get by tonight without a fire, and I don't want to waste the flashlight batteries. If we're here for any length of time, we'll need the flashlight."

"I have the lightsticks."

"We'll save those, too. Just in case."

Working together, they set up the tent. She could have done it herself; it was made for one person to handle, and she had practiced until she knew she could do it with a minimum of fuss, but with two people the job took only moments. Brushing away the rocks so they would have a smooth surface beneath the tent floor took longer, but even so, they weren't going to have a comfortable bed for the night.

When they were finished, she eyed the tent with misgivings. It was long enough for Chance, but… She visually measured the width of his shoulders, then the width of the tent. She was either going to have to sleep on her side all night long—or on top of him.

The heat that shot through her told her which option her body preferred. Her heart beat a little faster in anticipation of their enforced intimacy during the coming night, of lying against his strong, warm body, maybe even sleeping in his arms.

To his credit, he didn't make any insinuating remarks, even though when he looked at the tent he must have drawn the same conclusion as she had. Instead, he bent down to pick up the bag of nutrition bars and said smugly, "I knew you'd have dinner with me tonight."

She began laughing again, charmed by both his tact and his sense of humor, and fell a little in love with him right then.

She should have been alarmed, but she wasn't. Yes, letting herself care for him made her emotionally vulnerable, but they had lived through a terrifying experience together, and she *needed* an emotional anchor right now. So far she hadn't found a single thing about the man that she didn't like, not even that hint of danger she kept sensing. In this situation, a man with an edge to him was an asset, not a hindrance.

She allowed herself to luxuriate in this unaccustomed feeling as they each ate a nutrition bar—which was edible, but definitely not tasty—and drank some water. Then they packed everything except the two space blankets back in the bag, to protect their supplies from snakes and insects and other scavengers. They didn't have to worry about bears, not in this desertlike part of the country, but coyotes were possible. Her bag was supposedly indestructible; if any coyotes showed up, she supposed she would find out if the claim about the bag was true, because there wasn't room in the tent for both them and the bag.

Chance checked the luminous dial of his watch. "It's still early, but we should get in the tent to save our body heat, and not burn up calories trying to stay warm out here. I'll spread this blanket down, and we'll use your two blankets for cover."

For the first time, she realized he was in his T-shirt. "Shouldn't you get your jacket from the plane?"

"It's too bulky to wear in the tent. Besides, I don't feel the cold as much as you do. I'll be fine without it." He sat down and pulled off his boots, tossed them inside the tent, then crawled in with the blanket. Sunny slipped off her own shoes, glad she had the socks to keep her feet warm.

"Okay, come on in," Chance said. "Feet first."

She gave him her shoes, then sat down and worked herself feetfirst into the tent. He was lying on his side, which gave her room to maneuver, but it was still a chore keeping her skirt down and trying not to bunch up the blanket as she wiggled into place. Chance zipped the tent flaps shut, then pulled his pistol out of his waistband and placed it beside his head. Sunny eyed the big black automatic; she wasn't an expert on pistols, but she knew it was one of the heavier calibers, either a .45 or a 9mm. She had tried them, but the bigger pistols were too heavy for her to handle with ease, so she had opted for a smaller caliber.

He had already unfolded the space blankets and had them ready to pull in place. She could already feel his body heat in the small space, so she didn't need a blanket yet, but as the night grew colder, they would need all the covering they could get.

They both moved around, trying to get comfortable. Because he was so big, Sunny tried to give him as much room as possible. She turned on her side and curled her arm under her head, but they still bumped and brushed against each other.

"Ready?" he asked.

"Ready."

He turned off the flashlight. The darkness was complete, like being deep in a cave. "Thank God I'm not claustrophobic," she said, taking a deep breath. His scent filled her lungs, warm and... different, not musky, exactly, but earthy, and very much the way a man should smell.

"Just think of it as being safe," he murmured. "Darkness can feel secure."

She did feel safe, she realized. For the first time in her memory, she was certain no one except the man beside her knew where she was. She didn't have to check locks, scout out an alternate exit, or sleep so lightly she sometimes felt as if she hadn't slept at all. She didn't have to worry about being followed, or her phone being tapped, or any of the other things that could happen. She did worry about Margreta, but she had to think positively. Tomorrow Chance would find the problem was a clogged fuel line, he would get it cleared, and they would finish their trip. She would be too late to deliver the package in Seattle, but considering they had landed safely instead of crashing, she didn't really care about the package. The day's outcome could have been so much worse that she was profoundly grateful they were all in one piece and relatively comfortable—"relatively" being the key word, she thought, as she tried to find a better position. The ground was as hard as a rock. For all she knew the ground *was* a rock, covered by a thin layer of dirt.

She was suddenly exhausted. The events of the day—the long flight and fouled-up connections, the lack of food, the stress of being mugged, then the almost unbearable tension of those last minutes in the plane—finally took their toll on her. She yawned and unconsciously tried yet again to find a comfortable position, turning over to pillow her head on her other arm. Her elbow collided with something very solid, and he grunted.

"I'm sorry," she mumbled. She squirmed a little more, inadvertently bumping him with her knee. "This is so crowded I may have to sleep on top."

She heard the words and in shock realized that she had actually said them aloud. She opened her mouth to apologize again.

"Or I could be the one on top."

His words stopped her apology cold. Her breath tangled in her lungs and didn't escape. His deep voice seemed to echo in the darkness, that single sentence reverberating through her consciousness. She was suddenly, acutely, aware of every inch of him, of the sensual promise in his tone. The kiss—the kiss she could write off as reaction; danger was supposed to be an aphrodisiac, and evidently that was true. But this wasn't reaction; this was desire, warm and curious, seeking.

"Is that a 'no' I'm hearing?"

Her lungs started working again, and she sucked in a breath. "I haven't said anything."

"That's my point." He sounded faintly amused. "I guess I'm not going to get lucky tonight."

Feeling more certain of herself with his teasing, she said dryly, "I guess not. You've already used up your quota of luck for the day."

"I'll try again tomorrow."

She stifled a laugh.

"Does that snicker mean I haven't scared you?"

She should be scared, she thought, or at least wary. She had no idea why she wasn't. The fact was, she felt tempted. Very tempted. "No, I'm not scared."

"Good." He yawned. "Then why don't you pull off that sweater and let me use it as a pillow, and you can use my shoulder. We'll both be more comfortable."

Common sense said he was right. Common sense also said she was asking for trouble if she slept in his arms. She trusted him to behave, but she wasn't that certain of herself. He was sexy, with a capital SEX. He made her laugh. He was strong and capable, with a faintly wicked edge to him. He was even a little dangerous. What more could a woman want?

That was perhaps the most dangerous thing about him, that he made her want him. She had easily resisted other men, walking away without a backward look or a second thought. Chance made her long for all the things she had denied herself, made her aware of how lonely and alone she was.

"Are you sure you can trust me to behave?" she asked, only half joking. "I didn't mean to say that about being on top. I was half-asleep, and it just slipped out."

"I think I can handle you if you get fresh. For one thing, you'll be sound asleep as soon as you stop talking."

She yawned. "I know. I'm crashing hard, if you'll pardon the terminology."

"We didn't crash, we landed. Come on, let's get that sweater off, then you can sleep."

There wasn't room to fully sit up, so he helped her struggle out of the garment. He rolled it up and tucked it under his head, then gently, as if worried he might frighten her, drew her against his right side. His right arm curled around her, and she nestled close, settling her head in the hollow of his shoulder.

The position was surprisingly comfortable, and comforting. She draped her right arm across his chest, because there didn't seem to be any other place to put it. Well, there were other places, but none that seemed as safe. Besides, she liked feeling his heartbeat under her hand. The strong, even thumping satisfied some primitive instinct in her, the desire not to be alone in the night.

"Comfortable?" he asked in a low, soothing tone.

"Um-hmm."

With his left arm he snagged one of the space blankets and pulled it up to cover her to the shoulders, keeping the chill from her bare arms. Cocooned in warmth and darkness, she gave in to the sheer pleasure of lying so close to him. Sleepy desire hummed just below the surface, warming her, softening her. Her breasts, crushed against his side, tightened in delight, and her nipples felt achy, telling her they had hardened. Could he feel them? she wondered. She wanted to rub herself against him like a cat, intensifying the sensation, but she lay very still and concentrated on the rhythm of his heartbeat.

He had touched her breasts when he kissed her. She wanted to feel that again, feel his hard hand on her bare flesh. She wanted him, wanted his touch and his taste and the feel of him inside her. The force of her physical yearning was so strong that she actually ached from the emptiness.

If we don't get out of here tomorrow, she thought in faint despair just before she went to sleep, I'll be under him before the sun goes down again.

* * *

Sunny was accustomed to waking immediately when anything disturbed her; once, a car had backfired out in the street and she had grabbed the pistol from under the pillow and rolled off the bed before the noise had completely faded. She had learned how to nap on demand, because she never knew when she might have to run for her life. She could count on one hand the number of nights since she had stopped being a child that she had slept through undisturbed.

But she woke in Chance's arms aware that she had slept all night long, that not only had lying next to him not disturbed her, in a very basic way his presence had been reassuring. She was safe here, safe and warm and unutterably relaxed. His hand was stroking slowly down her back, and that was what had awakened her.

Her skirt had ridden up during the night, of course, and was twisted at midthigh. Their legs were tangled together, her right leg thrown over his; his jeans were old and soft, but the denim was still slightly rough against the inside of her thigh. She wasn't lying completely on top of him, but it was a near thing. Her head lay pillowed on his chest instead of his shoulder, with the steady thumping of his heart under her ear.

The slow motion of his hand continued. "Good morning," he said, his deep voice raspy from sleep.

"Good morning." She didn't want to get up, she realized, though she knew she should. It was after dawn; the morning light seeped through the brown fabric of the tent, washing them with a dull gold color. Chance should get started on the fuel pump, so they could get airborne and in radio contact with someone as soon as possible, to let the FAA know they hadn't crashed. She knew what she should do, but instead she continued to lie there, content with the moment.

He touched her hair, lifting one strand and watching it drift back down. "I could get used to this," he murmured.

"You've slept with women before."

"I haven't slept with *you* before."

She wanted to ask how she was different, but she was better off not knowing. Nothing could come of this fast-deepening attraction, because she couldn't let it. She had to believe that he could repair the plane, that in a matter of hours they would be separating and she would never see him again. That was the only thing that gave her the strength, finally, to pull away from him and straighten her clothes, push her hair out of her face and unzip the tent.

The chill morning air rushed into their small cocoon. "Wow," she said, ignoring his comment. "Some hot coffee would be good, wouldn't it? I don't suppose you have a jar of instant in the plane?"

"You mean you don't have coffee packed in that survival bag of yours?" Taking his cue from her, he didn't push her to continue their provocative conversation.

"Nope, just water." She crawled out of the tent, and he handed her shoes and sweater out through the opening. Quickly she slipped them on, glad she had brought a heavy cardigan instead of a summer-weight one.

Chance's boots came out next, then him. He sat on the ground and pulled on his boots. "Damn, it's cold. I'm going to get my jacket from the plane. I'll take care of business there, and you go on the other side of these boulders. There shouldn't be any snakes stirring around this early, but keep an eye out."

Sunny dug some tissues out of her skirt pocket and set off

around the boulders. Ten minutes later, nature's call having been answered, she washed her face and hands with one of the pre-moistened towelettes, then brushed her teeth and hair. Feeling much more human and able to handle the world, she took a moment to look around at their life-saving little canyon.

It was truly a slit in the earth, no more than fifty yards wide where he had landed the plane. About a quarter of a mile farther down it widened some, but the going was much rougher. The stream bed was literally the only place they could have safely landed. Just beyond the widest point, the canyon made a dog leg to the left, so she had no idea how long it was. The canyon floor was littered with rocks big and small, and a variety of scrub brush. Deep grooves were cut into the ground where rain had sluiced down the steep canyon walls and arrowed toward the stream.

All the different shades of red were represented in the dirt and rock, from rust to vermillion to a sandy pink. The scrub brush wasn't a lush green; the color was dry, as if it had been bleached by the sun. Some of it was silvery, a bright contrast against the monochromatic tones of the earth.

They seemed to be the only two living things there. She didn't hear any birds chirping, or insects rustling. There had to be small wildlife such as lizards and snakes, she knew, which meant there had to be something for them to eat, but at the moment the immense solitude was almost overwhelming.

Looking at the plane, she saw that Chance was already poking around in its innards. Shoving her cold hands into the sweater pockets, she walked down to him.

"Don't you want to eat something?"

"I'd rather save the food until I see what the problem is."

He gave her a crooked grin. "No offense, but I don't want to eat another one of those nutrition bars unless I absolutely have to."

"And if you can fly us out of here, you figure you can hold out until we get to an airport."

"Bingo."

She grinned as she changed positions so she could see what he was doing. "I didn't eat one, either," she confessed.

He was checking the fuel lines, his face set in that intent expression men got when they were doing anything mechanical. Sunny felt useless; she could have helped if he was working on a car, but she didn't know anything about airplanes. "Is there anything I can do to help?" she finally asked.

"No, it's just a matter of taking off the fuel lines and checking them for clogs."

She waited a few more minutes, but the process looked tedious rather than interesting, and she began getting restless. "I think I'll walk around, explore a bit."

"Stay within yelling distance," he said absently.

The morning, though still cool, was getting warmer by the minute as the sun heated the dry desert air. She walked carefully, watching where she placed each step, because a sprained ankle could mean the difference between life and death if she had to run for it. Someday, she thought, a sprain would be an inconvenience, nothing more. One day she would be free.

She looked up at the clear blue sky and inhaled the clean, crisp air. She had worked hard to retain her enjoyment of life, the way she had learned to rely on a sense of humor to keep her sane. Margreta didn't handle things nearly as well, but she already had to deal with a heart condition that, while it could be controlled with medication, nevertheless meant that she had to take certain precautions. If she were ever found, Margreta lacked Sunny's ability to just drop out of sight. She had to have her medication refilled, which meant she had to occasionally see her doctor so he could write a new prescription. If she had to find a new doctor, that would mean being retested, which would mean a lot more money.

Which meant that Sunny never saw her sister. It was safer if they weren't together, in case anyone was looking for sisters. She didn't even have Margreta's phone number. Margreta called Sunny's cell phone once a week at a set time, always from a different pay phone. That way, if Sunny was captured, she had no information her captors could get by any means, not even drugs.

She had four days until Margreta called, Sunny thought. If she didn't answer the phone, or if Margreta didn't call, then each had to assume the other had been caught. If Sunny didn't answer the phone, Margreta would bolt from her safe hiding place, because with the phone records her location could be narrowed down to the correct city. Sunny couldn't bear to think what would happen then; Margreta, in her grief and rage, might well throw caution to the wind in favor of revenge.

Four days. The problem *had* to be a clogged fuel line. It just had to be.

Chapter 6

Mindful of Chance's warning, Sunny didn't wander far. In truth, there wasn't much to look at, just grit and rocks and scraggly bushes, and those vertical rock walls. The desert had a wild, lonely beauty, but she was more appreciative when she wasn't stranded in it. When rain filled the stream this sheltered place probably bloomed with color, but how often did it rain here? Once a year?

As the day warmed, the reptiles began to stir. She saw a brown lizard dart into a crevice as she approached. A bird she didn't recognize swooped down for a tasty insect, then flew back off to freedom. The steep canyon walls didn't mean anything to a bird, while the hundred feet or so were unscalable to her.

She began to get hungry, and a glance at her watch told her she had been meandering through the canyon for over an hour. What was taking Chance so long? If there was a clog in the lines he should have found it by now.

She began retracing her steps to the plane. She could see Chance still poking around the engine, which meant he probably hadn't found anything. A chilly finger of fear prodded her, and she pushed it away. She refused to anticipate trouble. She would deal with things as they happened, and if Chance couldn't repair the plane, then they would have to find some other way out of the canyon. She hadn't explored far; perhaps the other end was open, and they could simply walk out. She didn't know how far they were from a town, but she was willing to make the effort. Anything was better than sitting and doing nothing.

As she approached, Chance lifted his hand to show he saw her, then turned back to the engine. Sunny let her gaze linger, admiring the way his T-shirt clung to the muscles of his back and shoulders. The fit of his jeans wasn't bad, either, she thought, eyeing his butt and long legs.

Something moved in the sand near his feet.

She thought she would faint. Her vision dimmed and narrowed until all she saw was the snake, perilously close to his left boot. Her heart leaped, pounding against her ribcage so hard she felt the thuds.

She had no sensation or knowledge of moving; time took on the viscosity of syrup. All she knew was that the snake was getting bigger and bigger, closer and closer. Chance looked around at her and stepped back from the plane, almost on the coiling length. The snake's head drew back and her hand closed on a coil, surprisingly warm and smooth, and she threw the awful thing as far as she could. It was briefly outlined against the stark rock, then sailed beyond a bush and dropped from sight.

"Are you all right? Did it bite you? Are you hurt?" She couldn't stop babbling as she went down on her knees and began patting his legs, looking for droplets of blood, a small tear in his jeans, anything that would show if he had been bitten.

"I'm all right. I'm all right. Sunny! It didn't bite me." His voice overrode hers, and he hauled her to her feet, shaking her a little to get her attention. "Look at me!" The force of his tone snagged her gaze with his and he said more quietly, "I'm okay."

"Are you sure?" She couldn't seem to stop touching him, patting his chest, stroking his face, though logically she knew there was no way the snake could have bitten him up there. Neither could she stop trembling. "I hate snakes," she said in a shaking voice. "They terrify me. I saw it—it was right under your feet. You almost *stepped* on it."

"Shh," he murmured, pulling her against him and rocking her slowly back and forth. "It's all right. Nothing happened."

She clutched his shirt and buried her head against his chest. His smell, already so familiar and now with the faint odor of grease added, was comforting. His heartbeat was steady, as if he hadn't almost been snakebitten. *He* was steady, rock solid, his body supporting hers.

"Oh my God," she whispered. "That was awful." She raised her head and stared at him, an appalled expression on her face. "Yuk! I *touched* it!" She snatched her hand away from him and held it at arm's length. "Let me go, I have to wash my hand. Now!"

He released her, and she bolted up the slope to the tent, where the towelettes were. Grabbing one, she scrubbed furiously at her palm and fingers.

Chance was laughing softly as he came up behind her. "What's the matter? Snakes don't have cooties. Besides, yesterday you said you weren't afraid of them."

"I lied. And I don't care what they have, I don't want one anywhere near me." Satisfied that no snake germs lingered on her hand, she blew out a long, calming breath.

"Instead of swooping down like a hawk," he said mildly, "why didn't you just yell out a warning?"

She gave him a blank look. "I couldn't." Yelling had never entered her mind. She had been taught her entire life not to yell in moments of tension or danger, because to do so would give away her position. Normal people could scream and yell, but she had never been allowed to be normal.

He put one finger under her chin, lifting her face to the sun. He studied her for a long moment, something dark moving in his eyes; then he tugged her to him and bent his head.

His mouth was fierce and hungry, his tongue probing. She sank weakly against him, clinging to his shoulders and kissing him in return just as fiercely, with just as much hunger. More. She felt as if she had always hungered, and never been fed. She drank life itself from his mouth, and sought more.

His hands were all over her, on her breasts, her bottom, lifting her into the hard bulge of his loins. The knowledge that he wanted her filled her with a deep need to know more, to feel everything she had always denied herself. She didn't know if she could have brought herself to pull away, but he was the one who broke the kiss, lifting his head and standing there with his eyes closed and a grim expression on his face.

"Chance?" she asked hesitantly.

He growled a lurid word under his breath. Then he opened his eyes and glared down at her. "I can't believe I'm stopping this a second time," he said with a raw, furious frustration. "Just for the record, I'm *not* that noble. Damn it all to hell and back—" He broke off, breathing hard. "It isn't a clogged fuel line. It must be the pump. We have other things we need to do. We can't afford to waste any daylight."

Margreta. Sunny bit her lip to hold back a moan of dismay. She stared up at him, the knowledge of the danger of their situation lying like a stark shadow between them.

She wasn't licked yet. She had four days. "Can we walk out?"

"In the desert? In August?" He looked up at the rim of the canyon. "Assuming we can even get out of here, we'd have to walk at night and try to find shelter during the day. By afternoon, the temperature will be over a hundred."

The temperature was probably already well into the seventies, she thought; she was dying of heat inside her heavy sweater, or maybe that was just frustrated lust, since she hadn't noticed how hot it was until now. She peeled off the sweater and dropped it on top of her bag. "What do we need to do?"

His eyes gleamed golden with admiration, and he squeezed her waist. "I'll reconnoiter. We can't get out on this end of the canyon, but maybe there's a way farther down."

"What do you want me to do?"

"Look for sticks, leaves, anything that will burn. Gather as much as you can in a pile."

He set off in the direction she had gone earlier, and she went in the opposite direction. The scrub brush grew heavier at that end of the canyon, and she would find more wood there. She didn't like to think about how limited the supply would be, or that they might be here for a long, long time. If they couldn't get out of the canyon, they would eventually use up their meager resources and die.

He hated lying to her. Chance's expression was grim as he stalked along the canyon floor. He had lied to terrorists, hoodlums and heads of state alike without a twinge of con-science, but it was getting harder and harder to lie to Sunny. He fiercely protected a hard core of honesty deep inside, the part of him that he shared only with his family, but Sunny was getting to him. She wasn't what he had expected. More and more he was beginning to suspect she wasn't working with her father. She was too… *gallant* was the word that sprang to mind. Terrorists weren't gallant. In his opinion, they were either mad or amoral. Sunny was neither.

He was more shaken by the episode with the snake than he had let her realize. Not by the snake itself—he had on boots, and since he hadn't heard rattles he suspected the snake hadn't been poisonous—but by her reaction. He would never forget the way she had looked, rushing in like an avenging angel, her face paper-white and utterly fo-cused. By her own admission she was terrified of snakes, yet she hadn't hesitated. What kind of courage had it taken for her to pick up the snake with her bare hand?

Then there was the way she had patted him, looking for a bite. Except with certain people, or during sex, he had to struggle to tolerate being touched. He had learned how to accept affection in his family, because Mom and Maris would *not* leave him alone. He unabashedly loved playing with all his nephews—and niece—but his family had been the only exception. Until now. Until Sunny. He not only hadn't minded, he had, for a moment, allowed himself the pure luxury of enjoying the feel of her hands on his legs, his chest. And that didn't even begin to compare to how much he had enjoyed sleeping with her, feeling those sweet curves all along his side. His hand clenched as he remembered the feel of her breast in his palm, the wonderful resilience that was both soft and firm. He ached to feel her bare skin, to taste her. He wanted to strip her naked and pull her beneath him for a long hard ride, and he wanted to do it in broad daylight so he could watch her brilliant eyes glaze with pleasure.

If she wasn't who she was he would take her to the south of France, maybe, or a Caribbean island, any place where they could lie naked on the beach and make love in the sunshine, or in a shaded room with fingers of sunlight slipping through closed blinds. Instead, he had to keep lying to her, because whether or not she was working with her father didn't change the fact that she was the key to locating him.

He couldn't change the plan now. He couldn't suddenly "repair" the plane. He thanked God she didn't know anything about planes, because otherwise she would never have fallen for the fuel pump excuse; a Skylane had a backup fuel pump, for just such an emergency. No, he had to play out the game as he had planned it, because the goal was too damned important to abandon, and he couldn't take the risk that she was involved up to her pretty ears, after all.

He and Zane had walked a fine line in planning this out. The situation had to be survivable but grim, so nothing would arouse her suspicion. There was food to be had, but not easily. There was water, but not a lot. He hadn't brought any provisions that might make her wonder why he had them, meaning he had limited himself to the blanket, the water and the pistol, plus the expected items in the plane, such as flares. Hell, she was a lot more prepared than he was, and that made him wary. She wasn't exactly forthcoming about her reason for toting a damn tent around, either. The lady had secrets of her own.

He reached the far end of the canyon and checked to make certain nothing had changed since he and Zane had been here. No unexpected landslide had caved in a wall, allowing a way out. The thin trickle of water still ran down the rock. He saw rabbit tracks, birds, things they could eat. Shooting them would be the easy way, though; he would have to build some traps, to save his ammunition for emergencies.

Everything was just as he had left it. The plan was working. The physical attraction between them was strong; she wouldn't resist him much longer, maybe not at all. She certainly hadn't done anything to call a halt earlier. And after he was her lover—well, women were easily beguiled by sexual pleasure, the bonds of the flesh. He knew the power of sex, knew how to use it to make her trust him. He wished he could trust *her*—this would be a lot easier if he could— but he knew too much about the human soul's capability of evil, and that a pretty face didn't necessarily mean a pretty person was behind it.

When he judged enough time had passed for him to completely reconnoiter the canyon, he walked back. She was still gathering sticks, he saw, going back and forth between the bushes and the growing pile next to the tent. She looked up when he got closer, hope blazing in her expression.

He shook his head. "It's a box canyon. There's no way out," he said flatly. "The good news is, there's water at the far end."

She swallowed. Her eyes were huge with distress, almost eclipsing her face. "We can't climb out, either?"

"It's sheer rock." He put his hands on his hips, looking around. "We need to move closer to the water, for convenience. There's an overhang that will give us shade from the sun, and the ground underneath is sandier, so it'll be more comfortable."

Or as comfortable as they could get, sleeping in that small tent.

Wordlessly she nodded and began folding the tent. She did it briskly, without wasted movement, but he saw she was fighting for control. He stroked her upper arm, feeling her smooth, pliant skin, warm and slightly moist from her exertion. "We'll be okay," he reassured her. "We just have to hold out until someone sees our smoke and comes to investigate."

"We're in the middle of nowhere," she said shakily. "You said so yourself. And I only have four days until—"

"Until what?" he asked, when she stopped.

"Nothing. It doesn't matter." She stared blindly at the sky, at the clear blue expanse that was turning whiter as the hot sun climbed upward.

Four days until what? he wondered. What was going to happen? Was she supposed to do something? Was a terrorist attack planned? Would it go forward without her?

The dogleg of the canyon was about half a mile long, and the angle gave it more shade than where they had landed. They worked steadily, moving their camp, with Chance hauling the heaviest stuff. Sunny tried to keep her mind blank, to not think about Margreta, to focus totally on the task at hand.

It was noon, the white sun directly overhead. The heat was searing, the shade beneath the overhang so welcome she sighed with relief when they gained its shelter. The overhang was larger than she had expected, about twelve feet wide and deep enough, maybe eight feet, that the sunshine would never penetrate its depths. The rock sloped to a height of about four feet at the back, but the opening was high enough that Chance could stand up without bumping his head.

"I'll wait until it's cooler to get the rest," he said. "I don't know about you, but I'm starving. Let's have half of one of your nutrition bars now, and I'll try to get a rabbit for dinner."

She rallied enough to give him a look of mock dismay. "You'd eat Peter Cottontail?"

"I'd eat the Easter Bunny right now, if I could catch him."

He was trying to make her laugh. She appreciated his effort, but she couldn't quite shake off the depression that had seized her when her last hope of getting out of here quickly had evaporated.

She had lost her appetite, but she dug out one of the nutrition bars and halved it, though she hid the fact that Chance's "half" was bigger than hers. He was bigger; he needed more. They ate their spartan little meal standing up, staring out at the bleached tones of the canyon. "Drink all the water you want," he urged. "The heat dehydrates you even in the shade."

Obediently she drank a bottle of water; she needed it to get the nutrition bar down. Each bite felt as if it was getting bigger and bigger in her mouth, making it difficult to swallow. She resorted to taking only nibbles, and got it down that way.

After they ate, Chance made a small circle of rocks, piled in some sticks and leaves, both fresh and dead, and built a fire. Soon a thin column of smoke was floating out of the canyon. It took him no more than five minutes to accomplish, but when he came back under the overhang his shirt was damp with sweat.

She handed him a bottle of water, and he drank deeply, at the same time reaching out a strong arm and hooking it around her waist. He drew her close and pressed a light kiss to her forehead, nothing more, just held her comfortingly. She put her arms around him and clung, desperately needing his strength right now. She hadn't had anyone to lean on in a long time; she had always had to be the strong one. She had tried so hard to stay on top of things, to plan for every conceivable glitch, but she hadn't thought to plan for this, and now she had no idea what to do.

"I have to think of something," she said aloud.

"Shh. All we have to do is stay alive. That's the most important thing."

He was right, of course. She couldn't do anything about Margreta now. This damn canyon had saved their lives yesterday, but it had become a prison from which she couldn't escape. She had to play the hand with the cards that had been dealt to her and not let depression sap her strength. She had to hope Margreta wouldn't do anything foolish, just go to ground somewhere. How she would ever find her again she didn't know, but she could deal with that if she just knew her sister was alive and safe somewhere.

"Do you have family who will worry?" he asked.

God, that went to the bone! She shook her head. She had family, but Margreta wouldn't worry; she would simply assume the worst.

"What about you?" she asked, realizing she had fallen halfway in love with the man and didn't know a thing about him.

He shook his head. "C'mon, let's sit down." With nothing to use for a seat, they simply sat on the ground. "I'll take two of the seats out of the plane this afternoon, so we'll be more comfortable," he said. "In answer to your question, no, I don't have anyone. My folks are dead, and I don't have any brothers or sisters. There's an uncle somewhere, on my dad's side, and my mom had some cousins, but we never kept in touch."

"That's sad. Family should stay together." *If they could,* she added silently. "Where did you grow up?"

"All over. Dad wasn't exactly known for his ability to keep a job. What about your folks?"

She was silent for a moment, then sighed. "I was adopted. They were good people. I still miss them." She drew a design in the dirt with her finger. "When we didn't show up in Seattle last night, would someone have notified the FAA?"

"They're probably already searching. The problem is, first they'll search the area I should have been over when I filed my flight plan."

"We were off course?" she asked faintly. It just kept getting worse and worse.

"We went off course looking for a place to land. But if anyone is searching this area, eventually he'll see our smoke. We just have to keep the fire going during the day."

"How long will they look? Before they call off the search?"

He was silent, his golden eyes narrowed as he searched the sky. "They'll look as long as they think we might be alive."

"But if they think we've crashed—"

"Eventually they'll stop looking," he said softly. "It might be a week, a little longer, but they'll stop."

"So if no one finds us within, say, ten days—" She couldn't go on.

"We don't give up. There's always the possibility a private plane will fly over."

He didn't say that the possibility was slight, but he didn't have to. She had seen for herself the kind of terrain they'd flown over, and she knew how narrow and easily missed this canyon was.

She drew up her knees and wrapped her arms around her legs, staring wistfully at the languid curls of gray smoke. "I used to wish I could go someplace where no one could find me. I didn't realize there wouldn't be room service."

He chuckled as he leaned back on one elbow and stretched out his long legs. "Nothing gets you down for long, does it?"

"I try not to let it. Our situation isn't great, but we're alive. We have food, water and shelter. Things could be worse."

"We also have entertainment. I have a deck of cards in the plane. We can play poker."

"Do you cheat?"

"Don't need to," he drawled.

"Well, I do, so I'm giving you fair warning."

"Warning taken. You know what happens to cheaters, don't you?"

"They win?"

"Not if they get caught."

"If they're any good, they don't get caught."

He twirled a finger in her hair and lightly tugged. "Yeah, but if they get caught they're in big trouble. You can take that as my warning."

"I'll be careful," she promised. A yawn took her by surprise. "How can I be sleepy? I got plenty of sleep last night."

"It's the heat. Why don't you take a nap? I'll watch the fire."

"Why aren't you sleepy?"

He shrugged. "I'm used to it."

She really was sleepy, and there was nothing else to do.

She didn't feel like setting up the tent, so she dragged her bag into position behind her and leaned back on it. Silently Chance tossed her sweater into her lap. Following his example, she rolled up the sweater and stuffed it under her head. She dozed within minutes. It wasn't a restful sleep, being one of those light naps in which she was aware of the heat, of Chance moving around, of her worry about Margreta. Her muscles felt heavy and limp, though, and completely waking up was just too much trouble.

The problem with afternoon naps was that one woke feeling both groggy and grungy. Her clothes were sticking to her, which wasn't surprising considering the heat. When she finally yawned and sat up, she saw that the sun was beginning to take on a red glow as it sank, and though the temperature was still high, the heat had lost its searing edge.

Chance was sitting cross-legged, his long, tanned fingers deftly weaving sticks and string into a cage. There was something about the way he looked there in the shadow of the overhang, his attention totally focused on the trap he was building while the light reflected off the sand outside danced along his high cheekbones, that made recognition click in her brain. "You're part Native American, aren't you?"

"American Indian," he corrected absently. "Everyone born here is a native American, or so Dad always told me." He looked up and gave her a quick grin. "Of course, 'Indian' isn't very accurate, either. Most labels aren't. But, yeah, I'm a mixed breed."

"And ex-military." She didn't know why she said that. Maybe it was his deftness in building the trap. She wasn't foolish enough to attribute that to any so-called Native American skills, not in this day and age, but there was something in the way he worked that bespoke survival training.

He gave her a surprised glance. "How did you know?"

She shook her head. "Just a guess. The way you handled the pistol, as if you were very comfortable with it. What you're doing now. And you used the word 'reconnoiter.'"

"A lot of people are familiar with weapons, especially out-doorsmen, who would also know how to build traps."

"Done in by your vocabulary," she said, and smirked. "You said 'weapons' instead of just 'guns,' the way most people—even outdoorsmen—would have."

Again she was rewarded with that flashing grin. "Okay, so I've spent some time in a uniform."

"What branch?"

"Army. Rangers."

Well, that certainly explained the survival skills. She didn't know a lot about the Rangers, or any military group, but she did know they were an elite corps.

He set the finished trap aside and began work on another one. Sunny watched him for a moment, feeling useless. She would be more hindrance than help in building traps. She sighed as she brushed the dirt from her skirt. Darn, stranded only one day and here she was, smack in the middle of the old sexual stereotypes.

She surrendered with good grace. "Is there enough water for me to wash out our clothes? I've lived in these for two days, and that's long enough."

"There's enough water, just nothing to collect it in." He unfolded his legs and stood with easy grace. "I'll show you."

He led the way out of the overhang. She clambered over rocks in his wake, feeling the heat burn through the sides of her shoes and trying not to touch the rocks with her hands. When they reached more shade, the relief was almost tangible.

"Here." He indicated a thin trickle of water running down the face of the wall. The bushes were heavier here, because of the water, and the temperature felt a good twenty degrees cooler. Part of it was illusion, because of the contrast, but the extra greenery did have a cooling effect.

Sunny sighed as she looked at the trickle. Filling their water bottles would be a snap. Washing off would be easy. But washing clothes—well, that was a different proposition. There wasn't a pool in which she could soak them, not even a puddle. The water was soaked immediately into the dry, thirsty earth. The ground was damp, but not saturated.

The only thing she could do was fill a water bottle over and over, and rinse the dust out. "This will take forever," she groused.

An irritating masculine smirk was on his face as he peeled his T-shirt off over his head and handed it to her. "We aren't exactly pressed for time, are we?"

She almost thrust the shirt back at him and demanded he put it on, but not because of his comment. She wasn't a silly prude, she had seen naked chests more times than she could count, but she had never before seen *his* naked chest. He was smoothly, powerfully muscled, with pectorals that looked like flesh-covered steel and a hard, six-pack abdomen. A light patch of black hair stretched from one small brown nipple to the other. She wanted to touch him. Her hand actually ached for the feel of his skin, and she clenched her fingers hard on his shirt.

The smirk faded, his eyes darkening. He touched her face, curving his fingers under her chin and lifting it. His expression was hard with pure male desire. "You know what's going to happen between us, don't you?" His voice was low and rough.

"Yes." She could barely manage a whisper. Her throat had tightened, her body responding to his touch, his intent.

"Do you want it?"

So much she ached with it, she thought. She looked up into those golden-brown eyes and trembled from the enormity of the step she was taking.

"Yes," she said.

Chapter 7

She had lived her entire life without ever having lived at all, Sunny thought as she mechanically rinsed out his clothes and draped them over the hot rocks to dry. She and Chance might never get out of this canyon alive, and even if they did, it could take a long time. Weeks, perhaps months, or longer. Whatever Margreta did, she would long since have done it, and there wasn't a damn thing Sunny could do about the situation. For the first time in her life, she had to think only about herself and what *she* wanted. That was simple; what she wanted was Chance.

She had to face facts. She was good at it; she had been doing it her entire life. The fact that had been glaring her in the face was that they could very well die here in this little canyon. If they didn't survive, she didn't want to die still clinging to the reasons for not getting involved that, while good and valid in civilization, didn't mean spit here. She already *was* involved with him, in a battle for their very lives. She certainly didn't want to die without having known what it was like to be loved by him, to feel him inside her and hold him close, and to tell him that she loved him. She had a whole world of love dammed up inside her, drying up because she hadn't had anyone to whom she could give it, but now she had this opportunity, and she wasn't going to waste it.

A psych analyst would say this was just propinquity: the "any port in a storm" type of attraction, or the Adam and Eve syndrome. That might be part of it, for him. If she had to guess, Sunny would say that Chance was used to having sex whenever he wanted it. He had that look about him, a bone-deep sexual confidence that would draw women like flies. She was currently the only fly available.

But it wasn't just that. He had been attracted to her before, just as she had been to him. If they had made it to Seattle without trouble, she would have been strong enough to refuse his invitation and walk away from him. She would never have allowed herself to get to know him. Maybe they had met only twenty-four hours before, but those hours had been more intense than anything else she had ever known. She imagined it was as if they had gone into battle together; the danger they had faced, and were still facing, had forged a bond between them like soldiers in a war. She had learned things about him that it would have taken her weeks to learn in a normal situation, weeks that she would never have given herself.

Of all the things she had learned about him in those twenty-four hours, there wasn't one she didn't like. He was a man willing to step forward and take a risk, get involved, otherwise he wouldn't have stopped the cretin in the airport. He was calm in a crisis, self-sufficient and capable, and he was more considerate of her than anyone else she had ever known. On top of all that, he was so sexy he made her mouth water.

Most men, after hearing something like what she had

told him, would have immediately gone for the sex. Chance hadn't. Instead, he had kissed her very sweetly and said, "I'll get the rest of the things from the plane, so I can change clothes and give you my dirty ones to wash."

"Gee, thanks," she had managed to say.

He had winked at her. "Any time."

He was a man who could put off his personal pleasure in order to take care of business. So here she was, scrubbing his underwear. Not the most romantic thing in the world to be doing, yet it was an intimate chore that strengthened the link forming between them. He was working to feed her; she was working to keep their clothes clean.

So far, Chance was everything that was steadfast and re-liable. So why did she keep sensing that edge of danger in him? Was it something his army training had given him that was just *there* no matter what he was doing? She had never met anyone else who had been a ranger, so she had no means of comparison. She was just glad of that training, if it helped keep them alive.

After his clothes were as clean as she could get them, she hesitated barely a second before stripping out of her own, down to her skin. She couldn't tolerate her grimy clothes another minute. The hot desert air washed over her bare skin, a warm, fresh caress on the backs of her knees, the small of her back, that made her nipples pinch into erect little nubs. She had never before been outside in the nude, and she felt positively decadent.

What if Chance saw her? If he was overcome with lust by the sight of her naked body, nothing would happen that hadn't been going to happen, anyway. Not that it was likely he would be overcome, she thought wryly, smiling to her-self, her curves were a long way from voluptuous. Still, if a man was faced with a naked, available woman—it could happen.

She poured a bottle of water over herself, then scooped up a handful of sand and began scrubbing. Rinsing off the sand was a matter of refilling the bottle several times. When she was finished she felt considerably refreshed and her skin was baby smooth. Maybe the skin-care industry should stop grinding up shells and rock for body scrubs, she thought, and just go for the sand.

Naked and wet, she could feel a slight breeze stirring the hot air, cooling her until she was actually comfortable. She didn't have a towel, so she let herself dry naturally while she washed her own clothes, then quickly dressed in the beige jeans and green T-shirt that she always carried. They were earth colors, colors that blended in well with vegetation and would make her more difficult to see if she had to disappear into the countryside. She would have opted for actual camouflage-patterned clothing, if that wouldn't have made her more noticeable in public. Her bra was wet from its scrubbing, so she hadn't put it back on, and the soft cotton of the T-shirt clung to her breasts, clearly revealing their shape and their soft jiggle when she walked, and the small peaks of her nipples. She wondered if Chance would notice.

"Hey," he said from behind her, his voice low and soft.

Startled, she whirled to face him. It was as if she had conjured him from her thoughts. He stood motionless about ten yards away, his eyes narrowed, his expression focused. His whiskey-coloured gaze went straight to her breasts. Oh, he noticed all right.

Her nipples got even harder, as if he had touched them. She swallowed, trying to control a ridiculous twinge of her nerves. After all, he had already touched her breasts, and she had given him permission to do more. "How long have you been there?"

"A while." His eyelids were heavy, his voice a little rough. "I kept waiting for you to turn around, but you never did. I enjoyed the view, anyway."

Her breath hitched. "Thank you."

"You have the sweetest little ass I've ever seen."

Liquid heat moved through her. "You sweet talker, you," she said, not even half kidding. "When do I get a peep show?"

"Any time, honey." His tone was dark with sensual promise. "Any time." Then he smiled ruefully. "Any time except now. We need to move these clothes so I can set the trap up here. Since this is where the water is, this is where the game will come. I'll set the traps now and try to catch something for supper, then wash up after I clean whatever we catch—if we catch anything at all."

He wasn't exactly swept away with lust, but there was that reassuring steadfastness again, the ability to keep his priorities straight. In this situation, she didn't want Gonad the Barbarian; she wanted a man on whom she could depend to do the smart thing.

He began gathering the wet clothes off the rocks, and Sunny moved to help him. "Let me guess," she said. "The clothes still smell like humans."

"There's that, plus they're something different. Wild animals are skittish whenever something new invades their territory."

As they walked back to the overhang she asked, "How long does it normally take to catch something in a trap?"

He shrugged. "There's no 'normal' to it. I've caught game

before within ten minutes of putting out the trap. Sometimes it takes days."

She wasn't exactly looking forward to eating Peter Cottontail, but neither did she want another nutrition bar. It would be nice if some big fat chicken had gotten lost in the desert and just happened to wander into their trap. She wouldn't mind eating a chicken. After a moment of wishful thinking she resigned herself to rabbit—if they were lucky, that is. They would have to eat whatever Chance could catch.

When they reached "home," which the overhang had become, they spread their clothes out on another assortment of hot rocks. The first items she had washed were already almost dry; the dry heat of the desert was almost as efficient as an electric clothes dryer.

When they had finished, Chance collected his two handmade traps and examined them one last time. Sunny watched him, seeing the same intensity in his eyes and body that she had noticed before. "You're enjoying this, aren't you?" she asked, only mildly surprised. This was, after all, the ultimate in primitive guy stuff.

He didn't look at her, but a tiny smile twitched the corners of his mouth. "I guess I'm not all that upset. We're alive. We have food, water and shelter. I'm alone with a woman I've wanted from the first minute I saw her." He produced a badly crushed Baby Ruth candy bar from his hip pocket and opened the wrapper, then pinched off small pieces of it and put them in the traps.

Sunny was instantly diverted. "You're using a candy bar as bait?" she demanded in outraged tones. "Give me that! You can use my nutrition bar in the traps."

He grinned and evaded her as she tried to swipe the remainder of the candy bar. "The nutrition bar wouldn't be a good bait. No self-respecting rabbit would touch it."

"How long have you been hiding that Baby Ruth?"

"I haven't been hiding it. I found it in the plane when I got the rest of the stuff. Besides, it's melted from being in the plane all day."

"Melted, schmelted," she scoffed. "That doesn't affect chocolate."

"Ah." He nodded, still grinning. "You're one of those."

"One of those *what?*"

"Chocoholics."

"I am not," she protested, lifting her chin at him. "I'm a sweetaholic."

"Then why didn't you pack something sweet in that damn survival bag of yours, instead of something that tastes like dried grass?"

She scowled at him. "Because the idea is to stay alive. If I had a stash of candy, I'd eat it all the first day, then I'd be in trouble."

The golden-brown gaze flicked at her, lashing like the tip of a whip. "When are you going to tell me why you packed survival gear for an overnight plane trip to Seattle?" He kept his tone light, but she felt the change of mood. He was dead serious about this, and she wondered why. What did it matter to him why she lugged that stuff everywhere she went? She could understand why he would be curious, but not insistent.

"I'm paranoid," she said, matching his tone in lightness. "I'm always certain there will be some sort of emergency, and I'm terrified of being unprepared."

His eyes went dark and flat. "Bull. Don't try to blow me off with lies."

Sunny might be good-natured almost to a fault, but she

didn't back down. "I was actually trying to be polite and avoid telling you it's none of your business."

To her surprise, he relaxed. "That's more like it."

"What? Being rude?"

"Honest," he corrected. "If there are things you don't want to tell me, fine. I don't like it, but at least it was the truth. Considering our situation, we need to be able to totally rely on each other, and that demands trust. We have to be up front with each other, even when the truth isn't all sweetness and light."

She crossed her arms and narrowed her eyes, giving him an "I'm not buying this" look. "Even when you're just being nosy? I don't think so." She sniffed. "You're trying to psych me into spilling my guts."

"Is it working?"

"I felt a momentary twinge of guilt, but then logic kicked in."

She sensed he tried to fight it, but a smile crinkled his eyes, then moved down to curl the corners of that beautifully cut mouth. He shook his head. "You're going to cause me a lot of trouble," he said companionably as he picked up the traps and started back to their little water hole, if a trickle could be called a hole.

"Why's that?" she called to his back.

"Because I'm afraid I'm going to fall in love with you," he said over his shoulder as he walked around a jutting curve of the canyon wall and disappeared from sight.

Sunny's legs felt suddenly weak; her knees actually wobbled, and she reached out to brace her hand on the wall. Had he really said that? Did he mean it? Would a man admit to something like that if he wasn't already emotionally involved?

Her heart was pounding as if she had been running. She could handle a lot of things most people never even thought of having to do, such as running for her life, but when it came to a romantic relationship she was a babe in the woods—or in the desert, to be accurate. She had never let a man get close enough to her to matter, because she had to be free to disappear without a moment's notice or regret. But this time she couldn't disappear; she couldn't go anywhere. This time she was in a lot more trouble than Chance was, because she was already in love—fully, falling-down-a-mine-shaft, terrifyingly in love.

The feeling was a stomach-tightening mixture of ecstasy and horror. The last thing she wanted to do was love him, but it was way too late to worry about that now. What had already begun had blossomed into full flower when he *didn't* make love to her after she had said he could. Something very basic and primal had recognized him then as her mate. He was everything she had ever wanted in a man, everything she had ever dreamed about in those half-formed thoughts she had never let fully surface into her consciousness, because she had always known that life wasn't for her.

But those circumstances held sway up in the world, not down here in this sunlit hole where they were the only two people alive. She felt raw inside, as if all her nerve endings and emotions had been stripped of their protective coverings, leaving her vulnerable to feelings she had always before been able to keep at bay. Those emotions kept sweeping over her in exhilarating waves, washing her into unknown territory. She wanted very much to protect herself, yet all the shields she had used over the years were suddenly useless.

Tonight they would become lovers, and one last protective wall would be irrevocably breached. Sex wasn't just sex to her; it was a commitment, a dedication of self, that would be part of her for the rest of her life.

She wasn't naive about what else making love with him could mean. She wasn't on any form of birth control, and while he might have a few condoms with him, they would quickly be used. The bell couldn't be un-rung, and once they had made love they couldn't go back to a chaste relationship. What would she do if she got pregnant and they weren't rescued? She had to hold out hope that they wouldn't be down here forever, yet a small kernel of logic told her that it was possible they wouldn't be found. What would she do if she got pregnant even if they *were* rescued? A baby would be a major complication. How would she protect it? Somehow she couldn't see herself and Chance and a baby making a normal little all-American family; she would still be running, because that was the only way to be safe.

Keeping him at a distance, remaining platonic, was the only safe, sane thing to do. Unfortunately, she didn't seem to have a good grip on her sanity any longer. She felt as if those waves had carried her too far from shore for her to make it back now. For better or worse, all she could do was ride the current where it would take her.

Nevertheless, she tried. She tried to tell herself how stupidly irresponsible it was to risk getting pregnant under any circumstances, but particularly in *this* circumstance. Yes, women all over the world conceived and gave birth in primitive conditions, but for whatever reasons, cultural, economic or lack of brain power, they didn't have a choice. She did. All she had to do was say "no" and ignore all her feminine instincts shrieking "yes, yes."

When Chance returned she was still standing in the same spot she had been when he left, her expression stricken. He was instantly alert, reaching for the pistol tucked into his waistband at the small of his back. "What's wrong?"

"What if I get pregnant?" she asked baldly, indicating their surroundings with a sweep of her hand. "That would be stupid."

He looked surprised. "Aren't you on birth control?"

"No, and even if I was, I wouldn't have an unlimited supply of pills."

Chance rubbed his jaw, trying to think of a way around this one without tipping his hand. He knew they wouldn't be here for long, only until she gave him the information he needed on her father, but he couldn't tell her that. And why in the hell wasn't she on some form of birth control? All of the female agents he knew were on long-term birth control, and Sunny's circumstances weren't that different. "I have some condoms," he finally said.

She gave him a wry smile. "How many? And what will we do when they're gone?"

The last thing he wanted to do now was make her hostile. Deciding to gamble a little, to risk not being able to make love to her in exchange for keeping her trust, he put his arms around her and cradled her against his chest. She felt good in his arms, he thought, firm with muscle and yet soft in all the right places. He hadn't been able to stop thinking about the way she looked naked: her slender, graceful back and small waist, and the tight, heart-shaped—and heart-stopping—curve of her butt. Her legs were as slim and sleekly muscled as he had expected, and the thought of them wrapping around his waist brought him to full, instant arousal. He held her so close there was no way she could miss his condition, but he didn't thrust himself at her; let her think he was a gentleman. *He* knew better, but it was essential she didn't.

He kissed the top of her head and took that gamble. "We'll do whatever you want," he said gently. "I want you— you know that. I have about three dozen condoms—"

She jerked back, glaring at him. *"Three dozen?"* she asked, horrified. "You carry around three dozen condoms?"

There it was again, that urge to laugh. She could get to him faster than any other woman he knew. "I had just stocked up," he explained, keeping his tone mild.

"They have an expiration date, you know!"

He bit the inside of his jaw—hard. "Yeah, but they don't go bad as fast as milk. They're good for a couple of years."

She gave him a suspicious look. "How long will thirty-six condoms keep you supplied?"

He sighed. "Longer than you evidently think."

"Six months?"

He did some quick math. Six months, thirty-six con-doms…he would have to have sex more than once a week. If he were in a monogamous relationship, that would be nothing, but for an unattached bachelor…

"Look," he said, letting frustration creep into both his voice and his expression, "with you, three dozen might last a week."

She looked startled, and he could see her doing some quick math now. As she arrived at the answer and her eyes widened, he thrust his hand into her hair, cupping the back of her head and holding her still while he kissed her, ruth-lessly using all his skill to arouse her. Her hands fluttered against his chest as if she wanted to push him away, but her hands wouldn't obey. He stroked his tongue into her mouth, slow and deep, feeling the answering touch of her tongue and the pressure of her lips. She tasted sweet, and the fresh smell of her was pure woman. He felt her nipples peak under the thin fabric of her T-shirt, and abruptly he had to touch them, feel them stabbing into his palm. He had his hand under her shirt almost before the thought formed. Her breasts were firm and round, her skin cool silk that warmed under his touch. Her nipples were hard little nubs that puckered even tighter when he touched them. She arched in his arms, her eyes closed, a low moan humming in her throat.

He had intended only to kiss her out of her sudden attack of responsibility. Instead, the pleasure of touching her went to his head like old whiskey, and suddenly he had to see her, taste her. With one swift motion he pulled her shirt up, baring her breasts, and tilted her back over his arm so the firm mounds were offered up to him in a sensual feast. He bent his dark head and closed his mouth over one tight, reddening nipple, rasping his tongue over it before pressing it against the roof of his mouth and sucking. He heard the sound she made this time, the cry of a sharply aroused woman, a wild, keening sound that went straight to his loins. He was dimly aware of her nails biting into his shoulders, but the pain was small, and nothing in comparison with the urgency that had seized him. Blood thundered in his ears, roared through his veins. He wanted her with a savage intensity that rode him with sharp spurs, urging him to take instead of seduce.

Grimly he reached for his strangely elusive self-control. Only the experience and training of his entire adulthood, spent in the trenches of a dirty, covert, on-going war, gave him the strength to rein himself in. Reluctantly he eased his clamp on her nipple, giving the turgid little bud an apologetic lick. She quivered in his arms, whimpering, her golden hair spilling back as she hung helplessly in his grasp, and he almost lost it again.

Damn it all, he couldn't wait.

Swiftly he dipped down and snagged the blanket from the ground, then hooked his right arm under her knees and lifted her off her feet, carrying her out into the sunlight. The golden glow of the lowering sun kissed her skin with a subtle sheen, deepened the glitter of her hair. Her breasts were creamy, with the delicate blue tracery of her veins showing through the pale skin, and her small nipples were a sweet rosy color, shining wetly, standing out in hard peaks. "God, you're beautiful," he said in a low, rough voice.

He set her on her feet; she swayed, her lovely eyes dazed with need. He spread out the blanket and reached for her before that need began to cool. He wanted her scorching hot, so ready for him that she would fight him for completion.

He stripped the T-shirt off over her head, dropped it on the blanket, and hooked his fingers in the waistband of her jeans. A quick pop of the snap, a jerk on the tab of the zipper, and the jeans slid down her thighs.

Her hands gripped his forearms. "Chance?" She sounded strangely uncertain, a little hesitant. If she changed her mind now—

He kissed her, slow and deep, and thumbed her nipples. She made that little humming sound again, rising on her toes to press against him. He pushed her jeans down to her ankles, wrapped both arms around her and carried her down to the blanket.

She gasped, her head arching back. "Here? Now?"

"I can't wait." That was nothing more than the hard truth. He couldn't wait until dark, until they had politely crawled into the tent together as if they were following some script. He wanted her now, in the sunlight, naked and warm and totally spontaneous. He stripped her panties down and freed her ankles from the tangle of jeans and underwear.

It seemed she didn't want to wait, either. She tugged at his shirt, pushing it up. Impatiently he gripped the hem and wrenched the garment off over his head, then spread her legs and eased his weight down on her, settling into the notch of her open thighs.

She went very still, her eyes widening as she stared up at him. He fished in his pocket for the condom he'd put there earlier, then lifted himself enough to unfasten his jeans and shove them down. He donned the condom with an abrupt, practiced motion. When he came back down to her, she braced her hands against his shoulders as if she wanted to preserve some small distance between them. But any distance was too much; he grasped her hands in one of his and pulled them over her head, pinning them to the blanket and arching her breasts against him. With his free hand he reached between them and guided his hard length to the soft, wet entrance of her body.

Sunny quivered, helpless in his grasp. She had never before felt so vulnerable, or so alive. His passion wasn't controlled and gentle, the way she had expected; it was fierce and tumultuous, buffeting her with its force. He held her down, dwarfed her with his big muscular body, and she trembled as she waited for the hard thrust of penetration. She was ready for him, oh, so ready. She ached with need; she burned with it. She wanted to beg him to hurry, but she couldn't make her lungs work. He reached down, and she felt the brush of his knuckles between her legs, then the stiff, hot length of him pushing against her opening.

Everything in her seemed to tighten, coiling, focusing on that intimate intrusion. The soft flesh between her legs began to burn and sting as the blunt pressure stretched her. He pushed harder, and the pressure became pain. Wild frustration filled her. She wanted him *now*, inside her, easing the ache and tension, stroking her back into feverish pleasure.

He started to draw back, but she couldn't let him, couldn't bear losing what his touch had promised. She had denied herself so many things, but not this, not now. She locked her legs around his and lifted her hips, fiercely impaling herself, thrusting past the resistance of her body.

She couldn't hold back the thin cry that tore from her throat. Shock robbed her muscles of strength, and she went limp on the blanket.

Chance moved over her, his broad shoulders blotting out the sun. He was a dark, massive silhouette, his shape blurred by her tears. He murmured a soft reassurance even as he probed deeper, and deeper still, until his full length was inside her.

He released her hands to cradle her in both arms. Sunny clung to his shoulders, holding as tight as she could, because without his strength she thought she might fly apart. She hadn't realized this would hurt so much, that he would feel so thick and hot inside her, or go so deep. He was invading all of her, taking over her body and commanding its responses, even her breathing, her heartbeat, the flow of blood through her veins.

He moved gently at first, slowly, angling his body so he applied pressure where she needed it most. He did things to her with his hands, stroking her into a return of pleasure. He kissed her, leisurely exploring her with his tongue. He touched her nipples, sucked them, nibbled on the side of her neck. His tender attention gradually coaxed her into response, into an instinctive motion as her hips rose and fell in time with his thrusts. She still clung to his shoulders, but in need rather than desperation. An overwhelming heat swept over her, and she heard herself panting.

He pushed her legs farther apart and thrust deeper, harder, faster. Sensation exploded in her, abruptly convulsing her flesh. She writhed beneath him, unable to hold back the short, sharp cries that surged upward, past her constricted throat. The pounding rhythm wouldn't let the spasms abate; they kept shuddering through her until she was sobbing, fighting him, wanting release, wanting more, and finally—when his hard body stiffened and began shuddering—wanting nothing.

Chapter 8

A virgin. Sunny Miller had been a *virgin*. He tried to think, when he could think at all, what the possible ramifications were, but none of that seemed important right now. Of far more immediate urgency was how to comfort a woman whose first time had been on a blanket spread over the rough ground, in broad daylight, with a man who hadn't even taken off his boots.

He lay sprawled on his back beside her on the blanket. She had turned on her side away from him, curling in on herself while visible tremors shook her slender, naked body. Moving was an effort—*breathing* was an effort—as he pulled off the condom and tossed it away. He had climaxed so violently that he felt dazed. And if it affected him so strongly, with his experience, what was she thinking? Feeling? Had she anticipated the pain, or been shocked by it?

He knew she had climaxed. She had been as aroused as he; when he had started to pull back in stunned realization, she had hooked her legs around his and forced the entry herself. He had seen the shock in her eyes as he penetrated her, felt the reverberations in her flesh. And he had watched her face as he carefully aroused her, holding himself back with ruthless control until he felt the wild clenching of her loins. Then nothing had been able to hold him back, and he had exploded in his own gut-wrenching release.

For a woman of twenty-nine to remain a virgin, she had to have some strongly held reason for doing so. Sunny had willingly, but not lightly, surrendered her chastity to him. He felt humbled, and honored, and he was scared as hell. He hadn't been easy with her, either in the process or the culmination. At first glance the fact that she had climaxed might make everything all right with her, but he knew better. She didn't have the experience to handle the sensual violence her body and emotions had endured. She needed holding, and reassuring, until she stopped shaking and regained her equilibrium.

He put his hand on her arm and tugged her over onto her back. She didn't actively resist, but she was stiff, uncoordinated. She was pale, her eyes unusually brilliant, as if she fought tears. He cradled her head on his arm and leaned over her, giving her the attention and the contact he knew she needed. She glanced quickly up at him, then away, and a surge of color pinkened her cheeks.

He was charmed by the blush. Gently he smoothed his hand up her bare torso, stroking her belly, trailing his fingers over her breasts. The lower curves of her breasts bore the marks of his beard stubble. He soothed them with his tongue, taking care not to add more abrasions, and made a mental note to shave when he washed.

Something needed to be said, but he didn't know what. He had talked his way into strongholds, drug dens and government offices; he had an uncanny knack for making a lightning assessment of any given person and situation, and then saying exactly the right thing to get the reaction he wanted. But from the moment he had seen Sunny, lust had gotten in the way of his usual expertise. No amount of prep work could have prepared him for the impact of her sparkling eyes and bright smile, or told him he could be so disarmed by a sense of humor. "Sunny" was a very apt nickname for her.

Just now his sunshine was very quiet, almost stricken, as if she regretted their intimacy. And he couldn't bear it. He had lost count, over the years, of the women who had tried to cling to him after the sex act was finished and he slipped away, both physically and mentally, but he couldn't bear it that this one woman wasn't trying to hold him. For some reason, whether this was simply too much too soon or for some deeper reason, she was trying to hold her distance from him. She wasn't curling in his arms, sighing with repletion; she was retreating behind an invisible wall, the one that had been there from the beginning.

Everything in him rejected the idea. A primitive, possessive rage swept over him. She was his, and he would not let her go. His muscles tightened in a renewed surge of lust, and he mounted her, sliding into the tight, swollen clasp of her sheath. She inhaled sharply, the shock of his entry jarring her out of her malaise. She wedged her hands between them and sank her nails into his chest, but she didn't try to push him away. Her legs came up almost automatically, wrapping around his hips. He caught her thighs and adjusted them higher, around his waist. "Get used to it," he said, more harshly than he'd intended. "To me. To this. To us. Because I won't let you pull away from me."

Her lips trembled, but he had her full attention now. "Even for your own sake?" she whispered, distress leaching the blue undertones from her eyes and leaving them an empty gray.

He paused for a fraction of a second, wondering if she was referring to her father. "Especially for that," he replied, and set himself to the sweet task of arousing her. This time was totally for her; he wooed her with a skill that went beyond sexual experience. His extensive training in the martial arts had taught him how to cripple with a touch, kill with a single blow, but it had also taught him all the places on the human body that were exquisitely sensitive to pleasure. The backs of her knees and thighs, the delicate arches of her feet, the lower curve of her buttocks, all received their due attention. Slowly she came alive under him, a growing inner wetness easing his way. She began to move in time with his leisurely thrusts, rising up to meet him. He stroked the cluster of nerves in the small of her back and was rewarded by the reflexive arch that took him deeper into her.

She sighed, her lips parted, her eyes closed. Her cheeks glowed; her lips were puffy and red. He saw all the signs of her arousal and whispered encouragement. Her head tossed to the side, and her hardened nipples stabbed against his chest. Gently, so gently, he bit the tender curve where her neck met her shoulder.

She cried out and began climaxing, her peak catching him by surprise. So did his own. He hadn't meant to climax, but the delicate inner clench and release of her body sent pleasure roaring through him, bursting out of control.

He tried to stop, tried to withdraw; his body simply wouldn't obey. Instead, he thrust deep and shuddered wildly as his seed spurted from him into the hot, moist depths of her. He heard his own deep, rough cry; then both time and thought stopped, and all that was left of him sank down on her in a heavy sprawl.

Shadow had crept across the canyon floor when he

wrapped her in the blanket and carried her back to the sheltering overhang. The surrounding rock blocked the sun during the day, but it also absorbed its heat so that at night, when the temperature dropped, it was noticeably warmer in their snug little niche than it was outside. Sunny yawned, drowsy with satisfaction, and rested her head on his shoulder. "I can walk," she said mildly, though she made no effort to slide her feet to the ground.

"Hey, I'm doing my macho act here," he protested. "Don't ruin it."

She tilted her head back to look at him. "You aren't acting, though, are you?"

"No," he admitted, and earned a chuckle from her.

Time had gotten away from him while they drifted in the sleepy aftermath of passion. The sun was so far down in the sky that only the upper rim of the canyon was lit, the reds and golds and purples of the rock catching fire in the sunset, while the sky had taken on a deep violet hue.

"I'm going to check the traps while there's still a few minutes of light left," he said as he deposited her on the ground. "Sit tight. I won't be long."

Sunny sat tight for about two seconds after he disappeared from view, then bounced to her feet. Quickly she washed and dressed, needing the protection of her clothing. She had the uneasy feeling that nothing was the same as it had been before Chance carried her out into the sunlight. She had been prepared for the lovemaking, but not for that overwhelming assault on her senses. She had hoped for pleasure, and instead found something so much more powerful that she couldn't control it.

And most of all, Chance had revealed himself for the marauder he was.

She had seen glimpses of it before, in moments when the force of his personality broke through his control. She should have realized then; one didn't bolt a steel gate on an empty room. His control had given her the rare, luxurious feeling of safety, and she had been so beguiled that she had ignored the power that gate held constrained, or what would happen if it ever broke loose. This afternoon, she had found out.

He had said he'd been in the Army Rangers. That should have told her everything she needed to know about the kind of man he was. She could only think she'd let the stress of the situation, and her worry about Margreta, blind her to his true nature.

A shiver rippled down her spine, a totally sensual reaction as she remembered the tumultuous hour—or hours—on the blanket. She had been helpless, totally blindsided by the force of her reaction. She had known from the beginning that she responded to him as she never had before to any man, but she still hadn't been prepared for such a complete upheaval of her senses. He wasn't the only one accustomed to control; her very life had depended on her control of any given situation, and with Chance, she had found that she couldn't control either him or herself.

She had never been more terrified in her life.

The way she had felt about him before was nothing compared to now. It wasn't just the sex, which had been so much more intense and harsh than she had ever imagined. No, it was the part of his character he had revealed, the part that he had tried to keep hidden, that called to her so strongly she knew only her own death would end the love she felt for him. Chance was one of a very special breed of men, a warrior. All the little pieces of him she had sensed were now settled into place, forming the picture of a man who would always have something wild and ruthless inside him, a man willing to put himself at risk, step into the line of fire, to protect what he loved. He was the complete antithesis of her father, whose life was devoted wholly to destruction.

Sunny hadn't had a choice in a lot of the sacrifices of her life. Their mother had given her and Margreta away in an effort to save them, but hadn't been able to completely sever herself from her daughters' lives. Instead, she had taught them all her hard-learned skills, taught them how to hide, to disappear—and, if necessary, how to fight. By necessity, Pamela Vickery Hauer had become an expert in her own brand of guerrilla warfare. Whenever she thought it safe she would visit, and the kindly Millers would go out of their way to give her time with her girls.

When Sunny was sixteen, Pamela's luck had finally run out. Their father's network was extensive, and he had many more resources at his disposal than his fugitive wife could command. Logically, it had been only a matter of time before he found her. And when she was finally run to ground, Pamela had killed herself rather than take the chance he would, by either torture or drugs, be able to wring their location from her.

That was Sunny's legacy, a life living in shadows, and a courageous mother who had killed herself in order to protect her children. No one had asked her if this was the life she wanted; it was the life she had, so she had made the best of it she could.

Nor had it been her choice to live apart from Margreta; that had been her sister's decision. Margreta was older; she had her own demons to fight, her own battles to wage, and she had never been as adept at the survival skills taught by their mother as Sunny had been. So Sunny had lost her sister, and when the Millers died, first Hal and then Eleanor, she had been totally alone. The calls on her cell phone from Margreta were the only contact she had, and she knew Margreta was content to leave it at that.

She didn't think she had the strength to give up Chance, too. That was why she was terrified to the point of panic, because her very presence endangered his life. Her only solace was that because he was the man he was, he was very tough and capable, more able to look after himself.

She took a deep breath, trying not to anticipate trouble. If and when they got out of this canyon, then she would decide what to do.

Because she was too nervous to sit still, she checked the clothes she had washed out and found they were already dry. She gathered them off the various rocks where they had spread them, and though the little chore had taken only minutes, by the time she walked back to the overhang there was barely enough light for her to see.

Chance hadn't taken the flashlight with him, she remembered. It was a moonless night; if he didn't get back within the next few minutes, he wouldn't be able to see.

The fire had been kept smoldering all day, to maximize the smoke and conserve their precious store of wood, but now she quickly added more sticks to bring up a good blaze, both for her own sake and so he would have the fire as a beacon. The flickering firelight penetrated the darkness of the overhang, sending patterns dancing against the rock wall. She searched through their belongings until she found the flashlight, to have it at hand in case she had to search for him.

Total blackness came suddenly, as if Mother Nature had dropped her petticoats over the land. Sunny stepped to the front of the overhang. "Chance!" she called, then paused to listen.

The night wasn't silent. There were rustlings, the whispers of the night things as they crept about their business. A faint breeze stirred the scrub brush, sounding like dry bones rattling together. She listened carefully, but didn't hear an answering call.

"Chance!" She tried again, louder this time. Nothing. "Damn it," she muttered, and flashlight in hand set off for the deep end of the canyon where their life-giving water trickled out of a crack in the rock.

She walked carefully, checking where she put her feet. A second encounter with a snake was more than she could handle in one day. As she walked she periodically called his name, growing more irritated by the moment. Why didn't he answer her? Surely he could hear her by now; sound carried in the thin, dry air.

A hard arm caught her around the waist and swung her up against an equally hard body. She shrieked in alarm, the sound cut off by a warm, forceful mouth. Her head tilted back under the pressure, and she grabbed his shoulders for support. He took his time, teasing her with his tongue, kissing her until the tension left her body and she was moving fluidly against him.

When he lifted his head his breathing was a little ragged. Sunny felt obliged to complain about his treatment of her. "You scared me," she accused, though her voice sounded more sultry than sulky.

"You got what you deserved. I told you to sit tight." He kissed her again, as if he couldn't help himself.

"Is this part of the punishment?" she murmured when he came up for air.

"Yeah," he said, and she felt him smile against her temple. "Do it some more."

He obliged, and she felt the magic fever begin burning again deep inside her. She ached all over from his previous lovemaking; she shouldn't feel even a glimmer of desire so soon, and yet she did. She wanted to feel all the power of his superbly conditioned body, take him inside her and hold him close, feel him shake as the pleasure overwhelmed him just as it did her.

Finally he tore his mouth from hers, but she could feel his heart pounding against her, feel the hard ridge in his jeans. "Have mercy," he muttered. "I won't have a chance to starve to death. I'm going to die of exhaustion."

Starving reminded her of the traps, because she was very hungry. "Did you catch a rabbit?" she asked, her tone full of hope.

"No rabbit, just a scrawny bird." He held up his free hand, and she saw that he held the plucked carcass of a bird that was quite a bit smaller than the average chicken.

"That isn't the Roadrunner, is it?"

"What's this thing you have with imaginary animals? No, it isn't a roadrunner. Try to be a little more grateful."

"Then what is it?"

"Bird," he said succinctly. "After I spit it and turn it over the flames for a while, it'll be roasted bird. That's all that matters."

Her stomach growled. "Well, okay. As long as it isn't the Roadrunner. He's my favorite cartoon character. After Bullwinkle."

He began laughing. "When did you see those old cartoons? I didn't think they were on anywhere now."

"They're all on disk," she said. "I rented them from my local video store."

He took her arm, and they began walking back to camp, chatting and laughing about their favorite cartoons. They both agreed that the slick animated productions now couldn't match the older cartoons for sheer comedy, no matter how realistic the modern ones were. Sunny played the flashlight beam across their path as they walked, watching for snakes.

"By the way, why were you calling me?" Chance asked suddenly.

"It's dark, in case you didn't notice. You didn't carry the flashlight with you."

He made a soft, incredulous sound. "You were coming to *rescue* me?"

She felt a little embarrassed. Of course, a former ranger could find his way back to camp in the dark. "I wasn't thinking," she admitted.

"You were thinking too much," he corrected, and hugged her to his side.

They reached their little camp. The fire she had built up was still sending little tongues of flame licking around the remnants of the sticks. Chance laid the bird on a rock, swiftly fashioned a rough spit from the sticks, and sharpened the end of another stick with his pocket knife. He skewered the bird with that stick, and set it in the notches of the spit, then added some small sticks to the fire. Soon the bird was dripping sizzling juice into the flames, which leaped higher in response. The delicious smell of cooking meat made her mouth water.

She shoved a flat rock closer to the fire and sat down, watching him turn the bird. She was close enough to feel the heat on her arms; as chilly as the night was already, it was difficult to remember that just a few short hours ago the heat had been scorching. She had camped out only once before, but the circumstances had been nothing like this. For one thing, she had been alone.

The amber glow of the flames lit the hard angles of his face. He had washed up while he was gone, she saw; his hair was still a little damp. He had shaved, too. She smiled to herself.

He looked up and saw her watching him, and a wealth of knowledge, of sensual awareness, flashed between them. "Are you all right?" he asked softly.

"I'm fine." She had no idea how her face glowed as she wrapped her arms around her legs and rested her chin on her drawn-up knees.

"Are you bleeding?"

"Not now. And it was only a little, at first," she added hastily when his eyes narrowed in concern.

He returned his gaze to the bird, watching as he carefully turned it. "I wish I had known."

She wished he didn't know now. The reasons for her recently lost virginity weren't something she wanted to dissect. "Why?" she asked, injecting a light note into her tone. "Would you have been noble and stopped?"

"Hell, no," he said. "I'd have gone about it a little differently, is all."

Now, that was interesting. "What would have been different?"

"How rough I was. How long I took."

"You took long enough," she assured him, smiling. "Both times."

"I could have made it better for you."

"How about for you?"

His dark gaze flashed upward, and he gave a rueful smile. "Sweetheart, if it had been any better for me, my heart would have given out."

"Ditto."

He turned the bird again. "I didn't wear a condom the second time."

"I know." The evidence had been impossible to miss.

Their gazes met and locked again, and again they were linked by that silent communication. He might have made her pregnant. He knew it, and she knew it.

"How's the timing?"

She rocked her hand back and forth. "Borderline." The odds were in their favor, she figured, but it wasn't a risk she wanted to take again.

"If we weren't stuck here—" he began, then shrugged.

"What?"

"I wouldn't mind."

Desire surged through her, and she almost jumped his bones right then. She got a tight grip on herself, literally, and fought to stay seated. Hormones were sneaky devils, she thought, ready to undermine her common sense just because he mentioned wanting to make her pregnant.

"Neither would I," she admitted, and watched to see if he had the same reaction. Color flared high on his carved cheekbones, and a muscle in his jaw flexed. His hand tightened on the spit until his knuckles were white. Yep, it went both ways, she thought, fascinated by his battle to remain where he was.

When he judged the bird was done, he took the skewer off the spit and kicked another rock over to rest beside hers, then sat down on it. With his pocket knife he cut a strip of meat and held it out to her. "Careful, don't burn yourself," he warned as she reached eagerly for the meat.

She juggled the strip back and forth in her hands, blowing on it to cool it. When she could hold it, she took her first tentative bite. Her taste buds exploded with the taste of wood and smoke and roasted fowl. "Oh, that's good," she moaned, chewing slowly to get every ounce of flavor.

Chance cut off a strip for himself and took his first bite, looking as satisfied as she with their meal. They chewed in silence for a while. He was careful to divide the meat equally, until she was forced to stop eating way before she was satisfied. He was so much bigger than she was that if they each ate the same amount, he would be short-changed.

He knew what she was doing, of course. "You're taking care of me again," he observed. "You're hell on my image, you know that? I'm supposed to be taking care of you."

"You're a lot bigger than I am. You need larger portions."

"Let me worry about the food, sweetheart. We won't starve. There's more game to catch, and tomorrow I'll look for some edible plants to round out our diet."

"Bird and bush," she said lightly. "What all the trendy people are eating these days."

Her quip made him grin. He persuaded her to eat a little more of the meat, then they finished off one of the remaining nutrition bars. Their hunger appeased, they began getting ready to turn in for the night.

He banked the fire while she got the tent ready. They brushed their teeth and made one last nature call, just like old married folks, she thought in amusement. Their "home" wasn't much, really nothing more than a niche in the rock, but their preparations for the night struck her as very domestic—until he said, "Do you want to wear my shirt tonight? It would be more like a nightgown on you than the shirt you're wearing."

There was nothing the least bit tamed in the way he was looking at her. Her heartbeat picked up in speed, and the now familiar heat began spreading through her. That was all he had to do, she thought; one look and she was aroused. He had taught her body well during the short time she had been sprawled beneath him on the blanket. Now that she knew exactly how it felt to take his hard length inside her, she craved the sensation. She wanted that convulsive peak of pleasure, even though it had frightened her with its intensity. She hadn't realized she would feel as if she were flying apart, as if her soul was being wrenched from her body. In a blinding, paralyzing moment of clarity, she knew that no other man in the world would be able to do that for her, to her. He was the One for her, capital O, big letter, underlined and italicized. The [BXU6,11p8,.2,1p4]One. She would never again be whole without him.

She must have looked stricken, because suddenly he was by her side, supporting her with an arm around her waist as he gently but inexorably guided her to the tent. He would be considerate, she realized, but he didn't intend to be refused.

She cleared her throat, searching for her equilibrium. "You'll need your shirt to keep warm—"

"You're joking, right?" He smiled down at her, the corners of his eyes crinkling. "Or did you think we were through for the night?"

She couldn't help smiling back. "That never crossed my mind. I just thought you'd need it *afterward*."

"I don't think so," he said, his hands busy unsnapping her jeans.

They were both naked and inside the tent in record time. He switched off the flashlight to save the batteries, and the total darkness closed around them, just as it had the night before. Making love when one was going totally by feel somehow heightened the other senses, she found. She was aware of the calluses on his hands as he stroked her, of the heady male scent of his skin, of the powerful muscles that bunched under her own exploring hands. His taste filled her; his kisses were a feast. She reveled in the smooth firmness of his lips, the sharp edges of his teeth; she rubbed his nipples and felt them contract under her fingers. She loved the harsh groan he gave when she cupped the soft, heavy sacs between his legs, and the way they tightened even as she held them.

She was shocked when she closed her hand around his pulsing erection. How on earth had she ever taken him inside her? The long, thick column ended in a smooth, bulbous flare, the tip of which was wet with fluid. Entranced, she curled down until she could take the tip in her mouth and lick the fluid away.

He let out an explosive curse and tumbled her on her back, reversing their positions. The confines of the small tent restricted their movement, but he managed the shift with his usual powerful grace.

She laughed, full of wonder at the magic between them, and draped her arms around his neck as he settled on top of her. "Didn't you like it?"

"I almost came," he growled. "What do you think?"

"I think I'll have my way with you yet. I may have to overpower you and tie you up, but I think I can handle the job."

"I'm positive of it. Let me know when you're going to overpower me, so I can have my clothes off."

That afternoon, caught in the whirlpool of his lovemaking, she wouldn't have believed she would be so at ease with him now, that they could indulge in this sensual teasing. She wouldn't have believed how naturally her thighs parted to accommodate his hips, or how comfortable it was, as if nature had designed them to fit together just so. Actually nature had; she just hadn't realized it until now.

He gave her a taste of her own medicine, kissing his way down her body until his hair brushed the insides of her thighs and she discovered a torture so sweet she shattered. When she could breathe again, when the colored pinpoints of light stopped flashing against her closed eyelids, he kissed her belly and laid his head on the pillowing softness. "My God, you're easy," he whispered.

She managed a strangled sound that was almost a laugh. "I guess I am. For you, anyway."

"Just for me." The dark tones of masculine possessiveness and triumph underlaid the words.

"Just for you," she whispered in agreement.

He put on a condom and slid into place between her thighs. She fought back a cry; she was sore and swollen, and he was big. He moved gently back and forth until she accepted him more easily and the discomfort faded, but gradually his thrusts quickened, became harder. Even then she sensed he was holding himself back to keep from hurting her. When he climaxed, he pulled back so only half his length was inside her, and held himself there while shudders racked his strong body.

Afterward, he tugged his T-shirt on over her head, immediately enveloping her in his scent. The roomy garment came halfway to her knees—or it would have if he hadn't bunched it around her waist. He cradled her in his arms, one big hand on her bare bottom to keep her firmly against him. He used her rolled-up cardigan for a pillow, and she used him. Oh, this was wonderful.

"Is Sunny your real name, or is it a nickname?" he asked sleepily, his lips brushing her hair.

Even as relaxed as she was, as sated, a twinge of caution made her hesitate. She never told anyone her real name. It took her a moment to remember that none of that made any difference here now. "It's a nickname," she murmured. "My real name is Sonia, but I've never used it. Sonia Ophelia Gabrielle."

"Good God." He kissed her. "Sunny suits you. So you're saddled with four names, huh?"

"Yep. I never use the middle ones, though. What about you? What's your middle name?"

"I don't have one. It's just Chance."

"Really? You aren't lying to me because it's something awful, like Eustace?"

"Cross my heart."

She settled herself more comfortably against him. "I suppose it balances out. I have four names, you have two—together, we average three."

"How about that."

She could hear a smile in his voice now. She rewarded him with a small, sneaky pinch that made him jump. His retaliation ended, a long time later, in the use of another condom.

Sunny went to sleep to the knowledge that she was happier now, with Chance, than she had ever before been in her life.

Chapter 9

The next morning the traps were empty. Sunny struggled with her disappointment. After such an idyllic, pleasure-filled night, the day should have been just as wonderful. A nice hot, filling breakfast would have been perfect.

"Could you shoot something?" she asked as she chewed half of one of the tasteless nutrition bars. "We have eight of these bars left." If they each ate a bar a day, that meant they would be out of food in four days.

In three days, Margreta would call.

Sunny pushed that thought away. Whether or not they got out of here in time for her to answer Margreta's call was something she couldn't control. Food was a more immediate problem.

Chance narrowed his eyes as he scanned the rim of the canyon, as if looking for a way out. "I have fifteen rounds in the pistol, and no extra cartridges. I'd rather save them for emergencies, since there's no telling how long we'll be here. Besides, a 9mm bullet would tear a rabbit to pieces and wouldn't leave enough left of a bird for us to eat. Assuming I could hit a bird with a pistol shot, that is."

She wasn't worried about his marksmanship. He was prob-

ably much better with a rifle, but with his military background, he would be more than competent with the pistol.
She looked down at her hands. "Would a .38 be better?"

"It isn't as powerful, so for small game, yeah, it would be
better. Not great, but better—but I have a 9mm, so it's a
moot point."

"I have one," she said softly.

His head whipped around. Something dangerous flashed
in his eyes. "What did you say?"

She nodded toward her bag. "I have a .38."

He looked in the direction of her gaze, then back at her.
His expression was like flint. "Would you like to tell me,"
he said very deliberately, "just how you happen to have a
pistol of any kind with you? You were on a commercial
flight. How did you get past the scanners?"

She didn't like giving away all her secrets, not even to
Chance. A lifetime on the run had ingrained caution into
her very bones, and she had already given him more of herself than she ever had anyone else. Still, they were in this
together. "I have some special containers."

"Where?" he snapped. "I saw you unpack everything in
your bag and there weren't any—ah, hell. The hair spray
can, right?"

Unease skittered along her spine. Why was he angry?
Even if he was a stickler for rules and regulations, which she
doubted, he should be glad they had an extra weapon, no
matter how they came by it. She straightened her shoulders.
"And the blow-dryer."

He stood over her like an avenging angel, his jaw set.
"How long have you been smuggling weapons on board
airplanes?"

"Every time I've flown," she said coolly, standing up. She

was damned if she would let him tower over her as if she was a recalcitrant child. He still towered over, just not as much. "I was sixteen the first time."

She walked over to the bag and removed the pertinent items. Chance leaned down and snagged the can of spray from her hands. He took the cap off and examined the nozzle, then pointed it away from him and depressed it. A powder-fine mist of spray shot out.

"It's really hair spray," she said. "Just not much of it." She took the can and deftly unscrewed the bottom. A short barrel slid out of the can into her hands. Putting it aside, she lifted the hair-dryer and took it apart with the same deft twist, yielding the remaining parts of the pistol. She assembled it with the ease of someone who had done the task so often she could do it in her sleep, then fed the cartridges into the magazine, snapped it into place, reversed the pistol and presented it to him butt-first.

He took it, his big hand almost swallowing the small weapon. "What in *hell* are you doing with a weapon?" he bit out.

"The same thing you are, I imagine." She walked away from him and missed the look of shock that crossed his face. With her back to him she said, "I carry it for self-protection. Why do you carry yours?"

"I charter my plane to a lot of different people, most of whom I don't know. I fly into some isolated areas sometimes. And my weapon is licensed." He hurled the words at her like rocks. "Is yours?"

"No," she said, unwilling to lie. "But I'm a single woman who travels alone, carrying packages valuable enough that a courier service is hired to deliver them. The people I deliver the packages to are strangers. Think about it. I'd have to be a fool not to carry some means of protection." That was the truth, as far as it went.

"If your reason for carrying is legitimate, then why don't you have a license?"

She felt as if she were being interrogated, and she didn't like it. The tender, teasing lover of the night was gone, and in his place was someone who sounded like a prosecutor.

She had never applied for a license to carry a concealed weapon because she didn't want any background checks in the national data system, didn't want to bring herself to the notice of anyone in officialdom.

"I have my reasons," she retorted, keeping her tone very deliberate.

"And you aren't going to tell me what they are, right?" He threw her a look that was almost sulfuric in its fury and stalked off in the direction of the traps. His stalking, like everything else he did, was utterly graceful—and completely silent.

"Good riddance, Mr. Sunshine," she hurled at his back. It was a childish jab, but she felt better afterward. Sometimes a little childishness was just what the doctor ordered.

With nothing better to do, she set off in the opposite direction, toward the plane, to gather more sticks and twigs for the all-important fire. If he tried to keep her pistol when they got out of here—and they *would* get out, she had to keep hoping—then it would be war.

Chance examined the compact pistol in his hand. It was unlike any he had ever seen before, for the simple reason that it hadn't come from any manufacturer. A gunsmith, a skilled one, had made this weapon. It bore no serial number, no name, no indication of where or when it was made. It was completely untraceable.

He couldn't think of any good reason for Sunny to have it, but he could think of several bad ones.

After yesterday, he had been more than halfway convinced she was innocent, that she was in no way involved with her father. Stupid of him, but he had equated chastity with honor. Just because a woman didn't sleep around didn't mean she was a fine, upstanding citizen. All it meant was that, for whatever reason, she hadn't had sex.

He knew better. He was far better acquainted with the blackness of the human soul than with its goodness, because he had chosen to live in the sewers. Hell, he came from the sewers; he should be right at home there, and most of the time he was. The blackness of his own soul was always there, hidden just a few layers deep, and he was always aware of it. He used to make his way in the dangerous world he had chosen, shaped it into a weapon to be used in defense of his country and, ultimately, his family. And being on such intimate terms with hell, with the twisted evil humans could visit on one another, he should know that golden hair and bright, sparkling eyes didn't necessarily belong on an angel. Shakespeare had hit the nail on the head when he warned the world against smiling villains.

It was just—*damn* it, Sunny got to him. She had slipped right past defenses he would have sworn were impregnable, and she had done it so easily they might as well not have been there at all. He wanted her, and so he had almost convinced himself that she was innocent.

Almost. There was just too much about her that didn't add up, and now there was this untraceable pistol that she smuggled on board airplanes, concealed in some very effective but simple containers. Airport scanners would show metal, but if a security guard was suspicious enough to check, he or she would find only the normal female styling aids. The hair spray can actually sprayed, and he didn't doubt the blow-dryer would work, too.

If Sunny could get a pistol on board a plane, then others could, too. He went cold at the thought of how many weapons must be flying around at any given time. Airport security wasn't his line of work, but damn if he wasn't going to make it a point to kick some asses over this.

He shoved his anger aside so he could concentrate on this assignment. He hoped he hadn't blown it by losing his temper with her, but his disillusionment had been too sharp for him to contain. The pleasure of the night they had just spent together should more than outweigh their first argument. Her inexperience with men worked against her; she would be easy to manipulate, where a seasoned veteran of the mattress wars would be more wary and blasé about their lovemaking. He still held all the trump cards, and soon he would be playing them.

He reached a particular point in the canyon and positioned himself so he was in the deepest morning shadows. Sunny couldn't catch him unawares here, and he had a clear line of sight to a certain rock on the rim of the canyon. He took a laser light from his pocket, a pencil-thin tube about two inches long that, when clicked, emitted an extraordinarily bright finger of light. He aimed it at the rock on the rim and began clicking, sending dashes of light in the code he and Zane had agreed on at the beginning of the plan. Every day he signalled Zane, both to let him know that everything was all right and that they shouldn't be rescued yet.

There was an answering flash, message received. No matter how closely he watched that rock, he never saw any movement, though he knew Zane would have immediately pulled back. He himself was damn good at moving around undetected, but Zane was extraordinary even for a SEAL. There was no one else on this earth Chance would rather have beside him in a fight than Zane.

That mission accomplished, Chance settled down in some cover where he could watch the trickle of water. Since the traps hadn't been productive overnight, he really did need to shoot something for supper. He was willing to starve to achieve his ends—but only if he had to. If a bunny rabbit showed its face, it was history.

As Sunny walked the canyon floor, picking up what sticks she could find, she studied the rock walls, looking for a fissure that might have escaped notice, an animal trail, anything that might point the way to freedom. If they only had some rock-climbing gear, she thought wistfully. A rope, cleats, anything. She had tried to anticipate any possible need when she packed her bag, but somehow being trapped in a box canyon hadn't occurred to her.

For the most part, the walls were perpendicular. Even when they slanted a little, the angle wasn't much off ninety degrees. Erosion from wind and rain had, over millions of years, cut grooves in the rock that looked like ripples in water. The only sign the canyon wasn't impregnable was the occasional little heap of rubble where smaller rocks had crumbled and fallen.

She had passed several of those small heaps before the light went on.

A fragile stirring of hope made her stomach tighten as she investigated one scattered pile of rock. It looked as if a larger boulder had fallen from the rim and shattered on impact. She picked up a fist-sized rock and rubbed her thumb over the surface, finding it gritty, the texture of sandpaper. Sandstone, she thought. It was a lovely pink color. It was also soft.

Just to be certain, she banged the rock down on a larger rock, and it broke into several pieces.

This site was no good; it was too steep. She walked along the wall, looking up at the rim and trying to find a place where the wall slanted back just a little. That was all she asked; just a little slant, enough that the angle wasn't so extreme.

There. One of the ripples curved backward, and when she picked her way through rocks and bushes to investigate she saw the opportunity for which she had been looking. She ran her hand over the rock, exulting in the sandpaper texture of it under her palm. Maybe, just maybe…

She ran back to the camp and grabbed the curling iron out of the bag. Chance hadn't asked, but the pistol wasn't the only weapon she carried. Quickly she unscrewed the metal barrel from the handle and removed a knife from the interior. It was a slender blade, made for slicing rather than hacking, but sharp and almost indestructible.

Her idea registered somewhere between being a long shot and just plain crazy, but it was the only idea she'd had that was even remotely possible. At least she would be doing *something*, rather than just waiting around for a rescue that might never happen.

She needed gloves to protect her hands, but she didn't have any. Hastily she opened the first-aid box and took out the roll of gauze. She wrapped the gauze around her palms and wove it in and around her fingers, then taped the loose ends. The result was crude but workable, she thought. She had seen the gloves rock climbers wore, with their fingers and thumbs left free; this makeshift approximation would have to do. She might wear blisters on her hands, anyway, but that was a small price to pay if they could get out of here.

Knife in hand, she went back to her chosen point of attack and tried to figure out the best way to do this. She needed another rock, she realized, one that wasn't soft. Anything that crumbled would be useless. She scouted around and finally found a pitted, dark gray rock that was about the size of a grapefruit, heavy enough to do the job.

Digging the point of the knife into the soft sandstone of the wall, she gripped the rock with her right hand and pounded it against the knife, driving the blade deeper. She jerked the blade out, moved it a little to the right, and pounded it in again. The next time she drove the knife in at a right angle to the original gouge, and hammered it downward. A chunk of sandstone broke loose, leaving a nice little gouge in the rock.

"This just might work," Sunny said aloud, and set herself to the task. She didn't let herself think how long it would take to carve handholds out of the rock all the way to the top, or if it was even possible. She was going to try; she owed it to Margreta, and to herself, to do everything she could to get out of this canyon.

Almost two hours later, the sharp crack of a pistol shot reverberated through the canyon, startling her so much that she nearly fell. She clung to the rock, her cheek pressed against the rough surface. Her heart pounded from the close call. She wasn't that high, only about ten feet, but the canyon floor was jagged with rock, and any fall was certain to cause injuries.

She wiped the sweat from her face. The temperature was

rising by the minute, and the rock was getting hotter and hotter. Standing with her toes wedged into the gouges she had hammered out of the rock, she had to lean inward against the rock to brace herself, because she had to have both hands free to wield the knife and the rock. She couldn't put nearly as much effort into it now, or the impact would jar her from her perch.

Panting, she reached over her head and blindly swung the rock. Because she had to press herself to the rock to keep her balance, she couldn't see to aim. Sometimes she hit the target and the knife bit into the rock; sometimes she hit her own hand. There had to be a better way to do this, but she couldn't think of one. She was an expert at working with what she had; she could do it this time, too. All she had to do was be careful, and patient.

"I can do this," she whispered.

Chance carried the skinned and cleaned rabbit back to the camp. He had also found a prickly pear cactus and cut off two of the stems, sticking himself several times as he removed the spines. The prickle pear was both edible and nutritious; it was usually fried, but he figured roasting would do just as well.

His temper had cooled. All right, so she had taken him in. He hadn't blown the plan; everything was still on track. All he had to do was remember not to be fooled by that oh-so-charming face she presented to the world and the plan would work just as he had expected. Maybe he couldn't make her love him, but he could make her think she did, and that was all he needed. A little trust, a little information, and he was in business.

He stepped beneath the overhang, grateful for the relief

the shade afforded, and took off his sunglasses. Sunny wasn't here. He turned around and surveyed what he could see of the canyon but couldn't spot her. Her green T-shirt and beige jeans didn't exactly stand out in the terrain, he thought, and abruptly realized what effective camouflage her clothing was. Had she chosen it for that exact purpose? She must have; everything she carried in that bag had been geared toward survival, so why should her clothing be any different?

"Sunny!" he called. His voice echoed, then died. He listened, but there was no answer.

Damn it, where was she?

The fire had died down, which meant she hadn't tended it in quite a while. He bent down and added more sticks, then skewered the rabbit and set it on the spit, more to keep it away from insects than anything else. The fire was too low to cook it, but the smoke wafting over the meat would give it a good flavor. He wrapped the prickly pear stems in his handkerchief and walked back under the over-hang to keep them out of the sun until he was ready to cook them.

The first thing he saw was the open first aid kit.

Alarm punched him in the gut. The paper wrapping had been torn off the roll of gauze; the tape was lying in the lid of the box, and it had also been used, because the end had been left free rather than stuck back to the roll.

Another detail caught his eyes. The curling iron had been taken apart; the two halves of it lay in the sand.

He swore viciously. Damn it, he should have remembered the curling iron and not assumed the pistol was the only weapon she had. She couldn't have hidden another pistol in the curling iron, but a knife would fit.

He didn't see any blood, but she must have injured herself somehow. Where in the hell was she?

"Sunny!" he roared as he stepped back out into the sun. Only silence answered him.

He studied the ground. Her footprints were everywhere, of course, but he saw where she had walked to her bag, presumably to get the first aid kit; then the prints led back out into the canyon. She was headed toward the plane.

He wasn't aware of reaching for his pistol. He was so accustomed to it that he didn't notice the weight of it in his hand as he followed her tracks, everything in him focusing on finding her.

If it hadn't been for the tracks, he would have missed her. She was almost at the far end of the canyon, past where the plane sat baking in the sun. The rock walls were scored with hundreds of cuts, and she was tucked inside one of them, clinging to the rock about a dozen feet off the ground.

Astonishment, anxiety, relief and anger all balled together in his gut. In speechless fury he watched her reach over her head and stab a wicked-looking blade into the soft rock, then, still keeping her face pressed against the hot stone, use another rock to try to pound the knife deeper. She hit her hand instead of the knife handle, and the curse she muttered made his eyebrows rise.

Strips of gauze were wound around her hands. He didn't know if she had wrapped her hands because she had hurt them, or if the gauze was an effort to keep them from being hurt. All he knew was that if she fell she would likely maim herself on the rocks, and that he really, *really* wanted to spank her.

He ruthlessly restrained the urge to yell at her. The last thing he wanted to do was startle her off her precarious perch. Instead, he stuck the pistol in his waist-band at the small of his back and worked his way over until he was standing beneath her, so he could catch her if she fell.

He forced himself to sound calm. "Sunny, I'm right beneath you. Can you get down?"

She stopped with her right hand drawn back to deliver another blow with the rock. She didn't look down at him. "Probably," she said. "It has to be easier than getting up here."

He was fairly certain what she was doing, but the sheer magnitude of the task, the physical impossibility of it, left him stunned. Just for confirmation he asked, "What are you doing?"

"I'm cutting handholds in the rock, so we can climb out of here." She sounded grim, as if she also realized the odds against success.

His hands clenched into fists as he fought for control. He looked up at the towering wall, at the expanse stretching above her. The dozen feet she had climbed was only about one tenth of the distance needed—and it was the easiest tenth.

He put his hand on the rock and almost jerked back at the heat radiating from it. A new concern gnawed at him. He didn't yell at her that this was the stupidest idea he'd ever heard of, the way he wanted. Instead, he said, "Sweetheart, the rock's too hot. Come down before you're burned."

She laughed, but without her usual humor. "It's too late."

To hell with cajoling. "Throw the knife down and get off that damn rock," he barked in sharp command.

To his surprise, she dropped the knife, then the rock she held in her right hand, tossing both to the side so they wouldn't land near him. Every muscle in her body was taut with strain as she reached for the handholds she had cut and began to work her way down, feeling with her toes for the gouges. He stood directly beneath her, reaching up for her in case she fell. The muscles in her slender arms flexed, and he realized anew just how strong she was. One didn't get that kind of strength with a once-in-a-while jog or the occasional workout in a gym. It took dedication and time; he knew, because he kept himself in top physical condition. Her normal routine would be at least an hour of work, maybe two, every day. For all he knew, while he had been checking the traps she had been doing pushups.

For all the gut-deep burn of his anger, it was overridden by his concern as he watched her inch her way down the face of the rock. She was careful and took her time, despite the fact that he knew the rock was scorching her fingers. He didn't speak again, not wanting to distract her; he simply waited, not very patiently, for her to get within his reach.

When she did, he caught her feet and guided them to the next gouges. "Thanks," she panted, and worked her way down another foot.

That was enough. He caught her around the knees and scooped her off the rock. She shrieked, fighting for her balance, but now that he had her in his grip he wasn't about to let her go. Before she could catch her breath, he turned her and tossed her face down over his shoulder.

"Hey!" The indignant protest was muffled against his back.

"Just shut up," he said between his teeth as he dipped down to pick up her knife, then set off for the camp. "You scared the hell out of me."

"Good. You had too much hell in you, anyway." She

clutched him around the waist to steady herself. He just hoped she didn't grab the pistol out of his waistband and shoot him, since it was so close to hand.

"Damn it, don't you dare joke about it!" Her upturned bottom was very close to his hand. Temptation gnawed at him. Now that he had her down, he was shaking, and he wanted some retribution for having been put through that kind of anxiety. He put his hand on her butt and indulged in a few moments of fantasy, which involved her jeans around her knees and her bent over his lap.

He realized he was stroking his palm over the round curves of her buttocks and regretfully gave up on his fantasy. Some things weren't going to happen. After he tended her hands and got through raising hell with her for taking such a risk, he fully intended to burn off his fright and anger with an hour or two on the blanket with her.

How could he still want her so much? This wasn't part of the job; he could live with it, if it had been. This was obsession, deep and burning and gut-twisting. He had tried to put a light face on it, for her benefit, but if she had been more experienced, she would have known a man didn't make love to a woman five times during the night just because she was available. At this rate, those three dozen condoms wouldn't last even a week. He had already used six, and it might take two or three more to get him settled down after the scare she had given him.

The hard fact of it was, a man didn't make love to a woman that often unless he was putting his brand on her.

This wouldn't work. Couldn't work. He had to get himself under control, stay focused on the job.

He heard her sniffing as they neared the camp. "Are you *crying?*" he demanded incredulously.

She sniffed again. "Don't be silly. What's that smell?" She inhaled deeply. "It smells like...food."

Despite himself, a smile quirked the corners of his mouth. "I shot a rabbit."

There was a small disruption on his shoulder as she twisted around so she could see the fire. Her squeal of delight almost punctured his eardrums, and his smile grew. He couldn't stop himself from enjoying her; he had never before met anyone who took such joy in life, who was so vibrantly alive herself. How she could be a part of a network devoted to taking lives was beyond his understanding.

He dumped her on the ground under the overhang and squatted beside her, taking both her hands in his and turning them up for his inspection. He barely controlled a wince. Her fingers were not only scorched from the hot rock, they were scraped raw and bleeding.

Fury erupted in him again, a flash fire of temper at seeing the damage she had done to herself. He surged to his feet. "Of all the stupid, lame-brained...! What in hell were you thinking? You weren't thinking at all, from the looks of it! Damn it, Sunny, you risked your life pulling this stupid stunt—"

"It wasn't stupid," she shouted, shooting to her feet to face him, her brilliant eyes narrowed. She clenched her bleeding hands into fists. "I know the risks. I also know it's my only hope of getting out of this damn canyon before it's too late!"

"Too late for what?" he yelled back. "Do you have a date this weekend or something?" The words were heavy with sarcasm.

"Yeah! It just so happens I do!" Breathing hard, she glared at him. "My sister is supposed to call."

Chapter 10

A sister? Chance stared at her. His investigation hadn't turned up any information about a sister. The Millers hadn't had any children of their own, and he had found adoption papers only on Sunny. His mind raced. "You said you didn't have any family."

She gave him a stony look. "Well, I have a sister."

Yeah, right. "You'd risk your life for a phone call?" Some terrorist act was being planned after all, he thought with a cold feeling in the pit of his stomach. That was why she'd been lugging the tent around. He didn't know how the tent fit into the scheme, but evidently she had been planning to drop out of sight.

"I would for this one." She wheeled away, every line of her body tense. "I have to try. Margreta calls my cell phone every week at the same time. It's how we know the other is still alive." She turned back to him and shouted, "If I don't answer that call, she'll think I'm dead!"

Whoa. Once again, the pieces of the puzzle that was Sunny had been scattered. Margreta? Was that a code name? He searched his memory, which was extensive, but couldn't find anything or anyone named Margreta. Sunny was so damned convincing....

"Why would she think you're dead?" he demanded. "You might just be in a place that doesn't have a signal—like here. What is she, some kind of nutcase?"

"I make certain I'm always somewhere that has a signal. And, no, she isn't a *nutcase!*" She threw the words back at him like bullets, her mouth twisted with fury at him, at the situation, at her own helplessness. "Her problem is the same as mine—we're our father's daughters!"

His pulse leaped. There it was, out in the open, just like that. He hadn't needed seduction; anger had done the job. "Your father?" he asked carefully.

Tears glittered in her eyes, dripped down her cheeks. She dashed them away with a furious gesture. "Our father," she said bitterly. "We've been running from him all our lives."

The pieces of the puzzle jumped about a little more, as if a fist had slammed down and jarred them. Easy, he cautioned himself. Don't seem too interested. Find out exactly what she means; she could be referring to his influence. "What do you mean, running?"

"I mean running. Hiding." She wiped away more tears. "Father dear is a terrorist. He'll kill us if he ever finds us."

Chance gently cleaned her hands with the alcohol wipes from the first aid kit, soothed the red places with burn ointment and the raw spots with antibiotic cream. The gauze she'd wrapped around her hands had protected her palms, but her fingers were a mess. Sunny felt a little bewildered. One minute they had been yelling at each other, the next she had been locked against him, his arms like a vise around her. His heart had been pounding like a runaway horse.

Since then he had been as tender as a mother with a child, rocking her in comfort, cuddling her, drying her tears. The emotional firestorm that had burned through her had left her feeling numb and disoriented; she let him do whatever he wanted without offering a protest, not that she had any reason to protest. It felt good to lean on him.

Satisfied with the care he had given her hands, he left her sitting on the rock while he added some fuel to the fire and turned the rabbit on the spit. Coming back under the overhang, he spread the blanket against the wall, scooped her into his arms, and settled on the blanket with her cradled against him. He propped his back against the wall, arranged her so she was draped half across his lap and lifted her face for a light kiss.

She managed a shaky smile. "What was that? A kiss to make it better?"

He rubbed his thumb over her bottom lip, his expression strangely intent as if studying her. "Something like that."

"I'm sorry for crying all over you. I usually handle things better than this."

"Tell me what's going on," he said quietly. "What's this about your father?"

She leaned her head on his shoulder, grateful for his strength. "Hard to believe, isn't it? But he's the leader of a terrorist group that has done some awful things. His name is Crispin Hauer."

"I've never heard of him," Chance lied.

"He operates mostly in Europe, but his network extends to the States. He even has someone planted in the FBI." She was unable to keep the raw bitterness out of her voice. "Why do you think I don't have a license for that pistol? I don't know who the plant is, how high he ranks, but I do know he's in a position to learn if the FBI gets any information Hauer wants. I didn't want to be in any database, in case he found out who adopted me and what name I'm using."

"So he doesn't know who you are?"

She shook her head. She had spent a lifetime keeping all her fear and worry bottled up inside her, and now she couldn't seem to stop it from spewing out. "My mother took Margreta and left him before I was born. I've never met him. She was five months pregnant with me when she ran."

"What did she do?"

"She managed to lose herself. America's a big place. She stayed on the move, changing her name, paying with cash she had taken from his safe. When I was born, she intended to have me by herself, in the motel room she'd taken for the night. But I wouldn't come, the labor just kept on and on, and she knew something was wrong. Margreta was hungry and scared, crying. So she called 911."

He wound a strand of golden hair around his finger. "And was there something wrong?"

"I was breech. She had a C-section. While she was groggy from the drugs, they asked her the father's name and she didn't think to make up a name, just blurted out *his*. So that's how I got into the system, and how he knows about me."

"How do you know he knows?"

"I was almost caught, once." She shivered against him, and he held her closer. "He sent three men. We were in…Indianapolis, I think. I was five. Mom had bought an old car and we were going somewhere. We were always on the move. We got boxed in, in traffic. She saw them get out of their cars. She had taught us what to do if she ever told us to run. She dragged us out of the car and screamed 'Run!' I did, but Margreta started crying and grabbed Mom. So Mom took off running with Margreta. Two men went after them, and one came after me." She began shuddering. "I hid in an alley, under some garbage. I could hear him calling me, his voice soft like he was singing. 'Sonia, Sonia.' Over and over. They knew my name. I waited forever, and finally he went away."

"How did your mother find you again? Or was she caught?"

"No, she and Margreta got away, too. Mom taught herself street smarts, and she never went anywhere that she wasn't always checking out ways to escape."

He knew what that was like, Chance thought.

"I stayed in my hiding place. Mom had told us that sometimes, after we thought they were gone, the bad men would still be there watching, waiting to see if we came out. So I thought the bad men might be watching, and I stayed as still as I could. I don't think it was winter, because I wasn't wearing a coat, but when night fell I got cold. I was scared and hungry and didn't know if I'd ever see Mom again. I didn't leave, though, and finally I heard her calling me. She must have noticed where I ran and worked her way back when she thought it was safe. All I knew was that she'd found me. After that was when she decided it wasn't safe to keep us with her anymore, so she began looking for someone to adopt us."

Chance frowned. He hadn't found a record of any adoption but hers. "The same family took both of you?"

"Yes, but I was the only one adopted. Margreta wouldn't." Her voice was soft. "Margreta… remembers things. She had lost everything except Mom, so I guess she clung more than I did. She had a hard time adapting." She shrugged. "Having grown up the way I did, I can adjust to pretty much anything."

Meaning she had taught herself not to cling. Instead, with her sunny personality, she had found joy and beauty wherever she could. He held her closer, letting her cling to him. "But…you said he was trying to kill you. It sounds as if he was trying very hard to get you back."

She shook her head. "He was trying to get *Margreta* back. He didn't know me. I was just a means he could have used to force Mom to give Margreta back to him. That's all he would want with me now, to find Margreta. If I was caught, when he found out I don't know where she is, I'd be worthless to him."

"You don't know?" he asked, startled.

"It's safer that way. I haven't seen her in years." Unconscious longing for her sister was in her voice. "She has my cell phone number, and she calls me once a week. So long as I answer the call, she knows everything is all right."

"But you don't know how to get in touch with her?"

"No. I can't tell them what I don't know. I move around a lot, so a cell phone was the best way for us. I keep an apartment in Chicago, the tiniest, cheapest place I could find, but I don't live there. It's more of a decoy than anything else. I suppose if I live anywhere it's in Atlanta, but I take all the assignments I can get. I seldom spend more than one night at a time in one place."

"How would he find you now, since your name has been changed? Unless he knows who adopted you, but how could he find that out?" Chance himself had found her only because of the incident in Chicago, when her courier package was stolen and he checked her out. As soon as he said it, though, he knew that the mole in the FBI—and he would damn sure find out who *that* was—had probably done the same checking. Had he gone as deep in the layers of bureaucracy as Chance had, to the point of hacking into those sealed adoption records? Sunny's cover might have been blown. He wondered if she realized it yet.

"I don't know. I just know I can't afford to assume I'm safe until I hear he's dead."

"What about your mom? And Margreta?"

"Mom's dead." Sunny paused, and he felt her inhale as if bracing herself. "They caught her. She committed suicide rather than give up any information on us. She had told us she would—and she did."

She stopped, and Chance gave her time to deal with the bleakness he heard in her voice. Finally she said, "Margreta is using another name, I just don't know what it is. She has a heart condition, so it's better if she stays in one location."

Margreta was living a fairly normal life, he thought, while Sunny was on the move, always looking over her shoulder. That was what she had known since birth, the way she had been taught to handle the situation. But what about the years they had spent with the Millers? Had her life been normal then?

She answered those questions herself. "I miss having a home," she said wistfully. "But if you stay in one place you get to know people, form relationships. I couldn't risk someone else's life that way. God forbid I should get married, have children. If Hauer ever found me—" She broke off, shuddering at the thought of what Hauer was capable of doing to someone she loved in order to get the answers he wanted.

One thing didn't make sense, Chance thought. Hauer

was vicious and crazy and cunning, and would go to any lengths to recover his daughter. But why Margreta, and not Sunny, too? "Why is he so fixated on your sister?"

"Can't you guess?" she asked rawly, and began shuddering again. "That's why Mom took Margreta and ran. She found him with her, doing…things. Margreta was only four. He had evidently been abusing her for quite a while, maybe even most of her life. By then Mom had already found out some of what he was, but she hadn't worked up the nerve to leave. After she found him with Margreta, she didn't have a choice." Her voice dropped to an agonized whisper. "Margreta remembers."

Chance felt sick to his stomach. So in addition to being a vicious, murdering bastard, Hauer was also a pervert, a child molester. Killing was too good for him; he deserved to be dismembered—slowly.

Worn out by both physical labor and her emotional storm, Sunny drifted to sleep. Chance held her, content to let her rest. The fire needed more fuel, but so what? Holding her was more important. Thinking his way through this was more important.

First and foremost, he believed every word she'd said. Her emotions had been too raw and honest for any of it to have been faked. For the first time, all the pieces of the puzzle fit together, and his relief was staggering. Sunny was innocent. She had nothing to do with her father, had never seen him, had spent her entire life running from him. That was why she lugged around a tent, with basic survival provisions; she was ready to disappear at any given moment, to literally go to ground and live out in the forest somewhere until she thought it was safe to surface and rebuild her life yet again.

She had no way of contacting Hauer. The only way to get to him, then, was to use her as bait. And considering how she felt about her father, she would never, under any circumstances, agree to any plan that brought her to his attention.

He would have to do it without her agreement, Chance thought grimly. He didn't like using her, but the stakes were too high to abandon. Hauer couldn't be left free to continue wreaking his destruction on the world. How many innocent people would die this year alone if he wasn't caught?

There was no point in staying here any longer; he'd found out what he needed to know. Zane wouldn't check in again, though, until tomorrow morning, so they were stuck until then. He adjusted Sunny in his arms and rested his face against the top of her head. He would use the time to formulate his game plan—and to use as many of those condoms as possible.

"Get away from me," Sunny grumbled the next morning, turning her head away from his kiss. She pried his hand off her breast. "Don't touch me, you—you *mink.*"

Chance snorted with laughter.

She pulled his chest hair.

"Ouch!" He drew back as far as he could in the small confines of the tent. "That hurt."

"Good! I don't think I can walk." Quick as a snake, her hand darted out and pulled his chest hair again. "This way, you can have as much fun as I'm having."

"Sunny," he said in a cajoling tone.

"Don't 'Sunny' me," she warned, fighting her way into her clothes. Since they barely had room to move, he began dodging elbows and knees, and his hands slipped over some very interesting places. "Stop it! I mean it, Chance! I'm too sore for any more monkey business."

More to tease her than anything else, he zeroed in on an interesting place that had her squealing. She shot out of the tent, and he collapsed on his back, laughing—until she raised the tent flap and dashed some cold water on him.

"There," she said, hugely satisfied by his yelp. "One cold shower, just what you needed." Then she ran.

If she thought the fact that he was naked would hamper his pursuit, she found out differently. He snatched up a bottle of water as he passed by their cache of supplies and caught her before she had gone fifty yards. She was laughing like a maniac, otherwise she might have gotten away. He held her with one arm and poured the water over her head. It was ice-cold from having been left out all night, and she shrieked and sputtered and giggled, clinging to him when her legs went weak from so much laughter.

"Too sore to walk, huh?" he demanded.

"I w-wasn't walking," she said, giggling as she pushed her wet hair out of her face. Cold droplets splattered on him, and he shivered.

"Damn, it's cold," he said. The sun was barely up, so the temperature was probably in the forties.

She slapped his butt. "Then get some clothes on. What do you think this is, a nudist colony?"

He draped his arm around her shoulders, and they walked back to the camp. Her playfulness delighted him; hell, everything about her delighted him, from her wit to her willingness to laugh. And the sex—God, the sex was unbelievable. He didn't doubt she was sore, because *he* was. Last night had been a night to remember.

When she awakened yesterday afternoon she had been

naturally melancholy, the normal aftermath of intense emotions. He hadn't talked much, letting her relax. She went with him to check the traps, which were still empty, and they had bathed together. After a quiet supper of rabbit and cactus they went to bed, and he had devoted the rest of the night to raising her spirits. His efforts had worked.

"How are your hands?" he asked. If she could pull his chest hairs and slap his butt, the antibiotic cream must have worked wonders.

She held them out, palms up, so he could see. The redness from the burns was gone, and her raw fingertips looked slick and shiny. "I'll wrap Band-Aids around them before I get started," she said.

"Get started doing what?"

She gave him a startled look. "Cutting handholds in the rock, of course."

He was stunned. He stared at her, unable to believe what he was hearing. "You're not climbing back on that damn wall!" he snapped.

Her eyebrows rose in what he now recognized as her "the-hell-you-say" look. "Yes, I am."

He ground his teeth. He couldn't tell her they would be "rescued" today, but no way was he letting her wear herself out hacking holes in rock or put herself at that kind of risk.

"I'll do it," he growled.

"I'm smaller," she immediately objected. "It's safer for me."

She was trying to protect him again. He felt like beating his head against a rock in frustration.

"No, it isn't," he barked. "Look, there's no way you can cut enough handholds for us to climb out of here in the next two days. You got, what, twelve feet yesterday? If you managed twelve feet a day—and you wouldn't get that much done today, with your hands the way they are—it would take you over a week to reach the top. That's if—*if*—you didn't fall and kill yourself."

"So what am I supposed to do?" she shot back. "Just give up?"

"Today you aren't going to do a damn thing. You're going to let your hands heal if I have to tie you to a rock, is that clear?"

She looked as if she wanted to argue, but he was a lot bigger than she was, and maybe she could tell by his expression that he meant exactly what he said. "All right," she muttered. "Just for today."

He hoped she would keep her word, because he would have to leave her alone while he went to the spot where he signaled Zane. He would just have to risk it, but there would be hell to pay if he came back to find her on that rock.

He quickly dressed, shivering, and they ate another cold breakfast of water and nutrition bar, since there wasn't anything left of the rabbit from the night before. Tomorrow morning, he promised himself, breakfast would be bacon and eggs, with a mountain of hash browns and a pot of hot coffee.

"I'm going to check the traps," he said, though he knew there wouldn't be anything in them. When he'd checked them the afternoon before, knowing they would be leaving here today, he had quietly released them so they couldn't be sprung. "Just tend to the fire and keep it smoking. You take it easy today, and I'll wash our clothes this afternoon." That was a safe promise to make.

"It's a deal," she said, but he could tell she was thinking about Margreta.

He left her sitting by the fire. It was a good ten-minute

walk to the designated spot, but he hurried, unwilling to leave her to her own devices for so long. Taking the laser light from his pocket, he aimed it toward the rock on the rim and began flashing the pickup signal. Immediately Zane flashed back asking for confirmation, to make certain there wasn't an error. After all, they hadn't expected this to happen so fast. Chance flashed the signal again and this time received an okay.

He dropped the light back in his pocket. He didn't know how long it would take for Zane to arrange the pickup, but probably not long. Knowing Zane, everything was already in place.

He was walking back to the camp when the small twin-engine plane flew over. A grin spread across his face. That was Zane for you!

He began running, knowing Sunny would be beside herself. He heard her shrieking before he could see her; then she came into view, jumping in her glee as she came to meet him. "He saw me!" she screamed, laughing and crying at the same time. "He waggled the wings! He'll come back for us, won't he?"

He caught her as she hurled herself into his arms and couldn't stop himself from planting a long, hard kiss on that laughing mouth. "He'll come back," he said. "Unless he thought you were just waving hello at him." The opportunity to tease her was too great to resist, considering she had pulled his chest hair and poured cold water on him. He'd retaliated for the cold water; this was for the hair-pulling.

She looked stricken, the laughter wiped from her face as if it had never been. "Oh, no," she whispered.

He didn't have the heart to keep up the pretense. "Of

course he'll come back," he chided. "Waggling the wings was the signal that he saw you and would send help."

"Are you sure?" she asked, blinking back tears.

"I promise."

"I'll get you for this."

He had to kiss her again, and he didn't stop until she had melted against him, her arms locked around his neck. He hadn't thought he would be interested in sex for quite a while, not after last night, but she proved him wrong.

He huffed out a breath and released her. "Stop manhandling me, you hussy. We have to get packed."

The smile she gave him was brilliant, like the sun rising, and it warmed him all the way through.

They gathered their belongings. Chance returned her pistol to her, and watched her break it down and store the pieces in their hiding places. Then they walked back to the plane and waited.

Rescue came in the form of a helicopter, the blades beating a thumping rhythm in the desert air, the canyon echoing with the sound. It hovered briefly over them, then lowered itself like a giant mosquito. Sand whipped into their air, stinging them, and Sunny hid her face against his shirt.

A sixtyish man with a friendly face and graying beard hopped out of the bird. "You folks need some help?" he called.

"Sure do," Chance answered.

When he was closer, the man stuck out his hand. "Charlie Jones, Civil Air Patrol. We've been looking for you for a couple of days. Didn't expect to find you this far south."

"I veered off course looking for a place to land. Fuel pump went out."

"In that case, you're mighty lucky. That's rough territory

out there. This might be the only spot in a hundred miles when you could have landed. Come on. I expect you folks are ready for a shower and some food."

Chance held out his hand to Sunny, and she gave him that brilliant smile again as she put her hand in his and they walked to the helicopter.

Chapter 11

Sunny was almost dizzy with mingled relief and regret; relief because she wouldn't miss Margreta's call, regret because this time with Chance, even under such trying conditions, had been the happiest, most fulfilling few days of her life and they were now over. She had known from the beginning that their time together was limited; once they were back in the regular world, all the old rules came back into play.

She couldn't, wouldn't risk his life by letting him be a part of hers. He had given her two nights of bliss, and a lifetime of memories. That would have to be enough, no matter how much she was already aching at the thought of walking away from him and never seeing him again. At least now she knew what it was to love a man, to revel in his existence, and she was richer for it. She wouldn't have traded these few days with him for any amount of money, no matter the price in loneliness she would have to pay.

So she held his hand all during the helicopter flight to a small, ramshackle air field. The only building was made of corrugated metal, rounded at the top like a Quonset hut, with a wooden addition, housing the office, added to one side. If the addition had ever seen a coat of paint, the evidence of it had long since been blasted off by the wind-driven sand. After living under a rock for three days, Sunny thought the little field looked like heaven.

Seven airplanes, of various makes and vintage, were parked with almost military precision along one side of the air strip. Charlie Jones landed his helicopter on a concrete pad behind the corrugated building. Three men, one wiping his greasy hands on a stained red rag, left the building by the back door and walked toward them, ducking their heads against the turbulence of the rotor blades.

Charlie took off his headset and hopped out of the chopper, smiling. "Found 'em," he called cheerfully to the approaching trio. To Chance and Sunny he said, "The two on the left fly CAP with me. Saul Osgood, far left, is the one who spotted your smoke this morning and radioed in your position. Ed Lynch is the one in the middle. The one with the greasy hands is Rabbit Warren, the mechanic here. His real name's Jerome, but he'll fight you if you call him that."

Sunny almost laughed aloud. She controlled the urge, but she was careful not to look at Chance as they shook hands with the three men and introduced themselves.

"I couldn't believe it when I saw your bird in that little bitty narrow canyon," Saul Osgood said, shaking his head after Chance told them what had happened. "How you ever found it is a miracle. And to make a dead stick landing—" He shook his head again. "Someone was sure looking out for you, is all I can say."

"So you think it was your fuel pump went out, huh?" Rabbit Warren asked as they walked into the hangar.

"Everything else checked out."

"It's a Skylane, right?"

"Yeah." Chance told him the model, and Rabbit stroked his lean jaw.

"I might have a pump for that. There was a feller in here last year flying a Skylane. He ordered some parts for it, then left and never did come back for 'em. I'll check while you folks are refreshing yourselves."

If "refreshing" themselves had anything to do with a bathroom, Sunny was more than ready. Chance gave her the first turn, and she almost crooned with delight at the copious water that gushed from the faucet at a turn of the handle. And a flush toilet! She was in heaven.

After Chance had his turn, they indulged in ice-cold soft drinks from a battered vending machine. A snack machine stood beside it, and Sunny surveyed the offerings with an eager eye. "How much change do you have?" she asked Chance.

He delved his hand into his front pocket and pulled out his change, holding it out for Sunny to see. She picked out two quarters and fed them into the machine, punched a button, and a pack of cheese and crackers fell to the tray.

"I thought you'd go for a candy bar," Chance said as he fed more quarters into the machine and got a pack of peanuts.

"That's next." She raised her eyebrows. "You didn't think I was going to stop with cheese and crackers, did you?"

Ed Lynch opened the door to the office. "Is there anyone you need to call? We've notified the FAA and called off the search, but if you have family you want to talk to, feel free to use the phone."

"I need to call the office," Sunny said, pulling a wry face. She had a good excuse—a very good one—for not making her delivery, but the bottom line was that a customer was unhappy.

Chance waited until she was on the phone, then strolled over to where Rabbit was making a show of looking for a fuel pump. His men were good, Chance thought; they had played this so naturally they should have been on the stage. Of course, subterfuge was their lives, just as it was his.

"Everything's good," Chance said quietly. "You guys can clear out after Charlie takes us back to the canyon with the fuel pump."

Rabbit pulled a greasy box from a makeshift shelf that was piled with an assortment of parts and tools. Over Chance's shoulder he eyed Sunny through the windowed door to the office. "You pulled a real hardship assignment this time, boss," he said admiringly. "That's the sweetest face I've seen in a while."

"There's a sweet person behind it, too," Chance said as he took the box. "She's not part of the organization."

Rabbit's eyebrows went up. "So all this was for nothing."

"No, everything is still a go. The only thing that's changed is her role. Instead of being the key, she's the bait. She's been on the run from Hauer her entire life. If he knows where she is, he'll come out of hiding." He glanced around to make certain she was still on the phone. "Spread the word that we're going to be extra careful with her, make sure she doesn't get hurt. Hauer has already caused enough damage in her life."

And he himself was going to cause more, Chance thought bleakly. As terrified as she was of Hauer, when she learned Chance had deliberately leaked her location to the man she was going to go ballistic. That would definitely be the end of *this* relationship, but he'd known from the beginning this was only temporary. Like her, he wasn't in any position for permanent ties. Sunny's circumstances would change when her father was gone, but Chance's wouldn't; he would move on to another crisis, another security threat.

Just because he was her first lover didn't mean he would be her last.

The idea shot a bolt of pure rage through him. Damn it, she was *his*—he caught the possessive thought and strangled it. Sunny wasn't his; she was her own person, and if she found happiness in her life with some other man, he should be happy for her. She more than deserved anything good that came her way.

He wasn't happy. Her laughter, her passion—he wanted it all for himself. Knowing he couldn't have her was already eating a huge hole out of his insides, but she deserved far better than a mongrel with blood on his hands. He had chosen his world, and he was well-suited for it. He was accustomed to living a lie, to pretending to be someone he wasn't, to always staying in the shadows. Sunny was…sunny, both by name and by nature. He would enjoy her while he had her—by God, he'd enjoy her—but in the end he knew he would have to walk away.

Sunny ended the call and left the office. Hearing the door close, he turned to watch her approach, and he let himself savor the pleasure of just watching her.

She wrinkled her nose. "Everyone's glad the plane didn't crash, that I'm alive—but the fact that I didn't die makes it a little less forgivable that I didn't deliver the package on time. The customer still wants it, though, so I still have to go to Seattle."

She came to him as naturally as if they had been together for years, and just as naturally he found himself slipping his arm around her slender waist. "Screw 'em," he said dismissively. He lifted the box. "Guess what I have."

She beamed. "The keys to the kingdom."

"Close enough. Charlie's going to take me back to the plane so I can swap out the fuel pump. Do you want to go with me, or stay here and rest until I get back?"

"Go with you," she said promptly. "I don't know anything about airplanes, but I can keep you company while you work. Are we coming back here, anyway?"

"Sure. This is as good a place to refuel as any." Plus she wouldn't find out they weren't in Oregon as he'd told her.

"Then I'll leave my bag here, if that's all right with Rabbit." She looked inquiringly at Rabbit, who nodded his head.

"That'll be just fine, ma'am. Put it in the office and it'll be as safe as a baby in the womb."

Sunny walked away to get the bag. She felt safe, Chance realized, otherwise she would never let the bag out of her possession. Except for her worry for Margreta, these last few days she must have felt free, unburdened by the need to constantly look over her shoulder.

He had enjoyed their little adventure, too, every minute of it, because he had known they weren't in any danger. Sunny made him feel more alive than he ever had before, even when he was angry at her because she had just scared him half to death. And when he was inside her—then he was as close to heaven as he was ever likely to get. The pleasure of making love to her was so intense it was almost blinding.

He grinned to himself as he hefted his own overnight bag. No way was he leaving it here; after all, the condoms were in it. No telling what might happen when he and Sunny were alone.

The afternoon was wearing on when Charlie set the helicopter down in the canyon again. He looked up at the light with an experienced pilot's eye. "You think you have enough time to get that fuel pump put on before dark?"

"No problem," Chance said. After all, as he and Charlie both knew, there was nothing wrong with the fuel pump, anyway. He would tinker around for a while, make it look realistic. Sunny wasn't likely to stand at his elbow the entire time, and if she did he would distract her.

He and Sunny jumped out of the helicopter, and he leaned in to get his bag. "See you in a few hours."

"If you don't make it back to the airfield, we know where you are," Charlie said, saluting.

They ducked away from the turbulence as the helicopter lifted away. Sunny pushed her hair away from her face and looked around the canyon, smiling. "Home again," she said, and laughed. "Funny how it looks a lot more inviting now that I know we aren't stuck here."

"I'm going to miss it," he said, winking at her. He carried his bag and the box containing the fuel pump over to the plane. "But we'll find out tonight if a bed is more fun than a tent."

To his surprise, sadness flashed in her eyes. "Chance... once we're away from here..." She shook her head. "It won't be safe."

He checked for a moment, then very deliberately put down the bag and box. Turning back to her, he put his hands on his hips. "If you're saying what I think you're saying, you can just forget about it. You aren't dumping me."

"You know what the situation is! I don't have a choice."

"*I* do. You're not just a fun screw who was available while we were here. I care about you, Sunny," he said softly. "When you look over your shoulder, you're going to see my face. Get used to it."

Tears welled in her brilliant eyes, filling them with diamonds. "I can't," she whispered. "Because I love you. Don't ask me to risk your life, because I can't handle it."

His stomach muscles tightened. He had set out to make her love him, or at least get involved in a torrid affair with him. He had succeeded at doing both. He felt humbled, and exhilarated—and sick, because he was going to betray her.

He had her in his arms before he was aware of moving, and his mouth was on hers. He felt desperate for the taste of her, as if it had been days since he'd kissed her instead of just hours. Her response was immediate and wholehearted, as she rose on her tiptoes to fit her hips more intimately to his. He tasted the salt of her tears and drew back, rubbing his thumbs across her wet cheeks.

He rested his forehead against hers. "You're forgetting something," he murmured.

She sniffed. "What?"

"I was a ranger, sweetheart. I'm a little harder to kill than your average guy. You need someone watching your back, and I can do it. Think about it. We probably made the news. When we get to Seattle, don't be surprised if there's a television camera crew there. Both our faces will be on television. Besides that, we were reported missing to the FAA, which is federal. Information would have been dug up on both of us. Our names our linked. If the mole in the FBI tumbles to who you are, your father's goons will be after me, anyway—especially if they can't find you."

She went white. "Television?" She looked a lot like her mother; Chance had seen old photos of Pamela Vickery Hauer. Anyone familiar with Pamela would immediately notice the resemblance. As sharp as she was, Sunny also knew the danger of being on television, even a local newscast.

LINDA HOWARD

"We're in this together." He lifted her hand to his mouth and kissed her knuckles, then grinned down at her. "Lucky for you, I'm one mean son of a bitch when I need to be—lucky for you, unlucky for them."

Nothing she said would sway him, Sunny thought with despair late that night as she showered in the hotel suite he had booked them into for the night—a suite because it had more than one exit. He had been exactly right about the television news crew. Crews, she corrected herself. News had been slow that day, so every station in Seattle had jumped on the human-interest story. The problem was, so had both national news channels.

She had evaded the cameras as much as possible, but the reporters had seemed fixated on her, shouting questions at her instead of Chance. She would have thought the female reporters, at least, would be all over Chance, but he'd worn such a forbidding expression that no one had approached him. She hadn't answered any questions on camera, though at Chance's whispered suggestion she had given them a quick comment off-camera, for them to use as a filler on their broadcast.

Her one break was that, since it had been so late when they landed, the story didn't make even the late news. But unless something more newsworthy happened soon, the story would air in just a few hours over millions of breakfast tables countrywide.

She had to assume her cover had been blown. That meant leaving the courier service, moving—not that she had much to move; she had never accumulated many possessions—even changing her name. She would have to build a new identity.

She had always known it could happen, and she had prepared for it, both mentally and with actual paperwork.
Changing her name wouldn't change who she was; it was
just a tool to use to escape her father.

The real problem was Chance. She couldn't shake him,
no matter how she tried, and she knew she was good at that
kind of thing. She had tried to lose him at the airport,
ducking into a cab when his back was turned. But he
seemed to have a sixth sense where she was concerned, and
he was sliding in the other door before she could give the
driver the address where she had to deliver the courier
package. He had remained within touching distance of her
until they walked into the hotel room, and she had no
doubt that, if she opened the bathroom door, she would find
him sprawled across the bed, watching her.

In that, she underestimated him. Just as she began lath-
ering her hair, the shower curtain slid back and he stepped
naked into the tub with her. "I thought I'd conserve water
and shower with you," he said easily.

"Hah! You're just afraid I'll leave if you shower by yourself," she said, turning her back on him.

A big hand patted her bottom. "You know me so well."

She fought a smile. Damn him, why did he have to be so
well-matched to her in every way? She could, and had, run
rings around most people, but not Chance.

She hogged the spray, turning the nozzle down to rinse
her hair. He waited until she was finished with that, at
least, then adjusted the nozzle upward so the water hit him
in the chest. It also hit her full in the face. She sputtered
and elbowed him. "This is my shower, and I didn't invite
you. I get control of the nozzle, not you."

She knew challenging him was a mistake. He said, "Oh,

yeah?" and the tussle was on. Before she knew it she was giggling, he was laughing, and the bathroom was splattered with water. She had played more with Chance than she had since she'd been a little girl; she felt lighthearted with him, despite her problems. Their wet, naked bodies slid against each other, and neither of them could get a good grasp on any body part. At least, she couldn't. She suspected he could have won the tussle at any time simply by using his size and strength and wrapping his arms around her, but he held back and played at her level, as if he were used to restraining his strength to accommodate someone weaker than himself.

His hands were everywhere: on her breasts, her bottom, sliding between her legs while she laughed and batted them away. One long finger worked its way inside her and she squealed, trying to twist away while excitement spiraled wildly through her veins. Their naked wrestling match was having a predictable effect on both of them. She grabbed for the nozzle and aimed the blast of water at his face, and while he was trying to deflect the spray she made her escape, hopping out of the tub and snatching up a towel to wrap around her.

He vaulted out of the tub and slammed the door shut just as she reached for it. "You left the shower running," she accused, trying to sidetrack him.

"I'm not the one who turned it on." He grinned and hooked the towel away from her.

"Water's getting all over the floor." She tried to sound disapproving.

"It needed mopping, anyway."

"It did not!" She pushed a strand of dripping wet hair out of her eyes. "We're going to be kicked out. Water will drip through the floor into the room below and we'll be kicked out."

He grabbed her and swung her around so she was facing the shower. "Turn it off, then, if you're worried."

She did, because she hated to waste the water, and it was making such a mess. "There, I hope you're satisfied."

"Not by a long shot." He turned her to face him, holding her lips against his and angling her torso away from him, so he could look his fill at her. "Have I told you today how damn sexy you are?"

"Today? You've never told me at all!"

"Have so."

"Have not. When?"

"Last night. Several times."

She tried not to be entranced by the way water droplets were clinging to his thick dark lashes. "That doesn't count. Everyone knows you can't believe anything a man says when he's in…uh—"

"You?" he supplied, grinning.

She managed a haughty look. "I was going to say 'extremis,' but I think that applies only to dying."

"Close enough." He looked down at her breasts, his expression altering and the laughter fading. Still holding her anchored to him with one arm, he smoothed a hand up her torso to cup her breasts, and they both watched his long brown fingers curve around the pale globes. "You're sexy," he murmured, a slow, dark note entering his voice. She knew that note well, having heard it many times over the past two nights. "And beautiful. Your breasts are all cream-and-rose colored, until I kiss your nipples. Then they pucker up and turn red like they're begging me to suck them."

Her nipples tightened at his words, the puckered tips

flushing with color. He groaned and bent his dark head, water dripping from his hair onto her skin as he kissed both breasts. She was leaning far back over his arm, supported by his arm around her hips and her own desperate grasp on his shoulders. She didn't know how much longer she would be able to stand at all. Her loins throbbed, and she gasped for breath.

"And your ass," he growled. "You have the sweetest little ass." He turned her around so he could stroke the aforementioned buttocks, shaping his palms to the full, cool curves. Sunny's legs trembled, and she grabbed the edge of the vanity for support. The cultured marble slab was a good six feet long, and a mirror covered the entire wall behind it. Sunny barely recognized herself in the naked woman reflected there, a woman whose wet hair dripped water down her back and onto the floor. Her expression was etched with desire, her face flushed and her eyes heavy-lidded.

Chance looked up, and his gaze met hers in the mirror. Electricity sparked between them. "And here," he whispered, sliding one hand around her belly and between her legs. His muscled forearm looked unbelievably powerful against her pale belly, and his big hand totally covered her mound. She felt his fingers sliding between her folds, rubbing her just as she liked. She moaned and collapsed against him, her legs going limp.

"You're so soft and tight," the erotic litany continued in her ear. "I can barely get inside you. But once I do—my heart stops. And I can't breathe. I think I'm going to die, but I can't, because it feels too good to stop." His fingers slid farther, and he pressed two of them inside her.

She arched under the lash of sensation, soaring close to climax as his fingers stretched her. She heard herself cry out, a strained cry that told him exactly how near she was to fulfillment.

"Not yet, not yet," he said urgently, sliding his fingers out of her and bending her forward. He braced her hands on the vanity. "Hold on, sweetheart."

She didn't know if he meant to the vanity, or to her control. Both were impossible. "I can't," she moaned. Her hips moved, undulating, searching for relief. "Chance, I can't—please!"

"I'm here," he said, and he was, dipping down and pushing his muscled thighs between her legs, spreading them. She felt his lower belly against her buttocks, then the smooth, hard entry of his sex. Instinctively she bent forward to aid his penetration, taking all of him deep within her. He began driving, and on the second hard thrust she convulsed, crying out her pleasure. His climax erupted a moment later, and he collapsed over her back, holding himself as deep as he could while he groaned and shook.

Sunny closed her eyes, fighting for breath. Oh God, she loved him so much she ached with it. She wasn't strong enough to send him away, not even for his own protection. If she had been really trying, she could have gotten away from him, but deep down she knew she couldn't give him up. Not yet. Soon. She would have to, to keep him safe.

Just one more day, she thought as tears welled. One more. Then she would go.

Chapter 12

Ten days later, Sunny still hadn't managed to shake him. She didn't know if she was losing her touch or if army rangers, even ex ones, were very, very good at not being shaken.

They had left Seattle early the next morning. Sunny was too cautious to fly back to Atlanta; as she had feared, the morning newscasts had been splashed with the "real-life romantic adventure" she and Chance had shared. His name was mentioned, but by some perverse quirk his face was never clearly shown; the camera would catch the back of his head, or while he was in a quarter profile, while hers was broadcast from coast to coast.

One of the a.m. news shows even tracked them down at the hotel, awakening them at three in the morning to ask if they would go to the local affiliate studios for a live interview.

"Hell, no," Chance had growled into the phone before he slammed it down into the cradle.

After that, it had seemed best they remove themselves from the reach of the media. They checked out of the hotel and took a taxi to the airport before dawn. The plane was refueled and ready to go. By the time the sun peeked over the Cascades they were in the air. Chance didn't file a flight plan, so no one had any way of finding out where they were going. Sunny didn't know herself until they landed in Boise, Idaho, where they refurbished their wardrobes. She always carried a lot of cash, for just such a situation, and Chance seemed to have plenty, too. He still had to use his credit card for refueling, so she knew they were leaving a trail, but those records would show only where they had last been, not where they were going.

Chance's presence threw her off her plan. She knew how to disappear by herself; Chance and his airplane complicated things.

From a pay phone in Boise, she called Atlanta and resigned her job, with instructions to deposit her last paycheck into her bank. She would have the money wired to her when she needed it. Sometimes, adrift from the familiar life she had fashioned for herself, she wondered if she was overreacting to the possibility anyone would recognize her. Her mother had been dead for over ten years; there were few people in the world able to see the resemblance. The odds had to be astronomical against one of those few people seeing that brief human-interest story that had been shown for only one day.

But she was still alive because her mother had taught her that any odds at all were unacceptable. So she ran, as she had learned how to do in the first five years of her life. After all, the odds were also against her getting pregnant, yet here she was, waiting for a period that hadn't materialized. They had slipped up twice, only twice: once in the canyon, and in the hotel bathroom in Seattle. The timing hadn't been great for her to get pregnant even if they hadn't used protection at all, so why hadn't her period started? It was due two days ago, and her cycle was relentlessly regular.

She didn't mention it to Chance. She might just be late, for one of the few times in her life since she'd starting having menstrual periods. She had been terrified when she thought they were going to crash; maybe her emotions had disrupted her hormones. It happened.

She might sprout wings and fly, too, she thought in quiet desperation. She was pregnant. There were no signs other than a late period, but she knew it deep down in her bones, as if on some level her body was communicating with the microscopic embryo it harbored.

It would be so easy just to let Chance handle everything. He was good at this, and she had too much on her mind to be effective. She didn't think he'd noticed how easily distracted she'd been these past few days, but then, he didn't know when her period had been due, either.

She had talked to Margreta twice, and told her she was going underground. She would have to arrange for a new cellular account under a different name, with a new number, and do it before the service she now had was disconnected. She had tried to tell Margreta everything that was going on, but her sister, as usual, kept the calls short. Sunny understood. It was difficult for Margreta to handle anything having to do with their father. Maybe one day they would be able to live normal lives, have a normal sisterly relationship; maybe one day Margreta would be able to get past what he had done to her and find some happiness despite him.

Then there was Chance. He had brought sunshine into her life when she hadn't even known she was living in shadows. She had thought she managed quite well, but it was as if B.C., Before Chance, had been in monochrome. Now, A.C., was in vivid tech- nicolor. She slept in his arms every night. She ate her meals with him, quarreled with him, joked with him, made plans with him—nothing long term, but plans nevertheless. Every day she fell more and more in love with him, when she hadn't thought it possible.

Sometimes she actually pinched herself, because he was too good to be true. Men like him didn't come along every day; most women lived their entire lives without meeting a man who could turn their worlds upside down with a glance.

This state of affairs couldn't last much longer, this aimless drifting. For one thing, it was expensive. Chance wasn't earning any money while they were flying from one remote airfield in the country to another, and neither was she. She needed to get the paperwork for her new name, get a job, get a new cellular number—and get an obstetrician, which would cost money. She wondered how her mother had managed, with one frightened, traumatized child in tow, pregnant with another, and without any of the survival skills Sunny possessed. Pamela must have spent years in a state of terror, yet Sunny remembered her mother laughing, playing games with them, and making life fun even while she taught them how to survive. She only hoped she could be half as strong as her mother had been.

She was full of wild hopes these days. She hoped she hadn't been recognized. She hoped her baby would be healthy and happy. Most of all, she hoped she and Chance could build a life together, that he would be thrilled about the baby even though it was unplanned, that he truly cared about her as much as he appeared to. He never actually said he loved her, but it was there in his voice, in his actions, in his eyes and his touch as he made love to her.

Everything had to be all right. It had to. There was too much at stake now.

Sunny slept through the landing as Chance set the plane down in Des Moines. He glanced at her, but she was soundly asleep, like a child, her breathing deep and her cheeks flushed. He let her sleep, knowing what was coming to a head.

The plan was working beautifully. He had arranged for Sunny's face to be broadcast worldwide, and the bait had been taken immediately. His people had tracked two of Hauer's men into the country and maintained discreet but constant surveillance on them. Chance hadn't made it easy for anyone to follow him and Sunny; that would have been too obvious. But he had left a faint trail that, if the bloodhounds were good, they would be able to follow. Hauer's bloodhounds were good. They had been about a day behind them for about a week now, but until Hauer himself showed up, Chance made sure the hounds never caught up with him.

The news he'd been waiting for had finally come yesterday. Word in the underground of terrorist organizations was that Hauer had disappeared. He hadn't been seen in a few days, and there was a rumor he was in the States planning something big.

Somehow Hauer had slipped out of Europe and into America without being spotted, but now that Chance knew there was a mole in the FBI helping Hauer, he wasn't surprised.

Hauer was too smart to openly join his men, but he would

be nearby. He was the type who, when Sunny was captured, would want to interrogate this rebellious daughter himself.

Chance would take him apart with his bare hands before he let that happen.

But he would have to let them think they had her, not knowing they were surrounded at all times, at a distance, by his men. Chance just hoped he himself wasn't shot at the beginning, to get him out of the way. If Hauer's men were smart, they would realize they could use threats to Chance to keep Sunny in line, and they had proven they were smart. This was the risky part, but he had taken all the safeguards he could without tipping his hand.

His interlude with Sunny would end tonight, one way or another. If all went well, they would both live through it, and she would be free to live her life out in the open. He just hoped that one day she wouldn't hate him, that she would realize he had done what he had to do in order to capture Hauer. Who knows? Maybe one day he would meet her again.

He guided the Cessna to a stop in its designated spot and killed the engine. Sunny slept on, despite the sudden silence. Maybe he'd cost her too much sleep and it had finally caught up with her, he thought, smiling despite his inner tension. He had glutted himself with sex for the past two weeks, as if subconsciously he had been trying to stockpile memories and sensations for the time when she was no longer there. But as often as he'd had her, he still wanted her. Again. More. He was half hard right now, just thinking about her.

Gently he shook her, and she opened her sleepy eyes with a look of such trust and love that his heart leaped. She sat up, stretching and looking around. "Where are we?"

"Des Moines." Puzzled, he said, "I told you where we were going."

"I remember," she said around a yawn. "I'm just groggy. Wow! That was some nap. I don't usually sleep during the daytime. I must not be getting enough sleep at night." She batted her eyelashes at him. "I wonder why."

"I have no idea," he said, all innocence. He opened the door and climbed out, turning around to hold his hands up for her. She clambered out, and he lifted her to the ground. Looking up at the wide, cerulean-blue sky, he stretched, too, twisting his back to get out the kinks. "It's a pretty day. Want to have a picnic?"

"A what?" She looked at him as if he were speaking a foreign language.

"A picnic. You know, where you sit on the ground and eat with your hands, and fight wild animals for your food."

"Sounds like fun. But haven't we already done that?"

He laughed. "This time we'll do it right—checkered tablecloth, fried chicken, the works."

"All right, I'm game. Where are we going to have this picnic? Beside the runway?"

"Smart-ass. We'll rent a car and go for a drive."

Her eyes began to sparkle as she realized he meant it. That was what he loved best about Sunny, her ability to have fun. "How much time do we have? What time are we leaving?"

"Let's stay for a couple of days. Iowa's a nice place, and my tail could use some time away from that airplane seat."

He handled his business with the airport, then went to a rental car desk and walked away with the keys to a sport utility.

"You rented a *truck?*" Sunny teased when she saw the

green Ford Explorer. "Why didn't you get something with style, like a red sports car?"

"Because I'm six-three," he retorted. "My legs don't fit in sports cars."

She had bought a small backpack that she carried instead of the bulky carry-on she had been lugging around. She could get her toiletries and a change of clothes into the backpack, and that was enough for the single night they usually spent in a place. That meant her pistol was always with her, fully assembled when they weren't having to go through x-ray scanners, and he didn't protest. He always carried his own pistol with him, too, tucked into his waistband under his loose shirt. She put the backpack on the floorboard and climbed into the passenger seat, and began pushing buttons and turning knobs, every one she could reach.

Chance got behind the wheel. "I'm afraid to start this thing now. There's no telling what's going to happen."

"Chicken," she said. "What's the worst that could happen?"

"I'm just thankful Explorers don't have ejection seats," he muttered as he turned the key in the ignition. The engine caught immediately. The radio blared, the windshield wipers flopped back and forth at high speed, and the emergency lights began blinking. Sunny laughed as Chance dived for the radio controls and turned the volume down to an acceptable level. She buckled herself into the seat, smiling a very self-satisfied smile.

He had a map from the rental car company, though he already knew exactly where he was going. He had gotten very specific directions from the clerk at the rental agency, so the clerk would remember where they had gone when

Hauer's men asked. He had personally scouted out the location before putting the plan into motion. It was in the country, to cut the risk of collateral damage to innocent civilians. There was cover for his men, who would be in place before he and Sunny arrived. And, most important, Hauer and his men couldn't move in without being observed. Chance had enough men in place that an ant couldn't attend this picnic unless he wanted it there. Best of all, he knew Zane was out there somewhere. Zane didn't usually do fieldwork, but in this instance he was here guarding his brother's back. Chance would rather have Zane looking out for him than an entire army; the man was unbelievable, he was so good.

They stopped at a supermarket deli for their picnic supplies. There was even a red-checkered plastic cloth to go on the ground. They bought fried chicken, potato salad, rolls, cole slaw, an apple pie, and some green stuff Sunny called pistachio salad. He knew he wasn't about to touch it. Then he had to buy a small cooler and ice, and some soft drinks to go in it. By the time he got Sunny out of the supermarket, over an hour had passed and he was almost seventy bucks lighter in the wallet.

"We have apple pie," he complained. "Why do we need apples?"

"I'm going to throw them at you," she said. "Or better yet, shoot them off your head."

"If you come near me with an apple, I'll scream," he warned. "And pickled beets? Excuse me, but who eats pickled beets?"

She shrugged. "Someone does, or they wouldn't be on the shelves."

"Have *you* ever eaten pickled beets?" he asked suspiciously.

"Once. They were nasty." She wrinkled her nose at him.

"Then why in hell did you buy them?" he shouted.

"I wanted you to try them."

He should be used to it by now, he thought, but sometimes she still left him speechless. Muttering to himself, he stowed the groceries—including the pickled beets—in the back of the Explorer.

God, he was going to miss her.

She rolled down the window and let the wind blow through her bright hair. She had a happy smile on her face as she looked at everything they passed. Even service stations seemed to interest her, as did the old lady walking a Chihuahua that was so fat its belly almost kept its feet from touching the ground. Sunny giggled about the fat little dog for five minutes.

If it made her laugh like that, he thought, he would eat the damn pickled beets. But he'd damn sure eat something else afterward, because if he got shot, he didn't want pickled beets to be the last thing he tasted.

The late August afternoon was hot when he pulled off the road. A tree-studded field stretched before them. "Let's walk to those trees over there," he said, nodding to a line of trees about a hundred yards away. "See how they're growing, in a line like that? There might be a little creek there."

She looked around. "Shouldn't we ask permission?"

He raised his eyebrows. "Do you see a house anywhere? Who do we ask?"

"Well, all right, but if we get in trouble, it's your fault."

He carried the cooler and most of the food. Sunny slung her backpack on her shoulders, then took charge of the ground cloth and the jar of pickled beets. "I'd better carry these," she said. "You might drop them."

"You could take something else, too," he grunted. This stuff was heavy.

She stretched up to peek in the grocery bag. The apple pie was perched on top of the other stuff. "Nah, you won't drop the pie."

He grumbled all the way to their picnic site, more because she enjoyed it than any other reason. This was the last day she would ever tease him, or he would see that smile, hear that laugh.

"Oh, there *is* a creek!" she exclaimed when they reached the trees. She carefully set the jar of beets down and unfolded the ground cloth, snapping it open in that brisk, economical movement all women seemed to have, and letting it settle on the thick, overgrown grass. A light breeze was blowing, so she anchored the cloth with her backpack on one corner and the jar of beets on the another.

Chance set the cooler and food down and sprawled out on the cloth. "I'm too tired now to enjoy myself," he complained.

She leaned over and kissed him. "You think I don't know what you're up to? Next thing I know you'll get something in your eye, and I'll have to get really, really close to see it. Then your back will need scratching, and you'll have to take off your shirt. Before I know it, we'll both be naked and it'll be time to leave, and we won't have had a bite to eat."

He gave her a quizzical look. "You have this all planned out, don't you?"

"Down to the last detail."

"Suits me." He reached for her, but with a spurt of laughter she scooted out of reach. She picked up the jar of beets and looked at him expectantly.

He flopped back with a groan. "Oh, man. Don't tell me you expect me to try them *now*."

"No, I want you to open the jar so *I* can eat them."

"I thought you said they were nasty."

"They are. I want to see if they're as nasty as I remember." She handed him the jar. "If you'll open them for me, I'll let you eat fried chicken and potato salad to build up your strength before I wring you out and hang you up to dry."

He sat up and took the jar. "In your dreams, little miss 'don't-touch-me-again-you-lech.'" He put some muscle behind the effort, twisting the lid free.

"I've been sandbagging," she said. "This time, don't even bother begging for mercy."

She reached for the jar. The loosened lid came off, and the jar slipped from her hands. He dived for it, not wanting beets all over everything. Just as he moved, the tree beside him exploded, and a millisecond later he heard the blast of the shot.

He twisted in midair, throwing himself on top of Sunny and rolling with her behind the cover of the tree.

Chapter 13

"Stay down!" Chance barked, shoving her face into the grass.

Sunny couldn't have moved even if she had wanted to, even if his two hundred-plus pounds hadn't been lying on top of her. She was paralyzed, terror freezing in her veins as she realized her worst nightmare had come true; her father had found them, and Chance was nothing more than an obstacle to be destroyed. That bullet hadn't been aimed at *her*. If she hadn't dropped the jar of beets, if Chance hadn't lunged for it, the slug that blew chunks of wood out of the tree would have blown off half his head.

"Son of a bitch," he muttered above her, his breath stirring her hair. "Sniper."

The earth exploded two inches from her head, clods of dirt flying in her face, tiny pieces of gravel stinging her like bees. Chance literally threw her to the side, rolling with her again; the ground dropped out from beneath her, and her stomach gave a sickening lurch. As suddenly as the fall began, it stopped. She landed hard in three inches of sluggish water.

He had rolled them into the creek, where the banks afforded them more cover. A twist of his powerful body and he was off her, his big pistol in his hand as he flattened himself against the shallow bank. Sunny managed to get to her knees, slipped on the slimy creek bottom, and clambered on her hands and knees to a spot beside him. She felt numb, as if her arms and legs didn't belong to her, yet they were working, moving.

This wasn't real. It couldn't be. How had he found them?

She closed her eyes, fighting the terror. She was a liability to Chance unless she got herself under control. She'd had close calls before and handled herself just fine, but she had never before seen the man she loved almost get killed in front of her. She had never before been pregnant, with so much to lose.

Her teeth were chattering. She clamped her jaw together.

Silence fell over the field. She heard a car drive by on the road, and for a wild moment she wondered why it didn't stop. But why would it? There was nothing the average passerby would notice, no bodies lying around on the highway, no haze of gun smoke hanging over the green grass. There was only silence, as if even the insects had frozen in place, the birds stopped singing; even the breeze had stopped rustling the leaves. It was as if nature held its breath, shocked by the sudden violence.

The shot had come from the direction of the road, but she hadn't seen anyone drive up. They had only just arrived themselves; it was as if whoever had shot at them had already been here, waiting. But that was impossible, wasn't it? The picnic was an impulse, and the location sheer chance; they could just as well have stopped at a park.

The only other explanation that occurred to her was if the shooter had nothing to do with her father. Maybe it was a crazy landowner who shot at trespassers.

If only she had brought her cell phone! But Margreta
wasn't due to call her for several more days, and even if she
had brought the phone, it would be in her backpack, which
was still lying on the ground cloth. The distance of a few
yards might as well be a mile. Her pistol was also in the pack;
though a pistol was useless against a sniper, she would feel
better if she had some means of protection.

Chance hadn't fired; he knew the futility of it even more
than she did. His dark gold eyes were scanning the countryside, looking for anything that would give away the assailant's position: a glint of sunlight on the barrel, the color
of his clothing, a movement. The extreme angle of the late
afternoon sun picked out incredible detail in the trees and
bushes, but nothing that would help them.

Only nightfall would help, she thought. If they could just
hold out for…how long? Another hour? Two hours, at most.
When it was dark, then they could belly down in the little
creek and work their way to safety, either upstream or down,
it didn't matter.

If they lived that long. The sniper had the advantage. All
they had was the cover of a shallow creek bank.

She became aware that her teeth were chattering again.
Again she clamped her jaw together to still the movement.
Chance spared a glance at her, a split-second assessment before he returned to once again scanning the trees for the
sniper. "Are you all right?" he asked, though he obviously
knew she was all in one piece. He wasn't asking about her
physical condition.

"S-scared spitless," she managed to say.

"Yeah. Me, too."

He didn't look scared, she thought. He looked coldly
furious.

He reached out and rubbed her arm, a brief gesture of comfort. "Thank God for those beets," he said.

She almost cried. The beets. She had thoroughly enjoyed teasing him about the beets, but the truth was, when she saw them in the supermarket she had been overcome by an almost violent craving for them. She wanted those beets. She felt as if she could eat the entire jar of them. Could cravings start this early in a pregnancy? If so, then he should thank God not for the beets, but for the beginnings of life forming inside her.

She wished she had told him immediately when her period didn't come. She couldn't tell him now; the news would be too distracting.

If they lived through this, she thought fervently, she wouldn't keep the secret to herself a minute longer.

"It can't be Hauer's men," she blurted. "It's impossible. They couldn't be here ahead of us, because we didn't know we were coming here. It has to be a crazy farmer, or a—a jerk who thought it would be funny to shoot at someone."

"Sweetheart." He touched her arm again, and she realized she was babbling. "It isn't a crazy farmer, or a trigger-happy jerk."

"How do you know? It could be!"

"The sniper's too professional."

Just four words, but they made her heart sink. Chance would know; he had training in this sort of thing.

She pressed her forehead against the grassy bank, fighting for the courage to do what she had to do. Her mother had died protecting her and Margreta; surely she could be as brave? She couldn't tell Hauer anything about Margreta, so her sister was safe, and if she could save Chance, then dying would be worth it....

Her child would die with her.

Don't make me choose, she silently prayed. *The child or the father*.

If it were just her, she wouldn't hesitate. In the short time she had known Chance—was it really just two weeks?—he had given her a lifetime of happiness and the richness of love. She would gladly give her life in exchange for his.

The life inside her wasn't really a child yet; it was still just a rapidly dividing cluster of cells. No organs or bones had formed, nothing recognizable as a human. It was maybe the size of a pin head. But the potential…oh, the potential. She loved that tiny ball of cells with a fierceness that burned through every fiber of her being, had loved it from the first startled awareness that her period was late. It was as if she had blinked and said, "Oh. Hello," because one second she had been totally unaware of its existence, and the next she had somehow known.

The child or the father. The father or the child.

The words writhed in her brain, echoing, bouncing. She loved them both. How could she choose? She couldn't choose; no woman should have to make such a decision. She hated her father even more for forcing her into this situation. She hated the chromosomes, the DNA, that he had contributed to her existence. He wasn't a father, he had never been a father. He was a monster.

"Give me your pistol." She heard the words, but the voice didn't sound at all like hers.

His head snapped around. "What?" He stared at her as if she had lost her mind.

"Give me the pistol," she repeated. "He—they—don't know we have it. You haven't fired back. I'll tuck it in the back of my jeans and walk out there—"

"The hell you will!" He glared at her. "If you think I—"

"No, listen!" she said urgently. "They won't shoot me. He wants me alive. When they get close enough for me to use the pistol I—"

"No!" He grabbed her by the shirt and hauled her close so they were almost nose to nose. His eyes were almost shooting sparks. "If you make one move to stand up, I swear I'll knock you out. Do you understand me? *I will not let you walk out there.*"

He released her, and Sunny sank back against the creek bank. She couldn't overpower him, she thought bleakly. He was too strong, and too alert to be taken by surprise.

"We have to do something," she whispered.

He didn't look at her again. "We wait," he said flatly. "That's what we do. Sooner or later, the bastard will show himself."

Wait. That was the first idea she'd had, to wait until dark and slip away. But if Hauer had more than one man here, the sniper could keep them pinned down while the other worked his way around behind them—

"Can we move?" she asked. "Up the creek, down the creek—it doesn't matter."

He shook his head. "It's too risky. The creek's shallow. The only place we have enough cover is flat against the bank on this side. If we try to move, we expose ourselves to fire."

"What if there's more than one?"

"There is." He sounded positive. A feral grin moved his lips in a frightening expression. "At least four, maybe five. I hope it's five."

She shook her head, trying to understand. Five to two were deadly odds. "That makes you happy?"

"Very happy. The more the merrier."

Nausea hit the back of her throat, and she closed her eyes, fighting the urge to vomit. Did he think sheer guts and fighting spirit would keep them alive?

His lean, powerful hand touched her face in a gentle caress. "Chin up, sweetheart. Time's on our side."

Now wasn't the time for explanations, Chance thought. The questions would be too angry, the answers too long and complicated. Their situation was delicately balanced between success and catastrophe; he couldn't relax his guard. If he was correct and there were five men out there hunting them—and that was the only explanation, that one of his own men was a traitor and had given Hauer the location of their supposedly impromptu picnic—then they could, at any time, decide to catch him in a pincer movement. With only one pistol, and Sunny to one side of him, he couldn't handle an attack from more than two directions. The third one would get him—and probably Sunny, too. In a fire fight, bullets flew like angry hornets, and most of them didn't hit their target. If a bullet didn't hit its target, that meant it hit something—or someone—else.

His own men would have been stood down, or sent to a bogus location. That was why there hadn't been any return fire when he and Sunny were fired on—no one was there. For that to have happened, the traitor had to be someone in a position of authority, a team leader or higher. He would find out. Oh, yeah, he'd find out. There had been several betrayals over the years, but they hadn't been traceable. One such breach had almost cost Barrie, Zane's wife, her life. Chance had been trying to identify the bastard for four years now, but he'd been too smart. But this time it was traceable. This time, his men would know who had changed their orders.

The traitor must have thought it was worth blowing his cover, to have this opportunity to kill Chance Mackenzie himself. And he should be here in person, to see the job done. Hauer's two men would bring the count to three. Hauer made it four. The only way Hauer could have gotten into the country and moved about as freely and undetected as he had was with inside help—the FBI mole. If Chance were really lucky, the mole was here, too, bringing the count to five.

But they'd made a big mistake. They didn't know about his ace in the hole: Zane. They didn't know he was out there; that was an arrangement Chance had made totally off the record. If Zane wasn't needed, no one would ever know he was there. Chance's men were damn good, world class, but they weren't in Zane's class. No one was.

Zane was a superb strategist; he always had a plan, and a plan to back up his plan. He would have seen in an instant what was going down and been on the phone calling the men back into position from wherever they'd been sent. How long it took them to get here depended on how far away they were, assuming they could get here at all. And after the call Zane would have started moving, ghosting around, searching out Hauer and his men. Every minute that passed increased the odds in Chance's favor.

He couldn't explain any of that to Sunny, not now, not even to ease the white, pinched expression that made him ache to hold her close and reassure her. Her eyes were haunted, their sparkle gone. She had worked her entire life to make certain she was never caught off guard, and yet she had been; he himself had seen to it.

The knowledge was bitter in his mouth. She was terrified of the monster who had relentlessly hunted her all her life, yet she had been willing to walk out there and offer herself as a sacrifice. How many times in the short two weeks he'd known her had she put herself on the line for him? The first time had been when she barely knew him, when she swooped down to grab the snake coiled so close to his feet. She was terrified of snakes, but she'd done it. She was shaking with fear now, but he knew that if he let her, she would do exactly what she'd offered. That kind of courage amazed him, and humbled him.

His head swiveled restlessly as he tried to keep watch in all directions. The minutes trickled past. The sun slid below the horizon, but there was still plenty of light; twilight wouldn't begin deepening for another fifteen, twenty minutes. The darker it was, the more Zane was in his element. By now, he should have taken out at least one, maybe two—

A man stepped out from behind the tree under which Chance and Sunny had intended to have their picnic and aimed a black 9mm automatic at Sunny's head. He didn't say "Drop it" or anything else. He just smiled, his gaze locked with Chance's.

Carefully Chance placed his pistol on the grass. If the gun had been aimed at his own head, he would have taken the risk that his reflexes were faster. He wouldn't risk Sunny's life. As soon as he moved his hand away from the pistol, the black hole in the man's weapon centered between his eyes.

"Surprised?" the man asked softly. At his voice Sunny gasped and whirled, her feet sliding on the slippery creek bottom. Chance reached out and steadied her without taking his gaze from a man he knew very well.

"Not really," he said. "I knew there was someone."

Sunny looked back and forth between them. "Do you *know* him?" she asked faintly.

"Yeah." He should have been prepared for this, he thought. Knowing one of his own men was involved, he should have realized the traitor would have the skill to approach silently, using the same tree that helped shield them as his own cover. Doing so took patience and nerve, because if Chance had happened to move even a few inches to one side, he would have seen the man's approach.

"H-how?" she stammered.

"We've worked together for years," Melvin Darnell said, still smiling. Mel the Man. That was what the others called him, because he would volunteer for any mission, no matter how dangerous. What better way to get inside information? Chance thought.

"You sold out to Hauer," Chance said, shaking his head. "That's low."

"No, that's lucrative. He has men everywhere. The FBI, the Justice Department, the CIA…even here, right under your nose." Mel shrugged. "What can I say? He pays well."

"I misjudged you. I never thought you'd be the type to get a kick out of torture. Or are you chickening out and leaving as soon as he gets his hands on her?" Chance nodded his head toward Sunny.

"Nice try, Mackenzie, but it won't work. He's her father. All he wants is his little girl." Mel smirked at Sunny.

Chance snorted. "Get a clue. Do you think she'd be so terrified if all he wanted was to get to know her?"

Mel spared another brief glance in her direction. She was absolutely colorless, even her lips. There was no mistaking her fear. He shrugged. "So I was wrong. I don't care what he does with her."

"Do you care that he's a child molester?" Keep him talking. Buy time. Give Zane time to work.

"Give it up," Mel said cheerfully. "He could be Hitler's reincarnation and it still wouldn't change the color of his money. If you think I'm going to develop a conscience— well, you're the one who needs to get a clue."

There was movement behind Mel. Three men approaching, walking openly now, as if they had nothing to fear. Two were dressed in suits, one in slacks and an open-necked shirt. The one in slacks and one of the suits carried hand guns. The suit would be the FBI informant, the one in slacks one of Hauer's bloodhounds. The man in the middle, the one wearing the double-breasted Italian silk suit, his skin tanned, his light brown hair brushed straight back—that was Hauer. He was smiling.

"My dear," he said jovially when he reached them. He stepped carefully around the spilled beets, his nose wrinkling in distaste. "It is so good to finally meet you. A father should know his children, don't you think?"

Sunny didn't speak for a moment. She stared at her father with unconcealed horror and loathing. Beside her, Chance felt the fear drain out of her, felt her subtly relax. Extreme terror was like that, sometimes. When one feared that something would happen, it was the dread and anxiety, the anticipation, that was so crippling. Once the thing actually happened, there was nothing left to fear. He took a firm grip on her arm, wishing she had remained petrified. Sunny was valiant enough when she was frightened; when she thought she had nothing left to lose, there was no telling what she would do.

"I thought you'd be taller," she finally said, looking at him rather dismissively.

Crispin Hauer flushed angrily. He wasn't a large man, about five-eight, and slender. The two men flanking him were both taller. Chance wondered how Sunny had known unerringly how to prick his ego. "Please get out of the mud—if you can bring yourself to leave your lover's side, that is. I recommend it. Head shots can be nasty. You wouldn't want his brains on you, would you? I hear the stain never comes out of one's clothes."

Sunny didn't move. "I don't know where Margreta is," she said. "You might as well kill me now, because I can't tell you anything."

He shook his head in mock sympathy. "As if I believe that." He held out his hand. "You may climb out by yourself, or my men will assist you."

There wasn't much light left, Chance thought. If Sunny could keep delaying her father without provoking him into violence, Zane should be here soon. With Hauer out in the open, Zane must be positioning himself so he could get all four men in his sights.

"Where's the other guy?" he asked, to distract them. "There *are* five of you, aren't there?"

The FBI man and the bloodhound looked around, in the direction of the trees on the opposite side of the road. They seemed vaguely surprised that no one was behind them.

Mel didn't take his attention from Chance. "Don't let him spook you," he said sharply. "Keep your mind on business."

"Don't you wonder where he is?" Chance asked softly.

"I don't give a damn. He's nothing to me. Maybe he fell out of the tree and broke his neck," Mel said.

"Enough," Hauer said, distaste for this squabbling evident

in his tone. "Sonia, come out now. I promise you won't like it if my men have to fetch you."

Sunny's contemptuous gaze swept him from head to foot. Unbelievably, she began singing. And the ditty she sang was a cruel little song of the sort gradeschoolers sang to make fun of a classmate they didn't like. "Monkey man, monkey man, itty bitty monkey man. He's so ugly, he's so short, he needs a ladder to reach his butt."

It didn't rhyme, Chance thought in stunned bemusement. Children, crude little beasts that they were, didn't care about niceties such as that. All they cared about was the effectiveness of their taunt.

It was effective beyond his wildest expectation.

Mel Darnell smothered a laugh. The two other men froze, their expressions going carefully blank. Crispin Hauer flushed a dark, purplish red and his eyes bulged until white showed all around the irises. "You bitch!" he screamed, spittle flying, and he grabbed for the gun in the FBI mole's hand.

A giant red flower bloomed on Hauer's chest, accompanied by a strange, dull splat. Hauer stopped as if he had run into a glass wall, his expression going blank.

Mel had excellent reflexes, and excellent training. In that nanosecond before the sound of the shot reached them, Chance saw Mel's finger begin tightening on the trigger, and he grabbed for his own weapon, knowing he wouldn't be fast enough. Then Sunny hit him full force, her entire body crashing into him and knocking him sideways, her scream almost drowning out the thunderous boom of Mel's big-caliber pistol. She clambered off him almost as fast as she had hit him, trying to scramble up the grassy bank to get to Mel before he could fire another round, but Mel never had another opportunity to pull the trigger. Mel never had anything else, not even a second, because Zane's second shot took him dead center of the chest just as his first had taken Hauer.

Then all hell broke loose. Chance's men, finally back in position and with the threat to Chance and Sunny taken care of, opened fire on the remaining two men. Chance grabbed Sunny and flattened her in the creek again, covering her with his own body, holding her there until Zane roared a cease fire and the night was silent.

Sunny sat off to the side of the nightmarish scene, brightly lit now with battery-operated spotlights that picked out garish detail and left stark black shadows. From somewhere, one of the small army of men who suddenly swarmed the field had produced a bucket that he turned upside down for her, providing her with a seat. She was wet and almost unbearably cold, despite the warmth of the late August night. Her muddy clothes were clammy, so the blanket she clutched around her with nerveless fingers didn't do much to help, but she didn't release it.

She hurt, with an all-consuming agony that threatened to topple her off the bucket, but she grimly forced herself to stay upright. Sheer willpower kept her on that bucket.

The men around her were professionals. They were quiet and competent as they dealt with the five bodies that were laid out on the ground in a neat row. They were courteous with the local law enforcement officers who arrived *en force*, sirens blasting, blue lights strobing the night, though there was never any doubt who held jurisdiction.

And Chance was their leader.

That man, the one who had first held a gun on them, had

called him "Mackenzie." And several times one or another of the locals had referred to him as Mr. Mackenzie; he had answered, so she knew there was no mistake in the name.

The events of the night were a chaotic blur in her mind, but one fact stood out: this entire scene was a setup, a trap—and she had been the bait.

She didn't want to believe it, but logic wouldn't let her deny it. He was obviously in charge here. He had a lot of men on site, men he commanded, men who could be here only if he had arranged it in advance.

Viewed in the light of that knowledge, everything that had happened since she met him took on a different meaning. She even thought she recognized the cretin who had stolen her briefcase in the Salt Lake City airport. He was cleaned up now, with the same quiet, competent air as the others, but she was fairly certain he was the same man.

Everything had been a setup. Everything. She didn't know how he'd done it, her mind couldn't quite grasp the sphere of influence needed to bring all of this off, but somehow he had manipulated her flights so that she was in the Salt Lake City airport at a certain time, for the cretin to grab her briefcase and Chance to intercept him. It was a hugely elaborate play, one that took skill and money and more resources than she could imagine.

He must have thought she was in cahoots with her father, she thought with a flash of intuition. This had all happened after the incident in Chicago, which was undoubtedly what had brought her to Chance's notice. What had his plan been? To make her fall in love with him and use her to infiltrate her father's organization? Only it hadn't worked out that way. Not only was she not involved with her father, she desperately feared and hated him. So

Chance, knowing why Hauer really wanted her, had adjusted his plan and used her as bait.

What a masterful strategy. And what a superb actor he was; he should get an Oscar.

There hadn't been anything wrong with the plane at all. She didn't miss the significance of the timing of their "rescue." Charlie Jones had just happened to find them first thing in the morning after she spilled her guts about her father to Chance the night before. He must have signaled Charlie somehow.

How easy she had been for him. She had been completely duped, completely taken in by his lovemaking and charm. He had been a bright light to her, a comet blazing into her lonely world, and she had fallen for him with scarcely a whisper of resistance. He must think her the most gullible fool in the world. The worst of it was, she was an even bigger fool than he knew, because she was pregnant with his child.

She looked across the field at him, standing tall in the glaring spotlights as he talked with another tall, powerful man who exuded the deadliest air she had ever seen, and the pain inside her spread until she could barely contain it.

Her bright light had gone out.

Chance looked around at Sunny, as he had been doing periodically since the moment she sank down on the overturned bucket and huddled deep in the blanket someone had draped around her. She was frighteningly white, her face drawn and stark. He couldn't take the time to comfort her, not now. There was too much to do, local authorities to soothe at the same time that he let them know he was the one in control, not they, the bodies to be handled, sweeps initiated at the agencies Mel had listed as having Hauer's moles employed there.

She wasn't stupid; far from it. He had watched her watching the activity around her, watched her expression become even more drawn as she inevitably reached the only conclusion she *could* reach. She had noticed when people called him Mackenzie instead of McCall.

Their gazes met, and locked. She stared at him across the ten yards that separated them, thirty feet of unbridgeable gulf. He kept his face impassive. There was no excuse he could give her that she wouldn't already have considered. His reasons were good; he knew that. But he had used her and risked her life. Being the person she was, she would easily forgive him for risking her life; it was the rest of it, the way he had used her, that would strike her to the core.

As he watched, he saw the light die in her eyes, draining away as if it had never been. She turned her head away from him—

And gutted him with the gesture.

Shaken, pierced through with regret, he turned back to Zane and found his brother watching him with a world of knowledge in those pale eyes. "If you want her," Zane said, "then don't let her go."

It was that simple, and that difficult. Don't let her go. How could he not, when she deserved so much better than what he was?

But the idea was there now. Don't let her go. He couldn't resist looking at her again, to see if she was still watching him.

She wasn't there. The bucket still sat there, but Sunny was gone.

Chance strode rapidly across to where she had been, scanning the knots of men who stood about, some working, some just observing. He didn't see that bright hair. Damn it, she was just here; how could she disappear so fast?

Easily, he thought. She had spent a lifetime practicing.

Zane was beside him, his head up, alert. The damn spotlights blinded them to whatever was behind them. She could have gone in any direction, and they wouldn't be able to see her.

He looked down to see if he could pick up any tracks, though the grass was so trampled by now that he doubted he would find anything. The bucket gleamed dark and wet in the spotlight.

Wet?

Chance leaned down and swiped his hand over the bucket. He stared at the dark red stain on his fingers and palm. Blood. Sunny's blood.

He felt as if his own blood was draining from his body. My God, she'd been shot, and she hadn't said a word. In the darkness, the blood hadn't been noticeable on her wet clothing. But that had been…how long ago? She had sat there all that time, bleeding, and not told anyone.

Why?

Because she wanted to get away from him. If they had known she was wounded, she would have to be bundled up and taken to a hospital, and she wouldn't be able to escape without having to see him again. When Sunny walked, she did it clean. No scenes, no excuses, no explanations. She just disappeared.

If he had thought it hurt when she turned away from him, that was nothing to the way he felt now. Desperate fear seized his heart, froze his blood in his veins. "Listen up!" he boomed, and a score of faces, trained to obey his every command, turned his way. "Did anyone see where Sunny went?"

Heads shook, and men began looking around. She was nowhere in sight.

Chance began spitting out orders. "Everyone drop what you're doing and fan out. Find her. She's bleeding. She was shot and didn't tell anyone." As he talked, he was striding out of the glare of the spotlights, his heart in his mouth. She couldn't have gone far, not in that length of time. He would find her. He couldn't bear the alternative.

Chapter 14

Chance blindly paced the corridor outside the surgical waiting room. He couldn't sit down, though the room was empty and he could have had any chair he wanted. If he stopped walking, he thought, he might very well fall down and not be able to stand again. He hadn't known such crippling fear existed. He had never felt it for himself, not even when he looked down the barrel of a weapon pointed at his face—and Mel's hadn't been the first—but he felt it for Sunny. He'd been gripped by it since he found her lying facedown in the grassy field, unconscious, her pulse thready from blood loss.

Thank God there were medics on hand in the field, or she would have died before he could get her to a hospital. They hadn't managed to stop the bleeding, but they had slowed it, started an IV saline push to pump fluid back into her body and raise her plummeting blood pressure, and gotten her to the hospital still alive.

He had been shouldered aside then, by a whole team of gowned emergency personnel. "Are you any relation to her, sir?" a nurse had asked briskly as she all but manhandled him out of the treatment room.

"I'm her husband," he'd heard himself say. There was no way he was going to allow the decisions for her care to be taken out of his hands. Zane, who had been beside him the entire time, hadn't revealed even a flicker of surprise.

"Do you know her blood type, sir?"

Of course he didn't. Nor did he know the answers to any of the other questions posed by the woman they handed him off to, but he was so numb, his attention so focused on the cubicle where about ten people were working on her, that he barely knew anyone was asking the questions, and the woman hadn't pushed it. Instead, she had patted his hand and said she would come back in a little while when his wife was stabilized. He had been grateful for her optimism. In the meantime, Zane, as ruthlessly competent as usual, had requested that a copy of their file on Sunny be downloaded to his wireless Pocket Pro, so Chance would have all the necessary information when the woman returned with her million and one questions. He was indifferent to the bureaucratic snafu he was causing; the organization would pay for everything.

But the shocks had kept arriving, one piling on top of the other. The surgeon came out of the cubicle, his green paper gown stained red with her blood. "Your wife regained consciousness briefly," he'd said. "She wasn't completely lucid, but she asked about the baby. Do you know how far along she is?"

Chance had literally staggered and braced his hand against the wall for support. "She's pregnant?" he asked hoarsely.

"I see." The surgeon immediately switched gears. "I think she must have just found out. We'll do some tests and take all the precautions we can. We're taking her up to surgery now. A nurse will show you where to wait." He strode away, paper gown flapping.

Zane had turned to Chance, his pale blue eyes laser sharp. "Yours?" he asked briefly.

"Yes."

Zane didn't ask if he was certain, for which Chance was grateful. Zane took it for granted Chance wouldn't be mistaken about something that important.

Pregnant? How? He pinched the bridge of his nose, between his eyes. He knew how. He remembered with excruciating clarity how it felt to climax inside her without the protective sheath of a condom dulling the sensation. It had happened twice—just twice—but once was enough.

A couple of little details clicked into place. He'd been around pregnant women most of his life, with first one sister-in-law and then another producing a little Mackenzie. He knew the symptoms well. He remembered Sunny's sleepiness this afternoon, and her insistence on buying the beets. Those damn pickled beets, he thought; her craving for them—for he was certain now that was why she'd wanted them—had saved his life. Sometimes the weird cravings started almost immediately. He could remember when Shea, Michael's wife, had practically wiped that section of Wyoming clean of canned tuna, a full week before she missed her first period. The sleepiness began soon in a pregnancy, too.

He knew the exact day when he'd gotten her pregnant. It had been the second time he'd made love to her, lying on the blanket in the late afternoon heat. The baby would be born about the middle of May…if Sunny lived.

She had to live. He couldn't face the alternative. He loved her too damn much to even think it. But he had seen the bullet wound in her right side, and he was terrified.

"Do you want me to call Mom and Dad?" Zane asked.

They would drop everything and come immediately if he said yes, Chance knew. The whole family would; the hospital would be inundated with Mackenzies. Their support was total, and unquestioning.

He shook his head. "No. Not yet." His voice was raw, as if he had been screaming, though he would have sworn all his screams had been held inside. If Sunny…if the worst happened, he would need them then. Right now he was still holding together. Just.

So he walked, and Zane walked with him. Zane had seen a lot of bullet wounds, too; he'd taken his share. Chance was the lucky one; he'd been cut a few times, but never shot.

God, there had been so much blood. How had she stayed upright for so long? She had answered questions, said she was all right, even walked around a little before one of the men had found that bucket for her to sit on. It was dark, she had a blanket wrapped around her—that was why no one had noticed. But she should have been on the ground, screaming in pain.

Zane's thoughts were running along the same path. "I'm always amazed," he said, "at what some people can do after being shot."

Contrary to what most people thought, a bullet wound, even a fatal one, didn't necessarily knock the victim down. All cops knew that even someone whose heart had been virtually destroyed by a bullet could still attack and kill *them*, and die only when his oxygen-starved brain died. Someone crazed on drugs could absorb a truly astonishing amount of damage and keep on fighting. On the other side of the spectrum were those who suffered relatively minor wounds and went down as if they had been poleaxed, then screamed unceasingly until they reached the hospital and were given enough drugs to quiet them. It was pure mind over matter, and Sunny had a will like titanium. He only hoped she applied that will to surviving.

It was almost six hours before the tired surgeon approached, the six longest hours of Chance's life. The surgeon looked haggard, and Chance felt the icy claw of dread. No. No—

"I think she's going to make it," the surgeon said, and smiled a smile of such pure personal triumph that Chance knew there had been a real battle in the O.R. "I had to remove part of the liver and resection her small intestine. The wound to the liver is what caused the extensive hemorrhage. We had to replace almost her complete blood volume before we got things under control." He rubbed his hand over his face. "It was touch and go for a while. Her blood pressure bottomed out and she went into cardiac arrest, but we got her right back. Her pupil response is normal, and her vitals are satisfactory. She was lucky."

"Lucky," Chance echoed, still dazed by the combination of good news and the litany of damage.

"It was only a fragment of a bullet that hit her. There must have been a ricochet."

Chance knew she hadn't been hit while he'd had her flattened in the creek. It had to have happened when she knocked him aside and Darnell fired. Evidently Darnell had missed, and the bullet must have struck a rock in the creek and fragmented.

She had been protecting him. Again.

"She'll be in ICU for at least twenty-four hours, maybe forty-eight, until we see if there's a secondary infection. I really think we have things under control, though." He grinned. "She'll be out of here in a week."

Chance sagged against the wall, bending over to clasp his knees. His head swam. Zane's hard hand gripped his shoulder, lending his support. "Thank you," Chance said to the doctor, angling his head so he could see him.

"Do you need to lie down?" the doctor asked.

"No, I'm all right. God! I'm great. She's going to be okay!"

"Yeah," said the doctor, and grinned again.

Sunny kept surfacing to consciousness, like a float bobbing up and down in the water. At first her awareness was fragmented. She could hear voices in the distance, though she couldn't make out any words, and a soft beeping noise. She was also aware of something in her throat, though she didn't realize it was a tube. She had no concept of where she was, or even that she was lying down.

The next time she bobbed up, she could feel smooth cotton beneath her and recognized the fabric as sheets.

The next time she managed to open her eyes a slit, but her vision was blurry and what seemed like a mountain of machinery made no sense to her.

At some point she realized she was in a hospital. There was pain, but it was at a distance. The tube was gone from her throat now. She vaguely remembered it being removed, which hadn't been pleasant, but her sense of time was so confused that she thought she remembered the tube being there after it was removed. People kept coming into the small space that was hers, turning on bright lights, talking and touching her and doing intimate things to her.

Gradually her dominion over her body began to return, as she fought off the effects of anesthesia and drugs. She managed to make a weak gesture toward her belly, and croak out a single word. "Baby?"

The intensive care nurse understood. "Your baby's fine," he said, giving her a comforting pat, and she was content.

She was horribly thirsty. Her next word was "Water," and slivers of ice were put in her mouth.

With the return of consciousness, though, came the pain. It crept ever nearer as the fog of drugs receded. The pain was bad, but Sunny almost welcomed it, because it meant she was alive, and for a while she had thought she might not be.

She saw the nurse named Jerry the most often. He came into the cubicle, smiling as usual, and said, "There's someone here to see you."

Sunny violently shook her head, which was a mistake. It set off waves of agony that swamped the drugs holding them at bay. "No visitors," she managed to say.

It seemed as if she spent days, eons, in the intensive care unit, but when she asked Jerry he said, "Oh, about thirty-six hours. We'll be moving you to a private room soon. It's being readied now."

When they moved her, she was clearheaded enough to watch the ceiling tiles and lights pass by overhead. She caught a glimpse of a tall, black-haired man and quickly looked away.

Settling her into a private room was quite an operation, requiring two orderlies, three nurses and half an hour. She was exhausted when everything, including herself, had been transferred and arranged. The fresh bed was nice and cool; the head had been elevated and a pillow tucked under her head. Sitting up even that much made her feel a hundred percent more normal and in control.

There were flowers in the room. Roses, peach ones, with a hint of blush along the edges of their petals, dispensed a spicy, peppery scent that overcame the hospital scents of antiseptics and cleaning fluids. Sunny stared at them but didn't ask who they were from.

"I don't want any visitors," she told the nurses. "I just want to rest."

She was allowed to eat Jell-O, and drink weak tea. On the second day in the private room she drank some broth, and she was placed in the bedside chair for fifteen minutes. It felt good to stand on her own two feet, even for the few seconds it took them to move her from bed to chair. It felt even better when they moved her back to the bed.

That night, she got out of bed herself, though the process was slow and unhappy, and walked the length of the bed. She had to hold on to the bed for support, but her legs remained under her.

The third day, there was another delivery from a florist. This was a bromeliad, with thick, grayish green leaves and a beautiful pink flower blooming in its center. She had never had houseplants for the same reason she had never had a pet, because she was constantly on the move and couldn't take care of them. She stared at the bromeliad, trying to come to grips with the fact that she could have all the houseplants she wanted now. Everything was changed. Crispin Hauer was dead, and she and Margreta were free.

The thought of her sister sent alarm racing through her. What day was it? When was Margreta due to call? For that matter, where was her cell phone?

On the afternoon of the fourth day, the door opened and Chance walked in.

She turned her head to look out the window. In truth,

she was surprised he had given her this long to recover. She had held him off as long as she could, but she supposed there had to be a closing act before the curtain could fall.

She had held her inner pain at bay by focusing on her physical pain, but now it rushed to the forefront. She fought it down, reaching for control. There was nothing to be gained by causing a scene, only her self-respect to lose.

"I've kept your cell phone with me," he said, walking around to place himself between her and the windows, so she had to either look at him or turn her head away again. His conversational opening had guaranteed she wouldn't turn away. "Margreta called yesterday."

Sunny clenched her fists, then quickly relaxed her right hand as the motion flexed the IV needle taped to the back of it. Margreta would have panicked when she heard a man's voice answer instead of Sunny's.

"I talked fast," Chance said. "I told her you'd been shot but would be okay, and that Hauer was dead. I told her I'd bring the phone to you today, and she could call again to-night to verify everything I said. She didn't say anything, but she didn't hang up on me, either."

"Thank you," Sunny said. He had handled the situation in the best possible way.

He was subtly different, she realized. It wasn't just his clothing, though he was now dressed in black slacks and a white silk shirt, while he had worn only jeans, boots, and casual shirts and T-shirts before. His whole demeanor was different. Of course, he wasn't playing a raffish, charming charter pilot any longer. He was himself now, and the real-ity was what she had always sensed beneath the surface of his charm. He was the man who led some sort of com-mando team, who exerted enormous influence in getting things done his way. The dangerous edge she had only glimpsed before was in full view now, in his eyes and the authority with which he spoke.

He moved closer to the side of the bed, so close he was leaning against the rail. Very gently, the touch as light as gossamer, he placed his fingertips on her belly. "Our baby is all right," he said.

He knew. Shocked, she stared at him, though she realized she should have known the doctor would tell him.

"Were you going to tell me?" he asked, his golden-brown eyes intent on her face, as if he wanted to catch every nuance of expression.

"I hadn't thought about it one way or the other," she said honestly. She had just been coming to terms with the knowledge herself; she hadn't gotten around to forming any plans.

"This changes things."

"Does it really," she said, and it wasn't a question. "Was *anything* you told me the truth?"

He hesitated. "No."

"There was nothing wrong with the fuel pump."

"No."

"You could have flown us out of the canyon at any time."

"Yes."

"Your name isn't Chance McCall."

"Mackenzie," he said. "Chance Mackenzie."

"Well, that's one thing," she said bitterly. "At least your first name was really your own."

"Sunny...don't."

"Don't what? Don't try to find out how big a fool I am? Were you really an army ranger?"

He sighed, his expression grim. "Navy. Naval Intelligence."

"You arranged for all of my flights to be fouled up that day."

He shrugged an admittance.

"The cretin was really one of your men."

"A good one. The airport security people were mine, too."

She creased the sheet with her left hand. "You knew my father would be there. You had it set up."

"We knew two of his men were trailing us, had been since the television newscast about you aired."

"You arranged that, too."

He didn't say anything.

"Why did we fly all over the country? Why didn't we just stay in Seattle? That would have been less wear and tear on the plane."

"I had to make it look good."

She swallowed. "That day…the picnic. Would you have made love—I mean, had sex—with me with your men watching? Just to make it look good?"

"No. Having an affair with you was necessary, but… private."

"I suppose I should thank you for that, at least. Thank you. Now get out."

"I'm not going anywhere." He sat down in the bedside chair. "If you've finished with the dissection, we need to make some decisions."

"I've already made one. I don't want to see you again."

"Sorry about that, but you aren't getting your wish. You're stuck with me, sweetheart, because that baby inside you is mine."

Chapter 15

Sunny was released from the hospital eight days after the shooting. She could walk, gingerly, but her strength was almost negligible, and she had to wear the nightgown and robe Chance had bought her, because she couldn't stand any clothing around her middle. She had no idea what she was going to do. She wasn't in any condition to catch a flight to Atlanta, not to mention that she would have to travel in her nightgown, but she had to find somewhere to stay. Once she knew she was being released, she got the phone book and called a hotel, made certain the hotel had room service, and booked herself a room there. The hotel had room service; until she was able to take care of herself again, a hotel was the best she could do.

In the hospital she had, at first, entertained a fragile hope that Margreta would come to stay with her and help her until she was recovered. With their father dead, they didn't have to hide any longer. But though Margreta had sounded happy and relieved, she had resisted Sunny's suggestion that she come to Des Moines. They had exchanged telephone numbers, but that was all—and Margreta hadn't called back.

Sunny understood. Margreta would always have problems relating to people, forming relationships with them. She was probably very comfortable with the long-distance contact she had with Sunny, and wanted nothing more. Sunny tried to fight her sadness as she realized she would never have the sister she had wanted, but melancholy too easily overwhelmed her these days.

Part of it was the hormonal chaos of early pregnancy, she knew. She found herself tearing up at the most ridiculous things, such as a gardening show she watched on television one day. She lay in her hospital bed and began thinking how she had always wanted a flower garden but had never been able to have one, and presto, all of a sudden she was feeling sorry for herself and sitting there like an idiot with tears rolling down her face.

Depression went hand in glove with physical recovery, too, one of the nurses told her. It would pass as she got stronger and could do more.

But the biggest part of her depression was Chance. He visited every day, and once even brought along the tall, lethal-looking man she had noticed him talking to the night she was injured. To her surprise, Chance introduced the man as his brother, Zane. Zane had shaken her hand with exquisite gentleness, shown her photos of his pretty wife and three adorable children, and spent half an hour telling her yarns about the exploits of his daughter, Nick. If even half of what he said about the child was true, the world had better brace itself for when she was older.

After Zane left, Sunny was even more depressed. Zane had what she had always wanted: a family he loved, and who loved him in return.

When he visited, Chance always avoided the subject

that lay between them like a coiled snake. He had done what he had done, and no amount of talking would change reality. She had to respect, reluctantly, his lack of any attempt to make excuses. Instead, he talked about his family in Wyoming, and the mountain they all still called home, even though only his parents lived there now. He had four brothers and one sister, a dozen nephews—and one niece, the notorious Nick, whom he obviously adored. His sister was a horse trainer who was married to one of his agents; one brother was a rancher who had married the granddaughter of an old family enemy; another brother was an ex-fighter pilot who was married to an orthopedic surgeon; Zane was married to the daughter of an ambassador; and Joe, his oldest brother, was General Joseph Mackenzie, chairman of the Joint Chiefs of Staff.

That couldn't all be true, she thought, yet the tales had a ring of truth to them. Then she remembered that Chance was a consummate actor, and bitterness would swamp her again.

She couldn't seem to pull herself out of the dismals. She had always been able to laugh, but now she found it difficult to even smile. No matter how she tried to distract herself, the knowledge was always there, engraved on her heart like a curse that robbed her life of joy: Chance didn't love her. It had all been an act.

It was as if part of her had died. She felt cold inside, and empty. She tried to hide it, tried to tell herself the depression would go away if she just ignored it and concentrated on getting better, but every day the grayness inside her seemed to spread and deepen.

The day she was released, the escort finally arrived with a wheelchair and Sunny called a taxi to meet them at the entrance in fifteen minutes. She gingerly lowered herself into the wheelchair, and the escort obligingly placed the small bag containing her few articles of clothing and her backpack on her lap, then balanced the bromeliad on top.

"I'm sure I have to sign some papers before I'm released," Sunny said.

"No, I don't think so," the woman said, checking her orders. "According to this, you're all ready to go. Your husband probably handled it for you."

Sunny bit back the urge to snap that she wasn't married. He hadn't mentioned it, and in truth she hadn't given a thought to how she would pay for her hospital care, but now that she thought about it, she realized Chance had indeed handled all of that. Maybe he thought the least he could do was pick up her tab.

She was surprised he wasn't here, since he'd been so adamant about being a part of the baby's life, and persistent in visiting. For all she knew, she thought, he had been called away on some mysterious spy stuff.

She underestimated him. When the escort rolled her to the doors of the patient discharge area, she saw a familiar dark green Ford Explorer parked under the covered entrance. Chance unfolded his long length from behind the steering wheel and came to meet her.

"I've already called a taxi," she said, though she knew it was a waste of breath.

"Tough," he said succinctly. He took her clothes and the bromeliad and put them in the back of the Explorer, then opened the passenger door.

Sunny began to inch herself forward in the wheelchair seat, preparatory to standing; she had mastered the art when seated in a regular chair, but a wheelchair was trickier. Chance gave her an exasperated look, then leaned down and scooped her up in his powerful arms, handling her weight with ease as he deposited her in the Explorer.

"Thank you," she said politely. She would at least be civil, and his method had been much less painful and time-consuming than hers.

"You're welcome." He buckled the seat belt around her, making certain the straps didn't rub against the surgical incision, then closed the door and walked around to slide under the steering wheel.

"I've booked a room in a hotel," she said. "But I don't know where it is, so I can't give you directions."

"You aren't going to a hotel," he growled.

"I have to go somewhere," she pointed out. "I'm not able to drive, and I can't handle negotiating an airport, so a hotel with room service is the only logical solution."

"No it isn't. I'm taking you home with me."

"No!" she said violently, everything in her rejecting the idea of spending days in his company.

His jaw set. "You don't have a choice," he said grimly. "You're going—even if you kick and scream the whole way."

It was tempting. Oh, it was tempting. Only the thought of how badly kicking would pull at the incision made her resist the idea.

The dime didn't drop until she noticed he was driving to the airport. "Where are we going?"

He gave her an impatient glance. "I told you. Hell, Sunny, you know I don't live in Des Moines."

"All right, so I know where you don't live. But I *don't* know where you *do* live." She couldn't resist adding, "And even if you had told me, it would probably be a lie."

This time his glance was sulfuric. "Wyoming," he said through gritted teeth. "I'm taking you home to Wyoming."

* * *

She was silent during the flight, speaking only when necessary and then only in monosyllables. Chance studied her when her attention was on the landscape below, his sunglasses hiding his eyes. They had flown around so much during the time they'd been together that it felt natural to once again be in the plane with her, as if they were where they belonged. She had settled in with a minimum of fussing and no complaints, though he knew she had to be exhausted and uncomfortable.

She looked so frail, as if a good wind would blow her away. There wasn't any color in her cheeks or lips, and she had dropped a good ten pounds that she didn't need to lose. The doctor had assured him that she was recovering nicely, right on schedule, and that while her pregnancy was still too new for any test to tell them anything about the baby's condition, they had taken all precautions and he had every confidence the baby would be fine.

As thrilled as he was about the baby, Chance was more worried that the pregnancy would sap her strength and slow her recovery. She needed all the resources she could muster now, but nature would ensure that the developing child got what it needed first. The only way he could be confident she was getting what *she* needed was if he arranged for her to be watched every minute, and coddled and spoiled within an inch of her life. The best place for that was Mackenzie's Mountain.

He had called and told them he was bringing Sunny there, of course. He had told them the entire situation, that she was pregnant and he intended to marry her, but that she was still mad as hell at him and hadn't forgiven him. He had set quite a task for himself, getting back in

Sunny's good graces. But once he had her on the Mountain, he thought, he could take his time wearing her down.

Mary, typically, was ecstatic. She took it for granted Sunny would forgive him, and since she had been prodding him about getting married and giving her more grandchildren, she probably thought she was getting everything she wanted.

Chance was going to do everything he could to see that she did, because what she wanted was exactly what he wanted. He'd always sworn he would never get married and have children, but fate had stepped in and arranged things otherwise. The prospect of getting married scared him—no, it terrified the hell out of him, so much so that he hadn't even broached the subject to Sunny. He didn't know how to tell her what she needed to know about him, and he didn't know what she would do when she found out, if she would accept his proposal or tell him to drop dead.

The only thing that gave him hope was that she'd said she loved him. She hadn't said it since she found out how he'd set her up, but Sunny wasn't a woman who loved lightly. If there was a spark of love left in her, if he hadn't totally extinguished it, he would find a way to fan it to life.

He landed at the airstrip on Zane's property, and his heart gave a hard thump when he saw what was waiting for them. Even Sunny's interest was sparked. She sat up straighter, and for the first time since she'd been shot he saw a hint of that lively interest in her face. "What's going on?" she asked.

His spirits lifting, he grinned. "Looks like a welcoming party."

The entire Mackenzie clan was gathered by the airstrip. Everyone. Josh and Loren were there from Seattle with their three sons. Mike and Shea and their two boys. Zane and Barrie, each holding one of the twins. And there was Joe, decked out in his Air Force uniform with more rows of fruit salad on it than should be allowed. How he had carved time out of his schedule to come here, Chance didn't know—but then, Joe could do damn near anything he wanted, since he was the highest ranking military officer in the nation. Caroline, standing beside him and looking positively chic in turquoise capri pants and white sandals—and also looking damn good for her age—had probably had a harder time getting free. She was one of the top-ranked physicists in the world. Their five sons were with him, and John, the oldest, wasn't the only one this time who had a girlfriend with him. Maris and Mac stood together; Mac had his arm draped protectively around Maris's slight frame. And Mom and Dad were in the middle of the whole gang, with Nick perched happily in Wolf's arms.

Every last one of them, even the babies, held a balloon.

"Oh, my," Sunny murmured. The corners of her pale mouth moved upwards in the first smile he had seen in eight days.

He cut the motor and got out, then went to the other door and carefully lifted Sunny out. She was so bemused by the gathering that she put her arm around his neck.

That must have been the signal. Wolf leaned down and set Nick on her feet. She took off toward Chance like a shot, running and skipping and shrieking his name in the usual litany. "UncaDance, UncaDance, Unca*Dance!*" The balloon she was holding bobbed like a mad thing. The whole crowd started forward in her wake.

In seconds they were surrounded. He tried to introduce everyone to Sunny, but there was too much of a hubbub for him to complete a sentence. His sisters-in-law, bless them, were laughing and chattering as if they had known her for years; the men were flirting; Mary was beaming; and Nick's piping voice could be heard above everyone. "Dat's a weally, weally pwetty dwess." She fingered the silk robe and beamed up at Sunny.

John leaned down and whispered something in Nick's ear. "*Dress*," she said, emphasizing the *r*. "Dat's a weally, weally pwetty *dress*."

Everyone cheered, and Nick glowed.

Sunny laughed.

Chance's heart jumped at the sound. His throat got tight, and he squeezed his eyes shut for a second. When he opened them, Mary had taken control.

"You must be exhausted," she was saying to Sunny in her sweet, Southern-accented voice. "You don't have to worry about a thing, dear. I have a bed all ready for you at the house, and you can sleep as long as you want. Chance, carry her along to the car, and be careful with her."

"Yes, ma'am," he said.

"Wait!" Nick wailed suddenly. "I fordot de sign!"

"What sign?" Chance asked, gently shifting Sunny so he could look down at his niece.

She fished in the pocket of her little red shorts and pulled out a very crumpled piece of paper. She stretched up on her tiptoes to hand it to Sunny. "I did it all by myself," she said proudly. "Gamma helped."

Sunny unfolded the piece of paper.

"I used a wed cwayon," Nick informed her. "Because it's de pwettiest."

"It certainly is," Sunny agreed. She swallowed audibly. Chance looked down to see the paper shaking in her hand.

The letters were misshapen and wobbly and all different

sizes. The little girl must have labored over them for a long time, with Mary's expert and patient aid, because the words were legible. "'Welcome home Sunny,'" Sunny read aloud. Her face began to crumple. "That's the most beautiful sign I've ever seen," she said, then buried her face against Chance's neck and burst into tears.

"Yep," Michael said. "She's pregnant, all right."

It was difficult to say who fell more in love with whom, Sunny with the Mackenzies, or the Mackenzies with her. Once Chance placed her in the middle of the king-sized bed Mary had made up for her—he didn't tell her it was his old bedroom—Sunny settled in like a queen holding court. Instead of lying down to sleep, she propped herself up on pillows, and soon all of the women and most of the younger kids were in there, sitting on the bed and on the floor, some even in chairs. The twins were working their way from one side of the bed to the other and back again, clutching the covers for support and babbling away to each other in what Barrie called their "twin talk." Shea had Benjy down on the floor, tickling him, and every time she stopped he would shriek, "More! More!" Nick sat cross-legged on the bed, her "wed cwayon" in hand as she studiously worked on another sign. Since the first one had been such a resounding success, this one was for Barrie, and she was embellishing it with lopsided stars. Loren, being a doctor, wanted the details of Sunny's wound and present condition. Caroline was doing an impromptu fashion consultation, brushing Sunny's hair and swirling it on top of her head, with some very sexy tendrils curling loose on her slender neck. Maris, her dark eyes glowing, was telling Sunny all about her own pregnancy, and Mary was overseeing it all.

Leaving his family to do what they did best, weave a magic spell of warmth and belonging, Chance walked down to the barn. He felt edgy and worried and a little panicked, and he needed some peace and quiet. When everything quieted down tonight, he had to talk to Sunny. He couldn't put it off any longer. He prayed desperately that she could forgive him, that what he had to tell her didn't completely turn her against him, because he loved her so much he wasn't certain he could live without her. When she had buried her face against him and cried, his heart had almost stopped because she had turned *to* him instead of away from him.

She had laughed again. That sound was the sweetest sound he'd ever heard, and it had almost unmanned him. He couldn't imagine living without being able to hear her laugh.

He folded his arms across the top of a stall door and rested his head on them. She had to forgive him. She had to.

"It's tough, isn't it?" Wolf said in his deep voice, coming up to stand beside Chance and rest his arms on top of the stall door, too. "Loving a woman. And it's the best thing in the world."

"I never thought it would happen," Chance said, the words strained. "I was so careful. No marriage, no kids. It was going to end with me. But she blindsided me. I fell for her so fast I didn't have time to run."

Wolf straightened, his black eyes narrowed. "What do you mean, 'end with you'? Why don't you want kids? You love them."

"Yeah," Chance said softly. "But they're Mackenzies."

"You're a Mackenzie." There was steel in the deep voice.

Tiredly, Chance rubbed the back of his neck. "That's the problem. I'm not a real Mackenzie."

"Do you want to walk in the house and tell that little woman in there that you're not her son?" Wolf demanded sharply.

"*Hell*, no!" No way would he hurt her like that.

"You're my son. In all the ways that matter, you're mine."

The truth of that humbled Chance. He rested his head on his arms again. "I never could understand how you could take me in as easily as you did. You know what kind of life I led. You may not know the details, but you have a good general idea. I wasn't much more than a wild animal. Mom had no idea, but you did. And you still brought me into your home, trusted me to be around both Mom and Maris—"

"And that trust was justified, wasn't it?" Wolf asked.

"But it might not have been. You had no way of knowing." Chance paused, looking inward at the darkness inside him. "I killed a man when I was about ten, maybe eleven," he said flatly. "That's the wild kid you brought home with you. I stole, I lied, I attacked other kids and beat them up, then took whatever it was they had that I wanted. That's the kind of person I am. That kid will always live inside me."

Wolf gave him a sharp look. "If you had to kill a man when you were ten, I suspect the bastard deserved killing."

"Yeah, he deserved it. Kids who live in the street are fair game to perverts like that." He clenched his hands. "I have to tell Sunny. I can't ask her to marry me without her knowing what she'll be getting, what kind of genes I'll be passing on to her children." He gave a harsh laugh. "Except I don't know what kind of genes they are. I don't know what's in my background. For all I know my mother was a drugged-out whore and—"

"Stop right there," Wolf said, steel in his voice.

Chance looked up at him, the only father he had ever known, and the man he respected most in the world.

"I don't know who gave birth to you," Wolf said. "But I do know bloodlines, son, and you're a thoroughbred. Do you know what I regret most in my life? Not finding you until you were fourteen. Not feeling your hand holding my finger when you took your first step. Not getting up with you in the night when you were teething, or when you were sick. Not being able to hold you the way you needed holding, the way all kids need holding. By the time we got you I couldn't do any of that, because you were as skittish as a wild colt. You didn't like for us to touch you, and I tried to respect that.

"But one thing you need to know. I'm more proud of you than I've ever been of anything in my life, because you're one of the finest men I've ever known, and you had to work a lot harder than most to get to where you are. If I could have had my pick of all the kids in the world to adopt, I still would have chosen you."

Chance stared at his father, his eyes wet. Wolf Mackenzie put his arms around his grown son and hugged him close, the way he had wanted to do all these years. "I would have chosen you," he said again.

Chance entered the bedroom and quietly closed the door behind him. The crowd had long since dispersed, most to their respective homes, some spending the night here or at Zane's or Michael's. Sunny looked tired, but there was a little color in her cheeks.

"How do you feel?" he asked softly.

"Exhausted," she said. She looked away from him. "Better."

He sat down beside her on the bed, taking care not to jostle her. "I have some things I need to tell you," he said.

"If it's an explanation, don't bother," she shot back. "You used me. Fine. But *damn* you, you didn't have to take it as far as you did! Do you know how it makes me feel that I was such a fool to fall in love with you, when all you were doing was playing a game? Did it stroke your ego—"

He put his hand across her mouth. Above his tanned fingers, her gray eyes sparked pure rage at him. He took a deep breath. "First and most important thing is: I love you. That wasn't a game. I started falling the minute I saw you. I tried to stop it but—" He shrugged that away and got back to the important part. "I love you so much I ache inside. I'm not good enough for you, and I know it—"

She swatted his hand aside, scowling at him. "What? I mean, I agree, after what you did, but—what do you mean?"

He took her hand and was relieved when she didn't pull away from him. "I'm adopted," he said. "That part's fine. It's the best. But I don't know who my biological parents are or anything about them. They—she—tossed me into the street and forgot about me. I grew up wild in the streets, and I mean literally in the streets. I don't remember ever having a home until I was about fourteen, when I was adopted. I could come from the trashiest people on the planet, and probably do, otherwise they wouldn't have left me to starve to death in the gutter. I want to spend the rest of my life with you, but if you marry me, you have to know what you'll be getting."

"What?" she said again, as if she couldn't understand what he was telling her.

"I should have asked you to marry me before," he said, getting it all out. "But—hell, how could I ask anyone to marry me? I'm a wild card. You don't know what you're getting with me. I was going to let you go, but then I found out about the baby and I couldn't do it. I'm selfish, Sunny. I want it all, you and our baby. If you think you can take the risk—"

She drew back, such an incredulous, outraged look on her face that he almost couldn't bear it. "I don't believe this," she sputtered, and slapped him across the face.

She wasn't back to full strength, but she still packed a wallop. Chance sat there, not even rubbing his stinging jaw. His heart was shriveling inside him. If she wanted to hit him again, he figured he deserved it.

"You fool!" she shouted. "For God's sake, my father was a *terrorist!* That's the heritage *I'm* carrying around, and you're worried because you *don't know who your parents were?* I wish to hell I didn't know who my father was! I don't believe this! I thought you didn't love me! Everything would have been all right if I'd known you love me!"

Chance uttered a startled, profound curse, one of Nick's really, really bad words. Put in those terms, it did sound incredibly trivial. He stared at her lovely, outraged face, and the weight lifted off his chest as if it had never been. Suddenly he wanted to laugh. "I love you so much I'm half crazy with it. So, will you marry me?"

"I have to," she said grumpily. "You need a keeper. And let me tell you one thing, Chance Mackenzie, if you think you're still going to be jetting all over the world getting stabbed and shot at while you get your adrenaline high, then you'd better think again. You're going to stay home with me and this baby. Is that understood?"

"Understood," he said. After all, the Mackenzie men always did whatever it took to keep their women happy.

Epilogue

Sunny was asleep, exhausted from her long labor and then the fright and stress of having surgery when the baby wouldn't come. Her eyes were circled with fatigue, but Chance thought she had never been more beautiful. Her face, when he laid the baby in her arms, had been exalted. Until he died, he would never forget that moment. The medical personnel in the room had faded away to nothing, and it had been just him and his wife and their child.

He looked down at the wrinkled, equally exhausted little face of his son. The baby slept as if he had run a marathon, his plump hands squeezed into fierce little fists. He had downy black hair, and though it was difficult to judge a newborn's eye color, he thought they might turn the same brilliant gray as Sunny's.

Zane poked his head in the door. "Hi," he said softly. "I've been sent to reconnoiter. She's still asleep, huh?"

Chance looked at his wife, as sound asleep as the baby. "She had a rough time."

"Well, hell, he weighs ten pounds and change. No wonder she needed help." Zane came completely into the room, smiling as he examined the unconscious little face. "Here, let me hold him. He needs to start meeting the family." He took the baby from Chance, expertly cradling him to his chest. "I'm your uncle Zane. You'll see me around a lot. I have two little boys who are just itching to play with you, and your aunt Maris—you'll meet her in a minute—has one who's just a little older than you are. You'll have plenty of playmates, if you ever open your eyes and look around."

The baby's eyelids didn't flicker open, even when Zane rocked him. His pink lips moved in an unconscious sucking motion.

"You forget fast how little they are," Zane said softly as he smoothed his big hand over the baby's small round skull. He glanced up at Chance and grinned. "Looks like I'm still the only one who knows how to make a little girl."

"Yeah, well, this is just my first try."

"It'll be your last one, too, if they're all going to weigh ten pounds," came a voice from the bed. Sunny sighed and pushed her hair out of her eyes, and a smile spread across her face as she spied her son. "Let me have him," she said, holding out her arms.

There was a protocol to this sort of thing. Zane passed the baby to Chance, and Chance carried him to Sunny, settling him in her arms. No matter how often he saw it, he was always touched by the communion between mother and new baby, that absorbed look they both got as if they recognized each other on some basic, primal level.

"Are you feeling well enough for company?" Zane asked. "Mom's champing at the bit, wanting to get her hands on this little guy."

"I feel fine," Sunny said, though Chance knew she didn't. He had to kiss her, and even now there was that flash of heat between them, even though their son was only a few hours old. She pulled back, laughing a little and blushing. "Get away from me, you lech," she said, teasing him, and he laughed.

"What are you going to name him?" Zane demanded. "We've been asking for months, but you never would say. It can't stay a secret much longer."

Chance trailed his finger down the baby's downy cheek, then he put his arms around both Sunny and the baby and held them close. Life couldn't get much better than this.

"Wolf," he said. "He's little Wolf."